When We Lost Touch

SUSAN KRAUS

Flint Hills Publishing

Original cover art, "The Days We Are Living In,"
by Dan McCarthy

Cover Design by Ashley Honey
www.ashleyhoney.com

Flint Hills Publishing
Topeka, Kansas
www.flinthillspublishing.com

Printed in the U.S.A.

ISBN Paperback: 978-1-953583-36-9
Ebook: 978-1-953583-37-6
Audio Book: 978-1-953583-42-0

Library of Congress Control Number: 2022914829

Dedication

When We Lost Touch is dedicated to two women I've never met but respect greatly for their fierce commitment to their principles: **Suzanne Brennan Firstenberg**, a social justice artist whose work shines light on issues when words fail; and **Heather Cox Richardson**, a historian for whom truth matters, facts matter, as she provides daily doses of context and hope in troubled times.

Introduction

When We Lost Touch is a genre-bending novel primarily set in the first 18 months of a deadly pandemic. It will be read as historical fiction in the future but as contemporary fiction now for readers who will find their own pandemic experiences mirrored in the challenges and lives of the characters. In any war, so much of what happens on the front lines, or with separated and grieving families, is invisible. To understand more fully, we have to listen to the stories of survivors. And, in this COVID-19 war, we are all, in diverse and different ways, survivors.

During COVID, time became less linear. We lost the daily habits and protocols that ground us. So much changed so quickly—and then so slowly. While unconventional for fiction, I found it essential to follow each chapter with fact-based *historical context*. It is that juxtaposition of what really happened or was said, with what we were told was happening or would happen, then juxtaposed with what the characters experience, that bring this novel to life.

Some of the characters evolved from the experiences of real people. For the most part, however, any character's thoughts and feelings are fiction—my projections, assumptions, and imagination. And any behavior that might be perceived as illegal, unethical, or simply inappropriate is totally fiction. That said, there is much that reflects the emotional and psychological journeys that we, our families, and friends, have taken during COVID-19.

Thank you for choosing this book, for reading it. I hope that you find it a journey in itself.

Prologue

Across the world, a virus was gathering strength, invisible tentacles reaching out across countries, continents, oceans, and borders. It originated in Wuhan, China, a city of 11 million people that most Americans, nationalistic and self-absorbed as we tend to be, had never heard of.

Wuhan is the capital city of the Hubei province, lying inland, in central China. It's 745 miles south of Beijing—and about 7,500 miles from New York City and Washington, D.C. The population of Wuhan is bigger than Los Angeles, Chicago, Houston, and Philadelphia combined.

But Americans, when asked to describe Wuhan, let alone Hubei province, often visualize it as backwards—rural and isolated. Not a massive, thriving metropolis with skyscrapers that rival Dubai and a metro system that makes New York City look antiquated.

While most Chinese, adults and children alike, can name numerous states and cities in the United States, as well as locate them on a map, most Americans are ignorant of the geography, history, culture, and political structure of most foreign countries. China is no exception.

Two years later, coming up for air, still breathing through masks, most Americans will still be unable to place Wuhan on a map.

Grace McDonald was one of them.

So was Donald Trump.

Historical Context: 2017-2019

January 13, 2017: Joint Obama-Trump transition teams run an exercise on pandemic preparedness, using pandemic scenarios and pandemic preparedness notebooks that the Obama administration was passing on to the Trump administration. The Trump Administration team is briefed on every aspect of pandemic concerns and issues, all based on years of scientific evaluation of viral spread and contagion. There are ultimately four critical takeaways:

1) A collective understanding of the science and disease must drive response decisions;
2) Days, even hours, are paramount to build as much lead time as possible. Delay, obfuscation, or denial will cause far more deaths;
3) A coordinated and unified *national* response and message is essential;
4) Consistent, strategic, and mandatory medical countermeasures to interrupt viral spread are key for viral control (i.e. masking, social distancing, adequate stockpiles of personal protective equipment (PPE) and ventilators for the entire country).

However, the pandemic response protocols, notebooks, and briefing data are ignored by the Trump administration.

Feb. 2017: President Trump halts a six-year process of developing targeted OSHA regulations to prepare health care facilities (hospitals, nursing homes, etc.) to combat airborne infectious diseases. It is part of his massive agenda of "deregulation." Years of meticulous work by highly experienced physicians and scientists goes into the digital dumpster.

Mar. 2017: President Trump proposes massive cuts, $136 million, to agencies and programs that dealt with pandemic preparedness. With bi-partisan support, Congress rejects many of the cuts.

Dec. 2017: President Trump bans the CDC from using "evidence-based" and "science-based" to describe CDC guidance and replace with "The CDC bases its recommendation on science in consideration with community standards and wishes..."

May 2018: The Trump administration disbands the existing White House pandemic response team.

Jul. 2019: The CDC epidemiologist embedded in China's disease control agency leaves the position. The Trump administration subsequently eliminates the position.

Oct. 2019: "Currently, there are insufficient funding sources designated for the Federal Government to use in response to a severe influenza pandemic."
– Draft report from 2019 Trump Administration's training simulations for a hypothetical pandemic caused by a virus.

January 2020

Grace & John Martin

"And then what happened?" Grace McDonald asked. Her client, John Martin, a slender man in his mid-40s, shifted uncomfortably in his chair. He'd never talked to a therapist before but had just disclosed that he'd yelled at his mother on the phone, telling her she sounded like a damn paranoid schizophrenic who was off their meds.

He was a minister who prided himself on respectful and tactful communication, so this self-disclosure had not come easily.

"She hung up on me. She's never done that before," he replied.

"Had you ever called her a 'paranoid schizophrenic who...'" Grace asked.

"No, of course not," the man replied, cutting her off in mid-sentence. "I haven't yelled at my mother since I was a teenager."

"Then you must have some serious concerns," Grace said. "What has you so worried?"

With that, John seemed to deflate.

"I don't know where to start. After my dad died—a heart attack—Mom was kind of lost. Dad took care of the bills and money, gave her an allowance to 'run the house,'" John replied. "Old school. But not mean. More a Biblical understanding of roles."

"Did she resent the roles?"

"No, I never got that sense. She took pride in being a wife and mother, and could take charge: Scout troops, church rummage sales, a hundred committees. Which is why this has been such a shift."

"What is 'this' and when did 'this' start?" Grace asked.

"A year after Dad died, when she was about 55, she met a man, Fred, at some church conference. We were Lutherans, so maybe a synod meeting? But he was a lot more conservative, more Missouri or Wisconsin, so..."

"Back up," Grace interrupted. "How is Missouri or Wisconsin more conservative?"

John shook his head. "Not the states, the synods. Lutheran synods are groupings of like-minded churches, with different degrees of values and beliefs. Wisconsin and Missouri are most conservative."

"Okay, keep going."

"Within five months they were married," John continued. "And within a year, she sold the family home, moved to Slinger, Wisconsin, dropped her old friends and started a new life. That was a decade ago."

"Sometimes that's a good thing after a loss," Grace said.

"Well, not here. Fred requires total conformity to his beliefs, and cut off from people who do not share those beliefs. Maybe Mom saw having someone who would take care of her as worth the trade-off."

"Or maybe she didn't understand that part of his personality. It sounds kind of whirlwind. Were they living in different states at that time?"

"Yes, a long distance 'courtship' with weekend visits."

"It can be easy to get confused when people don't have daily face-to-face contact, let alone not sharing a bathroom. So, does Fred take care of her?"

"Hard to know," John answered. "It's like a wall has been built, brick by brick, between Mom and her kids, her extended family. Her friends were the first to go, and I feel like a shit for not paying attention back then when maybe I could have influenced her. At the time, I think we—her kids, three of us—were taking it personally that she seemed so invested in this new life."

"Invested how?"

"We'd call to chat, and she could talk for maybe five minutes, but then there was always something. They were going out, or Fred was expecting supper. She'd say she'd call back, but she never did."

"What else?"

"We'd offer to come visit, but it was never a good time. We'd invite her to come down for a week with the grandkids, but she didn't want to travel without Fred. Or Fred didn't want her traveling alone. Or Fred was tied up so maybe in another month. Then that…"

"I get the picture," Grace interrupted. "So how does 'paranoid schizophrenic off her meds' fit in?"

"It's these crazy ideas she's latched on to. We thought it was just political, or some self-help stuff, but it's way weirder than that. I'm not even sure where to start. But she keeps talking about these conspiracies, and how Trump was sent by God to get rid of the pedophiles."

"Huh?" Grace asked, her eyebrows knotting. "What conspiracies?"

"Like Hillary Clinton and George Soros are part of an international cabal trafficking children? The Deep State? And Obama, Oprah Winfrey, and Ellen DeGeneres? The Pope? They're all in on it. Mainstream news is a front. The Storm is coming..."

"What 'Storm?'"

"I googled that one. Back in October 2017, Trump was posing for a photo op with some military generals. And he said, 'You know what this represents? Maybe the calm before the storm.' And that blew up like a mushroom cloud."

"Has your mother been talking about this since 2017?"

"No, if she did, she wasn't pushing it at us and then cutting us off if we question anything. That's just been for the last six to nine months."

"So that paranoid schizophrenic comment?"

"Mom had just informed me that the military got Trump elected to face down The Cabal, and there will be a day of reckoning, and summary executions, and it will be violent, but that violence and a hard moral line are needed to purify the country," John reiterated. "And Guantanamo Bay was in there somewhere."

Grace sighed, deeply and slowly.

"Yes, that would qualify for the diagnosis *if* the conspiracy theory was not shared by—did you say *thousands* of people?"

"Yes, and, by now, maybe millions."

"Which makes it less an individual mental illness and more a collective, albeit distorted, belief system. Like a cult maybe? I need to think about this."

Grace looked down at her pages of scribbled notes.

"Can we get together in about two weeks?" Grace asked. "In the meantime, would you talk with your siblings about specific experiences with your mom? And can concerns and goals be prioritized so we can move forward strategically? I don't want to make anything worse than it is."

Grace pulled out her planner, and they selected a date and time.

John turned as he was leaving the office. "My mom is a caring person," he said. "She's the one who always made sure the church food closet was full, and that it was open anytime so people did not have to be embarrassed to use it. She followed the Beatitudes as much as the Commandments."

"You miss her a lot, don't you?" Grace asked.

"Yes, I do. I feel ashamed that I didn't understand what was happening, that I dismissed her. And for losing it with her and attacking," John concluded. "But what I feel for Fred, who dragged her into this, is very un-Christian."

"Welcome to the club," Grace replied, "when you want bad things to happen to bad people."

After John left, Grace sat and looked out the window of her office. The holiday lights had just come on. Every tree that lined the sidewalk on Main Street was covered in white twinkle lights. Grace wished they could stay up until spring.

She put away the files, grabbed her coat off the hook on the back of the door, slid her Baggallini over her shoulder, and looked around the office for a final check. It was a simple office: scuffed wooden floors, a comfy sofa, a desk, and a few chairs. It was over a shoe store, but right in the middle of town, so people could anonymously slip up the staircase.

Her office fit her, like an old pair of jeans or a soft flannel shirt. Worn, but functional. Reassuring.

I think I'll walk downtown for a while, Grace thought. *Savor the lights. Maybe stop for a drink.*

"I don't understand all that the guy was talking about," Grace told Molly the next morning.

"Sounds like QAnon," her daughter replied, looking up from the sink where she was washing the breakfast dishes.

"That much I figured. But I'd pegged QAnon as just a fringe cult."

Molly stopped scrubbing and gave her mother a pointed look. "If a cult has millions of people who wait every day for a new secret message, and spend half their lives on the internet looking at articles or in chat rooms? Then, sure, it's *just* a cult."

"How do you know this and I don't?" Grace asked.

"Google, Mom. I googled it after a friend at school said her brother was telling the rest of the family that they were enabling pedophiles if they voted for a Democrat. Then I followed the breadcrumbs. I can see the addictive component because I ended up staying up until 2 a.m. one night after intending to take one quick look."

"Did you feel drawn to it?" Grace asked, keeping her voice neutral.

Molly snorted. "Get real. I was more horrified, but also curious in a sick way. Like when you pass a bad accident on the highway and the cops make you slow down? And you want to not look, but then go even slower so you can look?" Molly said in one long breath. "Like that. I was all alone in the dark and couldn't stop reading."

"Okay, then. I'll do some research and then we can talk."

"It changes every day, Mom. That's part of the addiction. Hang back and you miss stuff. Or at least people get scared they'll be left out."

"But it's not religious? No dogma?"

"Not religious like you'd think, but it does feel like a religion. And it doesn't help that Tucker Carlson, Sean Hannity, and then Fox News legitimize this stuff by offering it as an 'alternative' perspective," Molly explained. "But the connections, what ties it all together, are hypothetical. Somebody imagines *something* and then searches the universe for clues to make it be, well, not *impossible*. Just hypothetical. Like, hey, this *could* have happened. Once stated, it starts to mushroom and magnify. It's an alternate universe. And people are being manipulated and exploited."

"Well," Grace said, standing up to leave, "sometimes things that cannot be proven or seen have the most power. Especially if we have a need to believe."

"Are you knocking God?" Molly asked with a grin. "Because it sounds like..."

"No, smartass. I am not knocking God. I have it in the best authority that..." but the rest of the sentence was lost as the back door swung closed behind her.

Molly finished up in the kitchen, wiping down the counters, putting the dishes away. She was like her mother in how she liked to clean up as she went along. Not leave messes. Keep it fresh.

Molly

Molly was relieved that winter break was over. She dropped Max off at school and then celebrated by going straight to a coffee shop and ordering a grande peppermint mocha with extra chocolate curls and whipped cream. She slid into a booth in the back room, closed her eyes, and inhaled the coffee. Then she sat, both hands on the large, warm cup and smiled.

2020, she'd decided, was going to be the best year ever.

Molly had been a freshman in college those many years ago when her father had been killed, her mother indicted, and normal life imploded. She'd returned to college after her mother had, rather literally, run away from home. Then she'd fallen into a relationship with Jeff, gotten pregnant, and had Max. Jeff, as it turned out, was not cut out for parenting, or monogamy, and she was a single mom within a year

Now, Molly was in grad school doing a two-year program in clinical social work. She had ten days between when her university classes would resume and today, when Max was back in school. Having any time when she did not have to care for Max or stay up half the night to read or write papers was a rare gift.

She intended to savor every hour.

It was parenting Max, who was on the autism spectrum, that drew her to psychology. She wanted to understand what made people behave as they did and make the choices they made. Molly was insecure, having made a series of "bad choices," but most of those were in the past. In recent years, she'd felt that she could, *maybe*, trust her own judgment.

And today, having time to savor the treat of an overpriced coffee, to sit in a booth with her calendar and a journal, to reflect on what she wanted to accomplish this semester? *This* almost felt like a blessing.

Breathe, she told herself. *It's all good.*

Grace & Mickey & Molly & Max & Katrina

January 19th was the third Sunday of the month. Third Sundays were reserved for a family dinner, the category of family being loosely defined. It generally meant Grace, Molly, Max, Katrina, Mickey.

Katrina was Grace's "BFF" since before the acronym came into existence. They'd met when their own children were young, each juggling work, childcare, marriages, and laundry. Katrina was Creole, raised in New Orleans. An attorney, she'd segued into elder law, not just wills and inheritance, but the challenges of helping multi-generational families balance self-determination with the progression of dementia.

They'd weathered tough times: Katrina's divorce; Grace's husband's death; years of long-distance friendship. Their bond went deep. Over the years, Katrina had become Molly's "matant"—her Creole auntie—as much as Grace's friend.

Mickey Donahue, however, was a recent addition to their family.

Grace and Mickey had a link of lives bruised and almost broken. They each had dead spouses: one for Grace, two for Mickey. They'd reconnected after Grace returned to Kaw Valley, at first through work, and then, tentatively, as more.

It had not been hasty. Mickey had waited a few years to clean out his dead wife Joanne's closet, and even longer to tackle the rest of the house. Grace had recommended using Marie Kondo as a guide, but Mickey found that going through every item, asking "Does this spark joy?" was too depressing.

The Gentle Art of Swedish Death Cleaning was a better fit for Mickey. No sparking joy, no woo-woo, as Grace would say. Just ruthless purging.

Before his house even sold, he'd moved from Kansas City to Kaw Valley, renting a small ranch home a half mile from Grace. They each felt a need for private time and space, and Grace's one-bedroom casita, a renovated three-car garage behind Molly's bungalow, was perfect for one but tight for two.

They were, in their own peripatetic fashion, constructing their relationship. Neither had anticipated ever feeling as they did for someone new. They'd been reconciled to being alone, thus were cautious. Caution was compounded by a reluctance to open themselves to the inevitable pain that comes with a late-in-life love. Officially married or not, it would be a "until death do us part" commitment.

"I've had two wives die already," Mickey had told Grace. "You have to promise me that I get to die first. I can't survive another dead wife."

"No promises, Mickey," Grace had replied. "But as long as you brought it up, I feel the same. I want to die first. Maybe we'll get lucky and go at the same time? Or, if we come to a fork in the road, we separate without being dickheads about it?"

"Look," Grace told Molly one night after two margaritas. "I think I love the man. What we have feels good. I look forward to seeing him and talking with him. When he does sleep over, I like waking up to him being there. But if it were *every* day? *Every* night? *All* the time? I don't want to screw up a good thing."

"Okay, but, just so you know, if you dump him," Molly retorted, "I'm on *his* side."

On January 19ᵗʰ, they gathered at Molly's at 6 p.m., hugging and kissing as if they hadn't seen each other a year, when it had been, at the most, a week.

Max set the table. Katrina brought a salad. Molly and Max were in charge of the carrot cake. Mickey brought two bottles of red wine. Grace was stirring a crockpot of beef stew.

"My God, Gracie," Katrina exclaimed, leaning in to the crock pot to inhale slowly and deeply. "This stew smells seriously fantastic."

"Tripled the herbs and garlic," Grace explained, reaching across for a final stir. "And tossed in extra merlot. Did you know that 'merlot' translates to 'little blackbird?'"

"No, I did not, but I'll hang on to that nugget. In case I'm ever desperate for a cocktail party ice breaker?"

"I made cream cheese icing," Max announced from a stool by the counter, holding out a bowl with a big spoon. "Wanna' taste?"

They all did, taking licks, making slurpy noises of satisfaction, as Max giggled.

HISTORICAL CONTEXT: JANUARY 2020

Jan. 5: China announces that the unknown pneumonia cases in Wuhan are not SARS or MERS. Two days later they identify the virus as a novel coronavirus.

Jan. 20: "The NIH is in the process of taking the first steps towards the development of a vaccine." – *Dr. Anthony Fauci, Director of the National Institutes of Allergy and Infectious Diseases.*

Jan. 21: Officials in the state of Washington confirm first case in the U.S.

Jan. 22: "We have it totally under control. It's one person coming in from China. It's going to be just fine." – *Donald Trump.*

Jan. 29: The White House announces the formation of a new task force to help monitor and contain viral spread, as well as provide Americans accurate data for health and travel.

Jan. 29: The first 911 call describing coronavirus symptoms from the Life Care Center in Kirkland, WA. Dozens of requests for emergency aid from Life Care are made in the following weeks.

Jan. 30: World Health Organization declares "a public emergency of international concern" regarding the outbreak of the novel coronavirus.

Jan. 30: The U.S. confirms the first case of person-to-person transmission of the coronavirus.

Jan. 31: Trump suspends entry for foreign nationals who had been in China in the last two weeks. No restrictions, not even home quarantine, are placed on U.S. citizens returning from China or overseas.

February 2020

Grace & John Martin

"**I talked to my** sisters and brother," John said. "We know what we want but don't see how to get it with Fred in the middle."

"And what do you want?" Grace asked.

"We want our mother back. We want her to stop pushing all of this conspiracy bullshit and come back to the real world. We want Fred gone."

"That's one hell of agenda. Anything more realistic?"

"My middle sister drove to Wisconsin last week for a weekend with her two teen daughters to see Mom. She lives outside Chicago, so an easy drive. She booked a hotel room for a few nights, then showed up at mom's door. Like, 'Surprise! We missed you!' When we were kids, mom was *big* on surprises."

"And now? How was she *now* with this surprise?"

"Not so much. But they were on the front stoop, so Mom invited them in. Barb said she was uneasy. And the house didn't look right."

"What do you mean 'didn't look right?'"

"The dining room table was covered with newspapers and magazines. Piles of them. Mom hated that. Always wanted the table clear so you could sit down and eat or have tea with a friend. 'Cozy is not clutter,' she'd say."

"What else?"

"Fred came down the stairs and Barb said that Mom kind of froze. Like waiting for what he might do? Then he said to Barb, 'Did you just expect we'd be here? Ever think to call to ask if it's convenient?' But then he pretended like he was just joking when she tried to explain about surprises."

"And what did your mom say?"

"Nothing. Put on some coffee."

"Did they have a good visit?"

"Some moments, yes. When Barb told Mom they were taking her out shopping and to lunch, Fred said, 'So I'm not invited?' Mom started to say, 'Of course you are if you want to,' but Barb butted in, 'No, this is a girl's day out, Fred. The girls have it all planned for their grammy.'"

"And your mother went along?"

"Yes, but Barb said that around 5:30 she started to get anxious, looking at her watch, then said she needed to get back and fix Fred's supper. Didn't invite them in, didn't ask about the next day or anything."

"And then?"

"The next morning, they drove back to Mom's, but there was a note on the door. They rang and knocked but no answer." John reached into his jacket pocket and pulled out his phone, showing her a photo on the screen. "Barb took a photo of it. 'Not sure if you stayed around but I forgot to tell you that we had medical appointments in Milwaukee today. Next time, call first,'" he read.

"And that doesn't sound like your mom?"

"Well, it sure isn't her handwriting," he replied.

Grace took a few minutes to digest this data. She did not want to alarm John, but this had signs of a seriously controlling, if not abusive, relationship. Confrontation could make it worse. And letters and emails were probably being censored.

It was a pickle. Unless their mother asked for help.

"Is there one sibling your mother is more likely to listen to?" Grace asked. "Or confide in?"

"Probably me," John said. "She sees me as a bit closer to God. But maybe not now, maybe not after calling her..."

"Could you get her away for a day, or, better yet, a weekend?"

"Tried that. I emailed *and* phoned. Said I'd be in Milwaukee for work and wanted to come up for a few days to visit. Asked her to join me for a drive up to Door County. That was last October. But once I gave a date, she said, 'Oh dear, we have plans for that weekend.'"

"And what did you say?"

"To tell me when she was open, and I'd accommodate." John sighed. "She never called back."

Grace nodded, tapping her pen against her paper. "Have you ever directly asked her if she feels safe?"

"I think Fred listens in on our calls. I can't be sure. Or she says, 'Oh, let me put you on speaker. Fred is right here too.'"

"John," Grace said, taking off her glasses and resting them on her lap. "I'm stumped. You can't kidnap her, and, if you get confrontational, it sounds like she retreats. I'd just say to consistently reach out: cards, emails, letters, calls. Ignore the QAnon stuff. Share memories, like, 'I was driving and heard that song…remember how we all sang it in the car that summer on vacation?' Provide small, consistent reminders of what you shared as a family."

John looked away. "That feels like too little, too late."

"It may be. But your mother is an adult. She may be embarrassed about the choices she made, even feel trapped or cornered. But she's married. I'm assuming that there was no prenup? She may have lost control of her finances because she trusted this man."

As Grace spoke, she watched John, his jaw clenching, hands going from fists to open to fists to...

"Or, John, and you will be pissed at me for saying this, but she may have marital issues separate from her beliefs. You're seeing everything in terms of Fred—an evil Fred—and it's not that black and white. She may believe these conspiracy theories. Perhaps if one of the siblings were to 'back-door' her, ask her to explain more? Like, 'You've always been a smart cookie, Mom, so I want to understand. Can we start over?' Employ delicate and respectful probing."

"I'm not feeling very respectful right now, but I'll ask who's willing."

"Do your siblings also feel responsible for not somehow preventing this relationship?"

"We all had concerns back then. The courtship and wedding? It seemed rushed premature, but we didn't feel we had a right to say no. She looked happy. Told us they'd planned a bucket list of adventures."

"Have they been having those adventures?"

"None that I know, unless fishing counts. But nothing she'd need a passport for."

"I'm sorry," Grace said. "I do wish I could be more helpful. It might be useful to talk to an elder care attorney, but, at this point, I'm not hearing a threshold for guardianship or—well, anything."

"I appreciate your time. I didn't expect a miracle. Hoped, maybe, but..."

"You have my number and email if anything happens that you want to discuss. And tell your sibs to make copies of every communication, and keep a logbook for calls, dates, and times, in case you ever need documentation."

"That sounds so—ominous."

"Just practical. Probably never need it, but just in case."

John got his coat, shook Grace's hand, and headed for the door. Before he reached the stairs, Grace called after him.

"I just realized that I don't know your mother's name. She's just been *Mom*."

"Anna Marie," he replied. "Anna Marie Martin. Fred is a Schlinder, but she'll never be a Schlinder to me."

Listening, Grace felt that his very footsteps on the stairs sounded defeated.

Where the hell was an epiphany when she needed one?

Grace

Grace was looking at packing cubes on Etsy. She was preparing for a cruise, out of Ft. Lauderdale, to the southern Caribbean. It was for 12 nights, on Holland America, and already that did not seem long enough.

Grace was going with Chelle, an old friend who'd never been on a cruise but whose husband was adamant that he was not interested in being "stuck on a boat with a few thousand strangers and no privacy." His vacation of choice was skiing, or biking, or even hiking, each of which was a lot more solitary than cruising. Chelle thought he might change his mind when he was 85 or so, but she didn't want to wait that long to experience one herself.

Three months earlier, Chelle had asked, "Would you ever consider going on a cruise with me?" It had taken Grace three seconds to respond. "Yes, yes, yes. When and where?"

Grace hadn't been on a cruise since Gil, her husband, had died. Without Gil, Grace had thought that every aspect of a cruise would be tainted, weighted down with memories. That missing Gil would dominate the experience.

But this would be different. Sharing a cabin with Chelle, seeing the ship, the whole cruise experience, through her eyes? Like taking a kid to Disney World, she hoped she'd get caught up in the magic.

Grace was already visualizing strolling the promenade deck, lazy breakfasts seated by a big picture window, lazy afternoon naps with the smell of salt air on a chaise lounge, cocktail hours before four-course dinners served by attentive waiters. Exploring Caribbean islands. White sand beaches and swimming in turquoise seas.

It was all so *not* Kansas.

With two weeks until boarding, Grace had plenty of work to wrap up. Getting away for a vacation was always a challenge. As soon as she announced she was going to be gone, therapy clients felt the need to book an appointment. Divorcing couples who'd procrastinated on their parenting plans or settlements decided that another two-week delay was unacceptable. She usually found herself working extra evenings and some weekends just to get everyone settled enough so that she could leave without a crisis tracking her down.

Then Grace got an email from Holland America:

IMPORTANT NOTIFICATION: We are monitoring the situation with the coronavirus that originated in mainland China, and our medical experts are working with global health authorities. As a precaution, anyone who has traveled from or through mainland China, Macau, or Hong Kong (including airport transits), or has had contact with a suspected or confirmed case of coronavirus (2019-nCoV) within 14 days of the start of this cruise will not be allowed to board the ship. If this applies to you or your client, please contact us with proof of this travel for a full refund of the amount paid to Holland America Line. All guests will also be subject to preboarding health reporting and enhanced screening at check-in. Guest passports will be scanned to verify compliance. False responses on forms will result in immediate debark at the next opportunity, and you may face legal consequences. We may change requirements to safeguard guests and crew.

Well, that certainly did not apply to her, Grace thought. *Haven't been through China, Hong Kong, or Macau—where exactly is Macau anyway?—and no coronavirus around here.* Grace wondered what the enhanced screening would be. She made a note to buy zinc supplements and cough drops at the pharmacy. *Nothing to fret about,* she thought. And it was comforting that the cruise line was taking such precautions. It was probably because of that ship in Japan. It felt a little extreme, but they must know what they're doing.

Katrina

A week later, Katrina sat on a chair in Grace's bedroom and consulted as Grace packed. She was sipping the Mojito that Grace had made to generate a little pre-cruise ambiance.

"So, do you think that this could pass for dinner as well as a bathing suit cover-up?" Grace asked, waving a black—something.

"Is that a muumuu?" Kat asked. "If so, then, absolutely not. Put it back in the closet. Or should we start a giveaway pile?"

Grace frowned. "It's practical," she replied. "It multi-tasks. And it covers up a lot..."

Kat cut her off. "Enough with the covering up bullshit. You're an attractive woman. Stop hiding."

"My goal is to blend in, not stand out. Comfort and invisibility. And there is *plenty* to cover up."

"Then buy yourself a beach wrap on the ship. Then you'll really blend in. Half the ship will be wearing the same damn thing."

Grace paused to consider the suggestion.

"That's not the worst idea you've ever had. I never bought on ship because they have a high mark-up, but some of it was cute."

"Cute is better than black," Kat retorted. "It's not a funeral, it's a cruise."

Kat took another sip of her Mojito. She was second-guessing her decision a few months before to decline Grace's invitation to come along.

"Cruises are not my thing," she'd told Grace. "I lack impulse control. I'll come back with 10 extra pounds that it takes me months to get off." Grace had tried to persuade Kat, explaining she could avoid the Lido Deck, whatever that was, and only eat in the dining room, doted on by waiters bringing small, visually appealing portions.

"It's about being nurtured, quality not quantity," Grace had said. "And being on the ocean. I do love the ocean."

But Katrina was not persuaded. She was a woman who recycled religiously, contributed to a variety of environmental causes, and was aware of her "footprint." To go on a cruise had felt hypocritical.

But now Kat was pondering whether one more passenger floating the Caribbean instead of consuming electricity and gas to stay warm in February in Kansas made a measurable difference as the planet moved inexorably toward a tipping point and extinction.

Perhaps she'd been over-zealous.

Grace & Chelle

Mickey drove Grace and Chelle to the Kansas City airport to fly to Ft. Lauderdale. They were going down a day early, spending one night in a hotel close to the port with a free shuttle.

The next morning, they were both excited. The boarding process was seamless: check in, show passports, provide credit cards, sign a few forms, get room keys, passenger ID, answer some medical questions, have a temperature check. In 30 minutes, voila! They were walking up a ramp to the gangplank.

"Is there really a gangplank?" Chelle asked.

"Yeah, but it's covered, like airplanes. Not what you see in the old movies."

They were greeted by staff with trays of mimosas and shown where their room was on maps of the ship. Grace could see Chelle trying to grasp the enormity of the ship: a 13-story building, with busy elevators and a capacity larger than the populations of many towns. They dumped their carry-on luggage in the room and took off with their maps. They wandered until they got lost, then consulted their maps and kept going. It was like a treasure hunt with many treasures: lounges, dining rooms, bars, pools, fitness center, spa, library, reading rooms, music venues.

When the ship pulled out of the dock, escorted out of the bay by a tender, they stood on deck and waved to nameless strangers on the beach and rocks below, all of whom were waving back at them.

Across the United States, another ship, the *Grand Princess*, was headed to Hawaii from San Francisco. Over 50 countries were represented in the roughly 2,400 passengers and 1,100 crew.

Its passengers had heard the *Diamond Princess* was in quarantine in Japan. Some wondered if they'd have medical checks prior to boarding. But they were only asked a few questions: "Do you have a fever? Do you feel sick?" and then allowed to board.

The mood had been festive as the *Grand Princess* headed out of the bay, beneath the Golden Gate Bridge and onto the Pacific Ocean. There were four days at sea before the first port, a glorious time for everyone to party and relax. For many days, the cruise was wonderful. The Hawaiian Islands, excursions, candlelit suppers…

It was on the return voyage that things began to go downhill.

On March 3rd, passengers noticed that the buffets were no longer self-serve and staff were now filling their plates. On March 4th, a note slipped under each stateroom door informed passengers that the final port, Ensenada, Mexico, was cancelled. Anyone with any fever, cough, chill, or respiratory symptoms should contact the ship's medical center. About 20 people on the *Grand Princess* had developed flu-like symptoms.

Abruptly, everything escalated. Passengers were restricted to their cabins. Meals were delivered by crew in homemade PPE. The governor of California prohibited the ship from docking as scheduled. A National Guard helicopter hovered above the ship and lowered a white cooler with some coronavirus test kits. Of the 45 people who were tested, 21 were positive.

On March 9th, the ship was permitted to dock at the Port of Oakland, one of the busiest cargo ports in the country, but not a passenger port. It would take two days to evacuate the passengers.

The messaging was confusing. Some passengers assumed that only symptomatic people would be quarantined. Others thought they could self-quarantine, just go home and stay at home. Like an honor system.

U.S citizens are not used to being detained. Especially white ones.

They were processed by personnel in full hazmat gear. In sum, a few thousand people who'd expected their cruise to end on March 7th, who needed to get back to their jobs and kids and families, were transported to military bases for two more weeks of quarantine.

Many wouldn't be released until March 25th.

Some never made it home.

HISTORICAL CONTEXT: FEBRUARY 2020

Feb. 4: The Japanese Heath Ministry announces that ten people aboard the *Diamond Princess* cruise ship moored in Yokohama Bay have confirmed cases of the coronavirus.

Feb. 7: The United States donates almost 18 tons of medical supplies (masks, gowns, respirators, etc.) to China despite facing pending and predictable shortages within the U.S. The U.S. population remains ignorant of the state of our own supplies and PPE, assuming, as we tend to do, that the people in charge of such things have it under control.

Feb. 7: Li Wenliang, a physician in Wuhan who sounded an alarm about the virus in December, alerting international epidemiologists, but was then forced to recant by his government, dies of the coronavirus.

Feb. 10: "Looks like by April, you know in theory when it gets a little warmer, it miraculously goes away." – *Donald Trump on the coronavirus.*

Feb. 11: The World Health Organization names the coronavirus COVID-19, per World Health Agency policy, with no reference to any people, place, or country as viruses can morph and manifest on any continent, at any time, from multiple sources and for uncountable and invisible reasons.

Feb. 13: Japan reports that the *Diamond Princess* has 218 positive cases for coronavirus By February 19th, there are over 600 positives.

Feb. 14: Mardi Gras celebration begins in New Orleans with more than one million people attending the 12-day event. According to a later study led by Scripps Research, the virus spread from one person to become "one of the worst early outbreaks of COVID-19 in the United States," and "was responsible for tens of thousands of coronavirus cases."

Feb. 23: Ahmaud Arbery, a 25-year-old Black man, is murdered while jogging in a neighborhood near Brunswick, Georgia. Assuming he was a burglar, three white men pursued and shot him.

Feb. 25: "You should ask your children's schools about plans for school dismissals or school closures." – *Dr. Nancy Messonier, CDC, states at a press briefing.*

Feb. 26: "Well, we're testing everybody that we need to test. And we're finding very little problem. Very little problem." – *Donald Trump.*

Feb. 26: "The 15 [cases in the U.S.] within a couple of days is going to be down close to zero." – *Donald Trump*

Feb. 28: The first positive COVID-19 test results come back at the Life Care Center. In total, 129 people including 81 residents, about two-thirds of its population, will test positive for the virus and 35 people will die.

March 2020

Katrina

It was mid-afternoon on March 3rd that Katrina was first hit by a wave of exhaustion. It felt pervasive, not just her head, but her limbs and torso too. The intensity vaguely reminded her of pregnancy. She felt like her body had been invaded and forces outside her control had taken over.

I need a nap, she thought. *Maybe I'll cut out early from work.*

"I'm coming down with something," she told Mitzi, the office receptionist, on her way out.

"Not that virus, I hope," Mitzi replied.

"Well, don't think so. No cough. Chest feels fine. I'm just tired and achy. I may work from home tomorrow. Nothing urgent on the agenda."

But within two hours, the fatigue morphed into deep aches, as if every muscle had been pushed to its limit, like after a strenuous hike or cycle.

By bedtime she'd already been lying down for hours, and despite taking a double dose of ibuprofen, she felt no better. If anything, she felt worse.

I'll call the doctor in the morning, she told herself.

Which she did.

"Any fever?" the nurse practitioner asked the next day when returning her message. "Dry cough? Trouble breathing?"

"Not very high. About 102.2," Kat replied. "You don't think it could be that virus, do you? We've hardly had any cases here."

"Just asking to be on the safe side," the nurse said. "Call us if you develop a *high* fever or cough, okay? Otherwise, just do the usual: rest, fluids, over-the-counter meds for discomfort."

The next week was a blur. Katrina could barely get out of bed to go to the bathroom. Every time she tried to change positions in bed, to roll over, she felt pain. Even when lying perfectly still, her body throbbed. She took the maximum doses of ibuprofen and acetaminophen, but they didn't touch the deep muscle ache.

On day four when her son, MJ, who lived in Kansas City, called to say "Hi," Kat was too sick to pretend otherwise. "You sound weird, Mom. I'm coming over." he said. "Be there in a few hours and I'll stay until you're better."

Katrina called the doctor's office three times but was told that unless she had a *high* fever, racking cough, or couldn't catch her breath, she needed to stay home. Also, that due to very limited availability, coronavirus tests were being saved for people with those specific symptoms.

So, no test, no treatment.

"Call us if *those* symptoms develop," the nurse said. "Or just go to the ER."

But Kat did not have *those* symptoms. She had *different* symptoms.

She shivered even when buried under blankets and then felt as if her skin was on fire, burning from the inside out. It felt like she had sand under her eyelids but rubbing made it worse and rinsing them with water made no difference. Her tongue felt thick and swollen, and she could not taste anything. It was only texture: slimy or gravelly or hard. Chewing on a chicken breast made her choke.

On day seven, Kat realized she could not smell.

MJ came to her bedroom door, masked and gloved, carrying a tray with soup and toast. He walked in and immediately wrinkled his nose.

"Mom," he said, "you gotta' get in the shower. This place stinks like a boy's locker room."

Kat sniffed the air—nothing. No smell. She lifted her arm to sniff her armpit and pajamas, still damp from the last round of sweat. Nada. She looked at the overflowing wastebasket, a stew of the unwanted, could-not-swallow food: lasagna and mashed potatoes and scrambled eggs.

MJ watched her from the doorway.

"You don't smell this?" he asked, uncomprehending. Kat had always been a hard ass when it came to smells in her son's room.

"I can't smell anything," Kat said.

"That is so bizarre. This room stinks worse than my room did when you threatened to throw everything on the front lawn if I didn't clean it up."

"That bad?" Kat asked. "No way."

"Way, Mom. Trust me," he said. "Look, I'll start a hot shower for you. Just toss the PJs out the door and I'll get clean ones. Do you need help getting up?"

Katrina glared at him. "No, I do not need help getting up. I'm not an invalid. I'm just sick."

But, as she pushed back the comforter, she felt a wave if dizziness and had to stop and let her head catch up to her body.

"Start that shower and then leave," she told MJ.

"Not until I have your PJs to put in the wash," he retorted.

Forty-five minutes later, Katrina was showered, hair washed, body soaped. She had to sit on the toilet seat, wrapped in a towel, before she had the energy to carefully extend one leg at a time and pull on the fresh pajama bottoms MJ had placed on the towel rack. She inserted one arm at a time into the top, pulling it over her damp hair.

Opening the bathroom door into the bedroom, she saw that her room had been attacked—but in a good way.

The overflowing wastebaskets were empty. The clothes, pajamas, and robes were cleared from the back of the armchair. The bed had been stripped and remade with clean sheets. It even looked as if MJ had vacuumed the rug, which she did not remember hearing. The dresser top and side table were wiped down. A plastic bin next to her bed now contained Kleenex and assorted meds.

Katrina sniffed, to test if there was anything different. "Nope," she muttered.

"Back to the land of the living," MJ commented suddenly from the doorway. "She has risen."

Kat tried sniffing again. Nothing. "Did you use Lysol?" she asked.

"Yes, Mom, I used Lysol. And I changed my mask, wore gloves, even put the clothes I wore cleaning your pit of a room into the machine with your stuff."

"If I'd known you could accomplish this much in under an hour, I'd have been on your ass a lot more to keep *your* pit of a room clean when you..."

"Stop complaining," MJ interrupted. "Just say thank you. And, for the record, you trained me well."

Katrina stopped debating, as she literally did not have the breath to continue. She needed to lie down, curl into fetal position, swallow some more pills, and not move.

"I have soup here," MJ said. "Chicken noodle, from scratch. Molly dropped it off."

"Not now," Kat replied. "Maybe later." She did not say that the mention of food, even if Molly's outstanding creation, had no appeal. None.

Katrina wondered if she would ever want to eat again.

Grace

Across the Caribbean, with only five days remaining on their cruise, Grace felt disconnected from the world. All the hassles and anxieties of work, all her responsibilities, felt amorphous and distant.

The ship crew was being scrupulous about the virus thing, with sanitizer stations everywhere she turned. It seemed that staff were wiping down handrails and tables every twenty minutes. Grace disinfected her hands every time she passed a station.

In the ports, however, crowds of people jostled together with no indication that anything was amiss.

Grace knew that a ship docked in Japan had developed a lot of cases, but that ship was on the other side of the globe. And another ship had a few cases, but wasn't that in California? No cases in the Caribbean, she reassured herself.

The lingering concern she'd had—that memories of her husband Gil would trigger sadness—was the opposite of what happened. It was as if he was watching her, encouraging her to laugh, to not look back.

Best of all, Chelle was enjoying herself. And they'd proven to be good roommates. Neither required all the lights off to fall asleep or snored enough to wake the other up. They shared the bathroom seamlessly. They preferred the more intimate classical music Carnegie Hall evening venue to the flamboyant stage shows. And they relished the leisurely cruise dinners.

Chelle's delight was infectious.

Grace felt lighter, emotionally and psychologically, than when she'd boarded. She wanted these feelings to last when she returned home. She craved more joy, more laughter. She'd carried a backpack of guilt and regret for years. What good did it do?

The last evening of the cruise, they listened to the reggae band playing under the stars. Grace found herself humming, smiling, swaying to the rhythm as the music filled her head.

When Grace and Chelle disembarked in Ft. Lauderdale, on March 8th, they had no idea how lucky they had been.

Molly

Back in Kansas, Molly was missing Grace. It was the longest vacation that Grace had taken since her return to Kaw Valley. Life without Grace was harder. Max was crankier.

Get real, Molly thought. *No need to blame Max. I'm the cranky one.*

Molly startled a bit as her phone made the soft chime of a text arriving, but then relaxed. It was only Mike, a friend who lived in Florida with his son David.

Mike was also a single parent of a son with special needs. Their kids were a few years apart in age, the issues were different, but the challenges resonated: always feeling vigilant, anxious, anticipating what could go wrong.

Mike's parents lived near him, to help, just like her mom.

They'd been introduced in a circuitous way: Molly's friend, Leah, was David's cousin. They'd only met in person when Leah invited Molly and Max to join her on a road trip—a drive to Florida to visit Mike and David.

But the backdrop was that before Mike had left Kaw Valley, Grace had been the court-appointed mediator in his custody case.

That was a messy story that would take a book to cover.

Mike and Molly were now each other's sounding board for single parenting, family boundaries, college, and balancing all of the above while staying sane. Sometimes they just bitched about life, or the WTF of the week.

Since Grace had left, he'd been calling and texting more often to check in.

MIKE: Can you talk tonight?

MOLLY: Give me 30 mins to make sure Max is asleep. I'll pour some wine and then call you.

Ian & Nell

Ian Thomas received a call, in early March, from the administrative assistant of the Commander of DMORT. Teams were being assembled. DMORT usually rolled out *after* a disaster, but this time, they were forming crews in anticipation of one.

Ian was part of a national program—*Disaster Mortuary Operational Response Team*—composed of various types of mortuary professionals. It was created in the 1980s to manage "mass casualty events."

Ian grew up in a multi-generational family that owned one of the oldest African American funeral homes in Houston. As a boy, he'd been joined at the hip to his grandfather, following him around, watching how to console without intruding, to listen without judgment. He'd learned to sense when a family needed direction, suggestions, and when to hold back. When to touch, when to simply pass a box of Kleenex.

Ian was proud of his family history: his great-grandfather had been a gravedigger, his great-grandmother one of the first women, maybe the first Black woman, to be licensed as a funeral home director and embalmer in Texas. His grandfather was born in the small house they'd lived in on the cemetery grounds. They did difficult work, essential work.

Death was, for Ian, a natural and inevitable part of life. A body was what remained after the spirit had moved on. But the rituals centered around the body helped people grieve.

After high school, Ian had enlisted in the Army. That too, was a family tradition: to serve your country. After a deployment in Iraq, he'd returned home. College was a cakewalk after Iraq. He'd taken courses in anatomy, physiology, business management, psychology. He'd looked at mortuary science programs, but they felt superficial compared to his years of on-the-job training. Still, he completed a program to be certified as an autopsy assistant, a diener, and another in forensic pathology.

Ian had worked with the county coroner's office. He'd found forensic work challenging. And he'd had positions with major hospitals, working in morgues or anatomy labs and managing autopsies. But, by his late 30s, he'd assumed his place in the family business.

DMORT was like the National Guard. Ian could get called up at any time. He'd get a USERA letter—*Uniformed Services Employment Rights Act*—to provide his employers. Now that meant his father and grandfather.

Ian had been called up for Hurricane Katrina in New Orleans. He'd spent weeks doing work that would horrify and traumatize most people. Cataloging and identifying bodies. Unrecognizable bodies. Bodies that had been in filthy water for days. Bodies with limbs torn off. Bodies that had left "human" far, far behind.

Ian did this, recognizing that each body was a person who'd never imagined that they would drown in their own attics, or be swept away in waves of debris and floodwaters. His job was to identify and process bodies so that their families would have closure. Not that Ian believed in closure. Some doors, once opened, could never close.

Ian had to keep a wall between his head and his heart, or he couldn't do his job. The challenge was taking the wall down after he returned home.

When he was called up for Hurricane Maria in Puerto Rico, in September 2017, Ian had thought that after Katrina, he was prepared. But it was worse. There was no electricity. There was no place to store bodies. The stench was overpowering.

Ian had worked 12 to 14-hour shifts every day for a month. Dental X-rays of faces no longer recognizable. Body inventory. Body assembly. Supporting local medical examiners with whatever they needed.

But now, Ian didn't know why they were being called up. He was just told to pack up, board a plane to Atlanta, pick up a rental car, and drive to Dobbins Air Reserve Base in Marietta, Georgia.

Ian's flight to Atlanta on March 11th was strange. There were very few passengers. No lines. No crowds. The Atlanta airport was deserted.

It was like a movie set before a director yelled, "action!" He'd been through the Atlanta airport many times but had never seen how white it was. White walls, towering white ceilings, sunlight bouncing off the whiteness.

After picking up his rental car, he headed to Marietta. Traffic was light. It was rush hour without the rush.

Ian hoped a hotel room was waiting. He wanted to grab a nap before getting to work. Further orders would be provided upon arrival. That's what he'd been told.

On March 11th, charter flights landed at Dobbins Air Reserve Base filled with passengers from the *Grand Princess*.

It had been a long day, a few long days. Passengers shared being woken up in the middle of the night by people in PPE taking temps and asking medical questions. The cruise line had experience unloading huge numbers of passengers, so that part had been smooth. But once on land, it was messier. Authorities were coordinating between the feds, military, different states and cities, Port of Oakland, CDC, and more.

Mike Pence had announced that all disembarking passengers would be tested. But that never happened.

After being processed, passengers were loaded on buses, then had to wait. There were safety corridors from the ship to the charter planes. They boarded the planes and waited on the tarmac. By the time they got to Georgia, got to Dobbins, they just wanted a clean bed and a shower.

They also wanted clean clothes. They wanted a lot of things that, for some, were in suitcases piled somewhere on a dock in Oakland.

At Dobbins, passengers were quarantined in unused barracks. Fencing encircled the buildings. White tents were pitched outside the fencing to store supplies, water, toiletries—when the supplies arrived. It was a rocky start. There weren't enough beds. Nor enough toilet paper, or bedding, or towels or soap.

Passenger temperatures were checked, but no treatment provided for mild symptoms other than "Take a few Tylenol and..." It was not lack of caring, but insufficient knowledge. Medical staff were scrambling.

Only staff in hazmat suits, full PPE, were allowed in the quarantine buildings. Every time anyone entered or exited, there was a full "don and doff." Put hazmat gear on, totally cover up, do their tasks, and then take it all off.

"Did you see that movie *Contagion*?" one of Ian's co-workers asked the first day. "It's creepy how much this is reminding me of that movie."

"A lot of dying going on in that movie," another DMORT team member chimed in. "Not so sure I wanna' star in *Contagion Two*."

The quarantined passengers had urgent needs for "stuff"—and Ian had a car, and a team, who could go get stuff. "Concierge" was not in his job description, but he wanted to be useful. The quarantined wrote lists of what they needed—Kleenex, toilet paper, ibuprofen, chocolate, potato chips, batteries, paperbacks, notebooks, underwear, diapers, over-the-counter meds, board games —and put the list by the fence with money or a credit card. Ian and team members collected the lists, did store runs and delivered. Most urgent was the need for medications, prescriptions that their physicians from home were now faxing to a Marietta pharmacy.

The passengers, nor anyone outside the fencing, could get within six feet of the fence when anyone was there. They had to distance. And a lot of disinfectant was being used.

"It's not the usual," Ian texted his wife, Nell. "No casualties, just people needing shampoo and toilet paper. Not to worry."

Nell, an elementary school teacher, understood that DMORT was difficult, exhausting work. But Ian knew what he was doing. He had the skills.

Over the years, Ian had shared some of what he saw and did, often with the dark humor that all the DMORT teams used to cope. But there were parts he never disclosed. Like front line combat troops, he held back the worst.

This time felt different to Nell.

If DMORT teams were at Dobbins, then the feds wanted to be prepared, just in case, for a mass casualty event. Ian would then be smack in the *middle* of *that* storm, not called up afterwards to pick up the remains.

Meanwhile, at Dobbins, staff from the cruise line arrived. They immediately got to work arranging meal deliveries from local restaurants, doing whatever they could to make this "two-weeks-from-hell" mandated quarantine a little less frustrating for their passengers.

"I don't believe that I'm saying this, but I think we have it better than some friends we made on ship who are in quarantine in California," one passenger told Ian. "They aren't allowing cruise ship staff to facilitate takeout meals or do errands."

In a white tent, the cruise ship staff created what looked like a little general store. Toiletries, over the counter meds, snacks, toilet paper, and Kleenex. Whatever anyone wanted, they stocked it. They distributed menus to the barracks. They did everything possible to be accommodating. They had no idea what had happened on that ship, what decisions were being made in Washington, what the politics were. They didn't know what their own futures were, or if they'd even have jobs next week. They just smiled and hustled, working as best they could under challenging circumstances with frustrated and frightened people— *their* passengers.

With each day that passed, the heightened vigilance that was part of every DMORT rotation lessened, just a bit.

"Are people getting sick? What will they do then?" Nell asked Ian. "Take them to military hospitals? Can local hospitals manage that degree of contagion?"

Ian reassured her. He did not mention the ambulance that had left the day before, sirens blaring as a man was rushed to the hospital.

Among the arriving ship passengers was a woman who'd felt ill on the ship, but had been placed on a bus and then the charter flight, with other passengers. Her husband had also felt sick. Yesterday, the husband, unresponsive, had been rushed to a hospital in an ambulance. Two weeks later he would be dead.

Ian would not know that last part until after the rotation.

But that was why the feds wanted DMORT on-site. They didn't know how many people might get sick. Or how sick. Or die.

Ian was involved in meetings at the command center to discuss protocols and decision trees. "What if..." scenarios. Coordinating with the CDC. A video meeting with Mike Pence.

It was, he felt, way above his pay grade.

When the quarantine period ended, the passengers were out-processed. They received proof of quarantine certificates. There was a passenger "Graduation Board"—an attempt at humor—and a table of treats next to a temperature check. There were balloons, a lot of near-hysterical laughter, and tears. All of the staff—CDC people, DMORT people, military—were gowned and masked.

The passengers carried their luggage down to be loaded on buses that would take them to airports. They just wanted to go home.

In the end, the DMORT team would return to their respective homes and assume their usual work. A few casualties—COVID cases—had been transported to hospitals. Dobbins, nor the other military bases used for quarantine, did not become mass casualty events.

The last passenger would leave Dobbins on March 26th.

Ian brought home one souvenir, Blue Can Water, with a "50 Year Shelf Life." The label read: "Municipal water processed to remove chemicals and particles using twelve step multi-stage filtering, dual reverse-osmosis under high pressure, micron traps, high intensity UV light and ozone disinfectant resulting in pure water with contaminates less than one PPM."

It was the worst thing Ian had ever tasted.

Grace

When Grace and Chelle walked down the gangplank, tanned and relaxed, they didn't grasp all that they'd missed in the hour-by-hour fluctuating responses of governments and agencies and corporations to the viral spread. When they boarded their Southwest flight back to Kansas, they were surprised to find an empty middle seat.

There were, they observed, many empty middle seats.

"This never happens," Chelle said with a chuckle as she hoisted her carry-on into the overhead compartment. "We lucked out."

It wasn't until they landed, as Mickey drove them back to Kaw Valley, that they heard the word "lockdown."

At 10 a.m. the next morning, sitting at Molly's kitchen table over coffee and a scone from Wheatfield's Bakery, Molly told Grace that Katrina was sick.

"What do you mean sick?" Grace asked. "How sick?"

"Well, she started feeling crappy last week and she has not gotten better."

"That's not like Kat," Grace muttered. "She hardly ever gets sick. She was just skiing in Colorado after Christmas." Grace looked at her watch. "I'll just run over there. I didn't schedule any clients for re-entry day."

"She won't let you in," Molly said. "I brought her soup and had to leave it on the front steps."

Grace's head shot up. "What are you talking about? Why won't she let me in?"

"I mean she will not answer the door and will not let you come into her house," Molly explained, slowly, as if her mother were dim-witted. "She'll talk to you on your cell if she is awake and hears the ring. Kat thinks she may have that coronavirus."

"She *thinks* she *may* have it? Hasn't she been tested?" Grace asked in frustration.

"Tests are hard to come by. And it takes weeks for results. Without spiking a very high fever, she isn't eligible."

"Has she gone to the emergency room? Wouldn't they have to test her then?"

"Going to the ER could be dangerous, Mom," Molly retorted. "It's a hot spot, especially if she has to wait to get examined."

"Is she alone?" Grace's brows furrowed, her frustration turning to worry.

"No, MJ is there. He probably infected her, but he's recovered. He thinks he was infected at his dad's house during a birthday party."

MJ was Martin, Jr., named after his father, Martin, who divorced Katrina (although Katrina's version was "I threw his sorry ass out") after Crystal (a 20-something secretary at his office and his latest in a series of "friendships") got pregnant. The divorce had been years ago when their sons were in their early teens. Martin was now married to Crystal with his "second family."

"Whose birthday?"

"Crystal's mom."

"Why does MJ think he caught the virus there?" Grace was confused, as if she'd stepped back into her life but with missing pieces.

"Martin now says he woke up feeling achy but didn't want to 'ruin' the party. Then Crystal's brothers admitted that they'd also felt 'something coming on.' But they didn't tell anyone. It wasn't until MJ texted his dad that Katrina was really sick that Martin texted back, 'Hey, I've been sick, and Crystal's brothers too. Maybe it's that virus from China?'"

"Those stupid assholes," Grace muttered, finally catching up.

"Exactly," Molly added

"But MJ is better?" Grace asked.

"Yeah. But Kat still feels pretty awful. And all for a birthday party?"

Grace sipped her coffee, wishing that it had a shot of whiskey with a pile of whipped cream on top. First day back and this was a lot to take in without alcohol. The world had shifted somehow while she was gone, and it did not feel right.

"I'll call Kat now and see what I can do," she told Molly, standing up from the table to bring her cup to the sink. "For now, I'll make her some soup."

That first day back was consumed by "re-entry" tasks: sorting mail, scheduling clients, reading back issues of the daily newspaper so she could get some sense of what the hell had happened. She left the soup on Kat's back porch with a note to call. The rest of the soup she brought over for dinner with Max and Molly, hearing Max's accounts of the important elements of his life, like his favorite TV shows and his latest obsession with Fortnite. Whatever that was.

Then, finally, much needed quiet time: a late evening drink on her couch with Mickey, Coltrane playing in the background, trying to de-stress and, if it were possible, to recapture just a smidgen of the peace she'd felt while at sea.

"It's like I got on the ship in one world and came back to a different one," Grace explained to Mickey. "Molly said at dinner that there's talk about canceling school. Is that true? The kids are out for spring break, but she heard that the break might be extended."

"Molly is right. This virus is scary. We don't understand it yet, so everyone is going in circles over what to do. They're talking about a lockdown like they've done in some other countries."

"A national lockdown? Isn't that extreme?" Grace asked, still struggling to make sense of it all. "But, yeah, I guess it would be pretty dumb to shut down one state and have the next one over open."

"I don't see this administration having the cajones to piss the idiots off, and a national lockdown will do that. Trump's more a 'kick the can down the road' kind of guy. Never 'the buck stops here.'"

"You are so mixing metaphors, but I get the point." Grace sighed.

Mickey just looked at her, assessing this perplexed, tan, well-rested woman whose worry lines were becoming more pronounced by the minute.

"Come here, Gracie," he said, patting the couch beside him.

She slid over, and he put his arm around her shoulders and the other across her chest, holding her to him.

"We're going to be okay. This is scary, but we're smart people. We've survived a lot worse. We're resilient."

"Speak for yourself," Grace replied, but, at the same time, she tucked her head even closer into his neck. They sat for a few minutes in silence, inhaling and then exhaling until their breathing synchronized and settled.

"We're going to get up now and go to bed," Mickey said. "And after we turn off the light, you're going to tell me stories about the cruise, and what Chelle liked best, and your favorite ports. And then we're going to sleep for nine hours."

Grace lifted her head to look into his eyes. "I'm not happy to come home to the rest of it, but I happy you're here," she said.

Molly

On March 11th the World Health Organization declared COVID-19 as a pandemic. Molly had no idea what that meant, but it sure was making people nervous. She went out for her usual weekly grocery shopping but found it more chaotic than when a snowstorm was coming in.

Molly pulled out her phone to text her mom: Line at the checkout is SUPER long. Need anything? A moment passed: Toilet paper. Heard there's going to be a shortage. Hand sanitizer.

Toilet paper? Seriously? Sometimes her mother was so over-the-top in the worry department.

On March 13th there was an announcement that all the schools in

Kansas were closing for two weeks. Molly couldn't believe what she was reading. *The schools are closing? All of the schools? K-12?*

Kansas had 18 cases and only one man had died. But he was really old so it could have been anything, maybe a heart attack or some underlying condition. That was *it*.

How the hell was she supposed to manage Max being home for two entire weeks on top of her own work and classes?

Molly impulsively texted Mike.

MOLLY: WTF? They just closed all the schools in Kansas for two weeks. Are they doing that in Florida?

MIKE: Same here. Dept of Ed said all schools closed for two weeks starting the 16th. What about your classes?

MOLLY: KU says to stay home after spring break – but campus is open?

MIKE: You can do this. It's just for a few weeks, right?

MOLLY: I hate it. We have 18 cases in the whole state. What is the big deal?

Grace felt as if *everyone* was scrambling. Molly had make-up time at work and grad classes online. Max was home from school when he should've been in a classroom. Katrina was still isolating and sick.

On top of that, every one of her clients wanted an appointment as soon as possible, which made sense since everyone was now in a state of heightened anxiety.

On March 17th, on top of dealing with Max—who was upset because the St. Patrick's Day Parade had been cancelled—the governor announced that all public schools in Kansas would close for in-school learning for the remainder of the academic year. Since Kansas was the first state to make this announcement, there were thousands of parents who had not seen this coming and were blindsided.

Molly was one of them.

"I don't know how I can take care of Max while I have school," Molly told Grace. "How will I get any of my work done? And my practicum? Is that going to be virtual too? It's crazy."

Molly's grad school program in clinical social work was a hands-on program. At least it had been until the virus.

"I can help some," Grace replied. "And Mickey called this afternoon after the announcement and said to tell you that he'll take some shifts."

Molly looked at her mother. Before Grace had moved back to Kansas, every small crisis with Max had felt overwhelming. She'd felt so terrifically alone. But now...

"Have I told you that Mickey is a good catch?" she asked Grace. "Definitely a keeper."

Grace

Five nights later, Grace was putting her phone on the charger when she saw a text from Katrina: "Call me ASAP. Marty in hospital. Need to call MJ and Malcolm. Want to talk to you first."

She called Kat immediately.

"Start at the beginning," she said as soon as Kat picked up.

"I got a call from Crystal about 6 p.m. I knew Marty had been sick, but he was getting better," Katrina said. "Then, last night, he couldn't breathe. Crystal said it was different from anything she'd seen, like he was trying to get air, but he couldn't. She called 911 and the EMTs took him to the hospital. They immediately put him on oxygen, but by late afternoon today, they said he needed to be on a ventilator."

Grace was listening but her mind was racing. This was the first person she personally knew who was seriously ill from coronavirus. The usual platitudes, like, "Oh, don't you worry, he'll be okay," had a hollow echo. Most diseases were treatable.

But coronavirus? Everyone, even the healthcare workers, felt lost. It felt like a new hypothesis was being tested every day.

"How do I tell the boys?" Katrina asked. A muffled sound came from her mouth, as if she was stifling a cough.

"Is there anything they can do?"

"Crystal said family isn't allowed in the hospital."

"Where are the boys now?"

"Malcolm is in New Orleans and can't leave. MJ is back in Kansas City."

"Look, there isn't *anything* either of them can do if family isn't allowed in the hospital."

"A part of me doesn't want to tell them because they'll worry and want to come. MJ is just an hour away. But Malcolm is high-risk. Remember how he had pneumonia three times when he was in middle school?" Katrina was speaking fast, words stumbling. "I can't let him be exposed to this. I need to protect him."

Grace started to say, *There is no way you are going to be able to protect your adult male sons,* but clamped her teeth together before the words could slip out. She was already anxious about Molly and Max, and they were right under her nose.

"I think you just tell them that their dad is in the ICU, and the medical staff here is great, and it will just take some time to beat this thing. Give them the facts. But there's nothing that they can do at this point."

"Yeah, that's what I was thinking. But I wanted to hear it from you," Katrina paused. "I haven't felt this shaken in years. I mean, Marty has always been such a force. Aggravating as hell, but nothing knocked him down. Look at the man: old enough to be a grandpa but he's going to parent-teacher conferences with his trophy wife? And now he's in an ICU? And from *what*? Not cancer. Not a heart attack. From a damn virus?"

With that, Grace heard what else was fueling the panic and fear in Kat's voice.

"You are not Marty, Katrina Baptiste. You come from a long line of strong women who have faced down worse than this."

"I'm scared, Gracie," Kat said, her voice choking up. "I've never been this sick and, as soon I think that I'm turning the corner, I get slammed again."

"It hasn't even been three weeks, right? Your body is dealing with a devil, and you need to stop fighting. Everything you think is so important can wait. If the schools stay closed for the rest of the year, *everyone* will be scrambling. And since the courts shut down today, whatever hearings you had coming up are in limbo."

"What do you mean 'the courts shut down today?'" Kat asked, with urgency and surprise. "I've been asleep a lot of the day, and national news does not cover local Kansas."

"I mean that Douglas County Courts have suspended all in-person trials and hearings, civil and criminal, until further notice. They'll keep doing CINC, PFAs, PFSs, but even those may be remote."

"Holy shit," Kat muttered. "I don't remember this ever happening before. This is getting scarier and scarier."

Four days later, Grace emailed her clients to discuss how they wanted to move forward. She said she was willing to meet in person, but outside. She was considering trying the gazebo in the park by the courthouse. It was up 10-15 steps and usually deserted. And it was, after all, public property—and she was part of the public. She could bring a few camp chairs and sit six feet apart. No one could approach without being seen. And it was covered, so appointments wouldn't get rained out. Or, she wrote, they could have sessions on FaceTime or over the phone. Molly wanted to teach her how to Zoom, but Grace wasn't quite ready. It was enough learning the language: Zoom as verb—"Do you want to Zoom?"—or noun.

Grace had never heard of it until now.

Zed

Zed was not looking for QAnon. He was not looking, really, for anything. He was just scrolling on his phone, waiting for Cherry, his wife, to pick him up at work because the truck was in the shop again.

He looked over some dumb news release and then clicked a link to another piece and then another. One was talking about Hilary Clinton and how she pulled a fast one with her smooth-talking, screwing-around husband and a land deal that had been shady from the get-go and then got washed away after some pseudo investigation. He didn't remember most of it, but he'd been a kid back then.

He'd read the sports section of the paper those days, if anything at all.

Zed paid his taxes because they were taken out of his paycheck. But, if he had a choice, he'd prefer to find a loophole like the rich people seemed able to do. As far as Zed was concerned, the rules were made by rich people for rich people. He figured he'd behave exactly like they did if he ever got hold of some big bucks. Then the rules would be in his favor. Until then, life was going to be paycheck to paycheck and hoping the truck wouldn't give out.

Zed didn't vote. He'd never felt that anyone in any office gave a shit about what he felt or needed. And when he looked at who ended up shopping in Dollar General because the decent grocery stores were miles away, and how the lines at the food banks got longer after the 20th of every month, he knew he wasn't alone. He didn't know if any of the rest of the poor suckers voted, but, as far as he could see, if they did it never made a difference.

Over the next few days, Zed clicked on a few more links. Every time he opened his phone, a new one popped up. It was like he'd stumbled into a different world, but it made sense to him. Each site sounded urgent: what we see on TV is fake; the big name newspapers only "report" what they are told to write; there are people pulling the strings who are invisible; there is a Deep State, secret and corrupt, that benefits from keeping us all in the dark, that wants and needs us to believe the lies.

It was when he found forums, chat rooms, where ordinary people were communicating, that he got hooked.

There was something in the tone that resonated with Zed. To find that there were so many other people who also felt locked down—expected to swallow whatever was on the front page of the newspaper, or coming out of the mouth of a TV network so-called journalist, without question—made Zed feel less alone. He liked that no one had easy answers. Everyone was asking questions, following clues, helping each other out if they'd seen something that might make the puzzle connect. He was tired of the know-it-all political people, the smooth talkers, telling him what was best for him like they had any idea what his life was like.

The first time he answered someone's question, actually chimed in and contributed, was in some ways a first for him. He'd *never* been the kid who raised his hand to answer in class. He'd always hunkered down in his seat, not making eye contact with the teacher, staring at the floor, at his sneakers, at anything. Answering was risky, volunteering more so. He could be wrong. Kids could snicker or even laugh at him. The fear of being wrong had always been more powerful that any desire to be right. He'd learned young to keep his mouth shut.

But this was different. There was no one answer, no right answer. They were all hunting. There were a million questions, a million people, all venturing out, all looking for pieces of a puzzle that they were just starting to visualize. He felt acceptance and approval when he chimed into the conversation. Even, "Yeah, that's what I was wondering," coming from a stranger felt good. He felt curious when he got online in the evening after work. There were always people on the forums, no one condescending, no one in charge. Just adding to the conversation.

In the first few weeks, he was sporadic. There were evenings when he didn't think about it, when he and Cherry binge-watched some TV series. But then, the next day, he'd found himself wondering what he'd missed.

But it was—*more*? Like how he *felt* before logging in, a twinge of excitement, of anticipation. There were few things that Zed had ever really looked forward to other than sports games. And even with sports, he often felt like he was rooting for the wrong team.

There were never enough wins.

But Q was different. Sure, there were no clear answers, but he never knew when a break would come, some new "drop." Which was another part of it. He'd learned, mostly from just listening, what the lingo was. It was like a code, and he knew the language.

He wanted to talk about this with Cherry, but what if she thought he was bonkers? They were arguing enough already. Not like they needed something else to bicker about.

Zed had married Cherry when she was 19 and he was 23. They'd dated, on-and-off, since she was 17, only back then she'd lied to him and told him she was 18. Her dad was a cop and, when he found out his baby was getting screwed by some "older guy" who'd dropped out of high school and had no life-plans, well, Zed had almost found himself being charged with statutory rape, which made no sense as Cherry looked 18, acted 18, and clearly knew her way around a cock. She'd taught him a few things and he didn't want to think about where she'd learned them.

He'd hooked up with other girls, sure, but Cherry was different. She liked him, but she wanted more. So, he'd signed up for night classes and got his GED. He applied for a day job at Home Depot and landed it. 40

hours a week, steady, some shift changes but no big deal.

But it was moving out of his dad's basement and into a high-ceilinged, two-bedroom apartment in a big old house that got her attention. Remembering the day he'd shown Cherry the empty apartment, surprising her when it still had the wet paint smell, still made him smile.

"You know how you watch all those HGTV shows?" he'd said. "I think you could make this place into something special."

"This is your new apartment?" she'd asked, taking in the tall windows and hardwood floors, the wooden built-in cabinets. "Seriously?"

"Yeah," he'd replied. "And it could be ours if you're thinking the same way I am."

"Gee, Zed, you are such a romantic," she'd said, laughing. "Flattery *and* HGTV. That's a new angle."

But Cherry couldn't help herself from getting involved, especially when it was clear that he'd sleep on an air mattress for months if she didn't.

They started going together to yard sales on Saturday mornings, getting up at a ridiculously early hour when he used to sleep until at least noon. Zed had no idea what things were worth, but when Cherry whispered, "Oh shit, this is a great deal," he paid attention. She nabbed a "just like new" queen mattress and frame for $40, a sheet set for $5, a comforter and a rug for $20. A sofa that Cherry called "moss green" and looked like nobody had *ever* sat on it, was $35.

Cherry found large, old, framed prints of lakes and ocean scenes, at an estate sale for $4 each. Zed had never had art, but Cherry explained how perfectly this one would "bring together" the living room and that one would "pop" by the dining table.

Zed paid for everything. But, with every purchase, Cherry was creating a space that Zed hoped she might like enough to want to share.

And, if she didn't, well, he was going to end up with a chick-magnet of a place, nicer than anything he could have ever put together. He wouldn't come across as a "loser, empty-fridge, beer guzzling, mattress-on-the-floor-horny-dude." Those were not his words, but how Brenda, his cousin, had once described his basement space at his dad's.

Brenda had never minced words.

But she almost gushed at his new place.

"Damn, Zed, this looks great. Classy even. This is a place you can be proud to bring a girl," she said, perhaps realizing that her prior comments might have been a bit harsh. "Only problem is that any girl who can think past her nose will realize that another girl did it."

After Cherry started to stay over, first on Saturdays, then full weekends, Zed gave her a key on a little gold chain with her name on it. Without ever making a big deal of it, she started leaving clothing in one closet, and her "products," as she called them, in a red basket under the bathroom sink.

They were a couple.

When she missed her period, it had been sort of scary for both of them, but not the end of the world. It seemed more like the Universe showing them the next step. They talked about an abortion, but Cherry had been raised Catholic. And, as she logically explained, Catholics do get abortions, but only for really good reasons. Like getting raped. Or being halfway through college and knowing they could end up on welfare and never be able to give the baby a good life. Or being abandoned by the guy and scared that their family would cut them off for getting knocked up.

And Cherry had none of those "good" reasons.

So, it wasn't that they wanted a baby at that point, and they sure had not been "trying." It was more, "We'd probably end up married in a few years anyway, so this is just a change in the timeline."

Cody was born five months after their wedding and Colton fifteen months later. Their life of hanging out with friends, going to the bar to get a pitcher and watch games or play darts, disappeared. It was diapers and feedings, breasts sore from nursing, laundry that piled up in corners, and re-heated pizza. Zed tried to be a good dad, but he was working extra evening shifts at a McDonald's to meet the bills. Cherry missed working, but childcare for two kids cost so much they wouldn't break even.

It was tough all around. It was hard to have any conversation without resentments about money and time and their sheer exhaustion getting in the way.

MAX

Max was not struggling as much as most other kids were with the school closures and lockdowns. He did not play sports or have a social life in the way that other kids did.

"I'm fine," he told his mom when she asked him for the tenth time in three days how he was doing.

Once virtual school started, it took a few days to adjust. Max liked being able to lie on the floor of his room and not be expected sit at a desk all day. Nobody told him to get back in his chair. The teacher had way too much to deal with tracking a screen with 24 kids in 24 houses. His mom said that his teacher was "flustered." And "very stressed."

His teacher told his mom it was okay if he wanted to not be seen on video, to just watch the lesson. So, he could roll around on the floor or hang off the bed if he felt like it without distracting the other kids.

Some subjects were easier than others for him. He was able to follow history pretty well but got lost in math. Having his mom take notes for the hard subjects, then review with him later, helped.

His mom was never with him in class before the pandemic, so this was better. Mickey and his Grammy also came over on different days to help him stay on track. So, Max was having more time with the three people he liked best and did not have to get up as early to get ready for school. His mom let him sleep in and go to online school in his pajamas if he wanted.

"When do you think this will be over and we have to go back to school?" he asked his mom after a week.

"I have no idea," Molly replied. "Not soon enough."

But Max did not feel that way about it.

When the announcement had been on the TV that the governor of Kansas was declaring that all schools would be closed for the remainder of the year, his mother looked shocked, like when she'd seen a mouse run across the kitchen floor. She'd said, really loud, "Are you fucking kidding me?" even though she'd told him to never use the "F" word.

She apologized, but she still had to put a dollar in the swear jar.

"We're #1," Max told Mickey when he came over later that afternoon.

"How so?" Mickey asked.

"Kansas is #1. We're the first state to close the schools until next year. Do you think we will be the only state? That would be lucky, right?"

"I'm not sure your mom would agree with 'lucky,' buddy-boy," Mickey answered. "And I'm pretty sure that other states will be doing the same thing."

"Maybe schools will never open again, huh? Maybe everybody will need to learn stuff all by themselves?"

"No, Max, that is not going to happen. But this could mean new ways of doing things. We're going to have to adjust our ideas of what's normal."

"Normal is just a word," Max said. "Like when other kids tell me that I'm not normal, they mean that I'm not just like them. And I think they're a little strange because they don't think like me. I'm me and I'm my own normal."

Mickey listened to Max, watched his tapping left hand, his eyes that went past Mickey to fixate on the far wall.

"You are certainly that, kiddo," Mickey concluded.

HISTORICAL CONTEXT: MARCH 2020

Mar. 1: The first COVID-19 case is reported in New York.

Mar. 4: The CDC formally removes restrictions that limited coronavirus testing to people in the hospital or close contact with confirmed cases. According to the CDC, clinicians should now "use their judgment to determine if a patient has signs and symptoms compatible with COVID-19 and whether the patient should be tested." But that was only if tests were available, which was not the case.

Mar. 4: "If we have thousands or hundreds of thousands of people that get better by, you know, just sitting around and even going to work—some of them go to work, but they get better." – *Donald Trump*

Mar. 5: "I never said people that are feeling sick should go to work." – *Donald Trump*

Mar. 6: "I like this stuff. I really get it. People are surprised that I understand it. Every one of these doctors said, 'How do you know so much about this?' Maybe I have a natural ability. Maybe I should have done that instead of running for President." – *Donald Trump*

Mar. 8: "We have a perfectly coordinated and fine-tuned plan at the White House for our attack on coronavirus." – *Donald Trump*

Mar. 11: The World Health Organization categorizes the coronavirus as a pandemic.

Mar. 11: President Trump addresses the nation from the Oval Office in primetime—"On the Coronavirus Pandemic"—"We must put politics aside, stop the partisanship and unify together as one nation and one family." Trump outlined critical and essential steps to control the virus. Then he did the opposite.

Mar. 12: "The system is not really geared to what we need right now... That's a failing. Let's admit it." – *Dr. Anthony Fauci*

Mar. 13: The Atlantic reports that less than 14,000 tests have been done in the ten weeks since the Administration had first been notified of the virus, though Mike Pence had promised the week prior that 1.5 million tests would be available by this time.

Mar. 13: Breonna Taylor, a 26-year-old Black medical worker, is killed by police in her Louisville, Kentucky apartment in a botched no-knock warrant raid. She had nothing to do with the case.

Mar. 13: The cruise industry voluntarily suspends cruising, but dozens of ships had by then reported cases of symptomatic passengers. The *Miami Herald* would later report that 87 ships had had cases, and 111 crew and passengers died.

Mar. 16: "Respirators, ventilators, all of the equipment—try getting it yourselves." – *Donald Trump to state governors.*

Mar. 16: Laura Ingraham, on Fox News, introduces Gregory Rigano, a 34-year-old lawyer who self-published an article on Google Docs on the use of hydroxychloroquine to treat COVID-19, and argued for its use prophylactically.

Mar. 17: Anthony Fauci tells Laura Ingraham, on Fox News, that the "buzz" about hydroxychloroquine is unsubstantiated, only anecdotal reports from marginalized sources.

Mar. 17: Kansas becomes the first state to close its public schools for the remainder of the school year, by order of Governor Laura Kelly.

Mar. 18: Tucker Carlson brings Rigano back on Fox News. Rigano has acquired additional albeit false Stanford credentials. He continues to promote hydroxychloroquine, asserting 100% cure rate.

Mar. 19: President Trump announces at a press conference that he is ordering the FDA to "fast track" approval of the Fox News drug discovery.

Mar. 19: California becomes the first state to issue a stay-at-home order. Between March and April 2020, 42 additional states direct residents to stay at home in response to the pandemic.

Mar. 20: In a White House Task Force Briefing, Fauci refutes the use of hydroxychloroquine as a COVID-19 treatment. Trump overrides with "I feel good about it... That's all it is, just a feeling..."

Mar. 23: In his first post on the topic, the individual known as Q promotes two theories about COVID-19: It's both a Chinese bioweapon and an effort by the Democrats and China to stop Trump's re-election by destroying the economy.

Mar. 24: Tokyo postpones Olympic Games scheduled for summer 2020.

Mar. 26: The United States becomes the country with the most confirmed cases of COVID. It will remain so for the remainder of the Trump administration.

Mar. 27: Donald Trump signs the CARES act into law. The $2 trillion stimulus plan includes payments for $1,200 checks, with $500 for each eligible dependent under 16 years of age. Most of the funds designed to keep business afloat end up with big corporations while small business are frozen out. Minority-owned small businesses take the hardest hit.

Mar. 29: "Unfortunately the enemy is death...a lot of people are dying...it's very unpleasant." – *Donald Trump*

Mar. 23-Apr. 6: "During the two weeks between March 23 and April 6, Fox hosts and their guests promoted hydroxychloroquine nearly 300 times." – *Lawrence Wright, The Plague Year*

April 2020

Katrina

It had been a month since Kat had been blindsided by the virus. It took almost that long before Kat could get checked out by her physician.

She still could not get tested for COVID-19.

"The viral load will be too low to register since it's been a long time since you became symptomatic," the nurse said.

"So how do I know for sure?" Katrina asked.

"You can't."

Katrina didn't have the energy to argue.

The physical exam showed diminished lung function and muscle atrophy, but almost everything else that she could feel happening in her body was invisible.

"When will I get back to normal? How long can I expect to feel this shitty?" Kat asked.

"I have no idea," her physician said. "We don't understand this virus enough to make projections."

With those words, Katrina felt a visceral tremor of panic.

She was not getting better. Infinitely small, incremental changes, perhaps, but then even those seemed to relapse. The deep muscle pain had abated somewhat, but her joints felt swollen and ached. The fatigue was unrelenting. Her attempts to work from home had failed, as she read and re-read paperwork but then could not remember nor understand what it meant. Her memory, which had been laser sharp, had evaporated.

Katrina was frightened. She did not recognize the woman in her mirror, whose skin seemed too loose for her face, dark, deep circles under her eyes. She could not accept that this frail body, whose hands needed to grasp at the towel rack to step out of the tub or hold onto a chair for balance after walking across the room, belonged to her.

But worse than the physical challenges were the mental and

emotional ones.

Katrina had never felt the kind of fear that now consumed her. When faced with difficult circumstances, she took action. Tackled it head on. When she realized that her marriage was kaput, that nothing she could do would make Martin monogamous, she'd focused on getting the finances in order, documenting, developing a plan and making a checklist.

And when the checklist was completed, voila! Divorce final. Don't look back.

But action now was futile, even counter-productive. When she tried to power through, she paid a high price for days.

After her appointment, Katrina did follow up on one recommendation: to get a pulse oximeter and check her oxygen levels three times a day. It was a little device she could put over her fingernail that read oxygen levels. It might read a little lower than the hospital grade oximeter, but she was told to track levels for consistency. Below 90 and she should call her doctor. Immediately.

Katrina started calling local pharmacies, then the chains, Walgreens, CVS, Walmart. But they were *all* sold out.

Kat got on Amazon. There were several brands to pick from and she selected a mid-range one and placed an order. Then it popped up that delivery would be in five weeks. She clicked back to search but most of them were on back order. Then she spotted one that was more expensive, but it appeared to be available. Of course, what appeared available and what might actually get shipped as promised and not delayed for weeks, was a crapshoot. No matter, within two minutes she ordered three. Clearly this was going to be a hot item and either Grace, Molly, or the kids would want one.

Katrina had been told that she did not have a formal COVID diagnosis as she had not spiked a *high* fever—now considered to be over 104—or been hospitalized.

So, what the hell did they think had kept her out of work for a month?

She did not have the diagnosis because she had not been tested. She could not get tested when ill because the limited number of tests were reserved for people with high fevers and incapacitating coughing.

It was a Catch-22.

"Just have to ride it out," her doctor said. "The more you focus on it, the longer it may linger."

Right, Kat thought, *I'm dying here, but maybe it's psychosomatic? My anxiety about being sick is keeping me sick?* She did not know if she was more scared or angry. Her body was experiencing the battle of a lifetime, but she might not be taken seriously?

And Katrina had credentials. She'd thrown out the word "attorney" at times, and it did help. Especially if she just slipped it in, like, "I cannot imagine how difficult it is for you to deal all day with so many upset and frightened people," she'd said to the nurse who'd returned her call. "I've been an attorney for decades, but I've never had to deal with so much at one time. I'm used to helping people but now I can't stand upright without getting dizzy."

That time, she'd scored: one prescription for joint pain and another for dizziness.

Katrina had no idea how people were managing to get the medical care and support they needed without credentials to leverage.

Mickey

Mickey was reading up on "How to Coronavirus-Proof Your Home." As the only man in his "pod" (the new word to describe small units of family or close friends committed to safety protocols and mutual protection) composed of Grace, Molly, Max, and himself, he felt a responsibility to "secure the perimeter." Katrina would be joining their pod as soon as she felt a bit better.

Mickey felt as if they were under attack, the virus an alien invasion, and a more proactive defense strategy was needed. Everything he was reading vacillated between saying "Recommendations may change as officials learn more" to prescribing explicit, specific directives as if there was no possibility of any contradiction.

It was pretty much up to people to sort it out for themselves.

Mickey read that they were to "make a game plan" and "set up a disinfecting station" outside a door. Take off shoes and outerwear before entering the home. When they are out, avoid coming within six feet of anyone and wipe the handles on carts when shopping. No need to wear a mask or gloves, yet, but wash your hands frequently and avoid touching your face. Anything brought into the house needs to be disinfected, including take-out boxes, groceries, packages. Produce must be washed. Disinfect doorknobs, light switches, keys, phones, keyboards, remotes. This must be done with EPA approved disinfectants and surfaces left wet for 3 to 5 minutes. Clothes worn outside the pod are to be washed on the hottest possible setting, and even laundry hampers need to be disinfected. They were not to shake dirty laundry to avoid spreading any viral particles in the air.

Then the article expanded to people. First, there were to be no guests, period. If someone in the home got sick, they were to isolate, use a separate bathroom, and not share utensils or anything. No touching or hanging out in the same room.

Mickey stopped reading, went into his kitchen, and poured himself a double shot of whiskey over ice, then added ginger beer and lime. He leaned against the counter, took a long, slow sip, and looked through the back window to his yard.

Mickey took another sip, considering how much of this guidance assumed living quarters of middle-to-upper-middle-class families, with multiple bedrooms and bathrooms and "shared living space." It would be hard to set up a "disinfecting station" when you had no entry, just a small living room and kitchen, two bedrooms, one crowded bathroom, limited closets and four kids.

"Oh, sweet Jesus," Mickey muttered to himself. "This is not going to end well."

Katrina

Marty had been on a ventilator for almost three weeks. That's three weeks of having tubes going down his throat into his lungs, a machine that was breathing for him, muscles atrophying from not being used at all. And Marty was not getting better.

Katrina called Crystal every few days for updates, and to listen to whatever Crystal needed to vent. As much as she'd initially been pissed at Crystal for having an affair with Martin, and getting pregnant with Martin, that double whammy had been the final straw that Kat had needed to stop pretending that her marriage was okay and file for divorce.

Which, once Kat developed a different perspective, had proven to be a positive life transition for her.

Katrina had Crystal to thank for that. And there was more.

It had been a summer Saturday morning, years ago, Katrina dropping the boys off for a weekend with Dad. But, once again, Martin was not even there.

"He has a golf tournament," Crystal had told Kat. "He said he'll be back by 4 p.m."

"Did he remember that it's his weekend?" Kat had asked, her tone frustrated with an edge of sarcasm.

"Yes, but this is for work."

"Yeah, that's what I heard for years. Not sure I buy it."

And there had been a moment, unspoken, where the two women recognized they shared something. Being married to Martin meant loving a man who was charismatic, charming, even sweet, but who took his wives for granted. Who could be—evasive? A smooth talker?

"It's hard on the boys when they're told to *not* make their own plans with friends because it's 'Dad's time' but then he isn't here. And then, when he gets back, his focus is on the younger kids," Katrina had said. "I don't mean to come across bitchy. They'd be embarrassed to say it out loud, but they're jealous. The 'Daddy' your kids have was never that kind of dad to them. I know it's not anything you can control, but..."

"I realize that," Crystal had agreed. "They're in a tough position. I'll see what I can do. I don't want them hurting."

And Crystal had followed through. She'd told Martin that for at least one Sunday a month he was taking his older sons out alone for the day. No debate. No excuses. Crystal had "balls" that Kat, when she honestly reviewed her own marital history with Martin, had lacked. The two women were different generations. And Martin, perhaps more motivated in this marriage than the prior one, or perhaps appreciating how difficult his life would be to be twice divorced, paying child support for four kids to two different moms, was more receptive.

"Go for a drive, to a museum, or a game. Find something to share. But you can't have teenagers and toddlers lumped together and expect them to like it," Crystal had told him. "Your kids deserve a better dad, and *time* is the only way to show them that they matter to you."

Now that Crystal was overwhelmed, Kat wanted to be helpful. But how? She could barely take a shower and dress without needing to lie down. So, she called and listened. And ordered take-out delivered to Crystal.

She could do that much from her couch.

Grace & Alex & Graciella

Grace was on FaceTime with her son, Alex, and his wife, Graciella. They lived in Panama, in Gorgona, a beach town west of Panama City.

For years, too many years, Grace and Alex had been estranged. Each had blamed the other for—who knew exactly? Each had been both right *and* wrong. Mickey had been the one to push Grace to reconcile.

Grace owed Mickey big-time for that push. Without him, she wouldn't have flown to Panama a few years back to reconnect with her son. Since then, their connection had been repaired.

Now Grace talked on the phone with Alex every few weeks. Grace and Mickey had been scheduled to go to Panama for a visit, but COVID hit. They now hoped to go once the virus calmed down.

Panama had been ahead of the United States as far as reacting to the virus. They'd closed their borders in early March to all travelers from China and Europe. Soon after their first case, and when the virus started spreading worldwide, they closed their borders to all travel into the country.

"We had a curfew from 9 p.m. to 5 a.m., and they banned all alcohol sales," Alex explained. "I think people are more upset about no beer than the curfew."

"That's way more than we have here," Grace said. She could just imagine the response to the government closing liquor stores. Right now, they were at the top of the "essential providers" list along with groceries. And she could see the reasoning.

"Oh, that was weeks ago," Alex continued. "Then they made the curfew 5 p.m. to 5 a.m. Then they imposed a curfew where you can only leave your house for two hours a day based on the last number of your cedula."

"What's a cedula?" Grace asked.

"A national ID card, like a Social Security number in the United States."

"I cannot believe that people accept that," Grace said.

"Well," Alex continued, "the police are doing a lot of stop-and-check your cedula, and there are stiff fines for violations."

Grace shook her head, dumbfounded. "Here people would be screaming about their rights."

"Well, people in the United States haven't lived under a dictatorship—yet. Although down here people believe that Trump is a wannabe dictator in cahoots with Putin. Panama knows dictators and they have Trump pegged. Did I tell you the name 'Trump' is off the Trump Hotel in Panama City?"

"No, I missed that nugget."

"Anyway, we call a hotline or use WhatsApp if we think we could have the virus. We're interviewed and then, if they think you might have it, a nurse or medical person comes to your house to test you. If you need to go to a hospital, they send an ambulance to bring you. If you test positive, but are home, a doctor or nurse follows up with you every day."

"*Daily?*" Grace asked. "They follow up *daily*? How can they afford to do that?"

"National health system. Everything costs one-tenth what it is in the United States. Some drawbacks, but the rich can always do private pay. It works for the rest of us."

"How are people managing to pay bills if they're in lockdown?"

"No one has to make a house payment or rent, car payment, or credit card payment for four months. Utilities, internet, and cell phones will not be cut off for not paying bills. It's a safety net."

They chatted a bit more, about the weather (which was, Grace had observed, *always* better in Panama), COVID isolation, anxiety, and then clicked off. Grace considered how damn different the two countries were. Given that the U.S. could not even manage a coherent and consistent message from the CDC and the White House, mandating curfews and getting compliance seemed impossible.

Mickey

Mickey knew more than he was willing to share with Grace and Katrina about ventilators. He didn't want to tell them what Martin was enduring or how damaged his body would be when and if they weaned him off.

When he'd been on the police force, Mickey had had a partner, Vic, who'd been put on one. He'd developed complications when a routine surgery morphed into an infection.

What Mickey knew was that the man released from the hospital bore no resemblance to the man who'd entered it nine weeks before.

He couldn't walk because every muscle had atrophied. He couldn't dress, feed, or bathe himself. He couldn't talk well because his brain had forgotten how to make his tongue and jaw work to make words. And when he tried to talk, he could not remember words. He couldn't swallow because, apparently—and Mickey had felt stupid for not realizing it before kidding him—swallowing requires coordination of multiple systems to do the actions in a certain sequence, directed by the brain, to chew and then push the food down the esophagus. He couldn't track conversations or remember anything, except maybe the nightmares that had terrified him when he'd been on the ventilator. Vic's vision had unpredictable, intermittent blurring. There is pain in having a tube thrust down your throat all the way to your lungs, and pain when the body's position is changed, and pain when the sedative is almost working but not really. So, even without memory of being sedated and on the ventilator, his body had been traumatized.

Mickey remembered the look in Vic's eyes when he couldn't remember words, couldn't walk without assistance, or when he started to choke because he forgot *how* to swallow in the middle of *trying* to swallow. There had been a bewildered fear in the man who'd lunged into danger as a cop, courageous and determined, always willing to be the first one through a door when they didn't know what to expect on the other side. Vic had mentored young cops, making time to take them out for a beer and burger after a tough shift. He'd let them talk out whatever had happened, and then put it in a context.

Mickey remembered when Vic said to him, without self-pity, as a statement of fact, "I wished they'd let me die." He remembered feeling helpless about reassuring his friend that it was all going to work out, give it time, take it slow.

But time didn't make a difference. Vic was done as a cop. He took early retirement. And it did not all "work out." He was never the same man. He aged twenty years, and his heart broke, in the weeks on that ventilator. He was found dead in his apartment about five years later of an "accidental" overdose of his prescription meds.

Cherry

Cherry was feeling anxious. Zed had been weird lately about his phone and the computer. He was on them a lot, and never seemed to have a specific reason, like looking for which restaurants were having free delivery specials or "kids eat free specials."

They were not arguing as much, which, once Cherry noticed, made her question even more. What was Zed doing that made him less cranky? He'd even given the boys a bath and put them down without rolling his eyes or saying something like, "I did work all day, you know," as if her doing 24/7 with the kids, keeping them from killing each other, cooking, and picking up their messes, was a walk in the park.

When Cherry finally confronted Zed after he'd spent two hours on the computer late one evening, her tone was demanding, even accusative. "What the hell is going on? Are you watching porn?" she'd said, her eyes hot and angry, but keeping her voice low so she didn't wake the boys.

Zed had blustered up, defensive. That porn thing had been a few years ago and he'd never understood the big deal. Every guy he knew watched porn. But then he'd calmed down and said, "No, it's QAnon stuff. I'm trying to learn more and figure it out."

And Cherry had not gone off on him. Maybe she was relieved that it wasn't porn, or he wasn't texting—or sexting—another girl, one whose breasts were still perky because they hadn't nursed two insatiable kids, who could wear a bikini and flaunt her tight little ass. Cherry missed having *that* body.

Cherry had simply dropped to the floor, an overflowing basket of laundry in front of her, and said, "Well, your kids are finally asleep, and I need to fold this shit-pile, so you may as well help sort and tell me what you're getting into."

Cherry had listened, not interrupting, as he tried to put words to what he was thinking. She didn't tell him he was being stupid. She'd folded the laundry, her head cocked to one side, like she was trying to understand. When he'd finished, she'd asked for links to some of the websites.

When Zed got home from work the next evening, she'd told him that she'd checked out a few of the sites and chat rooms, and there was some stuff that made sense to her. How a lot of the people were concerned about children, and possible abuse. This hit home with her as she'd been sexually abused as a kid by a neighbor who her parents had believed when he'd denied such a ridiculous accusation.

Like she'd made it all up "for attention."

And from then on, like rain hoped for yet unexpected after a long drought, they fell back into talking, back to being friends.

Cherry always had something or other to report when he got home from work because she'd checked into some sites when Cody and Colton, now six and four, were napping. After supper, they cleaned up the kitchen together once the kids were down, talking, musing, wondering. They shared a curiosity, a desire to track and know, in this netherworld where anything could mean something different. They found acceptance and affirmation in the relationships that they started to build with other seekers.

Katrina

Katrina was sitting in her favorite chair looking out the window to her backyard. A couple of blue jays had settled in, and Kat hoped that they would build a nest. She'd closed her eyes and was starting to doze when the phone jarred her from her slumber.

It was Crystal.

"They want to take him off the ventilator," Crystal said, sobbing. "His other systems are shutting down and his lungs are too damaged. How could this happen? How can they just give up?"

Katrina listened as Crystal continued. She would never remember what else Crystal said.

In mere hours, it all got worse.

The ICU scheduled a time so that Crystal and the kids, all four of them, could say goodbye to Martin on FaceTime. Martin was in a coma and did not respond, but they proceeded. "Goodbye Daddy, I love you Daddy," his younger children yelled. His older sons watched in horrified disbelief.

Martin was pronounced dead 17 minutes after they took him off the ventilator. He never regained consciousness.

The body was double wrapped in body bags and brought down to the hospital morgue to be transported to a funeral home. There would be no viewing, no funeral, no rituals of mourning shared with family and friends. His body was cremated the next day. It was never removed from the body bags. The fear of contagion was high.

Crystal wrote an obituary, asking all the kids to contribute. They added that there would be a memorial service at some point in the future. They had no idea when that would be.

Katrina's focus was on MJ and Malcolm. MJ had been in his apartment in Kansas City when informed he had ten minutes to prepare to say goodbye to his father. Malcolm was still in New Orleans. Their relationship with their father, so strained years back, had gradually improved. Martin had made efforts to connect, and they'd each, individually, come to accept what he could give and yearn less for what they'd missed.

But both of them had expected that they had *time. More time.* They'd each counted on having their father in their lives until they were considerably older. They'd hoped to find a vicarious pleasure and joy when, perhaps, Martin would be an affectionate grandfather to children they might someday have.

To his family, it felt as if Martin had been erased.

His ashes were stored in a black cardboard container on a shelf at the funeral home. They would remain there, as the shelves in the back room got more and more crowded.

Mickey kept his mouth shut. He did not say, "Maybe this is for the best."

HISTORICAL CONTEXT: APRIL 2020

Apr. 2: "Massive amounts of medical supplies...are being delivered directly to states... Some states have insatiable appetites and are never satisfied... The complainers should have been stocked up and ready long before this crisis hit." – *Donald Trump*

Apr. 3: Trump administration recommends Americans wear "non-medical" cloth face coverings. Etsy reports a 79% jump in sales during the month, selling 12 million face masks.

Apr. 3: "I don't think I'm going to be doing it...I think wearing a face mask as I greet presidents, prime ministers, dictators, kings, queens...I don't see it for myself...Maybe I'll change my mind." – *Donald Trump*

Apr. 6: U.S death toll passes 10,000.

Apr. 7: "You are not going to die from this pill...I think it's a great thing to try." –*Donald Trump promoting Hydroxychloroquine as a treatment for COVID-19.*

Apr. 9: CDC Director Robert Redfield tells NPR that, "If we're going to get this country back to work," it will require more testing and very aggressive contact tracing.

Apr. 10: The state of New York records more than 160,000 COVID-19 cases. This is greater than the number of cases in any other country.

Apr. 15: A leaked CDC and FEMA report warns of "significant risk of resurgence of the virus" with phased re-openings in the United States.

Apr. 23: "And is there a way we can do something like that by injection inside or almost a cleaning*?*" – *Donald Trump asks about the use of disinfectant to kill COVID-19.*

Apr. 26: "The people that know me and know the history of our country say that I am the hardest working president in history." – *Donald Trump*

Apr. 27: "I can't imagine why." – *Donald Trump's response to an increase of poison control calls about disinfectant.*

Apr. 29: U.S death toll passes 60,000, with one million confirmed cases.

Apr. 30: By the end of April, 26.5 million Americans have filed for unemployment since mid-March.

May 2020

Ian

In Houston, the virus was taking hold. Ian's family's funeral home had experienced an increase in deaths, but it wasn't anything they couldn't handle.

Before the pandemic, they'd averaged six to ten funerals a week, that number was now approaching 15 to 20 a week. But the real challenge was not being able to do what they'd done for generations: face-to-face, hand-to-hand work with grieving families.

Ian hated feeling that he was letting people down when they most needed support.

The CDC provided protocols, such as what percentages of capacity were allowed for funerals. Families were faced with deciding who could be present in person, who would have to watch on a phone-in line, or Zoom. And the technology, which was new to everyone, was unreliable. Systems crashed, links were lost, phone lines reached capacity and went down. Clients were angry, frustrated, and hurt.

And funeral home staff got the brunt of it.

When Ian received his next call from DMORT, he was not surprised. He had seen the pictures on the news from New York City: overloaded hospital morgues, bodies in corridors, refrigerator trucks parked behind hospitals.

"How soon can you get there?" the DMORT coordinator asked.

"Send the flight info and tickets. I'll make it," Ian responded.

Ian was assigned to work out of the 39th Street Pier in Brooklyn.

The logistics were significant. Processing and intakes happened in large warehouses. There were giant freezers inside the warehouses. Outside, refrigerator trailers were lined up, dozens of them, numbered, each holding 50-100 bodies.

It was a lot to take in.

Each day was broken down into a 24-hour operational period with a briefing on logistics that was over 20 pages long. Every participating agency or department was involved: DOD; OCME; NYCEM; FDNY; DMORT.

Lots of acronyms.

Driving from hospital to hospital to pick up corpses, Ian saw a lot of the city. But more of the underbelly than what tourists saw.

Ian also worked intake at the in-processing warehouse. He'd open a body bag, never sure what to expect. He'd place a placard with an ID number below the person's jaw and take a photo. He'd enter the number and photo with any other data that had come with the body from the respective hospital. Hopefully that included contact info for family members, but some did not. A name or age or anything that could help with identification. Some had nothing.

Ian was told unidentified and unclaimed bodies would probably end up, after a period of time, in mass graves on Hart Island.

"You don't know about Hart Island?" a local cop asked him on his second day. "It's about a mile long, in Long Island Sound, off the Bronx. Used to be some asylums or prisons out there, but now just graves."

"The largest mass grave in the United States," his buddy chimed in. "Over one million-plus bodies buried there." He sounded almost proud, like here was one more example of New York City having the biggest or highest of something.

A year later, early May 2021, there would still be about 750 bodies in long-term storage in refrigerator trailers on Pier 39.

Each morning as Ian walked past the lines of refrigerator trailers to the warehouses to meet up with his team, he'd pause to look at the Statue of Liberty outlined against the early morning sky. From the yard there was also an exceptional view of Manhattan, sunlight dancing on the East River as it met up with the Hudson.

On May 6th, the *New York Daily News* had a screaming cover: "OLD-AGE HOME OF HORRORS: At least 20 bodies taken from Harlem nursing facility, but state reports only 5 died from COVID-19."

That makes no sense, Ian thought. *15 residents managed to all die at the same time but **not** from the highly contagious and deadly virus? Are* *they keeping stats down? Or wanting autopsy conclusions? They'll be waiting a long time because they can't autopsy that many bodies. Didn't one of their teams pick up bodies there yesterday?*

Ian flipped through the paper. Pages six and seven were about Donald Trump's visit to a factory in Phoenix making face masks. Trump, of course, was not wearing a face mask while all the essential workers in the factory were. He used the tour to announce that the economy had to reopen soon, even it meant that some people would be "affected badly."

Trump also said, offhandedly, that the Coronavirus Task Force was preparing to disband. Pence had told reporters earlier in the day that the goal was to dissolve the task force by Memorial Day.

All of which was news to Anthony Fauci.

It would help if they got their stories straight, Ian thought.

Ian was not that political, but he believed that the government's priority was to protect its citizens. Decent roads, clean air, clean water, regulations that saved lives and protected health even if folks got pissed. Or inconvenienced. Like seat belts.

Government needed to model and mandate the precautions and protocols that *everybody* needed to take to protect each other in a time of crisis.

Ian tossed the newspaper in a trash bin. Time to go collect the bodies of people who'd been "affected badly."

He wished he could take the Donald along for the ride.

Mike

Mike was sitting on his couch absentmindedly scrolling on his phone when he had the urge to text Molly.

MIKE: Can you talk tonight? David is with his abuela making enchiladas. Does 7 work?
MOLLY: Yeah but make it 7:15. Max is going to watch a movie with Mickey at his place. It's the first time we're trying this since the virus hit. Mickey sanitized and no one else has been in his house for a month. Are we crazy or what?

MIKE: 7:15 is fine. I'll grab a beer and a snack.
MOLLY: Good plan. If you're drinking, I'm making a margarita. Let's Zoom.
MIKE: I'll send an invite.

Mike found himself smiling. He and Molly had had a "moment" a few years ago when she and Max had driven to Florida at Christmas break with Leah, David's cousin. They'd both been feeling overwhelmed with their respective lives, questioning their judgment, just hanging on. Some very good rum had been involved, the kind that starts out like nothing at all—but then sneaks on you with a punch. Not quite frat boy Jungle Juice but close. A hug led to a cuddle, then a kiss.

A single kiss that lingered. Slow, tentative, intimate.

But before they might have moved toward hook-up ground, they'd taken a deep breath and stepped back.

"I'm not sure that this is a good idea," Molly had said. "What do you think?"

Then they'd actually talked, more openly than either ever had before, realizing quickly that neither of them were ready for a relationship. But what they needed, really *needed*, was a friend who could understand the tedious and exhausting list of "issues" they shared. That kind of friend was a lot harder to find than a hook-up. And they knew, without saying so, that they didn't want to be each other's hook-up.

So, they'd pinky-promised—Molly had insisted on the pinky thing—to be *that* friend, to never dump the friendship, and to call each other out on dumb decisions and crappy choices. They'd pinky-promised to be honest.

So that's what they'd done, about once a week, by phone, text, and email. And recently, by all of the above, almost every day, plus Zoom.

Molly, Max, and Leah had come another time to Florida, the following holiday break, when Kansas was blustery and cold. But Mike and Molly had maintained the friendship boundaries despite staying up until 2 a.m. talking on a blanket on the beach, leaving Leah to babysit the boys.

Mike remembered Leah asking, "Is there something going on with you and...?" Before she could even finish her question, he'd cut her off with an abrupt, "We're friends."

Leah smiled, "Okay. Got it. But just so you know, it wouldn't be the worst thing in the world. Seriously, you two sure can talk."

Which was true. He'd never talked to anyone, girl or guy friend, not even when he'd been in the military and deployed, like he talked to Molly.

But he'd pinky promised. And he would not mess up what they had.

Max

Max was excited to go to Mickey's house. Mickey had a humongous TV, and it was way better than at home. Mickey was cool.

Max understood that if he wanted to hang out with Mickey, he needed to—as Mickey put it— "go with the flow." That meant at least trying whatever Mickey cooked. Last week he'd eaten a whole plate of fettuccini, with crumpled bacon in a creamy-cheesy sauce, without realizing that he'd also eaten a bunch of peas. And peas usually made him gag.

Mickey had said that maybe it wasn't really peas he had a problem with, but the peas he saw in his head when he thought of peas. Max said he would think about it.

Mickey asked him a lot of questions, like about what he felt about things. Feelings were hard for Max. He was more comfortable with facts. But Mickey didn't rush him, just listened to NPR, and kept cooking as Max worked out an answer. And Mickey did what he said he would do.

"I don't like to promise what I might not be able to deliver," he'd told Max.

This was different for Max. His only experience with a grown-up man was his father, Jeff, who lived far away. Jeff had always made a lot of promises when Max was little, like that he was coming and where they would go and what they would do. His mother had explained that Jeff confused promises with wishes, that Jeff *wanted* to do those things, which was nice, but hadn't really thought it through as far as the time and cost and stuff. And then Jeff just stopped coming at all.

Molly

Molly dropped Max off at Mickey's house at 6 p.m. Mickey had asked if Max could have supper with him while they watched the movie.

That was a no brainer.

Now she was making her margarita: bottled low-cal mix from the grocery store tweaked with fresh squeezed lime, ounce of triple sec, and two ounces of tequila with lots of ice. Glass with a salted rim, of course.

It was when she was putting on a little lipstick and brushing out her hair from being clipped up all day that Molly realized she was—what, primping? For a Zoom? With Mike? No, she concluded, it was just to shake off the COVID blues. She'd do the same for a margarita chat with a girlfriend. In fact, she might be even more invested in not being a wreck with a girlfriend.

In the last two months, Mike had seen her at her worst. They'd Zoomed through her snot-dripping crying jags of hopeless angst and paper-writing-all-nighters when she hadn't taken a shower in two days and was sure she smelled all the way to Florida. She'd seen him in bleary-eyed despair, convinced that the lingering, residual memory challenges from a combat head injury and PTSD meant he would never finish *anything*.

Even harder was when he blamed himself for every depression, mood swing, or burst of anger that his son had, because *he* was the reason that David's mom had relinquished custody. The nights when he felt he'd ruined his kid's life drove him to the edge.

They were friends, she reminded herself. She'd never had a deep friendship with a man, not like this. Knowing he was there, that he would always make time to talk if she wanted to run something by him—or vent at 11 p.m.—made her feel secure. She had her mom, but there were times she needed to talk *about* her mom, and there were things she didn't want to share.

Because, well, Grace was her *mom*.

Grace

The debate was hot and heavy as to whether the coronavirus was like a bad flu or something completely different. Every day the experts, who had practiced medicine for decades, explained what needed to be done in every state, county, city, and town to stop the spread.

And, every day, it seemed that President Donald Trump made another undermining comment.

Grace was sorting her mail and bills while watching a YouTube video. A petite woman physician, who looked younger than Molly, was explaining how the coronavirus was different from the flu, and what the virus could do to a body.

"Now, everyone inhale," said the doctor, dressed in a white jacket with a stethoscope around her neck. "Hold that breath. Now exhale. Inhale again. Exhale again."

Grace did as directed.

"Now, here is what's happening. When you inhale, oxygen flows through your trachea, down branches that divide, again and again, a thousand-thousand times, and ends up in about 600 million itty-bitty air sacs called alveoli," the doctor continued. "The walls of the alveoli are only one cell thick, and the oxygen flits right through them and into the blood stream, where it is carried throughout the body."

The screen changed as a new power-point slide popped up.

"COVID-19 causes inflammation—visualize slime in a tiny pipe— making it hard for the oxygen to get where it needs to be. At the same time, this virus is burrowing into the lungs and churning out viral particles. The lungs turn into a battleground: immune system against foreign invader. Cells, tightly packed together, become more and more swollen, more inflamed. Then they simply stop working. For the person, it feels like drowning. No matter how deeply they try to breathe, they cannot 'get' oxygen."

Another slide change.

"The body is using every immune cell to defend against the invader. But when they try to destroy the cells invaded with the virus, they can end up damaging surrounding tissue also. While initially it may have only been a few sections of the lungs affected, as those sections cease functioning, the remaining are overwhelmed.

What we do not fully understand yet is how COVID affects other systems. We're observing consequences, but do not know if they are temporary or long-lasting."

Grace made a mental note not to share this video with Katrina.

"For example, is the disorientation—the 'fogginess' as far as brain function—a result of oxygen deprivation? Can it result in permanent cognitive deficits or is it a transient symptom? We don't understand the origin of some of the excruciating headaches, sensory losses, dizziness, and balance issues. There is much that we know—but just as much that we don't know."

Grace found herself becoming more and more tense and frightened as she listened. She desperately wanted to pretend that this was no big deal, that life would be back to normal in a few months.

When the talk was over, after a final PowerPoint slide demonstrated how masking and distancing interrupted the spread of invisible viral droplets, Grace pulled up Amazon and searched for masks. Nobody was requiring them, not yet, but better to be proactive. The word for now was that only sick people needed them. And there were not enough masks for medical staff.

The "good" ones, N95, were unavailable for at least a month. The basic ones could be delivered in about two weeks. She ordered 50 adult size and another 25 in a bright pattern in kid-size for Max.

Molly

It had been over two months of 24/7 parenting. Molly had completed two of her graduate classes but had taken an incomplete in the other two. This felt like a failure, although many other students were taking incompletes, especially students with kids.

But it was more. Molly was dissatisfied with the process: Zoom classes, especially Zoom teaching, fell short. And she felt her work, in return, was uninspired, more regurgitation. Her mind had gone flat.

Everyone was going through the motions. There was no excitement in learning. She sat alone in her room staring at a screen, checking the time every five minutes to see how much longer.

This was not the education she'd anticipated. And now they were facing the harsh realities. The virus was not going to just 'go away' when the weather changed, nor was it 'just like the flu.'

Molly had not yet told Max that the city pool, an almost daily escape every summer, was not opening. When she'd seen the newspaper headline "Pools Closed for Season," she'd put the paper in the trash and dumped coffee grinds on top.

Max still insisted that he was okay with not having in-person school, not being around other kids. But Molly thought he was regressing. The gains he'd made in social interaction, behaving age-appropriately, were slipping. It felt as if every month isolated equaled six months of regression. Molly was increasingly anxious about how Max would reintegrate when school reopened.

Even more, Molly was terrified that schools would not reopen.

It was a hot mess no matter what.

Grace & Mickey

"I need a project," Mickey said a few days later. He was stretched out on the couch, head on a pillow, watching Grace heat up soup and assemble a salad. "And have I mentioned how much I like watching you cook?" he added. "Makes me feel nurtured."

"Works for me," Grace countered. "I like watching you do dishes and wipe down the counters. And those vacuum skills? Takes a real man to dominate that machine."

Grace and Mickey had found a balance in their relationship that was satisfying: intimacy with space. They were "coupled up," the label coming from Molly, who had, with a smile, explained that to keep using "hooked up" could be misconstrued. In some ways, this was working so well that neither wanted to mess with it. They were committed, but they knew that life could dish out surprises that could rock any relationship. And now, with COVID, with no idea of what was coming next?

It felt as if their very lives were on hold.

"Soup is good," Mickey said between slurps, after moving to the table.

"Chicken corn chowder," Grace replied. "I even used a recipe."

Grace's cooking tended to be more spontaneous, less rule driven. She was a "toss it in a skillet and see what happens" cook.

"So, what were you thinking about when you said you needed a project? Do you have something specific in mind or is it more abstract?" Grace asked.

'Yeah, I have something specific. But since I rent and you own your lovely abode, it would have to be on your turf."

"Then that depends on the project. I do like the fence, so you get brownie points for that."

Mickey had built a privacy fence last year around Grace's side yard and back patio, then built some lower, horizontal sections in front of her door, more decorative, to separate it from Molly's bungalow. Grace had been hesitant at first, thinking she'd feel too "fenced in." But the fence made her space feel larger, not smaller. She still did not understand how that could be.

Mickey had not yet replied, so Grace looked at him inquisitively, raising one eyebrow.

"Hear me out before you start telling me all the reasons it makes no sense," he said. "Just let me explain in my own way."

Grace put down her spoon. This was getting interesting.

"I want to build a sauna. I'm not sure exactly what kind, but not one where you have to chop wood and tend a fire for three hours to get it hot enough. I'm thinking, well, with COVID, we can't really travel, and we don't know long this shit will last, and one of the things I really enjoyed when I was overseas in the military was the German saunas."

Mickey's voice faltered at the end as he was looking at Grace's face but could not read her expression.

"So, what do you think?" he asked.

"You're a very interesting man, Mickey Donahue," she said, looking at him as if he'd just said he wanted to build a spaceship. "I did not see that one coming."

Grace and Mickey were walking down the driveway to head to the river trail the following afternoon when they heard persistently honking horns. A fire truck turned the corner, followed by a car, then a pick-up, then another car, then...

Each vehicle was covered with posters: "Mrs. Elliot Misses YOU!!!" and "Honking for West Middle School." "First Grade Kids ROCK!" and "Your School Wants You Back!" Cans were tied to bumpers, and balloons. It was like Mardi Gras.

Grace and Mickey stood in the driveway, making high-fives and waving at every car and truck.

"Did you know this was happening?" Grace asked.

"A buddy mentioned it. Each school is covering their own area, their neighborhoods. Want to give the kids a pick-me-up," Mickey replied. "I think other school districts are doing parades too."

"Does Max know about it?" Mickey asked. "Want me to run up and ring the bell?"

"Molly took him to that enclosed area at the dog park," Grace said. "They bring chairs. Molly can read, and Max can play with the dogs."

Grace smiled as a truck passed with a blackboard and desks set in the bed with teachers on the kid-size chairs.

"How much longer do you think they can do this?" Grace asked.

"What? The parade?"

"No, trying to teach by computer and expecting kids to learn looking at a little screen instead of in person. It's got to get back to normal by August, right?"

"I have no idea," Mickey said. "But what we call 'normal' could be a long way off."

They kept cheering and hooting and waving until the very last car had passed.

Katrina

Katrina had been recuperating for ten weeks, with no end in sight. Her firm had approached her about an extended leave. Her cases had been assigned to other attorneys. She remained on salary, but her combined sick-time and vacation-time was up. They had some kind of policy for extended leave at half-salary, but that was yet to be discussed. It had never been used except for diseases like cancer, when recovery was anticipated following chemo.

"What the hell?" Kat muttered, staring at her cell phone after a conference call to inform her that the partners were "looking into it." While it had not been their intention—or at least she *hoped* it had not been their intention—their discussion had centered on how her symptoms did not have a label that fit the insurance policy's defined coverage. It was as if she was a malingerer, as if lying around her house and doing nothing—not even the dishes, not even making her bed—was preferable to work.

The call had triggered shame. It had been a long time since she'd felt the hot rush of shame. And this time it wasn't even anything she'd actually *done.*

Grace

Grace was lacing up her sneakers to go for a walk. Two miles a day in the early morning or weeding for an hour—those were the two options she was giving herself. It was like offering her inner child two alternatives: "Walk for forty minutes or weed the front yard?" Nothing like the prospect of weeding to make a walk appealing.

She was about halfway through her walk when her cell vibrated.

"Hello? Is this Grace McDonald?" a deep and somber male voice asked.

"Yes, this is Grace," she replied, trying not to sound breathless.

"Is this a good time?" he asked. "I'm Todd Barker with Barker Funeral Home."

Grace had not heard from the funeral home since her husband's funeral well over a decade ago. She had a flashback: picking out a coffin, Katrina almost holding her up. Or was it holding her together?

Grace wondered if coffins were in short supply these days.

"I'm out walking," Grace said cautiously. "This is fine. What can I do for you?"

Todd explained that their grief group, which had been meeting by Zoom, was scheduled to start meeting in person, outside, in the prayer garden adjacent to the funeral home, on Thursday. But, Todd continued, their social worker had COVID and was in quarantine. She also had four kids who would probably now also get COVID, so he did not expect her back for a while. He knew it was only five days out, but he wondered if she could possibly facilitate the group. It might only be for a few months. She would be paid, of course. The social worker, Ivy, had given Todd her name and highly recommended her.

"She said you were familiar with the grief process and that the clients would identify with you," Todd added. "That you've walked the walk."

Yeah, Grace thought, *Except I didn't just "walk the walk." I ran away as far as I could get from everything and everyone. I did the exact opposite of what every damn therapist and self-help book would advise. I'm so not the person for this work.*

Grace started to backpedal, explaining to Todd why she could not make this commitment at the moment. Todd listened, not interrupting, as she listed her private practice, responsibilities with her daughter and grandson, blah-blah-blah.

When she ran out of steam, he just said, "I understand, it's a hard time for all of us. It's just that these folks have all had someone they loved die of COVID. We separated out our COVID family members from other clients because their issues are different—a lot more anger and intensity We have a young social worker, just graduated, covering the other group. But we feel a responsibility to try to get someone more seasoned, with more life experience, for this group. But I do understand if you're simply over-extended."

Damn, Grace thought, *this guy is good.* He'd picked up on the "blah-blah" nature of her excuses. And he had, respectfully, called her out. He wouldn't pressure, but he was making clear that this was not a favor for him but to better meet the needs of people who were in COVID hell.

"Let me think about it and I'll call you back tomorrow. Is that okay?" Grace asked.

"That's all I can ask," Todd replied. "Thanks for reconsidering."

Later that afternoon, Grace walked across the patch of lawn that separated her casita from her daughter's bungalow.

"Molly?" she called. "Yoo-hoo?"

"I'll be right down," Molly called from upstairs. "Getting Max settled for a class."

She appeared a few minutes later. "What's up?" Molly asked, selecting some mugs from the cabinet to pour them both a cup of coffee.

"I want to run something by you, that's all."

"Shoot. What's it about?" she asked, putting a filter in the coffee pot.

"I got a call asking if I could facilitate a grief group. For the funeral home on 6th Street. Family members of COVID casualties. Just once a week for a few hours."

Molly raised an eyebrow. "What's the problem? It sounds like there's a problem."

Grace sighed. "I gave a bunch of excuses, but I'm wondering if it's more that I don't think I'm a good fit because of how I dealt with my own grief," she admitted.

Molly inhaled very, very slowly, as if counting to ten. She made it to seven before going off. "You mean like packing up your car, abandoning your kids, running away? For about a decade?" There was an edge in Molly's voice, rarely heard anymore.

The words stung. "Yes, Molly," Grace said. "I did not face my grief, could not face it, and I made a mess. So, how can I do a grief group with a straight face?"

"How can you not? Who else knows so intimately what *not* to do?" Molly retorted. "If you can help prevent even one person from making their own mess? If they can hear guidance not just because a book says so but because they really understand how much they could regret it later?"

"I hadn't considered myself the poster child for screwing up, but you made your point," Grace muttered.

Molly's face fell. "I'm sorry, Mom. That was harsh. I do understand better than I did back then, but..."

"It still hurts. I know it does," Grace conceded.

"The world is crazy right now, and I get that you want to not add anything more to your plate," Molly continued, "but I've seen your plate a lot more crowded than it is now. Your appointments are down. None of us have a social life."

"Yeah, I know, I know. It's just that..."

Molly cut her off with a wave. "Remember, just a few weeks ago, we were watching the news of refrigerator trucks lined up outside the hospitals in New York City, and you said that you wished you could do something to help, that the helplessness was crazy-making?"

"Yeah, but this is different..."

"No, it isn't," Molly snapped, "and I think you'll feel even better if you do it pro bono. Tell them that whatever they were going to pay you to donate it instead to the food pantry."

"You're on a roll, here, you know that? What's going on?"

"Karma, mother dearest," Molly replied with a wicked grin. "Your karma has finally arrived."

"I'm coming over," Grace announced when Katrina answered her cell. "We can sit in the backyard with masks and sanitizer and be six feet apart. But I made uber-healthy ratatouilles, plus olive bread from Wheatfields and a glass of Zinfandel."

"Yes, ma'am," Kat replied. She knew better than to argue with Grace on a mission of mercy.

"So, what are you binging?" Kat asked Grace about an hour later, the question somewhat muffled by chewing bread.

"Depends on the mood. I started watching *Schitt's Creek* because everyone said it was so funny but dropped it after two episodes because it was too dumb. But then last week I had a shitty day, wanted total distraction, and tried it again. Now I'm hooked. Watching two episodes a night. I channel the daughter, Alexis, sometimes when I'm talking to myself," Grace concluded. "Makes the conversation more fun."

Kat rolled her eyes.

"I haven't checked that out yet. But I started on *Vera,* a British series with a cranky older woman detective. It's formulaic. I like the characters and knowing that it will all get solved by the end of the show," Kat said. "And Vera drinks too much, which is a habit I enjoy even vicariously."

"We're all drinking too much," Grace added, reaching for the bottle of wine.

Grace was worried about Kat. She'd lost a lot of weight. Over the years, it had always been Grace who wanted to lose pounds, who tried out different diets and programs.

Kat didn't need to.

Katrina

After Grace left, Kat put the remaining ratatouille in the fridge. It was, she assumed, delicious. It was something she used to love, especially in summer, made from farmer's market eggplant, tomatoes and such. But now it felt rubbery, slimy even. So, she took small bites and made herself swallow. It was better than having to chew incessantly as with steak. Or grilled chicken. She'd had to spit that out.

Katrina had not tasted anything since March.

She still could not smell anything either—the spices that used to make her inhale with delight when cooking, the flowers in her garden, the loamy earth when she would take early morning walks past fields.

Two weeks ago, she'd gone to a stable outside of town because she'd thought, just maybe, that riding a horse, even touching a horse, which she used to love, would be therapeutic and pleasurable, and not *just* exhausting. But she'd gotten as far as inside the barn when she realized that she could not smell *anything*. The smell of a stable, hay and manure, and horses, usually overpowering, ripe with memories, was a void. She'd turned abruptly and left, her eyes tearing up.

It was yet another slam of discovering something else that she'd lost that she had once cherished.

Molly

Molly and Mike had their scheduled Zoom but also "in-between" calls. Molly called them "AA" calls—for "anxiety attack."

"I'm obsessing about what would happen to Max if I die," Molly shared. "I start to fall asleep and then it just floods my brain." Her voice ratcheted up.

"Your mom is there, and Mickey," Mike said, trying to reassure her.

"But they're old and vulnerable," Molly answered. "Haven't you felt anxious about what would happen to David if you..."

"That is such a dark hole that I can't let myself go there."

"Okay, then, at least you see what I mean. Legally, Jeff is Max's father, even if he hardly ever sees him. But does he *know* Max? Jeff sends a Christmas card with some cash, but he has no idea who Max is or how to parent him. *Max cannot live with Jeff.*"

"David's mom severed her rights, so I decide who'd be David's guardian," Mike said. "But, other than my parents?"

"I don't get why this particular anxiety is not being covered in the news. There have got to be thousands and thousands of parents who've never thought about wills and appointing legal guardians," Molly continued. "They figure they have time. Years of time."

"Shit, Molly, now I'm freaking out."

Molly continued as if Mike hadn't spoken.

"I'll talk to Mom. She knows a lot of attorneys and she does custody mediation."

"Yeah, I vaguely remember that experience..."

"If Jeff were out of the picture, and he might prefer to be out of the legal picture, Max would go to my brother."

"Put the brakes on, Molly. Your brother lives in Panama."

"Yes. Which isn't a bad thing except they speak a different language. But Alex is a teacher. He and Graciella would be good with Max. Maybe Alex and Graciella could come up and live here for six months, a time to transition Max? That might help. They could have my house."

"Molly," Mike said. "*Listen to yourself.* You have you, your mom, and Mickey all dead. That is NOT going to happen."

"I feel so vulnerable, Mike," Molly confessed. "The world feels dangerous. I liked it better when I could pretend we have some measure of control."

"It does feel more dangerous, but it's temporary," Mike said, in another attempt to reassure. "Did I tell you about an email I got from a buddy from Iraq? We were in the same platoon. Anyway, he just got back from working in New York City, mortuary work. And he was describing it as a battleground. Like combat but with a shitload more casualties. Hundreds and hundreds of bodies. I called him and we talked for an hour. He had a lot to unload."

"Is this supposed to help me feel better?" Molly asked.

"Yeah, sort of," Mike said. "You're not in New York. You're not stuck in an apartment surrounded by millions of other people. You have a yard and garden. Our lives now are a picnic compared to what those families are going through."

"Okay, Mike. I get it. And you're right. I'll try to soldier up."

Katrina

It was a holiday, but didn't feel like one to Katrina, just as Easter had not been Easter. It was a day just like every other day: mostly alone, at home, a slow walk along the river for some exercise if she felt well enough. But no barbecue, no backyard gathering with friends and family, no kids excited over the city pool's opening weekend.

The Memorial Days that she mostly remembered were when her sons had been young, when she'd been married to Martin. He'd always grilled, not one of the monster-sized gas ones, but a charcoal grill.

Most years, the afternoon had been shared with Grace and Gil, and their kids, and whatever other families wanted to join in.

"The taste isn't the same without the charcoal," Martin would explain when the kids complained about how long it was taking. But the burgers were always perfect, and everyone agreed, year after year, that Martin was right.

Katrina grabbed the remote and settled down on the couch with a Hurricane in a large wine glass. She would have preferred a Ramos Gin Fizz, her "fancy" drink of choice, but it took too much energy. The egg white alone would have done her in. The Hurricane was simple. She kept all the ingredients: dark rum, light rum, lemon juice, and passion fruit syrup—in arms reach, in the fridge or on the counter. Not that the ingredients made a difference anymore. She was in it for the buzz, not the flavor.

But just looking at a Hurricane made her remember times when she could taste. When taste was a reason to celebrate.

Katrina had been gravitating to the BBC in the last few weeks just to get away from the obsessive chronicles of Trump's tweets. She was about to change the channel from CNN when the reporter caught her attention.

They were showing a video of a Black man, face down on pavement, next to a car, with a cop kneeling. Was it next to him or on top of him? A smallish group of people encircled the scene and more cops seemed to be in the background. The voice-over was reporting that a man had died after a police officer kneeled on his neck after taking him into custody.

Katrina could not tell where it was, but her mind jumped to her default assumptions about states where it is not healthy to be a Black man—like Mississippi, Alabama, Georgia.

She flipped the channel. She was ready for a few episodes of *Vera,* not more shitty news.

By the next evening, Katrina could no longer look away.

This "incident" had not happened, as she'd wrongly assumed, somewhere in the south. It was in Minnesota. And it had not been the aftermath of, as she'd also wrongly assumed, a shoot-out, or intense car chase, or armed robbery. It had not been someone who'd attacked the police or hurt other people. It had started with a phone call from a cashier who thought a customer had, maybe, used a counterfeit $20 bill.

Did this customer *know* the bill was counterfeit? Nobody knew. Was the man armed and dangerous? No. Had he been threatening? No. He was sitting in a car with some friends when the police responded. Not fleeing like someone who'd done something wrong. Just hanging out. Probably headed for a barbecue later in the day.

And then, within 17 minutes, George Floyd was dead.

Katrina sat and watched as the videos ran, over and over. Different angles had been taken by bystanders. You could see and hear a small circle of people pleading with the policemen, saying that the man in their custody was in danger. That he couldn't breathe. That he was panting, trying to say he could not breathe. Some had pulled out their phones, and were pointing them as cameras, perhaps a futile attempt to do *something* when they felt helpless to intervene. It was in the middle of the day, a holiday, on a very public street, and women, men, children, cousins, siblings, friends were strolling to their neighborhood stores to get staples or treats.

During which an execution was taking place.

Katrina found herself fixated on the ever-emerging coverage, as assumptions made about why he was arrested, why multiple police officers were engaged with restraining him, what dangerous felony had he committed to elicit such a response, and many more, were countered with...facts.

Hour-by-hour, the gauzy curtains that usually veiled law enforcement treatment of Black citizens, that allowed for different "interpretations," like script changes adapting to an evolving movie, were being lifted. No curtains could cover the cell phone videos taken by witnesses. The usual room for "interpretation"—how officers felt threatened and thus reacted as they had—was contradicted by what the nation saw with their own eyes.

It was no big surprise that Derek Chauvin had had multiple complaints from citizens about aggressive tactics, some 18 complaints in 19 years. Yet he was still training rookie cops?

But what Katrina was processing was not just the brutality of killing a restrained citizen in broad daylight in front of a crowd begging the cops to listen and stop. She was processing how she, a Black woman, had made the same initial, gut assumptions that most white people did: the guy *must* have done *something* to get treated that way. *Something* else had to have happened in the past. Had he been known to be violent? Floyd was a big man, so maybe some precautions were protocol.

In her head, Katrina was unpacking a long-buried suitcase of what she'd been taught about being Black. It was a heavy, heavy suitcase, almost too much to lift. But she'd started, one memory a day.

Any more would have been too much to bear.

HISTORICAL CONTEXT: MAY 2020

May 1: The US Food and Drug Administration issues an emergency-use authorization for remdesivir in patients with severe COVID-19.

May 5: U.S. death toll passes 70,000.

May 5: "I don't want to be Mr. Doom-and-Gloom. It's a very bad subject... I'm not looking to tell the American people when nobody really knows what's happening yet— 'Oh, this is going to be so tragic.'" – *Donald Trump*

May 9: The FDA authorizes the use of a saliva-based test to detect COVID-19.

May 11: "Coronavirus numbers are looking MUCH better, going down almost everywhere. Big progress being made." – *Donald Trump*

May 19: "When we have a lot of cases, I don't look at that as a bad thing. I look at that as, in a certain respect, as being a good thing...because it means our testing is much better. I view it as a badge of honor..." – *Donald Trump*

May 21: Home mortgage delinquencies surged by 1.6 million in April, the biggest jump in history. 38 million unemployment claims have been filed.

May 25: A grocery store employee calls the police, accusing a Black customer, George Floyd, of using a counterfeit $20 bill. Floyd is then killed in police custody by Officer Derek Chauvin.

May 27: U.S death toll passes 100,000.

May 27: Minneapolis Mayor Jacob Frey calls for criminal charges against Officer Derek Chauvin. Protests erupt in at least 140 cities across the U.S. The National Guard is activated in at least 21 states.

May 29: Chauvin is charged with third-degree murder and manslaughter. President Donald Trump tweets about "thugs" in Minneapolis protests and warns: "When the looting starts, the shooting starts." Protests turn violent again in Minneapolis and elsewhere.

May 29: "We will be today terminating our relationship with the World Health Organization." – *Donald Trump*

June 2020

Covid Grief Group

Grace did not weasel out, which is how she came to be sitting in a pretty little garden with rock-wall raised beds around a gravel circle where eight chairs were arranged some feet apart. It was shaded, with hostas and coleus, alyssum and caladiums. On two sides of the circle were delicate Japanese maples, their leaves and branches a soft red.

There were five women and two men sitting on the lawn chairs, with appropriate social distancing, except for one man and one woman whose lawn chairs were pulled close to one another. He had his hand on her knee.

Everyone was masked. The couple was looking down, one woman was blinking quickly and jiggling her leg. Their eyes, peering over masks like raccoons, could not fully display what a face could by a mouth that tightened, cheeks sucked in, lips bit until they bled.

"Are we waiting for anyone else?" Grace asked.

A few on the group looked at each other as if appraising.

"I don't think so," a woman said.

"Then let's get started. Shall we?"

She looked around the circle quickly, waiting for their nods.

"You may know each other, but I don't know any of you," Grace started. "So, would you each introduce yourself? And share who you are grieving, and when they died. And then I'll introduce myself."

The members of the group looked at each other, waiting for one to begin.

"All right," one woman said, "I'll start. I'm Cheryl. My husband died in April after being sick for about two weeks. One day he was mowing the yard and the next he felt tired. He lay down for a nap and I swear he barely left the bed until he died. He never had an awful time breathing, but he went into cardiac arrest. By the time the EMTs got to the house it was too late."

Cheryl nodded to the next woman.

"I'm Beth. My father died May 1st. He believed that COVID was a hoax. He came down with it but didn't believe he had COVID. Kept saying how it wasn't so bad, COVID wasn't real, just a flu, until one night he couldn't breathe. Mom called me, crying, 'What should I do? He doesn't want to go to the hospital.' I called an ambulance. That was the last time she saw him, being taken out to the ambulance. He died nine days later, after being on a ventilator."

Beth spoke fast, rote, as if repeating a story she'd told too many times.

"But I'm not grieving him. No, ma'am. I'm grieving my mama. Ruthie. He infected her. The day after the ambulance came, she couldn't get out of bed. I was already calling into work, gonna' take a few days off and go be with her when she called me again. I drove 85-90 miles an hour on I-70 to Abilene. She'd felt sick but made herself keep going to take care of Dad. She died *before* Dad, only two days in the hospital, never got put on a ventilator, which may have been a mercy. He never knew what he'd done." She stopped, then added, "I wish he had known. I wish he'd known he killed her. All his stupid..."

Grace felt sucker punched. She looked around the circle. They'd heard this before, but they still looked punched as well.

"That's more than any one daughter can bear," Grace said. "It truly is."

"Yes," Beth said. "It is. And yet, here I am." She gestured to the man to her left. "Your turn."

"I'm Larry," he said. "My wife, Jasmine, died in April. She'd had cancer, was just finished with the chemo, feeling more herself again. We'd beat it. It was breast cancer, and we'd caught it early. Last November, in the middle of chemo, we booked a month in Italy. For June. Now. It was something to look forward to. We were practicing Italian on Duolingo. She'd waited her whole life to go."

Larry was focused on the gravel under his feet the entire time he spoke.

"She probably caught the COVID at her last chemo session. Three of the staff there had to quarantine later that week because... Anyway, she died in six days. Her body couldn't fight it. After the test came back, she knew she was dying. The doctors wanted to get her to the hospital, but she'd seen the TV and what was coming. She said, 'No hospital, Larry. No ventilators. It's too late, Larry. Keep me home, please, keep me home.' So, I did. I figured I'd get it, but I didn't much care. And I got it, of course, taking care of her. Hospice helped us some. I didn't mess with a mask. I was right there with her, holding her, managing the oxygen, and making sure she wasn't too scared. I had liquid drops of morphine, to help when she felt she couldn't breathe. I made sure she didn't suffer."

He looked up with those words, as if daring anyone to contradict him, to question him.

"After the funeral home came for her body, the COVID hit me. Maybe I'd been holding it off. Like your mom did," he added, gesturing toward Beth. "I was sicker than I've ever been in my life, like every muscle in my body was screaming, my lungs burning, but I didn't care. And to be honest, I wish I'd just died too."

The silence in the group was deep, so deep that they could hear the whisper of a breeze, and every birdcall.

Grace looked around the circle for who might follow. No one made eye contact with her.

A young woman, much younger than the rest, a girl, really, shifted in her chair and cleared her throat, looking sideways at the couple. They kind of nodded at her.

"Well, then," she started, "I'm Kayla. I'm new to the group. My mom, her name is Jolene, just died on May 25th. The same day that George Floyd died. He had the life smothered out of him by that cop, and my mom got the life smothered out of her too. Only my mom was killed by her customers, people she used to joke with, ask how they were doing, and if they'd got that pesky truck engine fixed."

Kayla stopped, as if even sharing this, out loud, was more than she could manage. Then she continued.

"Mom worked a second job at Chuck's Stop. She told me how people would come in, men mostly, and ignore the signs on the door that said, 'No Mask, No Entry.' Or wear their masks under their nose. They'd saunter over to the donut counter, make themselves coffee, just daring anybody to call them out, like they were itching for a showdown. I wanted her to quit, but she'd already gotten laid off from her hotel job.

She said she had to work."

Kayla paused, looking quickly at each of the other members of the group. "This is my first time coming. But I don't know, maybe I'm not a good fit."

At first glance, Grace thought, *Yeah, that might be accurate.* She estimated that the girl was in her late teens or early twenties. She had a delicate nose-ring and multiple earrings. She was dressed in black boots and a short skirt, but with a brightly colored top that laced up the front like you see in old oil paintings of goat herders in the Alps. She wore eye makeup, very dark, artfully applied, that flowed down the sides of her face from her eyes. Kabuki-esque?

She looked, Grace thought, like a goth-shepherdess. It was a look that was unique, with a cognitive dissonance. But before Grace could finish her thought and make an encouraging remark, Beth beat her to it.

"If you mean because you're young, have a different look, like that fancy eye thing you have going? Uh-uh. My daughter has twice as many ear holes as you do, and her hair is purple. And she would so get off on what you're doing with the clothes. So, girl, we may look different on the outside, but we both have dead mamas and we're both pretty damn angry about that. This group is to help us deal with the hand we just got dealt. So, I think you fit in just fine."

Excellent, Grace thought, wanting to pat Beth on the back. *You nailed it.*

"I agree with Beth," Grace added. "Give it a few times before you make any decisions?"

Kayla was still looking at Beth, but she nodded ever so slightly.

"I'm Shawnee," the next woman said. "I'm from Georgia. I moved here for a teaching position with the business school at the university. But my whole family is still there. It's a big family, but they're getting killed off, one-by-one: an aunt, then an uncle, grandma, another uncle, two cousins."

Shawnee paused, then continued.

"I don't answer the phone anymore. I wait to listen to the message," she explained. "They aren't having any funerals. Like it's just a bad dream. I'm numb."

Shawnee looked away, flipping her hand, like, *Move along, please.*

Grace turned to the remaining two people, the couple. She raised her eyebrows, inviting them to speak.

"I'm Bill and this is my wife, Debra," the man said, his hand still resting on his wife's knee. "Our son died May 5th. Dean was only 32, so damn healthy, a runner, made these green protein shakes with kale every morning. He was a doctor, finishing up his residency in thoracic surgery. At Columbia University Medical Center. Lord, he was so happy to get that residency. Said he would be working with the best, learning from the best. He was two weeks from the end of his contract."

Debra picked up. "It was two weeks, yes, but he'd already told us he wasn't abandoning ship if they still needed doctors. And they surely did. 'I can't leave until we get this under control, Mom. I couldn't live with that on my conscience.' That's what he told me three weeks before he died."

Grace sat, her hands clenched so tightly to the seat of the chair that they were red with strain, holding on, as it were, for dear life. With each person, she'd felt sucker punched. This was going to be harder work than she'd known in a long time. She'd done rotations for the military, working with troops returning from deployments, during the years she'd been gone from Kaw Valley. There had been intensive grief work, often survivor guilt for not dying, not having saved a buddy. Lots of PTSD.

But that had been the *military*. Combat was dangerous, even lethal. Everyone knew that when they signed on. But working the checkout at a Chuck's Stop? Doing a surgical residency? Making it through cancer only to die from a virus?

Grace felt, more viscerally than she had thus far, that *this* was *war*. People were being killed. But this war was with an invisible, insidious virus that did not respect rules of conduct, that could not be shot or bombed. It was sneaky and arbitrary, and a 9/11 was happening almost every day.

The bigger insanity was that people were dying, daily, from "friendly fire." People were turning on each other, blaming science for not knowing everything at the get-go. They got angry that experts didn't know *everything*, wanting absolute assurances even as they denied science.

How has this happened?

Grace wondered how it would be different if the virus had been shown to be deliberately planted by an identified enemy. Like, "This virus was brought to our country by terrorists from _____?"

Would citizens then be turning on each other or rejecting science? Or would masks and sanitizers and social distancing be patriotic? Would they all be giving each other thumbs-up for patriotic compliance?

"Ummm, ma'am, would you like to tell us about yourself some?"

Grace was startled. Bill was the one who'd spoken.

"Oh, damn, I'm sorry. I just went off in my head with what I was hearing. I've been doing that lately," she replied, in an apologetic tone.

"Anyway, I'm Grace. I've been a social worker, for decades it seems, and Ivy asked if I could cover for her..."

That night, trying to tell Mickey what the group had been like, Grace could not quite remember what they had discussed after the introductions. How grief is a unique journey for everyone, that there is no right or wrong way to feel or act, that it was one hour at a time, sometimes one minute. But it had felt like so many empty words, sounds leaving her mouth to float away, that there was nothing she could say or do that would make any difference to these grieving people.

All she knew was that they were meeting next week, they were all coming back, and whatever happened would happen.

"Did you tell them about Gil being murdered? And being indicted?" Mickey asked.

"No, I didn't. Maybe later."

"Don't wait too long," Mickey replied. "Don't make into a secret."

Mickey

Mickey spent over six hours online looking at "Build Your Own Sauna" videos before he acknowledged that starting from scratch was way more of a project than he wanted to tackle. Then he found the "My Sauna World" website, with a wide selection of "Almost Heaven" barrel saunas with Finnish stoves. He selected a four-person, chatted with a friendly young woman who assured him that this was a great choice, and then found it would take two to three months for delivery.

But that was okay. He needed time to prepare. Not like he'd plunk the sauna down in the middle of the yard. He needed to build a patio or base, get electrical outlets installed, and hire a plumber for the outdoor cold shower he'd decided was essential. And build more privacy fences. No need to advertise that they were getting naked in the middle of their suburban backyard.

Mickey wasn't even sure that Grace was aware of that factor.

"I went to Home Depot to get pavers and sand for the patio, and lumber for the privacy screens," he told Grace as she chopped onions. "Turns out there is a national lumber shortage. Home builders must be going nuts. Met a guy who works in that department, Zed something-or-other, and he suggested taking whatever cedar pieces I could scrounge, any length, any width. He said he'd call me if more cedar shows up. Nice guy. He said to buy whatever I can, wherever I can, then figure it out.

"That sounds challenging," Grace said, dumping the onions into a hot skillet.

"Yeah, but more design, more aesthetically interesting."

"You're into this, huh?" Grace asked. "Even the 'aesthetics?'"

"Don't be condescending. I can do aesthetics."

"It wasn't condescending, Mickey. Just sexist."

"And they differ how?" Mickey countered, grinning.

Grace looked up from the onions, eyes watering. "Not sure exactly, but I'll let you know. So, tell me more about this national lumber shortage."

Katrina

June 8th was a beautiful afternoon, sun filtering through tree branches, with a soft breeze. Grace texted Katrina that she was bringing over a surprise for a backyard picnic.

Any surprise was a crapshoot now. Kat had always been a "live-to-eat" person, loving ethnic foods, slurping up big bowls of pho at Little Saigon. Now she was "eat-to-live," and eating was a chore with little gratification. Nothing appealed.

The surprise was cheese soup from the brewery, with crusty bread for dipping. It wasn't an *awful* choice.

"Have you been tracking this whole thing with George Floyd?" Kat asked after Grace cranked up the umbrella over the wrought iron table and chairs. They'd settled down with the soup, bread, and a pitcher of iced tea.

"Yeah," Grace replied. "And it almost feels that the networks are jumping all over it because anything besides COVID or Trump is a change."

Katrina winced. "What do you mean? Like they should not give it so much coverage?"

"No," Grace answered. "More that it was one bad cop and a video that went viral."

Kat cringed. She took a moment to collect herself, wiping her mouth with a napkin. "One bad cop, huh?" she questioned. "You really believe that?"

"The guy is a bad cop. Obviously. But that doesn't make all law enforcement guilty of..."

"It's not one bad apple, Gracie, and it's naïve to think so," Kat snapped. "If George Floyd had been a white dude sitting in a car with his friends on a sunny holiday Monday, he would not be dead. Unarmed white men do not get killed by police..."

"Hold on, Kat, don't get mad at me," Grace protested. "I agree. I agree he was a bad cop, only this might not be getting so much coverage if the media wasn't so hungry for something to chew on besides COVID."

Kat tried to keep her voice steady. "But not that this deserves all the coverage? Because it keeps happening, over and over, and 90 percent of the time it gets little to nothing in attention?"

"That's not true," Grace countered. "Who was that kid in Ferguson? That got a lot of media coverage."

"*That kid* was Michael Brown, and he was unarmed and just 18, so, yeah, it got people pretty upset," she retorted. "But most of the coverage was about those awful Black folks rioting and not Michael Brown or how racist the Ferguson police had been for years!"

"Kat, what's going on?" Grace asked. "You sound pissed."

Katrina felt her chest tighten, her body tighten. She felt like she was on the edge of a cliff with nothing to hold on to.

Pissed? she thought. *Is that what this is? This is a planet away from pissed.*

"Why don't we ever talk about race?" Katrina asked, lowering her voice. "We've talked about everything else—kids, husbands, work, friends, politics—but not race. Why is that?" Her voice sounded disappointed, almost sad.

Grace's expression changed. "What do you mean, 'why is that?' You tell me," Grace objected, her tone defensive. "You could've brought it up anytime you wanted. I never shut you down."

Kat shook her head. "You never asked either, Gracie. Why didn't *you* ask? Why did I have to be the one to do it?"

Grace shifted in her chair, as if the metal had become hot to the touch. "Look, Kat, I don't know what's going on or what you want from me. I've always tried to be there for *you.*"

Kat pulled back from the table. "But how do *you* see *me*? Why do we never talk about how you're white and I'm Black? And what that means?"

"I don't see color when I see you, okay?" Grace defended. "I see Katrina, my *best* friend. Not my *Black* friend."

With that, Kat was silent.

Grace was silent.

Something had just been said that they each heard in very different ways. And there was no going back. And neither one of them could see or understand, in this particular moment, how to go forward either.

"I can't do this today," Katrina said. "Thanks for bringing over the food. I'm going to lie down."

"Sure, Kat, no problem. Get some rest. I'll check back in a few days," Grace said as she collected her things.

Grace

Later that evening, Grace tried to explain to Mickey what had happened with Kat.

"I screwed up, Mickey. She asked how I see her. And I said I see my *best* friend, not my *Black* friend."

Mickey looked up from his phone, tilting his head.

"What exactly did you intend to communicate with that?"

"That I love her for her, and race is not a factor in that?"

Mickey took off his reading glasses and placed them on the coffee table. "Can you really *know* her if you don't see and understand what being Black means to *her*?"

"But isn't racism about negative attribution? About assuming or projecting negative qualities onto someone because of race?" Grace pushed. "I've never done that with Katrina."

"It's bigger than that," he said. "Not just feelings about Katrina."

"Mickey, I am *not* racist," Grace retorted.

"And that kind of denial comes across as defensive. And dumb," Mickey pointed out. "Because we're all racist. It's impossible to be white or Black or brown without having deeply embedded beliefs about race."

"Are you saying that *you're* racist?"

"Yes, that is *exactly* what I'm saying. We all are. We were taught how to think and feel about race before we could put it into words.

Grace did not move. Until that moment she had not understood that this *learning* was mostly *unlearning*.

That she didn't know yet what all she didn't know.

Molly

Molly was looking at her day planner. The spaces that had always been scribbled in, with arrows and cross-outs, different colored pens for different parts of her life. Those spaces were eerily blank. Little white squares.

It was a relief to have school officially over, and to not have to cajole Max into doing his homework, stay focused during a virtual lesson, not slide off his chair and go limp on the floor under the table. But there were no summer camps at the art center, the city pool was closed, and Molly couldn't trade a morning a week with another mom so they each had a break and their kids got to play.

Each day felt interminable.

She and Grace were patching together a schedule. They'd agreed that taking full days felt too exhausting. But they could do 3-4 hours, with strategic breaks for TV and YouTube videos. Having the same show each day at 1 p.m. was something Max could anticipate, and they could plan a break.

Katrina had originally offered to also help with Max once she felt better. But Katrina was not recovering. Every good day was followed by a few bad days when fatigue would grab hold and her muscles would throb. One day she could sit in the sun, the next day any light felt like daggers poking her eyes.

Two days ago, Molly realized that Max was looking scruffy. Mickey was looking scruffy. Grace's ends needed a trim. Molly googled home haircutting YouTube videos and found hundreds. Then she googled haircutting scissors and sets. It was a lovely distraction for an hour or so, just comparing sets and descriptions, another hour looking at "how-to" videos. She ordered a set. Most were on backorder but this one would be delivered in a week or so.

Good, Molly thought, *one simple and useful thing that I can do.* Setting up a backyard "salon," complete with Mojitos, could end up being a fun evening. Maybe Katrina would feel up to coming over for a quick trim. Anything for a few laughs.

Mickey

They were adjusting to a COVID-19 reality: solo activities, outside, limited to people in their pod, were safe. Letting kids play with other kids? Not safe. Having friends over for dinner? Not safe. Seeing a client outdoors if distanced and masked? Probably safe. But no touching, and ample use of disinfectant afterwards.

The adults were responsible for any children in a pod. And kids needed more supervision and parental engagement—because the rest of their lives had disappeared.

Which is how Mickey came to complain to Grace about how sore and sunburned he was from walking the trails around the reservoir with Max.

"The kid is like the damn Energizer bunny. With new batteries every damn day."

"I bet you're wishing for your old life, hey, Mickey?" Grace teased, but there was a serious undertone in her voice. "Just yourself to take care of, no women asking for help every twenty minutes? No kid making you sweat?"

They were questions to ponder. Did a part of him want his old life back? He could be alone, no responsibilities, just take care of his own needs, no worrying about anyone else? It had definitely been easier.

They were getting into bed later that evening, sliding under the sheets, making sounds of gratitude, the "mmm" and exhalations that come with the release of a long day, when Mickey spoke.

"I thought about your questions," he said to Grace, their faces just a few inches apart on their pillows. Mickey saw a flash of panic in her eyes, that he might be about to tell her something she did not want to hear. "And here's my answer, so you don't have to worry. I may complain, because that's what men do, and you can tease me, because that's what women do. But I want you to know, in your heart, that I feel blessed to be here, with you and Molly and Max. You give me purpose, belonging, family. I never expected to have this, to not be alone. There is nothing I regret, nothing I yearn for. At the same time, I reserve the right to bitch and moan like an old man and you can just remind me that this is what I signed up for."

Speech over, Mickey stopped. Grace looked like she was holding something back, choking something back. Tears? Laughter?

Was Grace *laughing* at him?

"What *men* do? What *women* do?" she chuckled, her lips forming a pouty smile. "You are so damn cute when you go all serious, Mickey Donahue. But thank you for sharing"

Then she continued, in a low voice, almost gravelly, her eyes on his mouth, taking in his face, then locking into his eyes. "But are you sure that there is *nothing* else you *yearn* for? Because I may have a few *yearnings* myself..."

Zed

Zed was trying to sort out what was different about how he now felt about his life, about forces he could not name that were in motion. It was confusing, but he felt that, in time, it would all come together. He felt akin to the character in the old sci-fi movie, *Close Encounters of the Third Kind*.

"Remember," Zed asked Cherry, "when the guy starts to feel it in his gut, can see something forming, knows something is coming but can't say exactly what? And everyone thinks he is batshit crazy. But then people from all over the world feel the same way? They're all drawn to the same place? What was that line?" He paused to think. "Yeah, 'If you build it, they will come?'"

"I know what you're talking about," Cherry replied. "Only that line's from a different movie, about baseball, I think. But, Zed, you're on to something. People need to start trusting their gut and stop acting like zombies who accept whatever the TV news tells them."

When she said that, how he was on to something, he wanted to grab her up and kiss her. Zed had a hard time imagining how it would be if Cherry had reacted, back when he'd opened up to her, the way their families were reacting now whenever they tried to share what they'd been learning.

Over the past two months, they'd started to bring up important issues with their families, mostly emailing and texting links to articles and websites, saying that they thought this was important so just wanted to share it, so that their families could begin to understand what was happening that the media ignored.

Cherry's two sisters had emailed back, but they were just mean.

"You believe this shit?" one sister had asked. "It makes no sense."

"These are conspiracy theories, and if you buy into it, you're one of the wacko nut-jobs," the other wrote. "And just stop it because you're scaring Mom and Dad and they were already worried about you. This started with Zed, didn't it?"

Her mom had called and tried to find out what was *really* going on, like if Cherry was depressed or having a hard time with the kids home constantly and the pandemic.

"Do you need money?" her mom had asked. "We're tight also, but whatever we can do to be supportive. We're here for you."

Cherry had emailed her sisters, telling them that they were being disrespectful and condescending, like she had no brain when it was them that needed to wake up. "If you swallow everything that the media is feeding you without questioning it, then you're the sheep," she'd written.

With her mom, she just said, "Thanks, but we're doing fine."

Zed's family had not responded at all. They just pretended he hadn't said anything.

But that was no different from how it had always been.

His parents had divorced when he was about four years old. They each remarried within a year and went on to have more kids with their new spouses. Zed had two bio-parents, two stepparents, and five half-siblings—two sisters and a brother at Dad's house, and one of each at Mom's.

For his entire life, he was the only kid with two homes. His life was split down the middle: alternate weeks. Back and forth. It was 50/50.

"It's only fair," his parents had told him when he'd tried to explain that he didn't want to live like that. And, if he persisted, they took it personally, acted all hurt or disappointed or rejected. They said stuff like, "You're just saying that because your dad told you to," or "Your mom is trying to alienate you."

And it always came back to "fair." How the schedule was "fair," Fair for them, maybe. But it had never felt fair to him.

His younger siblings teased him—or maybe just tried to make him feel better—saying that he had it good because he got presents from two sets of parents at Christmas. But, every other year, he missed out. When there was a big Christmas reunion at his uncle's ranch, and his mom's brother and all his cousins from Illinois came? Zed had been with Dad that year. When his dad's parents took everyone on a cruise for their 50th wedding anniversary? Sorry, but that was Mom's holiday.

"We have to stick to the schedule," his mother said when he'd asked about a switch. "Your father will want to make all sorts of changes if we start to switch."

But it was more than that. It was not getting some of his own family's jokes, ordinary stuff, because it happened when he was gone. He didn't fit in like the other kids did. He could never really feel settled or get in a groove. He was there and then he was gone.

And now it was like he'd never belonged at all.

Theo

Theo Murphy was looking for a parking space between the county courthouse and downtown park where Kaw Valley's weekly summer concerts and arts and craft fairs were held. He had an appointment with a therapist, and this is where she'd told him to come.

"The gazebo in South Park," she'd said. "I'll bring the chairs."

Theo had just read that the concerts, as well as every other summer activity that his kids loved, were cancelled. Every summer, since the kids were babies, they'd gone to the Wednesday night concerts spreading out a king-size puffy comforter and pillows, bringing a picnic—plus two sippy cups with "parent-drinks" for he and Josie, his wife.

Their kids, Eli and Aimee, had looked disappointed when he'd told them about the concerts. But the hardest news had been about the public pool. They were stunned.

"You mean closed for a few more days, right?" Eli had asked.

"You mean the pool with the slides and fountains?" Aimee asked. "*That* pool?"

When he explained that, yes, it was *that* pool—they'd both started crying.

"But is won't be summer without the pool," they said, almost in unison.

Theo had never talked to a therapist, but a doctor he worked with had recommended this one. He said that she was pragmatic and direct. Being able to safely blow off steam after his divorce had helped. She'd suggested a few tips that had made a difference.

Theo had a lot of steam to blow off and could use a few tips.

He was both new to his profession, respiratory therapy, and burned out.

He remembered being a kid and wondering, when a doctor would listen with a stethoscope, *I'm obviously breathing so why do you need to listen?* It was just *breathing*.

But he quickly learned that listening was the first skill of his newly-chosen profession. It was a listening that required experience and discernment.

Theo had learned to distinguish vesicular breathing, the soft and low-pitched inhalations and exhalations of normal breathing, from breathing that would indicate inflammation or infection.

He'd learned to identify crackles, both fine crackles and coarse crackles. Then came the wheezing of bronchoconstriction, or inflammation secondary to asthma or bronchitis. There were rhonchi sounds that reflect secretion, lesions, and point to pneumonia or cystic fibrosis. Or the less common stridor sounds, noisy and high-pitched, that can come from obstructions, narrowing of the larynx, vocal cord abnormalities. And don't forget pleural friction rub.

Once you started listening, there was an orchestra of sounds. As indiscriminate noises became distinct, the type, duration, location, and intensity of each sound became part of a diagnostic tree.

And that was just the beginning. It had been a very demanding curriculum.

When he was starting his first clinical, Josie had bought him his own stethoscope. A 3M Littman Classic III. He used it every day, more than he'd ever imagined.

Because, what respiratory therapy had become, in this pandemic, was a job from hell.

Grace's outdoor office was working. Unconventional, for sure, but it met COVID-19 protocols: outdoor, socially distanced, lots of sanitizer available, and usually a breeze. Being tree-top level in a gazebo in the middle of a park meant she could see anyone approaching, but the steps up made it impossible to hear what was being said, or to see who was up there. As far as masks—that was up to her clients.

Now Grace was waiting in the gazebo for a new client. Not that she'd wanted a new client. She'd removed her name from any "find a therapist" websites, insurance company listings, and *Psychology Today*. She had all the clients she could handle, and former clients were lining up, wanting to schedule an appointment.

Everyone was experiencing stress beyond anything they had before, and each crack in a relationship was turning into a crevasse.

This new client had been referred by a physician, himself a former client. Grace didn't have any info other than, "He's holding a lot in, and I think he needs someone to talk to who is not a friend or coworker." Then he'd mentioned that the guy worked at the hospital—with mostly COVID patients.

Grace had been about to decline until the hospital had been mentioned. She'd privately decided that she would work, pro bono if needed, with anyone in a frontline position.

It was the least she could do.

Grace watched a man walking toward the gazebo from the parking lot. He looked up and she waved him toward the steps.

They went through a somewhat awkward COVID-style greeting: a pulling back, nodding of the head, never an extended hand—no shaking hands *ever*—then jutting out elbows to touch, or almost touch.

It reminded her of cranes, bobbing and weaving.

"I'm Theo Murphy," he said, looking at the two folding chairs in a space big enough for the bands and small orchestras that played the summer concerts. "I like what you've done with the place."

Grace smiled. "I picked it for the view," she replied, gesturing at a chair and handing him the intake paperwork.

"You can fill it out now, bring it next time, or scan and send to my email," she said.

"I'll scan," he replied, folding the papers and putting them in a pocket. He was tall, thin, LL Bean-ish in dress, curly dark brown hair that looked in need of a cut. But these days everyone looked like they needed a haircut.

And Theo Murphy felt tense. Tightly wound.

"How do we start?" he asked, suddenly. "I haven't done this before."

"How about I get some background, a little small talk, and then we get around to what's going on? I could give you the HIPPA spiel but it's all in the paperwork."

He smiled at the HIPPA reference. "I can't wait to read it," he said.

"Where are you from?" she started. "Where do you work and what do you do? Are you married? Kids?"

"From Salina. Been living in Kaw Valley for six years. I'm a respiratory therapist at a hospital in Kansas City. Married with two kids."

"That's a full plate," Grace said. "Why RT?"

"I was a philosophy major in college. But philosophy doesn't pay the bills. I tried some other things, but they were just pushing paper: insurance paper, sales paper. So, I stepped back to consider the long-term cost-benefits—like what kind of profession would benefit others, be stimulating and satisfying, and also take care of my family. I settled on RT and went back to school."

"That's both smart and difficult. How long have you done RT?"

"I graduated in December 2019. Got a job offer from KU Med about four days later. Started January 10, 2020."

Grace inhaled sharply.

"So, not exactly what you'd anticipated for your new profession, eh?"

"No. I wanted to help people recover. To develop the best possible lifestyle. Focus on positive outcomes," Theo said in a monotone voice. "Now I watch people suffer and die. Every single day it feels like someone is dying on my watch, in my care."

"I think we bypassed the small talk," Grace said. "Tell me more about what your life is like now and how it has been the last three months."

"When it all started, we didn't understand what we were dealing with," Theo said. "COVID was just so many unknowns. We weren't sure about transmission, so we looked at every possibility. Here, in Kansas, we watched what was happening in New York City. Ambulances lined up outside jammed emergency rooms. Refrigerator trucks to hold the bodies. It felt like there was this black wave that was going to move west and smother us. Drown us. And there's nothing we can do to stop it. And thousands of people are acting like they can't see the wave...." Theo's voice cracked, just a bit, and he stopped talking.

Grace noted that he'd moved from past tense to present tense in five or so sentences.

"What has been happening at home?" she asked.

"First the schools closed. Our oldest, Eli, suddenly had virtual school. Daycare shut down so our daughter, Aimee, was home as well. But that's what every family has been dealing with."

"Are you not like every...?"

"My wife, Josie, is a nurse. We work in high-risk environments, and we didn't want to infect our kids. So, we took them to their grandparents. Thought it would be a few days, maybe a week at the most. Like a mini vacation? Just until we knew what we were dealing with."

"But?"

"We didn't touch them for two months," Theo continued. "We did

FaceTime, and then Zoom, but we did not hold our kids for 64 days. We felt like we couldn't touch each other. We slept in separate rooms. We were too afraid of infecting each other not to. Our kids need a parent. We took our scrubs off and tossed them straight into the washing machine as soon as we got home, scrubbed ourselves raw in the shower, collapsed, woke up, and did it all over again. It was hell."

Grace had no words. She'd thought she'd understood what the medical staff were going through, but this was—more. It was like the combat troops she'd worked with after deployments: families separated, marriages strained, exhaustion and fear dominating every waking moment.

"And now?"

"We realized that this was not going to be over anytime soon. So, we cleaned our place like maniacs, disinfected everything, and brought the kids home. We booked a hotel room next to the hospital and Josie and I switch out every three or four days."

"What do you mean 'switch out?'"

"I crash there when I'm working, and then my wife does. She works in Kansas City also. We'd been commuting from Kaw Valley, no big deal, but it's too dangerous when we're that tired, takes time that we could sleep, and going in-and-out of the house every day puts the kids at more risk. This way we have one transition into our home each week."

"Who takes care of the kids?"

"We changed shifts to be off different days. I work Sunday, Monday, Tuesday, Wednesday, and Josie works Thursday, Friday, Saturday. We disinfect in-between. We were trying to get tested before coming home but it takes too long to get results."

"And when you're home?"

"Then we're full-time with the kids—supervising virtual school, keeping them from driving each other crazy, getting them out safely for exercise, cooking every meal at home."

"How many hours are you each working?"

"She's 25-35 hours over three days. I'm usually 40-50 over four. But I did over 60 last week. I never left the hospital between shifts. Crashed on cot in a basement room that is set up for that now. We're down three RTs, and there's nobody to cover."

"What do you mean 'we're down?'"

"COVID. They got infected. One is recovering at home. But two ended up in the ICU. Miguel died yesterday. He was due to retire but stayed on to help. Debbie made it home but is in no shape to return to work. She may never come back."

Theo's voice was flat, as if he were reporting the weather. It took Grace a moment to process the words—"Miguel died yesterday"—his co-worker died *yesterday*—with the absence of emotion.

"Oh, God, I'm so sorry. I didn't know if it just meant they'd been exposed and had to quarantine," Grace said, almost apologetically.

Theo looked at Grace and then laughed, but it came out as a harsh guttural sound.

"We're potentially *exposed* every minute of every workday," he said. "No matter if we have PPE—and there were days when we patched it together with duct-tape. We get exposed to high viral loads—that virus attached to every invisible particle. Not the viral load you get in passing someone or touching a surface. When we get infected, it's serious. Deadly serious."

Theo shook his head, like a "no-no-no," then spoke. "Quarantine? That's a luxury. A privilege. That's for the rest of the world."

Yes, Grace thought, *this is war.*

"I didn't understand, so thanks for explaining," she said. "So, you go to work every fucking day knowing that you could not only get infected, but that it could be very, very bad?"

"Yeah," Theo said, smiling just a bit. "*And I'm so fucking scared.*" He looked surprised that he'd spoken the words out loud. "I've never felt like this. I'm the fix-it guy. Problem solver. I used to be *fun*. I could *play*," he continued. "I could make my kids laugh until they were rolling on the floor. Now I want to grab my kids and wife and run away. But—where? COVID is everywhere."

"When was the last time you had any time with your wife without the kids?" Grace interrupted.

"When we're not working?"

"Yeah", Grace said. "Like 48 hours to be a couple? To really rest?"

"Before COVID," he said after thinking a minute. "Maybe summer of 2019 for a weekend? We had a real vacation planned for our tenth anniversary last April, but that couldn't happen."

Grace put down her clipboard and notes.

"Look, Theo, here it is. I'm just a therapist. Not God. Your challenges are real. It's not like you're exaggerating. Or worrying for no good reason. It would be an insult to suggest otherwise. We're in a war and people are dying every day. And you're on the front lines."

Grace paused. Could what she was about to say be unhelpful?

"I've worked with combat troops in the past. And you sound like them. Only by the time I met with them they were out of the war zone, returned to safety, their families tucked away in base housing. I was helping them transition from hyper-vigilance to 'normal.' Like not waking up every two hours to secure the perimeter, only now it's checking every door and window in the house. Or being unable to sit in a restaurant unless they have their back to a wall and can continually scan. But they were *out* of the war zone. They were back home. But your war zone and your home? They're all connected."

Theo was listening, but head down, staring at the floor. Grace thought that he'd deflated some when she said, "I'm just a therapist. Not God." Like he'd been hoping that this process would provide him— what? Magical insight? Hope?

She waited until he looked up.

"I hadn't worked this through in my head until the last few minutes," she continued. "But this war may be harder than combat. I think you're so bogged down in the mud that you can't even imagine what could make a difference. You're feeling trapped, cornered. And you're deeply in need of an R&R."

Grace waited for his slight nod.

"So, here goes. This is a prescription, not a suggestion. You ask your in-laws to take the kids for three days minimum. You tell work whatever you need to tell them, and 'I'm feeling ill' would not be lying. You tell your wife to do the same thing. And you find a little Airbnb within a few hours' drive and go curl up with your wife. Sleep. Walk. Swim in a lake."

Theo's eyes had focused in on her face, like he was trying to make sense of what she was saying.

"My in-laws have a camper," he mused. "I think we could borrow it. We like camping. Would that work?"

"Does it have a queen bed? This is not a single bed R&R."

"Yeah," he answered. "It's at least a double."

Grace looked at him appraisingly. "You're skinny enough," she concluded. "A double could work."

They talked some more about un-plugging, not checking email and messages every hour, mind-games that could help to let go of some of the worry.

"And no news," Grace added. "Nada. No TV. No talk shows. It will all be there when you get back. I know this is a Band-Aid. But sometimes wounds need to be covered up to stop oozing."

Katrina

It had been four months since Katrina had walked out of her office for what she thought would be a day or so. She tried to remember what her life had been like, what she had been able to accomplish in any given day. She juggled multiple cases, dozens of clients. She could flip through files, talk on speaker phone, and not miss a beat. She'd crammed before depositions and court, got by on a few hours' sleep when on deadlines, spent entire days plugging through research. And work had been satisfying. Not every day, every task, but much of it.

Plus, she'd somehow found time to get to the gym three to four times a week, have lunch with a friend and, more often than not, hit martini night at the Eldridge on the way home from work on Thursdays.

Damn, she missed martini night. The tasty half-price appetizers. The slow warmth that spread through her body and up to her over-active mind after the first few sips of straight gin with extra olives.

Katrina Baptiste used to have a life.

And now she did not. She was a ghost of her former self.

And the world was moving on without her.

HISTORICAL CONTEXT: JUNE 2020

Jun. 6: Massive, peaceful protests happen nationwide to demand police reform. Services are held for Floyd in Raeford, North Carolina, near Floyd's birthplace.

Jun. 6: "Hopefully George is looking down right now and saying this is a great thing that's happening for our country... This is a great day for him... This is a great, great day in terms of equality. " – *Donald Trump*

Jun. 8: New Zealand finds no new confirmed cases and plans to lift almost all coronavirus restrictions.

June. 18: "And it is dying out. The numbers are starting to get very good." – *Donald Trump*

Jun. 20: The NIH halts a clinical trial of the drug hydroxychloroquine as a treatment for the coronavirus, stating, "It was very unlikely to be beneficial to hospitalized patients with COVID-19."

Jun. 20: "When you do testing...you're going to find more cases, so I said to my people, 'Slow the testing down, please.'" – *Donald Trump*

Jun. 22: As many as 80% of Americans who sought care for flu-like illnesses in March were infected with the virus that causes COVID-19, according to a study in *Science*.

Jun. 22: U.S death toll passes 120,000.

Jun. 24: A grand jury indicts the three men involved in the murder of Ahmaud Arbery near Brunswick, Georgia.

Jun. 25: "Coronavirus deaths are way down. Mortality rate is one of the lowest in the world. Our economy is roaring back and will NOT be shut down." – *Donald Trump*

Jun. 30: In a Senate hearing, Anthony Fauci warns that COVID-19 cases in the U.S. could reach as high as 100,000 new cases per day. The U.S. reaches that milestone on Nov. 4, 2020.

Jun. 30: The U.S. has 25% of global coronavirus cases—but only 4% of global population—and the second highest death per capita rate.

July 2020

Grace

Grace and Katrina had not talked, not really, in weeks, although Grace continued to drop off meals and make email offers to help however Kat needed.

But Kat did not respond, other than a formulaic "Thank you for the food," or "Thank you, but I have that covered."

Grace and Mickey had reacted, initially, as Kat had to the death of George Floyd. They'd thought there had to be a *reason* for what they were seeing: the man must have been a wanted felon, armed and dangerous, or had attacked someone. But that wasn't how the people that encircled the police were reacting.

The people were pleading.

Grace found herself thinking, often, about the "bystanders." She knew from her work with the military, how much being a "bystander" to something horrific ate at the psyche. It became the stuff of nightmares. These bystanders did not realize that these few accidental moments would become part of their life-narrative, their history, for the rest of their lives. They would never shake the fear of what could happen when you least expect it.

They would carry an invisible blanket of guilt for not intervening, for not knowing what to do. But more than guilt—and more toxic—would be the shame. Shame for not risking more, shame for feeling the fear that they already carried, would always carry, when it came to the police. Shame for pleading, witnessing, but not rushing in, not facing down, with their unarmed bodies, cops with guns.

It was if they were *forced* to witness, as police officers stood back and did nothing. As a white man, in a blue uniform, with a twisted badge, slowly crushed a handcuffed Black man on the pavement until he stopped breathing.

But the bystanders had used their phones, had risked taking video, had created evidence. Not evidence just for a courtroom, but for a nation. Everyone who saw the videos was confronted with irrefutable evidence. The inequities of what constituted "equal justice under the law" played out on televisions and phones and laptops, over and over.

Was this the first time that the nation had all become bystanders? Or just the first time that they could not look away?

Zed & Cherry

It was also over four months into the pandemic for Zed and Cherry, but things were better than they had initially feared.

Actually, things were going pretty well.

Who knew that Home Depot would be considered an essential business and need to remain open? Zed thought. And that he'd be designated as an "essential worker?"

But Home Depot was doing great. With everybody in lockdown and stuck at home, *everybody* wanted to finally fix whatever it was that needed fixing. Some guy at work said that the stats for YouTube videos about home construction projects, like building a fence or any kind of repairs, had gone up like a million percent. No more extra shifts at McDonalds for Zed. Now he could get extra shifts at work whenever he wanted.

Not that it was all "peaches and cream," as Cherry would say. He was in the lumber and building supplies department. There was a national shortage of lumber. Prices were shifting every week. Builders were screaming, and everybody was pissed-off.

And it was only going to get worse.

But the silver lining was that that Zed discovered something that he'd never known about himself: he could listen to people who were mad, and yelling, and not react. He'd tell people that they were totally entitled to be pissed-off, but, as much as he wished he could make it right, and he'd do anything to help them, he couldn't make lumber out of thin air. He'd offer to check something out and call them back. And he'd call back even if just to tell them more bad news, which impressed the shit out of them since they'd been assholes before. So, despite getting the bad news that Home Depot had no idea when the lumber on back-order would actually show up, they appreciated not feeling jerked around. After that, when they called, they'd ask for Zed. And *that* made the higher-ups take notice.

Just two weeks ago, he'd been called into the front office and promoted. He'd not seen that coming. He was now training as an assistant manager for the lumber and building department.

What Zed was learning from QAnon, by asking and responding to questions, changed how he worked. He didn't wait to be told to do something, and he didn't feel the resentment he used to at being bossed around. Now he just stepped up to the plate. He felt he had something to offer. And every day customers said, "Hey, thanks. Appreciate your help." He almost *liked* going to work, which was different than he'd ever felt before.

Zed did not talk politics at work, but he noticed that what people believed, where their loyalties were, slipped out. Like when he wore his MAGA ball cap to work, and he'd remembered before got to the door he couldn't wear it at work, so he turned around to bring it back to his car. But he passed another guy heading in, who gave him a quick grin with a thumbs up. It was like code for "Yeah, go Trump," if not for Q.

Grace & Amber

Grace sat at her desk in her empty office and stared at the pile of files. She'd never felt so impotent as she did now.

Two days ago, she'd had a Zoom session with a woman in an abusive marriage. She'd briefly worked with the woman a few years ago, but then she hadn't been ready to separate or divorce. The kids had been in preschool, but now they were both in elementary. Having kids home 24/7 since March had been a tipping point. Her husband was more and more angry with her, with the kids.

"He occasionally loses it with me," Amber had shared. "But he hadn't been physical with the kids like this. Yelling, but not physical."

Grace noted that she said "physical" instead of hit. Or slapped. Or beat.

"Do you have some place to go?" Grace had asked. "I don't know if the shelter is taking families. Have you called?"

"He said that if I ever left with the kids, he'd get sole custody because that would be kidnapping," Amber had replied. "I'd go to jail."

"That's a lie, Amber. Protecting your kids is not kidnapping." Grace paused to look at her notes. "Do you have any way to document the abuse? Remember how we talked about..."

"Yeah, I remember. I have photos of bruises and a black eye, and I left the phone on 'record' a few weeks ago when I heard him coming in the back door stumbling drunk. He was mad. Yelling and threatening. Telling me how I was why he drank. You can hear him breaking stuff."

Grace didn't know whether to be grateful or scream. Amber's tone was so matter of fact. What she was describing was just a part of her day-to-day existence: being hit, threats and violence along with dishes, laundry and groceries.

By the time they finished the session, Amber had a plan: call her sister in Utah; pack up some of the kids' clothes, toys, books, and games, and drop them at a friend's house to hold for her; send multiple copies of the photos and recording to her sister and a friend in case something happened to her phone; withdraw at least half of the funds in the joint bank accounts but not until she was on her way out of town. Not the day before, but in the car, all packed up, with the kids, headed for I-70.

Leave no chance that he could check the balances while she was still in town.

Once she was away and safe, she could send her husband an email that described the abuse, why she left, and that she was not kidnapping the children but protecting them. Then he could never say he was not informed. Also, write that if he wanted to hire an attorney, go ahead. The attorney could contact her by this email. Get a second email address just for this process.

The good news was that her sister had only moved to Utah two months ago, so her husband didn't know her address.

"I don't think he even remembers me telling him," Amber said. "He's probably thinks she's in California."

As long as she didn't use credit cards, Grace explained, it could take him a while to locate her. In the meantime, she needed to find an attorney—but first decide what state she wanted to live in.

"I'm ready for a change," Amber said. "I'd like to live by my sister."

"Then hire an attorney in Utah who specializes in domestic abuse divorces," Grace concluded. "As soon as you get there. Then open a bank account and go get a Utah driver's license.

'We can Zoom when that's done, or if something comes up that we didn't discuss," Grace concluded.

Grace wondered how many other women were stuck in escalating domestic abuse with nowhere to turn. It was enough to bring her to tears. Or rage.

Ian & Nell

The funeral home was still doing almost double the number of funerals. There had been an incremental rise, and then—a surge. Ian looked at the COVID-19 stats from the county and state but felt that they were under-reported. So many people were dying at home, never getting to an ER. Black families often faced bias from medical institutions, so they were understandably reluctant. His own family had their "experiences" of misdiagnosis, or having symptoms minimized.

So many more Black families, Latino families, were being hit hard. There were theories about more underlying conditions, more vulnerabilities. Looking to explain what factors were influencing the higher rates of serious illness and death. But it didn't get the attention in the media, not like if white families were suffering more, if white people were dying at higher percentages. And medical science was so focused on developing a vaccine and finding what interventions worked better in treatment—well, they'd sort out the "factors" when they got the virus under control.

It wasn't the volume that made it harder with work, but how emotionally difficult it was for their clients. Families were not allowed in the hospital rooms with their loved ones. They were not able to be with them when they died. They did not see them in caskets.

Funerals were mostly on Zoom, and technology was unreliable. Ian felt that his purpose— to facilitate grieving with ritual and respect, to be fully present for families on the worst of days—was being sabotaged by the same tenacious virus that was killing everyone.

Nell was not teaching, but home for the summer and helping at the funeral home. Nell was good with talking to people on the phone, connecting with them, in ways that Ian could not. He'd watched her sitting at the front desk, her eyes closed, as if visualizing who was at the other end, closing off everything else in the world but that one person.

And Nell had taken charge of inventory—the boxes of ashes that they'd never needed to inventory before. But now black boxes of ashes were five deep on the backroom shelves. Nell came up with a system: letters for each shelf, numbers for the rows, another number for how far back on the shelf. So, if a family wanted the ashes of John Doe, they knew to go to shelf K, row 5, box 3. It beat having to sort through fifty labels.

For Nell, the funeral home was easier than the frustrating months of attempting to "teach-by-Zoom" to inner-city kids whose families often lacked both computers and computer access. The school district had been trying to reach families with "challenging circumstances" to loan a laptop, but it wasn't just a lack of computers. It was no Wi-Fi because some families could afford food or Wi-Fi. Not both. And no parent was around to supervise kids because the parents had to work.

Nell remembered calling the home number of a 4th grade boy who hadn't logged in for classes, and the child saying, so very politely, "I can't talk now, ma'am. I'm changing my brother's diaper. Maybe tomorrow?" Nell had heard a crying baby and at least one more young child's voice in the background. That boy never did log in. From March until June, he was, she assumed, the family's childcare provider. Nell wondered if he would have to repeat 4th grade or if catch-up tutoring would be provided.

Ian felt that there was an upside to the pandemic, although he would *never* say that out loud. Since being with friends or even family was potentially dangerous, and concerts, activities, conferences, and meetings had been cancelled, Ian and Nell found that they had more time together. As much as they enjoyed being with their extended families and friends, they'd felt like they needed a *valid* excuse, a *reason*, to say, "Oh, sorry, we can't make it..."

"We're tired and we need some couple time," was not *valid* enough. And neither of them was a good liar.

COVID took care of that. Their calendars went from black scribbles on every page, all the way to the margins, to white space. Nell now put in reminders like "Prep the lasagna" and "Watch old NYPD Blues."

But more, Ian and Nell were taking stock. Every day they faced reminders of the fragility of life. Nell had had uterine cancer in her late 20s. They'd accepted that they would not be having biological children but had vacillated on adoption.

"I saw this piece today on TV," Ian told Nell one evening in June as they chopped onions and peppers to make tacos. "About how hard it is for older kids to be adopted. Everybody wants a baby. But there are hundreds of kids over 10 years old that are trapped in the system."

"Some of those kids are pretty messed up," Nell pointed out.

"Yeah, but there are a lot of kids who just need a home, some security, to not be so messed up. Consistency. Predictability. Accountability."

"And love," Nell countered. "You could be describing the Army. A little young for boot camp, huh?"

"Maybe that's why so many kids in foster care end up in the Army. It gives them what they need to survive until they can figure things out."

"You're serious about this, Ian?"

"I want us to talk about it."

"You been thinking about what age kid? Boy or girl?" Nell asked.

"That's on the 'Talk About' list."

"Let's talk then," Nell answered, a warm flush of possibility filling her chest. "I'll pour some Pinot Noir. You get the crackers and cheese?"

They talked, on and off, for weeks. And then they started the paperwork to begin an adoption process. It was a bear: detailed application, financial statements, family and marital history, lifestyle, references, background and child abuse checks.

But they would not have to face an interminable wait, as when adopting a baby, hoping a pregnant woman would choose them to parent her child. Instead, there were websites with pages and pages of pictures and short bios of older kids "available to adopt."

"It makes me cry to see how many kids need a home," Nell said. "And every one of them looking at some camera with those hopeful, desperate eyes. *Pick me, please, choose me.*"

It would take time for all the paperwork to make its way through the system. Once they were approved, they could schedule a home study. They were looking at January 2021. They could have a child by next summer.

"Have to pass a home inspection," Nell said. "We're taking pictures that day because this house will be cleaner than it's ever been. And we're decluttering first."

But she grinned as she said it. They'd discussed what rooms to switch around. There would never be a nursery, but they were looking to create a space that would make a kid feel welcome.

It was still a little scary, but, after COVID, nothing was as scary as it used to be.

Max

It was hot, and Max missed the big town pool. It had slides and a rope walk and fountains to run through. His mom or Grammy had packed picnics and they'd eat at a picnic table under a big umbrella. He usually got to have one ice cream cone from the snack stand.

Max knew he needed to take more swim lessons. He was supposed to be in the intermediate class, but it was cancelled too. He wondered if he would ever learn to swim better.

Mickey was taking him on surprise drives. It was not the same day every week because that was part of the surprise. They would get in the car and Mickey would hand him a map. It would have a circle where he lived and then a circle around a destination. And Max had to figure out how to get there and tell Mickey where to turn and what roads to take. And when they got to wherever it was, they would either get take-out from a special place—like barbecue or fried chicken—or have a picnic in a state park. Some of the parks had lakes. Mickey packed their bathing suits, noodles, and towels. And Max's lake shoes. Max needed lake shoes because he did not like the squishy feel of the bottom of lakes. It was so gross.

Even when they got lost, because Max read the map wrong, it was fun. Mickey said that was when the adventure started, when you didn't know exactly where you were or how to get to where you were going.

Molly

Molly and Mike were having their weekly Zoom chat. They were talking about Zoom itself, how it was better than a phone, but also frustrating and limiting.

"My mom says that Zoom is much harder with her clients than then face-to-face, much more draining," Molly said. "Too much 'face' and not enough body language and context. Like if you look away from the screen for just a minute the other person can feel that you're not paying attention or getting bored or distracted."

"Is it like that for you on Zoom? Like with me?" Mike asked.

"Not really, but I think sometimes I'd like to just talk lying down on the couch, lights off, less intensely visual. Does that make any sense?"

"Yeah, it does. Less eye strain too," he chuckled. "So, any exciting news in your world?"

"I'm going to try to get our Third Sunday Suppers going again but flexing on the day. More spontaneous, like if Katrina is feeling good… then 'Let's have a supper.' Also, weather permitting as we'll be eating outside and socially distanced."

"That's good, right?" Mike asked. "You sound a little…"

"Mom and Kat have been sort of weird with each other. It started right after George Floyd. Mom said something and Katrina heard it one way. Mom tried to explain but made it worse. So, a little tense? Prickly?"

"Maybe the suppers will get them talking again. Not so one-on-one?"

"Yeah, that's what I hope. But, hey, what's going on in your life?" she asked, changing the subject. "How are your folks? And David?"

"My folks are managing. They have each other, and they were slowing down anyway, so this isn't as hard for them," Mike replied, folding his arms. "They go for a walk on the beach every day. They invite David and Moses too. I think that dog has become a second grandkid. It's a hassle cleaning off the sand—which blends so well with his golden retriever coat—but Moses does love the ocean and beach."

"Getting that dog was one of your brilliant moves," Molly said.

"I happen to know that getting a puppy for David was *your* idea," he corrected with a sly smile. "Your mother let it slip one time when I was thanking her for suggesting it. She couldn't take a compliment that she didn't deserve."

There was a split second of awkwardness, recalling Mike's prior professional relationship with Grace. Grace had known Mike before Molly ever did. And Grace was unaware that they were, well, "good friends."

Molly pivoted to another topic.

"Are people down there masking or are they in rebellion? It got crazy around the 4th of July. All these people acting like the virus was going to disappear when it got hot out."

"Yeah," Mike said. "Those viral posts from the Lake of the Ozarks? People crammed into pools and bars, no masks, waving and dancing."

"They're all idiots," Molly said, leaning into the screen. "They're asking to get sick. I'm angry that they'll all return home and infect people who are following CDC guidelines and not being assholes."

"They don't believe in the virus, Molly. There are so many who think it's a hoax. They're brainwashed."

With that, Molly lost it. "Bullshit! Every damn one of them has agency. They can read what scientists and epidemiologists are saying and not just swallow what they want to hear to rationalize their desire to party."

"Has anyone even mentioned that can come across as opinionated?" he grinned, wickedly.

"Don't try to distract me," she said, pointing a finger at him. "This is righteous indignation. I'm calling out evil."

Mike laughed. "Evil? Seriously?"

Molly glared at the screen. "Yeah, what do *you* call it when people put their 'right' to party, not mask, over protecting their community? That their 'freedoms'—more conveniences—take priority over the freedom of others to keep on breathing."

Molly's voice had escalated but now she put her face in her hands. "Jesus, Mike, I cannot carry this much anger in me. It's like bile that erupts up my throat, and I have to vomit it out."

"I get it. You see how bad Katrina still is and then you see bozos acting like COVID is no big deal."

"I don't think I've ever wanted to physically hurt anyone. But I want to slap their smug, unmasked faces, just haul off and let one fly," she blurted, gesturing wildly.

Molly saw Moses come into the frame. Mike gave him a scratch on the head as he continued speaking. "Not smart. These are people that could also believe in their right to carry a loaded gun anywhere that they please."

"Do not get me started on guns. We've got to talk about something else. Help me out here."

"Okay, here's something: I'm looking into grad school."

Molly pulled back in surprise. "No shit? After moaning all that time about how you couldn't wait to graduate, that it was never going to happen, that you'd never be able to focus or finish..."

"Shut up already," Mike cut her off. "I thought you social work people didn't pick on people with *disabilities*."

"Oh, is that what you have?" she teased, leaning towards the screen, as if getting closer meant she might be able to actually touch his arm. "And here I thought your challenges were due to your extra-thick skull."

I so see what Mom means about Zoom, Molly thought. *I want to be face-to-face, in a coffee shop, with twenty other people at other tables, with background noise. Like life used to be.*

"Are you going to ask *what* I may be going to graduate school to study?" Mike asked.

"Absolutely," Molly said, dropping her attitude. "What are thinking of studying in grad school? And where? And when would you start?"

"I have the BA in history. Not marketable. But paired up with a master's in education? I could do something with it. Something that I might even enjoy."

"Teaching," Molly replied, her voice lifting. "Those kids would be so lucky. To have someone teaching who wants to make history real and meaningful."

He shrugged. "Don't go overboard. But, yeah, I see how hard it is for David to just navigate being a kid. He'll be going to college in a few years. Then what do I do? I'm thinking I could do this."

Molly's eyes brightened. "You can definitely do this. You could rock at doing this. So where do you want to go to grad school?"

"I'm a Florida resident, so makes sense to stay local. And I want David to be able to finish high school here. No more uprooting. He's been through enough."

Molly reflected that David had been through hell. That he was still functioning and not a train-wreck was testament to the considerable love given by his dad and grandparents.

"Whatever the school, you'll run with it," Molly concurred. "You don't need to be spoon-fed."

"Well, a little spoon-feeding could be nice. Maybe that delicious tomato-basil soups you made when…"

"Don't change the subject," she said. "Where are you planning to go?"

"Florida Gulf Coast University. It's local, public, reasonable costs for Florida residents. Can do a combo remote and in-person. From a practical standpoint, it works."

"Mike, anything that's an easy commute and works with parenting is the right choice."

"That's what I'm thinking. Don't complicate life any more than necessary. The real learning happens in the trenches after you finish, anyway."

After she left the call, Molly thought about this shift in Mike. She felt in her gut that he'd be a solid teacher. He'd been through a lot of shit in his adult life, and he'd learned compassion.

Teaching could even bring him happiness, she thought. *I could use a little of that myself.*

She'd almost brought up a decision that she was leaning towards, to take a leave of absence from *her* grad school program. It wasn't just the strain of virtual school with Max, but what *she* wanted from *her* practicum in terms of experience. It was looking like she'd be working virtually. No team meetings in person or being able to talk about cases in the break room. She wanted to finish her degree. But would she feel unprepared? Miss out on the best part of grad school, the hands-on experience? Was it better to take a leave and return when she could get what she wanted from the program?

But she hadn't wanted to rain on Mike's parade. And it was still a "maybe."

For just a quick moment, Molly thought about Mike's comment on "spoon-fed." Had it been more personal, maybe even flirty? *Nah,* she concluded, *he isn't thinking like that. More just playing around.*

Grace

On Sunday, July 19ᵗʰ, Grace was reading the New York Times Magazine cover story, *"Why We're Losing the Battle With COVID-19,"* which was both illuminating and scary in explaining the underfunding of public health. But then she saw the other lead article: "Whiteness Lessons." It was about Robin DiAngelo and her book, *White Fragility.*

The article galvanized her. It was hard to articulate an experience or feeling without the right words. "Whiteness Lessons" could help with that.

She cut out the article and put it in a folder. Grace had also read, in the last few weeks, *How to Be An Anti-Racist* by Ibram X. Kendi, and was halfway through *Caste* by Isabel Wilkerson. More books were waiting on the shelf.

On July 20ᵗʰ, Grace drove over to Katrina's house, bringing a basket with curried squash soup and kalamata olive bread.

For so many years, they'd just checked the door, and, if not locked, walked in, calling out "Yoo-hoo? Anybody home? It's me."

They'd always known who "me" was.

This time Grace rang the doorbell.

Katrina answered, still in her PJs at 1 p.m. She looked surprised to see Grace. "I wasn't expecting you," she said. "Did you text?"

"No, dammit, I didn't text. Look, I miss you. I know I screwed up, but can we please talk it out?"

"I'm too tired to talk," Kat replied, her voice flat. "I don't even know where to start."

"I want to try. Call me when you're feeling up to it," Grace said, holding out the basket.

Molly

A few days later, Molly phoned Katrina.

"I'm not sure what's going on with you and Mom," she said. "But I'm ready to go back to our Third Sunday Suppers. They don't have to be on a third Sunday. More spontaneous. If you're having a few good days, then we have a supper."

"Don't schedule around me," Kat protested. "Just go ahead and plan and I'll see how…"

"No, dammit," Molly said. "My mother is moping around here like she lost her best friend, which she has, and I'm tired of her sad-sack face. Whatever she did, don't put that on me. If you don't come here, we're all going to show up at your door."

Kat paused to consider the threat. Molly was not past doing exactly that, and she would not stop at the door.

"So, when is this spontaneous supper happening?" Kat asked.

"Now there's the Kat I know and love," Molly replied. "Tomorrow at 7 p.m. Can you pick up a bottle of gin on the way over? We're eating outside, of course."

After hanging up, Molly walked the ten steps to Grace's casita.

"Yoo-hoo," she called out, walking in the front door. "Where are you?"

"We're starting Third Sunday Suppers again, just not on third Sundays," Molly said in a chipper, upbeat voice once they were seated at the counter with lemonade. "Tomorrow at 7 p.m. Mickey is grilling kabobs and I'm making Asian Slaw. Max wants to help you make strawberry shortcake. How does that sound?"

"What about Kat?" Grace immediately asked.

"Kat's bringing the gin. I think some G & T's are called for. So very refreshing in the heat, no?"

"Kat's coming?" Grace sounded surprised. And relieved. Maybe even hopeful?

"Yes, mother, Kat is coming." *And if she doesn't,* Molly thought, *I will march over there and…*

"Tell Max to come over tomorrow about 11, or by 8 if he wants to pick out the berries at the Farmer's Market," Grace said. "And we may need a different name if they aren't on the third Sunday."

"I'll leave that up to Max," Molly concluded. "He likes an assignment."

At 7 p.m. the next night, the picnic table was set with divided plates, so the food did not touch—one of Max's preferences—and the kabobs were on the grill. The slaw was in the fridge, and Molly was filling tall glasses with ice for their drinks. Katrina arrived, handing over a bottle of Bombay Sapphire. Molly had splurged on some Fever Tree Tonic. As she cut limes into quarters, she sent a brief prayer out to the Universe: *This has been a very shitty year, so please, please, please...let this work out.*

Max was sitting at the kitchen counter when Grace walked in with the strawberry shortcake. "Hi Grammy," he called out. "Auntie Kat is here. Our pod is back. For *'Pod-Potlucks.'* That's the new name. Do you like it? Mom says it has alliteration."

When Mickey poked his head in the back door announcing, "Kabobs are about done," there was a flurry of carrying out the slaw and bread and pickles and such. Once they were seated, Molly, Mickey, and Max carried the conversation, but there was an awkwardness, an absence of teasing. Voices were missing.

Halfway through supper, Molly looked over at Mickey and raised her eyebrows. Mickey gave the smallest of shrugs back. Molly lifted back up shoulders and plunged in.

"Auntie Katrina, I want to say something. We miss you. We love you. We know that Mom screwed up..."

"Hey, hold on a minute..." Grace interrupted, but was silenced by a glare from her daughter, who then continued.

"We know that Mom screwed up, but this is bigger than the two of you. It's been a wake-up call for me, and what I need to do to raise Max so he can see and understand better than I or my mother ever have. So, we want to have some conversations."

"Did your mother put you up to this?" Kat asked, shooting a look at Grace.

"I most certainly did not," Grace replied, ignoring that the question had been directed to Molly.

"She most certainly did not," Molly added, giving Grace a "shut up" glare. "I asked her *after* I asked you. And given how stubborn you both are, I'm almost surprised that neither one of you flaked out with some pathetic last-minute excuse."

"This doesn't involve you, Molly," Katrina said. "This is between your..."

"Bullshit, Kat," Molly interrupted. "We're family. You're my *matant*. So, whatever it is, we will talk it out. It may take a few years given what all has to be covered, and we will definitely hit some walls, but you are both—we are all—stuck with our skins. Stuck inside those skins in this godforsaken country. Mom said something dumb, but it took both of you to create the little bubble you've been living in..."

"Did you just say bubble?" Grace interrupted. "Yesterday I was thinking about how I grew up in a white bubble," Grace continued. "And in *that* bubble, there was *never* a discussion about race, just like there was nothing about sex. And, despite all my education, and skills at probing, and tackling uncomfortable subjects with clients..."

"Are you saying that your parents *never* talked to you about race?" Kat asked, her reluctance fading, and ire, mixed with incredulity, rising. "How is that possible? With *anything* we did, *anything,* race was front and center."

"I don't want to make excuses, but my parents *never* talked about race directly," Grace replied. "My dad hated conflict, so he'd mutter stuff like, 'Do they not realize that burning buildings will not help their goals? Change takes time.'"

Grace recalled how her mother or father would turn the TV channel whenever there was "disturbing" news. "Why can't people just get along?" her mother had often said with a sigh.

"Did your parents have Black friends?" Katrina asked.

"Hah! There were almost no Black people in our town," Grace replied. "None in my Catholic elementary school, and only a handful in public high school, maybe 2-3 per grade level."

"So, none in your neighborhood?"

Grace snorted. "Nope. There was one block on the far side of town that I never knew existed until I volunteered to bring over some books and assignments to the only Black girl in an English class who was sick. The road was gravel, and it took my mother 30 minutes to find it. I can't be sure, but I think she said something like, 'Grace, people just naturally like to live near their own kind. Irish like Irish. Italians like Italians. That's how it is.'"

"Well, there is truth in that," Kat agreed. "Unless it's less about 'like' and more about redlining and restrictive covenants."

Grace had made jokes about her white "Wonder Bread" childhood. It's easy to believe that you're color-blind when you never had color to see. At least no local color.

"What was your neighborhood like?" Molly asked, shifting to Katrina.

"Pretty Black. It had been white, decent houses, but back then if even one Black family moved in the white flight started. Only Black families couldn't *buy* the houses. Banks denied mortgages, because, if Black people lived there, it was rated as too risky. Developers exploited the racist fears, bought up whole neighborhood as whites sold out at way below the former market value. Then they turned them into rentals, invested nothing, and pocketed the money."

Katrina stopped talking but looked as if she was reaching for something in in the deep recesses of her memory. Her body shifted on the bench to face Grace more directly.

"Didn't your parents buy their first home with the GI Bill? Your Dad was in the Navy?" Katrina asked, connecting some dots in her head. "Didn't you tell me about Pearl Road?"

"Yeah, they did. My Dad used to say that it was the best thing the Navy ever did for him. They got into a brand-new house in a cookie-cutter neighborhood. I think half the street was veteran families. I have pictures of me, about two-years old, in a snowsuit, just the frame of the house up, while they were building it."

"I did a paper in college on the GI Bill," Kat continued, now looking past Grace at the back of the house. "And I never forgot the stats because they shocked me. The GI Bill was great for white veterans. But minority vets? Black vets? They were screwed over. The states, not the feds, had control. Banks had to approve loans first and *then* the VA would co-sign. And banks denied most Black applications for mortgages. Minority or inner-city neighborhoods were deemed 'high risk' and a lot of decent neighborhoods, the suburbs, had covenants against selling to Black people, or were 'inappropriate.' In New York and northern New Jersey, under 100 of 67,000 GI Bill mortgages went to Black vets. In

Mississippi, only 2 of 3,200 loans, in thirteen different cities, went to Black families. You think those Black families didn't want a pretty new house to raise their kids? Good schools? A backyard, garden, and a barbecue grill?" Her voice was not angry, but factual. Coldly factual.

Grace was stunned. Here, all these years, she'd thought of the GI Bill as something that had been her nation's finest expression of support and gratitude to *all* its veterans. That's what she'd read in her history books.

Maybe this is the truth, in history, that so many white legislators opposed and feared, Grace thought. *The statistics, the facts, that could tarnish the idealized...*

"What about the education part? College and vocational training? The free ride?" Molly jumped in. Her grandfather had told her when she was little about that benefit also. It was how he got his degree.

"Same shit. States administered. Programs and schools were segregated," Kat continued. "And Black education under segregation? So NOT equal. Many Black schools were unable to teach college-prep classes. They lacked resources like labs, equipment, and faculty. Could you learn chemistry with a twenty-year-old book and no lab? So Black vets didn't have the college-prep classes required by universities. And veterans had to get *accepted* to get the GI Bill. No 'transitional' classes available to help them. It was, 'Tough shit, but *thank-you-for-your-service.*' Even vocational training, to be an electrician or plumber? Apprenticeships went to white boys. Blacks should do the grunt work and leave the 'skilled work' to the whites."

"What grade did you get on your paper? Do you remember?" Max asked. He was always intrigued by grading.

"I got a B-," Kat retorted. "'Well constructed,' the prof wrote, 'but one-sided. Not balanced.' Not sure if those were the prof's exact words, but that was the message."

"So, stats and numbers are one-sided?" Molly queried. "Because I'm assuming you had plenty of verifiable data to back your thesis."

"I had pages and pages. And I'd worked hard to find them. No internet or Google back then. It was archives and dusty library shelves. But the prof taught the GI Bill as a great program for Americans, like the New Deal. Period. How it opened doors for veterans, provided a means to build equity. Generated a strong middle class."

"Your paper rained on his parade?" Grace asked.

"It was a frickin' downpour," Katrina concluded. Then she pointed her finger at Grace. "But it does explain why *you* grew up in an all-white neighborhood, with college-prep-all-white-schools, and had a comfy, subsidized suburban life with no Black folks on the block."

With that, Kat stood up and reached for some plates to start to clear the table. With each of them helping, it took all of four minutes. In the kitchen, Grace distributed leftovers for Katrina, Molly, herself, and Mickey. Molly filled the sink with soapy water to wash up.

"So, did your parents have to rent? Forever?" Molly asked Katrina.

"No, they bought, but in a person-to-person sale, which bypassed the banks and mortgage issues. It wasn't the neighborhood they wanted, but it was a home, and they could build equity. An older woman whose husband died wanted to go north to Michigan to live with her daughter. She put the word out. They all sat down at her kitchen table, with their pastor present, and set up their own arrangement: my parents gave her a down payment and promised a monthly payment. She signed the deed over. She moved to Detroit. They sent her a check every month for 14 years."

"But wasn't that risky?" Molly's voice was surprised. "To sign over a deed and just trust that someone would…"

"They felt that they could trust each other more than a white bank. Banks were notorious for foreclosing on Blacks at much higher rates than whites. Miss a payment and…boom! All in the fine print."

"I didn't realize," Molly said, slowly soaping the platters in the sink. "I get that it was never taught, but I never looked deeper either."

Katrina went up behind her and rested her head on Molly's shoulder. "You did good today, honey," she whispered. "I was a little pissed at first, but you pulled it off. Thank you."

"I'm keeping the gin," Molly whispered back. "You got a problem with that?"

Mickey

The patio base was coming along. Mickey had dug up an 8-by-8 section, leveled it, framed it with 8 foot 4-by-4 posts, screwed them together, put heavy duty plastic edging on the inside of the posts and filled it in with four inches of sand. Once that settled a bit, he'd lay pavers. As long as he was careful with the leveler, made sure it all stayed level, it would be a good base for the barrel sauna. He was planning an adjacent 8-by-8 section for two lounge chairs but wanted to get this finished first.

Mickey had a pile of fencing leaning against the side of the casita. Zed, the young guy at Home Depot had called him to say that they'd gotten some fencing materials in.

"I put 32 cedar boards aside under your name, but I can just hold them for 24 hours," his message had said.

Mickey had scored enough now to build a six-foot high fence on three sides, with the fourth side being the wall of the house—where the outlets would be. He was still playing around with the design. Maybe have the shower stall across the second patio square from the sauna?

It all looked workable on paper, but paper could be deceptive. Mickey didn't want to build a fence until the sauna kit arrived, was assembled, and worked.

Mickey had a friend, who'd retired from construction, to help with the assembly. They'd watched the instructional video together. And he'd found more on YouTube.

It looked doable.

Grace & Sofia

"I think I may have killed Mr. Huang," the woman, Sofia Dominguez, said. Her voice was soft, but her brown eyes looked intently at Grace as if to measure the impact of the words. It was her first session, and, until that point, Grace had just been getting background info.

The words did have an impact: a slight jerk upwards of Grace's head, a furrowing of her forehead, a pursing of her lips, all happening simultaneously as the words registered.

"Would you say that again, please?" Grace asked, shifting in her lawn chair. They were meeting in the gazebo in the park.

"I. Think. I. May. Have. Killed. Mr. Huang," the woman repeated.

"Like I told you, I do in-home health care. And one of my people is, or was, Mr. Huang. I went five mornings a week for three hours at a time, sometimes longer. You know, like cooking, groceries, cleaning, laundry, gardening, and keeping his medications organized. I sort his mail and help him pay his bills, take him to doctor visits, sometimes just for a drive to get out. He liked Sylas and Maddy's, the ice cream store downtown."

"And so how did you, *maybe*, kill him?"

Her eyes started to fill with tears. "My son lied to me about meeting some friends in the park when I thought he was just out for a run, staying in shape for track. I think he got infected with COVID, and then I caught it. I just felt tired and had a bad headache. No coughing or fever. I didn't think it was COVID. I kept caring for Mr. Huang."

Sofia paused, her voice growing softer with each sentence.

"Then, a few days later, Mr. Huang started getting sick. That night, when I was talking with my husband at supper about Mr. Huang being ill, and about whether to call Mr. Huang's nephew who lives in St. Louis, our son finally told us that his friend had tested positive for COVID. And he was probably contagious when they were hanging out in the park. Our son said he'd had a few symptoms, but nothing bad, and hadn't wanted to make us worry. But now I think my headache and fatigue... I slept all weekend which has never happened..."

Sofia was staring at the cement floor. When she looked back up, tears were inching down her cheeks.

"I'm the *only* person who consistently takes care of Mr. Huang. I drove him to the emergency room, and they admitted him, and he was put on a ventilator but died five days later."

Sofia's breath had grown choppy, like panting. And then came a sound, from her gut, a low moaning wail.

"I really liked Mr. Huang," she choked out. "He was a good man, always so polite and sweet with me, so appreciative. And I killed him. I didn't realize, but he's dead and I killed him."

Grace did not know where to go with this. It certainly was not intentional.

"Could he have had contact with someone else? A delivery person? Or he went out and you were not aware?"

"No," Sofia replied dismissively. "Other than the yard and garden, he was housebound. He used a walker. I helped him with showers and dressing. On days I wasn't there, he often stayed in his pajamas all day. I'd call in the morning to remind him to take his pills and describe what was in the refrigerator to warm up in the microwave, with big, printed instructions taped to the plate, and then call at night to make sure he was okay."

"You really did care for him," Grace said. "And I bet that what you just described was not all 'on the clock'."

Sofia flushed. "You're right. About two years ago there was one time when I called to tell him a favorite TV show was starting, and he didn't answer. After a few more calls not picked up, I got worried and ran over. And he'd fallen. He has an 'alert' button he could push, that I kept telling him to leave on, but he'd forget. I called the ambulance, and they took him to the hospital but released him after checking him out. I took him back home and stayed over there on the couch for a few nights."

"So, then you got into the habit of calling?"

"Yeah," Sofia nodded. "He was—he felt—like a dad? My father left when I was a kid, never took much interest in me." Sofia grimaced. "I think that's why I made some poor choices in men when I was younger. Too hungry for attention. Got married at 19, divorced at 23, with two kids to support. Met my husband, Tony, seven years later, when I could finally think straight. He's a good man."

Sofia paused, as if looking for the right words to explain.

"Mr. Huang respected me. He called me his 'meimei,' little sister, because I reminded him of the little sister that he had to leave behind in China. He told me over and over that I was smart. He taught me to play chess. We ate meals together. He told me stories about growing up in China, then being a refugee, and ending up in Kansas. His family had been fishermen for generations, but he ended up here."

Grace knew that they were talking around the real issue, but she was buying time to think. This was new territory.

"Did you wear a mask when taking care of him?"

"Mostly. But he couldn't understand what I was saying without seeing my mouth. Like reading lips? I'd start out with the mask on, but..."

Sofia's voice faltered. "Do you think he would still be alive if I hadn't taken it off. Do you think that? Is that why you asked?"

"No," replied Grace. "I was just thinking. There is no way to pinpoint what could have made any difference. But what I mostly hear is that you really cared for him, like a daughter for a father. And that you miss him. And there was never any intent to cause harm. So, there may have been an accidental transmission, but that's different from killing him," Grace concluded. She hoped these words might help.

"Except that he's dead," Sofia said. "Mr. Huang is dead."

That night, still troubled by the session, over pasta al pesto and a glass of Pinot Noir, Grace processed the session with Mickey.

Grace played a little loose when it came to some of the therapist regulations. She had a disclaimer on her intake papers that she reserved the right to process clinical issues, not using any personal or identifying information, with other professionals who might provide insight into issues of the client or case. It was a vague disclaimer but had never been challenged. And Mickey was a professional who always seemed able to provide insight into issues. Molly as well.

"It felt like a confession," she explained. "Like she was confessing to some crime, but there is nothing that I can say to contradict her. And what we didn't cover today was how angry she is with her son for lying to her about being with other kids and hiding his symptoms."

"Well, that's legitimate. Her son made a poor choice. In normal circumstances, that may have pissed-off his parents, but nothing serious. But this is different. His mom probably would have been super-cautious if she'd known. Maybe gotten someone else to cover. And Mr. Huang might still be alive. So, if anyone is to blame it's the kid. But the kid was just doing what kids do sometimes..." Mickey's voice drifted off.

They were silent, sipping their wine, reflecting on how, in such a very short time, the world had become such a dangerous place.

HISTORICAL CONTEXT: JULY 2020

Jul. 1: "I think we're going to be very good with the coronavirus. I think that, at some point, that's going to sort of disappear, I hope." – *Donald Trump.*

Jul. 1: The European Union announces it will allow travelers from 14 countries outside the bloc to visit EU countries. The U.S. is excluded.

Jul. 2: The U.S. records 50,000 new cases of COVID-19, the largest one-day spike since the beginning of the pandemic. Several states postpone or reverse plans to reopen.

Jul. 8: Donald Trump announces his administration "may cut off funding" for schools that don't resume face-to-face instruction.

Jul. 9: The World Health Organization announces that the COVID-19 virus can be transmitted through the air, linger in crowded indoor spaces, and might be spread by asymptomatic persons.

Jul. 19: "I think we have one of the lowest mortality rates in the world." – Donald Trump

Jul. 27: A vaccine being developed by the Vaccine Research Center at the National Institutes of Health's National Institute of Allergy and Infectious Diseases, in partnership with the biotechnology company Moderna, enters Phase 3 testing.

Jul. 28: "He's got this high approval rating. So why don't I have a high approval rating with respect—and the administration—with respect to the virus?" – *Donald Trump referring to Dr. Anthony Fauci*

Jul. 28: U.S. death toll passes 150,000.

Jul. 28: Dr. Anthony Fauci tells educators in a virtual town hall that there were still many unanswered questions about how the coronavirus is spread by children.

August 2020

Max

Max did not like masks. He did not like feeling his own breath under the mask. He did not like having something behind his ears.

But Mickey had explained that he was a soldier in a war against the virus, and wearing a mask was a shield that protected other people and himself. Mickey said he had to "soldier up."

On the other hand, Max did like the new rule about people staying at least six feet apart. He didn't like being touched when he didn't know it was coming. So, the six feet rule was good. Mom had told him that touching was a sign of affection, of liking him. But Max thought that if they liked him, they could ask first.

Max did not like the smell of hand sanitizer, or the sticky feeling when he put it on. His mom kept sanitizer in her purse, and in the door handles of the car. She was always holding out a little bottle, making a motion to hold up the palm of his hand so she could squirt sanitizer. His mom talked a lot about staying safe. For a while, she'd ordered the groceries online. They drove over to pick them up, getting in a line with other people who were picking up their orders. But she got frustrated, especially when she ended up with bags of cat food when they didn't even have a cat. "So, the cat people have my avocados and olive oil and rye bread and salad stuff," she'd told Mickey in a grumpy voice. "And the tomatoes are hard as cantaloupe and the bananas will only last a day or two."

Max had watched his mom shop for years. "You have to feel produce," she'd explained, picking up a tomato or avocado. "Just testing them," she'd told him. She'd also told him to never buy a banana with a single brown spot. "Go for the ones that are still green at the ends," she'd said. He wondered why the people who worked in the store didn't know that.

Now they go to the grocery store once a week. But Max is not allowed to run his hands along the shelves like he used to and touch all the boxes and cans. He must keep his hands in his pockets.

It is hard to walk straight with his hands in his pockets. He feels like he will lurch to one side and crash. The store has made the aisles like one-way streets, so you just see people's backs.

Shopping is not as much fun as it used to be.

Theo

Two months had passed since Theo had met in person with Grace. They'd exchanged a few emails. There had been a dip in hospitalizations, weeks where he'd worked more normal hours, but then the dreaded second wave had begun.

He and Josie had followed her prescription for the R&R, although it took almost a month to pull it off between the two jobs and staffing issues. It had been easier for Josie to arrange coverage, so they'd gone away for a Wednesday-Thursday-Friday-Saturday. Not far, just to a state park in southwest Missouri with a lake. They'd slept, hiked, napped, swam, then slept some more. They'd sat on lawn chairs and just looked—at the trees, the lake, the sunset, the moon.

"It was good," he told Grace. "We needed the break for sure. It made a difference."

That's what Theo shared with Grace. A summary. The rest felt too private.

Theo and Josie had not talked at first. They'd made coffee on the camping stove, grilled salmon for supper over a fire, frying potatoes, onions, and peppers in a cast iron skillet. They'd eaten voraciously, straight out of the skillet, and polished off a bottle of wine.

For the first 24 hours, they did not touch, curling into fetal positions in bed, back-to-back, saying, "I'm wiped, honey," and "I just want to sleep." It had been so long since they'd been intimate. The last time they'd tried, Josie's body could not relax, her mind could not quiet the racing thoughts. She'd felt nothing when Theo had cupped her breasts, had gently circled her nipples. Nothing. And Theo had felt impotent, not as far as an erection, but in being unable to arouse her. He did not want to just get off, he wanted to connect. *He wanted his touch to matter.* After another failed attempt, they hadn't tried again, each waiting for a sign, for room to breathe.

It was the second night, in the middle of the night, that Theo woke to see Josie awake also, just looking at him, her face inches from his. "Josie?" he said, her very name a question. And then he reached for her, softly, then hungrily. They slid their hands up and down each other's back. He tasted her skin, and his hands cupped her ass, pulling her toward him. She whimpered; the sounds of a scared child lost in the woods.

When they finished, Theo lay to one side, one leg still straddling her body, one hand against the side of her face. He felt the wetness before he saw the tears on his wife's face. And then he began also to weep, silently, with relief, with gratitude.

They fell back asleep, and slept, deeply, well into the next morning.

Then, over coffee, they talked. How they'd each felt they needed to be strong, their fear and anxiety a secret that they needed to hide. That every single day they'd thought about each other dying—a slow, excruciating COVID death. How they'd imagined being alone, a single parent, raising their kids.

"I've been distancing from you," Josie confessed. "Like, somehow, maybe, I'll hurt less if and when something happens to you if we're less connected."

"I felt so torn, because a part of me wants to grab you and run away," Theo added. "Never go back to work, not even call in, just disappear. I swear there were days when I was making packing lists in my head..."

Josie cackled, a throaty witch-cackle in the back of her throat.

"I got you beat on that. I have an 'Escape' notebook. It's filled with packing lists, even what to bring for the kids' schoolwork. Emergency contact info. What documents we'd need. I have it down to color-coded plastic tubs for clothing and bathroom stuff and meds and the kids' school stuff."

"Did you want to leave? Did I stop you?" he asked.

"No," Josie said. "It was just a way to make me feel some momentary control when everything was spinning out of control. Lists do that for me."

They talked on-and-off for six hours, disjointed pieces of themselves and their lives. But entire weeks had evaporated or been erased. Time was no longer sequential, weeks and months distinct. They'd been caught up in the wave where time meant nothing.

When Theo looked up, Grace was sitting, hands in her lap, waiting.

"How long was I gone?" he asked.

"A minute or two. Maybe a bit longer."

"That's been happening. I go off in my head."

"We're all going off in our heads," Grace said. "Either that or they might explode. Like opening a valve so some of the insanity is released."

"So," she continued, "how is work?"

Katrina

Katrina was googling websites and forums for people who'd survived COVID but not recovered.

There was a name for it now: "Long Haul COVID" and "Long Hauler."

Their residual symptoms varied tremendously, and the intensity of the initial infection varied as well. Long haulers could be people who'd been hospitalized, on oxygen or ventilators, or people who'd never had symptoms serious enough to be hospitalized but whose symptoms persisted months later.

Katrina found it comforting to know she wasn't crazy, and to know that thousands of otherwise competent, healthy, active people shared her struggle.

When it came to the "long haul" people, the diversity of symptoms was overwhelming. But she'd found an article, *"I've Been Sick with COVID-19 for Over 3 Months. Here's What You Should Know,"* written by an Ann Wallace, a college professor of English in New Jersey, that nailed it.

Katrina printed out copies for her doctor, MJ, Grace, and Molly. She emailed a link to Malcolm.

Kat did not want to be rude to Grace, who asked, "How are you feeling?" every single damn time they talked or saw each other. Kat knew the question came out of concern, maybe hope, but Kat felt that an honest response was a real downer. A few times she'd lied on a phone call, saying "I'm doing fine, heading out for a walk," and could tell that Grace was relieved.

Then Kat had collapsed on the couch, too tired to even read or watch TV.

The symptoms were never one thing, more a pervasive and arbitrary pain spectrum. It was a crapshoot as to which symptoms would dominate on any given day. Even more tiring was trying to express how frustrating and scary it was to not be recovering without feeling anger at whatever platitudes she heard in return.

When she'd first realized that she was not recovering in a matter of weeks, even a month, she'd told her doctor. Then there was no name for it, no consensus that this virus could insidiously linger. Many people felt dismissed, as if they were making it up.

But, with *this,* everyone affected could point to the same origin: they'd all had COVID. Researchers were uncertain what the prognosis was. As soon as they thought they had it nailed, COVID threw them a curve ball.

Meanwhile, millions of Americans were buying into Trump's mixed messages, his dismissive attitude about COVID. What Katrina found most infuriating was his refusal to mask, refusal to set executive orders, inability to understand that his arrogance, ego, and perverted nationalism were killing thousands and thousands of citizens every day.

Katrina was angry, an anger that vibrated in her bones.

This one man had had the once-in-a-generation opportunity to be a true leader, to go down in history as having led his country through a plague, to enlist the support of all Americans to defeat their common enemy. But he was too narcissistic, too vain. He had the emotional maturity of an angry adolescent, a bully who forever feels victimized if he doesn't get *everything* he wants exactly *when* he wants it.

Katrina watched the numbers rise, the surges in infections and deaths, the faces of the doctors and nurses who faced even more death in a day than they had before in months, even a year. It was their eyes, over the masks, their helplessness to save their patients, their exhaustion, that haunted Katrina.

Zed

It was a Thursday evening, August 6th, and the boys were already in bed, worn out by two hours of running around at the playground.

Zed and Cherry were packing to go to a rally and march over the weekend. It was a "Save the Children" event, one of over 200 scheduled to take place at the same time on Saturday. The rallies were being talked about all over the Internet, or at least the Facebook groups that Zed and Cherry were members of. There were helpful guidelines—like stick to talking points if interviewed by the press; that this was just about wanting stricter laws against pedophilia; and more media attention of the issues of sex trafficking of children—so that the core message would not get diffused or manipulated by the mainstream media. And all their signs were to be homemade, and issue focused.

Going to a march was different from anything they'd ever done. They'd never protested anything. They hadn't followed politics. But now? Last month they both registered to vote. They believed in Donald Trump.

For the first time, Zed and Cherry felt part of something bigger than themselves. This was about stopping the lies and cover-ups that powerful people used to do sick and sadistic things, to hurt children, to make money, to steal. They felt connected to people from all over the country, who were seeking the truths that the politicians and left-wingers had drowned with their big words and justifications. There were so many lies that they had never realized were lies. And everyone they were talking to felt the same way.

Cherry's parents were going to watch the boys for three days. After all, they'd offered: "Whatever we can do to be supportive..."

Zed and Cherry didn't tell them that they were going to a march, just that they needed a few days alone to "work on stuff without the kids." And that was not really a lie, because her parents got to fill in the blank on what they might think that "stuff" meant.

"We'll keep the kids quarantined for two weeks before they come," Cherry had reassured them. "I don't ever want to be the reason you get sick."

When they drove away after dropping off the kids, they whooped like teenagers and turned up the radio full blast. They were on an adventure.

There wasn't money for a hotel, so Cherry had reserved a campsite in a state park just outside St. Louis. They put up their family tent, which felt big without the boys. It seemed like other campers had also come for the march. Some campsites even had flags, and they felt dumb that they hadn't thought to bring one. But then a lady walked around handing out little flags to anyone who wanted one. Some guys built a bonfire on the little beach by the lake. People gathered around the fire on lawn chairs and talked about where they were from and why they had come.

When a park ranger walked up about 9 p.m., Zed thought he'd come to tell them to break it up. But he just asked them to not get too loud, and then tipped his hat and gave them a thumbs-up.

In their tent, later that night, they lay facing each other, on top of the comforters that they'd put over the air mattresses instead of sleeping bags. "Too sweaty for sleeping bags in August," Cherry had said, loading the car. They touched each other's faces, silent, gentle, their eyes half-closed.

The morning of the march was sunny and clear, which felt, to Cherry, as if the very Universe was approving.

Cherry had made signs for the march. "Save the Children" was in red on white posterboard. "Wake Up 4 Our Children," was in black on yellow board. But the one she was most proud of was the biggest, with cut out pictures of kids' faces like a border around all four sides, and "We Are Not For Sale." The words were in the middle, in a block print that looked like a child had written it.

"That's really good," other marchers told her. "You make the problem real for people who don't believe it yet."

She'd heard that over three million, maybe even four million people were talking in Facebook groups, chat rooms, and on Instagram about these issues. But others were trying to make it that QAnon had started it, and it wasn't really happening. Facebook had taken down a bunch of stuff related to QAnon, which felt to Cherry like censorship. People were getting too close to truths that Facebook wanted to hide. The people with the power were covering up something.

If the mainstream media and platforms like Facebook were coming down on QAnon, trying to silence them, that made Zed and Cherry question whether Q was on to something,

And by then, most of the info about the rallies, which were happening all over the country, was out. And talking about a rally didn't seem to trigger the censorship.

Just keep it ambiguous, never mention Q. That was the message.

"Every person is going to have their own freedoms and beliefs," was what one of the organizers for some of the rallies had written. Which is how Zed felt. That instead of being told what he had to think, told what was true and what was fake, he was developing his own beliefs. He was *seeking*, not just accepting what the talking heads on CNN parroted.

What mostly showed up in local papers where the rallies were held did not even mention QAnon. It was more about the issue, that was why they were marching: that children were missing. Missing kids was the pandemic that no one was talking about.

The media was obsessed with BLM and COVID.

But kids mattered too.

Zed and Cherry held their signs up proudly and chanted every slogan. They were going to change the world. They were in this together, in it for the long haul.

Pod-Potluck

Kat and Grace were back at Molly's picnic table. It was a steamy-hot day, and Max was jumping in and out of a small plastic pool that Mickey had brought over.

"I see myself lying in that before the evening is over," Kat said, gesturing at the pool.

Grace had set a pitcher on the table. "So, what all is in this?" Kat asked, as Grace poured punch over four tall glasses filled with ice.

"Light rum, dark rum, passion fruit juice, OJ, fresh lime, grenadine, and several maraschino cherries."

"Oh, a Hurricane?" Kat asked.

"No, because you New Orleans people are so particular about your damn Hurricanes. Always gotta' comment on what a real Hurricane tastes like," Grace teased. "This is just punch." But then Grace froze, as if she'd inadvertently crossed a line.

Katrina took a sip from her glass. "Good punch, Gracie."

It was a potluck, yes, but tonight was too hot to cook. Mickey was in the kitchen unwrapping take-out from the Greek place downtown: salads, gyros, pita, olives, and extra tzatziki. Grace and Kat had not gotten together in the meantime.

When their plates were overflowing, and their mouths full, Molly took the opportunity to announce that she'd enjoyed the discussion last time and learned a few things about her mother. So, since she was hosting, she wanted to ask more pesky questions.

"Anyone have a problem with that?" Molly asked, looking at each of them.

"Are we going to talk about race every time we eat?" Katrina asked, not looking up from her plate while methodically cutting the food into small bites.

"No. We can always talk about Trump and the global pandemic. Or whether our lives will ever…"

"Okay, okay. Race is fine. Ask away," Kat agreed.

"Can I ask questions too?" Max asked. "I had a question last time, but I never asked it, and now I can't remember."

"Yes, Max, anyone can ask a question, and anyone can answer a question," Molly said, but shifting on the bench to face Katrina. "But I get to start."

"So, Katrina, I'm assuming that your parents were more direct than my mom's parents in their messaging about race to you. Being Black was…"

"Black was who we were," Kat interjected. "When I was a kid, my mother was on me about always being polite, like I was the poster child for being a respectful, courteous Black girl. One mistake and the image would be ruined forever. And not just my image, but like it would hurt Black kids everywhere."

"Shit," Grace muttered. "That's a burden for a kid."

"I never questioned it. I resented it, sure, but never questioned it. Because she was right. Black kids were judged differently than white kids. A white boy doing a prank was 'Boys will be boys.' A Black kid doing the exact same thing could end up dead."

"Did you talk with her about how you felt?"

"Not really. I would've been disrespecting her experience and judgment. I knew she wanted the best for me, and 'image' mattered. I had to be the best—just never be obvious about it."

"But you changed at some point? Right?" Molly asked. "You went to law school. You need to be able to speak up for that."

"I started, very slowly, to have a voice. But I consciously made sure that I did not sound angry or aggressive or negative. Be nice. I remember in college, in a history class, saying that what we were studying felt to me like half the pages were missing, that we were getting a sanitized version. That this version of 'history' was not balanced. And the professor said that I sounded like I was advocating for a cause, and how I might want to consider that my tone wouldn't encourage people to listen or join that cause."

"Were you angry? Like loud or accusatory?" Molly probed.

"No, but I was being persistent. I hadn't shut up after the prof said, 'Interesting perspective, Ms. Baptiste.' I didn't just drop it. But the professor was so threatened that he had to make a statement to the whole class that said I was out of line."

"Damn, Kat, then what happened?" They'd all stopped eating, drawn into her narrative.

"After class, another student came up to me. 'I agree with you,' she said. 'But how you were saying it? It was like you were challenging the teacher. Maybe find a way to not sound so aggressive?'"

"What did you say?" Max asked.

"I told her, 'Thanks for telling me,' but I *was* challenging the teacher. Not being aggressive, but respectfully asserting that alternative data existed that was being ignored."

"What did she do?"

"She said, 'Okay, then, whatever' but seemed affronted that I was not taking her well-intentioned guidance about how to communicate with white people. And she never spoke to me again."

Grace was silent. Memories, like hammers, were banging around in her head.

"What?" Mickey asked, looking at Grace, aware that something was percolating.

"Your mother was right, Kat," Grace said. "I don't ever remember my folks talking about the content of what was being said, like when someone Black was being interviewed or talking on TV news. Never 'that's wrong.' Never a blatant derogatory comment. Or that they disagreed. It was how a Black person was talking that they critiqued."

"So how were Black people supposed to express their dissatisfactions with the system?" Kat's voice dripped with sarcasm.

"My mother loved Sidney Poitier," Grace continued. "We watched every movie. I remember her saying, 'If they would only talk like him, people might listen.'"

With that, Grace and Kat and Molly and Mickey paused, reflecting on the many-layered implications of that statement.

"Huh?" Max asked. "Who's Sidney Pwa-te-a?"

"So," Kat responded, picking her words carefully, "let me get this straight. If Black people in real life only sounded like a Black actor who had to talk a certain way to get any roles at all, roles where he modeled how honorable a Black man could be, and not threaten a white audience, then white people might listen?"

"Pretty messed up, huh?" Grace asked.

"Yeah, but, in a twisted way, spot on. I was learning that to make it in a white world I had to cover up the parts of me that were too 'Black' and adopt social niceties. To hold my tongue, and not, under any circumstances, show what I really felt."

"Do you remember the movie *Guess Who's Coming to Dinner?*" Grace asked, finding another memory. "Where Sidney Poitier plays this perfect doctor and..."

"Yeah, I do," Kat interrupted. "What about it?"

"It was the first time I saw interracial marriage. And it was so idealized, so 'love conquers all.' The white liberal parents had their values put to the test, while the Black parents were more opposed than the white parents. Which I do not think would ever have occurred to *my* relatives. They'd think any Black family should feel honored to be accepted. I fell hard for Sidney Poitier in that film," Grace mused. "Did you?"

"Did you know when it was being filmed, interracial marriage was still illegal in 17 states?" Kat asked. "Nobody remembers that now. People could be put on trial and imprisoned for that kind of 'love.' It wasn't until June '67, the Supreme Court ruling in *Loving v. Virginia*, that anti-miscegenation laws were struck down. The film was released six months later. But interracial couples are still harassed in many states."

"But what about Dr. John Spencer?" Grace persisted. "You didn't answer."

"What I felt, more when I saw it again, later, as a teen, was a sense of—hopelessness? This hunk of a Black man, a doctor for God's sake, picks a 23-year-old white girl to marry? Why not a peer, an educated, professional Black woman?" Katrina said slowly. "I knew it was a movie, but the message was clear: no matter how smart or accomplished I was, I'd never be as desired or valued as a young white girl."

"Ouch," Grace said. "That's harsh. You really felt that way?"

"Yeah, I did. Dr. Spencer was Hollywood perfect. Perfect Black men wanted white girls. Not Black girls. And I wasn't even Black-Black."

"What do you mean 'Black-Black?'" Max asked. "I never heard of that."

"Just what it sounds like," Kat replied, but then re-directed her next question back to Grace.

"Did you ever think, as you were 'falling hard,' that maybe this hunk of a Black actor/doctor would not be interested in a *white* girl? Did that ever mess with your head?"

Grace had no quick reply. It had been a crush. On a movie star. Of course, a movie star would not be interested in a kid. But that was not the question. The question was whether she ever ruled out a fantasy because of her skin. A teenage *fantasy*.

"No," Grace said. "I don't remember ever thinking that being white could be a dream-crusher. Other stuff, but not being white."

"And that, my white friend, is an example of white privilege that rarely gets covered. Our dreams? Our fantasies? Our aspirations? Even in those, you get your privilege."

"I never saw that movie, but perhaps we can have a 'classics' night?" Molly asked. "Dinner and a movie?"

"What's Black-Black?" Max asked again, but everyone was focused on cleaning their plates, and Mickey had cranked up the volume on Pandora.

Max

Grammy had discovered that there were not many people at Lone Star Lake in the evening. When they'd driven out in the middle of the day, there had been a lot of people. "It feels like Coney Island," she'd told him. "And too many people not wearing masks."

Max wasn't sure what Coney Island was but expected it was crowded. Then she'd turned around and driven home. He'd wanted to swim so he'd tried to explain that people couldn't wear masks if they were in and out of the water. Grammy kept driving.

But a few weeks ago, they'd started driving out about 7 p.m. They'd wear their suits and bring floatie-noodles. His mom showed him how to put two between his legs and pedal around the lake like he was on an underwater bicycle. She would pedal around too, sipping a water bottle with a lot of ice and tea that came from Long Island. They would watch the sun set over the trees at the far end of the lake, and then climb back up on the dock, wrap up in their towels, and drive home. Sometimes they stopped at Dairy Queen.

Mickey always treated, telling Max he could have anything he wanted. Grammy always shook her head at Mickey, but then would say, "I'll have a hot caramel sundae. As long as you're treating."

School was supposed to start again, with the desks more separated. Everyone seemed nervous about it.

His mom was going to take two classes and postpone something she called her "practicum." She said it was like a practice job, but because of COVID she'd have been doing it from home, on Zoom, and that would *not* be good practice.

Covid Grief Group

Two months later and the grief group was still meeting. No one had dropped out, and another man had joined.

Luis was in his mid-40s. He did computer repairs. His wife had died in June. She'd been pregnant, six months along. They'd met in their 30s, and Mariana did not think that, after years of endometriosis, she could get pregnant. But, at 41, she had.

Mariana had worked at the local hospital for eighteen years as a surgical nurse.

"We knew the exact night we conceived," he said, looking down at his folded hands. "Christmas Eve. We felt so blessed. She patted her belly every day and said '¿Cómo está mi pequeño milagro?'"

Each meeting, Grace would check in with everyone in the circle: how they were managing, what was the hardest time of the day to get through, what did they do that brought some relief. She asked them to bring any books they read that were helpful or quotes that helped then navigate the dark times.

Grace had let go of any lurking fantasies that *anything* she could say would make a significant difference. And the group members seemed to feel the same way. They expected little. They were each in their own corner of hell, and this group made them aware, for a few hours a week, that they were not alone in that hell. That was solace enough. Grace was the only one who had not lost someone she loved to this plague.

But she persisted in the role of facilitator. She talked about the differences between short-term stress bursts and chronic, prolonged stress. She brought handouts of articles. She reiterated, at every session, the basics: eat healthy, get enough sleep, get outside, exercise, breathe.

The last session she'd opened with a breathing exercise, for calming and relaxation: "Inhale-exhale-inhale-exhale. Feel your body. Use your breath to get centered and slow your mind."

But that had backfired big time.

"I can't do this," Beth had said after just a minute. "If I focus on breathing, all I can see is my mom drowning in air. She was fighting to breathe. She died because she couldn't breathe."

Beth looked around the circle. "Am I the only one? Anybody else here that cannot face a *breathing* exercise?" she asked

And most of the group had silently nodded. Anything centered on the most basic element of being alive—breathing—did not calm them down. It was more likely to elicit a PTSD response of helplessness, pain, and fear.

"Don't feel bad, dear," Larry had said after Grace apologized, profusely, for not recognizing that the exercise could be triggering. "We're just figuring it out ourselves. And we have no idea where we're going or where we'll end up."

In some ways, screwing up bad took the pressure off. They were all navigating a broken world. Not like anyone had been through a politicized global pandemic before in a country torn apart by a toxic narcissist who'd never wanted the responsibilities and work of being a president, just the trappings, glory, and adulation.

Grace was having a harder and harder time not going down the deep, dark rabbit holes of despair at the state of her country. She'd always been impatient with the pace of change, but now she was aghast at the nonchalant signing of executive orders, so random, inconsistent, and almost always to appease donors or "the base."

There were some small successes with the group, suggestions Grace made that people ran with.

"It's a lot harder to take seriously the stuff about eating healthy when you don't have the will to do anything but cereal," Grace had said a few weeks ago. "Can you share what you're doing, or what's been helpful?"

"I do pizza," Beth replied. "Breakfast, lunch, or dinner. It covers a lot of food groups."

"Ice cream with granola on top is my dinner of choice," tossed in Kayla.

"Frozen dinners. I can't taste them anyway," Larry added. "I just look for the protein count."

"What I'd like to suggest," Grace had continued, "is that perhaps you get together, just whoever wants to, like on a Saturday or Sunday, for a potluck. You can buy something at the deli if you don't want to cook. But at least there will be some variety and you aren't eating alone. And everyone takes home leftovers of what they didn't bring."

And they had. Without her saying anything else, someone had sent out an email inviting the others to their back yard for a Sunday potluck. Socially distanced and masked, but *together*. Not everyone. Not yet. But it was becoming a weekly thing.

Later that night, Grace was checking mail when an oversized postcard slipped out. It was of mountains, birch trees, in Utah. "Did what you said. At my sister's. Kids are fine. Got a job yesterday. School starts next week. Thanks." It was a succinct summary. Grace expected that a lot of stories were buried in making it happen. *Well, Amber*, Grace thought, *you did it. And lived to tell.*

Mickey

Mickey had a routine. He got up at 6 a.m., made coffee, threw on some clothes, and walked over to Grace's house—unless, of course, he'd slept at Grace's house, in which case it was less of a walk.

By 7 a.m. he was working on his project. The first 8-by-8 paver patio was completed, and the adjacent second one was in place, with gravel and sand down and half the pavers as well. One or two more days and it would be finished. He was taking it slow, and not working past 10 a.m. when the temperature got crazy hot. But that was August in Kansas for you. You'd think you were in a bayou, it got so humid.

Max often came over about 8 a.m., still in his PJs, and sat on a lawn chair and asked questions. Sometimes Mickey told him to run back to his mom and get dressed and come help spread the sand. Or to come with him to Home Depot to pick something out, like a showerhead, or copper tubing, or nails and screws for the fence. They didn't need much of an excuse.

Sometimes Grace had clients on her back patio, so she didn't want any hammering or such. But the worksite was against the side of the house, pretty much the whole side yard. Mickey could slip in and out without disturbing.

The electrician had come and installed some heavy-duty outlets and a new 220 circuit.

The sauna wasn't scheduled to be delivered for a month. It was so big and heavy that it required a forklift to move it once off the truck.

He anticipated a few logistical issues, but, overall, Mickey was feeling pretty good so far.

Mike

Mike and Molly had settled into at least one extended Zoom a week. On Tuesday evening. No interruptions, no kids.

Mike had explained that every Tuesday, David went to his abuela's house to cook with her. Abuela had apparently hooked him by explaining that none of her recipes were written down, none documented, and David could learn from her but also record them in a book for "posterity." Abuela was rather insightful in appreciating that David had a black hole in his heart when it came to family, and every crumb that could help fill it in made a difference. After eating and wrapping up leftovers to take home to his dad, they watched an old film or a few episodes of whatever they were bingeing.

In Kaw Valley, Molly had asked Mickey if he could possibly commit to Max being dropped off at 5 p.m. and Mickey returning him at about 9:30. It was enough time to feel like a break.

Mike and Molly had set their Zoom conference for 7 p.m. They did not tell their parents, just said that they had a conference call every Tuesday evening as that was the only time when the other people could make it. It was a discussion group.

All of which was true.

They made a joke of trying to remind themselves of what business casual would look like, and not just from the waist up. It was, they pointed out, practice for an eventual return to the real world. A return that felt more elusive with every day's infection and death statistics. On some level, it felt like playing dress-up.

Last week, they'd decided to not bring up anything serious. Or depressing. Just keep it light. So, they'd talked about what they were binge watching, what fantasies they had about travel when life returned to some semblance of normal. They compared the appeal of beaches and ocean vacations to mountains and lakes. They shared favorite childhood vacation memories. And if either decided to go off-script, they made a noise—eh-eh-eh—like warning a dog to back off from the table.

Binge watching was the new national past-time. "What are you binge watching?" was a universal conversation opener. People who'd taken pride in *never* watching mainstream television were now addicted to a nightly fix. Mike and Molly sometimes watched the same series during the week and then talked about it.

"We started watching *West Wing*," Molly reported. "Mom, Mickey, and me. It's new to me but they saw it all before. It's comforting pretending that ethical adults are in the White House. If I watch an episode, I think I sleep better."

"Ethical adults are better than narcissists with 4th grade vocabularies," Mike added. "My parents are in season five of West Wing, I think. They do subtitles because everyone talks so fast, and they don't want to miss out. Second language and all."

"Hey, I do subtitles because they talk too fast, but also because it keeps Mom from asking 'What did she just say?' every thirty seconds. The woman needs hearing aids bad once we're allowed to get back in each other's faces."

HISTORICAL CONTEXT: AUGUST 2020

Aug. 5: "If you look at children, children are almost—and I would say definitely—but almost immune from this disease." – *Donald Trump*

Aug. 12: U.S. reports highest number of COVID-19 deaths in one day since mid-May.

Aug.20: In his acceptance speech for the Democratic nomination, Joe Biden critiques President Trump's response to COVID-19, "The President keeps telling us the virus is going to disappear. He keeps waiting for a miracle. I have news for him: No miracle is coming."

Aug. 23: Donald Trump makes claims against ballot drop boxes, calling them a "voter security disaster," a "big fraud," "possible for a person to vote multiple times," and that they aren't "COVID sanitized."

Aug. 23: Protests erupt in Kenosha, Wisconsin after the shooting of an African American man, 29-year-old Jacob Blake. He was shot seven times by police and became paralyzed from the waist down.

Aug. 24: In his acceptance speech at the Republican National Convention: "The only way they can take this election away from us is if this is a rigged election."

Aug. 25: Kyle Rittenhouse, a 17-year-old from Antioch, Illinois, fatally shoots two men and wounds another in Kenosha. The shootings occurred during the civil unrest and protests that followed the shooting of Jacob Blake.

Aug. 26: U.S death toll passes 180,000.

Aug. 27: The CDC notifies U.S. public health officials to prepare to distribute a potential coronavirus vaccine as soon as late October.

Aug. 31: "We've done a great job in COVID but we don't get the credit."
– *Donald Trump*

September 2020

Katrina

Katrina still had no sense of taste or smell. It was one of those things that most people did not fully appreciate. Human senses have a hierarchy as far as loss, and taste and smell rarely made the news or a made-for-TV movie. Most people are terrified of losing sight or going deaf. Losing the ability to touch is a horrible part of paralysis.

But smell and taste? Not newsworthy.

When her senses had not returned in a month, in two months, she'd done some research. A word she'd never heard before, *ageusia,* was the loss of taste. And 20-30 percent of people who had COVID reported it as a symptom. Coupled with the loss of smell, it messed with not just enjoyment of food and eating, but with the ability to eat. Big meals were out, as a gag reflex kicked in. Super chewy foods were out (hard to accept as Katrina had been a carnivore with a deep appreciation for a perfect steak or smoked BBQ).

Visual appearance mattered, very small portions, eating every 2-4 hours, trying extra tart or sour or spicy foods to stimulate possible taste.

Texture mattered most, so nothing that would feel slimy or stick to the roof of the mouth. Potato chips, for example, absent the intense biting flavor of Kat's favorite, salt and vinegar, were disgusting. But Fritos were okay since they were crunchy and held their texture.

Katrina was still trying to keep on top of any developments with the damn "Long-COVID."

There was now a name for *emotional* long-haul symptoms. "PCSD" was a nickname, not a formal diagnosis, that was being used in forums. Post-COVID Stress Disorder.

Katrina was sticking with PTSD. This was so much more than "stress." This was traumatic.

Grace & Theo

"**Can you explain** to me how *exactly* COVID usually affects people, and your work with COVID patients?" Grace asked. "I want to be able to visualize and understand your workday."

"In how much detail?" Theo countered.

"As specifically as you can. Take your time."

"You know, no one asks that question," Theo said. "And when I'm working, everything happens so fast. We're running from patient to patient, assessing, evaluating, snap judgment, move on."

"No long-winded team discussions about alternate treatment modalities?" she asked, remembering her stints on hospital psych wards.

"Nope. We're just hoping there's enough 'treatment' to go around. We play musical chairs sometimes with ventilators."

"Is that still an issue?"

"Two days ago, we knew that two patients were dying, no chance of recovery. But their families wanted us to keep trying, as if we'd stumble into a miracle. But down the hall are people who *need* to be on a ventilator, like hours ago, or *they* will die. So, do we keep talking with the families of dying patients? Waste precious hours until they can say, 'Okay, take her off the ventilator' when we know those families will spend years second-guessing their decision, thinking they 'let Mama die'? Especially when they see some damn news story about the 'one-in-a-million' guy who was on a ventilator for months and lived?" Theo stopped, closing his eyes. His voice had escalated with each question.

"Or, do we make a medical decision, like triage in a war zone? If *we* assume that responsibility, we don't burden families with the guilt. But then we're not following the damn rules about suspending treatment without patient DNRs."

"What did you do?" Grace asked.

"My shift was ending. I'd worked 14 hours straight. I went home, showered, and crashed."

"And the next day?"

"There were new patients on the ventilators."

"What had the staff decided?"

"I never asked. We don't have time to talk about dead patients."

Grace pursed her lips.

"Do you still want to know about treating COVID patients?" Theo asked.

"Yes, Theo, I do," Grace replied, leaning in.

"Okay, then, here goes. Say, Walt and Wanda. Walt is 42, married, cop, three kids, Little League coach, former smoker. Wanda is 68, divorced, just retired, grandkids, had bucket-list-dream-trips booked into 2023 before COVID. She told me she'd saved her whole life to have five years of happy spending. She'd already booked a cruise for her 70th birthday—kids, grand kids, everyone. Told me I'd be amazed at how cheap it is with a group rate."

"Are Walt and Wanda real people?"

"Walt and Wanda are real, but not their names."

"Okay. Go on."

"By the time most people get to the ER they've been having symptoms for days. A lot can happen with COVID that's sneaky. Patients feel okay, but then, *suddenly,* they can't catch their breath. We immediately check oxygen saturation levels and get to work: supplemental oxygen of one to four liters a minute, steroids, antivirals, anticoagulants, or monoclonal antibodies *if* we have them."

Theo paused, looking out over the park before continuing.

"Walt and Wanda are like most people: treating with rest, pills for the aches and fever, chugging cough syrup. But, no, this shit is not 'just like the flu.' They are both admitted. Their families are told to go home and quarantine."

"And do they quarantine?"

"Many do. They're scared. What they've seen on the news is now in *their* family. It's real."

"But some do not?"

"No. They're more angry than scared. Like this *can't* be COVID because COVID is a *hoax.* They start telling the doctors to do more tests to find out what is *really* making their daddy so sick."

"Okay, so go back to Walt and Wanda."

"We monitor how they respond to treatment. They feel like they've been hit by a truck, but, if their lungs are healthy, and no chronic disease, they may wean off oxygen, catch a break, and get discharged. But there is no way to predict for sure. It feels arbitrary who goes home."

"Then what happens?"

"It gets clear that the bronchodilator treatments are not adequate. Walt and Wanda both feel like they're drowning. They're begging for more air. The need for oxygen goes up and up: four liters per minute to 10 to 15 to 20 to 40. Any movement is exhausting. It's way too hard to get out of bed to urinate so nurses put in catheters. Their oxygen saturation drops with *any* movement."

"Which means?"

"Time to transfer to ICU. *If* there are beds available. Where staff is stretched so thin that we're taking care of two to three times the usual patient load. We can be in the middle of a code when there's another code in the next room. We look at each other, like 'Who gets to play God today?' Maybe someone says something like '14B is only 38' and we look at the patient we're working on who is 67 and we have six seconds to decide."

Theo closed his eyes, focused on remembering.

"By now, Walt and Wanda are so exhausted they can't move, can't hardly open their eyes. The oxygen content in their blood is so low it's critical. They'll die soon without the last treatment possible: the infamous ventilator. We try to connect them with spouses or kids, usually a quick FaceTime before we intubate. Some patients realize they're dying but keep up a front, like, 'Don't worry, I'll be home in a week.' Some families and patients just cry together."

"What happens with intubation?"

"Walt and Wanda are sedated and paralyzed. They get nutrients through a feeding tube. Their body is completely limp. The team turns them to prevent pressure sores, rolls them on their stomach—proning—to help oxygenation. Whatever experimental treatments are available, we'll try, because..." Theo stopped mid-sentence.

"Because?" Grace repeated softly.

"Because. Just *because*. Some patients do improve with the machine breathing for them. But the less time a patient is on a ventilator, the better. Patients on ventilators have to be constantly monitored. And things happen."

"Things?"

"Air leaks into the chest cavity, so we put in tubes to draw it out. Kidneys fail. Fluid accumulates in lung sacs. Blood clots form.

Infections of any sort go wild because the immune system is in overdrive. Blood pressure drops. Hearts just stop. But we can't predict which of those may happen next and can't prevent them. So, it's whack-a-mole."

Theo gestured, his right hand illustrating a hammer. Bam-Bam-Bam.

"Then it's all downhill. Doctors talk to families about withdrawing life support. We may tell the patient we're taking out the tubes, and they will have limited time to communicate, if they're conscious. But if we take away sedation so they are conscious to know they're dying, they're also in pain, intense pain. Families are on FaceTime, screaming and crying goodbyes."

"It sounds horrible. Not just for patients and families but staff too."

Theo didn't bother to respond to that.

"And what happened with Walt and Wanda? Did they survive?" Grace asked.

"Walt did, but with a lot of damage. He'll never be a cop again. Don't think he'll ever play ball with his sons. He has long-term damage: lungs working at half capacity, on dialysis for kidney failure."

"So, recovery will take a long time? Like months?" Grace asked.

"I don't think you're getting it," Theo said. "When the *acute* COVID is over, it's just the start of a new reality for a lot of people. Like after a heart attack or stroke. COVID can cause permanent, long-term damage. And we have no idea what other long-term damage will show up years later in otherwise healthy-looking people who 'survived.'"

Theo paused to think of an example.

"Remember mumps?" he asked. "Some people thought 'no big deal' until testicular atrophy was discovered in young men when they wanted to have kids. Mumps left them sterile. Hell, *those* were guys who wished they'd been vaccinated."

"And Wanda?"

Theo froze. He'd been talking fast, spitting out things he'd never verbalized.

"Wanda died after being on the ventilator for three or four days."

"Did her family get to say goodbye?"

"No," Theo replied. "It was sudden. Her heart stopped."

Theo had not told anyone, and would not, ever, about Wanda.

And he'd lied to Grace. Wanda was her real name.

Wanda had been *his* patient. As she failed, she did not want to be ventilated. She saw what was happening around her. But her kids were pushing the doctors hard to do everything they could, to "save our mama." So, she agreed—maybe to keep the peace?

Theo had been explaining to her what was going to happen, sitting next to her bed, clipboard in his lap, covered in PPE.

Wanda had not been listening. Her eyes had gone off to someplace deep inside. But he'd kept talking in a low monotone.

"Wait," she'd said, looking again at his nametag. "Theo? That's a good name. I have a Theo, my youngest. And his son is a Theo, only we call him 'TJ' for Theo Junior."

Her voice was a gravelly whisper.

Wanda reached for his hand, which had a latex glove on, of course, no warm skin there, and said, "Theo, you have kind eyes behind that mask thing. Are you listening? I need you to listen. So, this is what I want: Don't let me die unconscious. I want to be awake even if I'm hurting bad. I'm okay with the pain. It won't be for long. I want to be present for my passing. Get the tubes out of me."

She'd stopped talking, for a moment, to try for more oxygen.

"But don't let my kids see me die. You just tell them that I went peaceful, but sudden, and my last words were, 'Tell my babies—and they're all my babies—that I love them all the way to the rainbow.' And that I said I want them to take every cent I saved for 40-plus years and use it to travel. Not buy more stuff. Not even education. My money is for adventures. Do what makes them feel alive. Every grandchild gets a graduation trip. Don't play it safe. Take some risks."

She was wandering, losing focus, her brain fogged by not enough oxygen. She stopped, searching for what she needed to say, then found it before it drifted off forever.

Then she said, "I need a big piece of paper. *Now!*"

Theo didn't ask why. He just waved at a nurse's aide, "I need a few pages of printer paper. In the nurses' station, bottom drawer to the left of the printer."

The aide ran and came back with several sheets of paper.

"I'm putting my signature at the bottom," Wanda continued, "Help me hold my arm up. I need you to write out what I told you and make eight copies. That's for my four kids and four nosy spouses. They all know my signature. And put Last Will and Testament at the top. Make it look serious."

"You could throw in that I'm leaving $10,000 to the nice white boy who took such good care of me, but that would get us both in trouble." She attempted a chuckle, but it came out a grunt.

"Now," she wheezed, "tell me what I said before I can't talk anymore."

Theo repeated, softly, quickly, making notes. Wanda listened and nodded.

"There's more." Her voice was a rasp. "If I have that tube down my throat and can't speak, you need to ask me questions. Ask me if I'm ready to go. Two blinks are yes. Three is no. One is just my body blinking. Too easy to misunderstand just one blink. You'll see my eyes mean business. And if I'm ready to go, ready to pass, you help me along. Treat me with the same compassion you'd treat a suffering dog. Slip me a shot."

Theo startled. He'd been tracking so far, but this?

"I can't do that," he whispered.

"I'm talking about when you know it's no use pretending. Don't rush it. But don't keep me alive on that machine waiting for my kids to stop bickering over who loves Mama best. They can't decide on what to have for Easter dinner without a debate. Give the damn machine to somebody who has a chance."

Theo was stunned, still processing everything Wanda had said. Without fighting her request, he said, "I'll write this up tonight and bring it back to you tomorrow."

"You know that's gonna' be too late," Wanda whispered. "They're putting me under soon. I trust you to do the right thing."

Mickey

It was the nineteenth anniversary of 9/11. About 3,000 people had died in the terrorist attacks on the Twin Towers of the World Trade Center. It took less than three days now for that many people to die in the war with COVID.

Mickey didn't talk about it, but he had a friend from high school whose son had been on Flight 93, the hijacked plane that had never made it to Washington, D.C. to crash into the Capitol. It was taken down in a field in Pennsylvania. The son was one of the men who'd stormed the cockpit, who faced down terrorists with box cutters and knives. Mickey thought he'd been an accountant. Or a teacher?

Flight 93 was what Mickey visualized when he heard the word "patriot." Ordinary citizens who, when faced with unfathomable circumstances, chose sacrifice. Which made them extraordinary.

Now, whenever he saw red-faced, angry men and women, spouting racist garbage or yelling into bullhorns about their "rights" and entitlements—like to not be "forced" to wear a mask or wash their damn hands—Mickey wanted to load *them* on a plane. Let them all go down together, bickering about their precious, selfish, *me-me-me*, rights.

Mickey was quietly incensed that the very word—*patriotic*—had been appropriated by the White supremacists. That a waving flag was now seen as a symbol of the far-right extremists. Those people weren't patriots. They were doing whatever they could to undermine democracy and the Constitution.

Mickey wanted a "National Flag for Democracy Day." He wanted every Democrat in the USA to get a flag, a big one, and fly it.

Take back our flag, he thought. *Just do it.*

Covid Grief Group

The group was sharing the ups and downs of the past week. Debra and Bill had had family drive in from Ohio, which made them nervous, but they'd also wanted to see them. Larry had a really hard day on Saturday because it was Jasmine's birthday. Shawnee had lost another cousin, although this one was older, and she hadn't known her that well. Luis had moved from the rental house he'd lived in with Mariana to a small one-bedroom apartment.

"I felt like I was leaving her, but also that it hurt too much to stay. It was more space than I need, and it was so empty. Like I am empty," Luis explained.

Grace looked around the group, nodding at whoever had not shared yet.

"Anything else?" she asked.

"I was arrested on Friday," Kayla announced. "But then they didn't know what to charge me with, so they just asked me not to do it again and let me go. The officers were very nice."

"Arrested for what?" Beth asked, as they all looked at Kayla.

"Sitting on a folding chair outside Chuck's Stop and holding up a sign every time someone walked past me without a mask, or with their mask down below their nose."

"What did the sign say?" Grace asked.

"Did YOU kill my mother?" Kayla deadpanned. "I had a picture of her, mostly her face with a big smile, so they could make the connection. Because these were the weekday morning regulars, the ones that Mom chatted with."

"It could have been anyone," Larry said. "There's no way to..."

"Yeah, I know that," Kayla ranted, "but they're still not masking, still playing games. And my mom, who went out of her way to be nice to them, is dead. I just wanted them to connect the dots. They probably didn't even notice she was gone."

"Who called the police?" Larry persisted.

"I have no idea. Someone working? Or someone who was pissed that I dared to make them think?"

"What did the police say?" Larry again.

"That it was private property and I needed to leave. I said I would sit in my car, which was parked right there in front. Then I'd be on my own property. I think one of them actually called in to the station to make sure they were in the right for making me stop."

"And then what happened?" Grace asked.

"They asked me to come down to the station to talk. So, I got in the police car and went with them, with my sign held up to the window as we drove off. Down at the station, they asked me to wait in a conference room, brought me a Coke, and asked what was going on and I told them."

"And then?" Grace asked.

"I think they didn't know if I was a minor, or whatever, so asked if there was anyone they could call or I could call. I said, 'No, sir, I'm an orphan.'"

"Do you feel better having done it?" Beth asked, as if she were weighing the pros and cons of her own private protest.

"Yeah," Kayla replied. "But I may need to do it more. I need to check first but I think they can't stop me if I stay on the sidewalk. I have another poster ready. It's a poster of a guy's face, with the mask below a big nose, only the nose is a penis, with the words, 'Are you hanging out?'"

Cheryl's eyes widened. Beth chuckled.

"Would you bring that next time?" Grace asked. "I think we need to see it to get the full effect. And bring the one with your mom's picture too."

Grace & Sofia

Sofia Dominguez had emailed for another appointment. Grace did not, at first, remember who she was when she received Sofia's email. Grace was at a loss with email addresses that weren't someone's name, clearly spelled out. She still expected people to identify themselves.

Grace had felt her cognitive functioning slipping since the lockdowns and start of COVID. Was it six months ago? Seven?

There was chatter on the web, in the news, about brain fog as a long-term consequence of COVID infection. She'd always had a hard time with names, placing names with faces. She'd spent her life apologizing for that deficit.

But with clients, her memory had been sharp. Each client was like a book, a narrative, and, once the file loaded in her head, it was all there. But now?

Grace did an email search and found it was Sofia. So, here they were, again, in the gazebo.

"Mr. Huang's nephew is upset. He wants to know how his uncle was infected when I was his only contact," Sofia started. "And I want to tell him, to explain, but my husband said to not do that. He wants me to lie. He is afraid that the nephew will make trouble."

"What kind of trouble?"

"He is saying that I was negligent. That he will report me to the licensing board. Say bad things about me on social media. The nephew has a company that manages social media for other companies." Sofia's eyes started to fill with tears.

"But we're in a pandemic," Grace replied. "You think you caught COVID from your son, but we can't say with certainty where anyone catches the virus."

"There is more," Sofia explained. "There was a will with Mr. Huang's attorney. His nephew is the executor but did not know that Mr. Huang had changed part of the will. Mr. Huang has left me his house. I knew nothing of this. He never mentioned it."

Grace startled a bit. This was no small thing. She leaned in closer, her tone shifting.

"What is the nephew alleging?" Grace asked, picking up her clipboard to take notes.

"That I knew about the change of the will, that I manipulated Mr. Huang to change his will, that I'm one of those home health people who exploit old people. Also, that I deliberately infected Mr. Huang to get Mr. Huang's house."

"But none of that is true, Sofia."

"But how can I prove that? And if I say that I did not know I had COVID, but that it was my son's lying that caused this? I am covering up."

"You *assume* you caught COVID from your son. And your symptoms were mild, inconsistent with what we knew then," Grace assured her.

"He says he will take me to court to break the will, and I will never work again."

Grace paused to think this through.

"Tell me about the house," she asked, changing directions.

"It's a pretty house. Not so big, but with many windows, so much sunshine. And the floors are all shiny wood," Sofia replied, starting to smile. "It's ranch style, three bedrooms, two bathrooms, and a big basement that has been finished to be a rec room. But the best part is the yard, a huge yard, with a garden. And pear trees and apple trees. And many different flowers."

"Why do you think he left you his house?"

"Because Mr. Huang was a kind and generous man," Sofia explained. "And we talked a lot. I told him how pretty his house was, but I meant it as a compliment for him, and his wife who died, nothing more. He loved his garden and would sit in a lawn chair and direct me—how to trim the roses in the fall, when to fertilize, what to plant in the garden each spring."

"Did he ever see where you lived?" Grace interrupted.

"Once, when we were on a drive. But only because he asked me to show him. Our home is much smaller, very small yard, but I had pots with flowers in front. I told Mr. Huang that I planted more flowers and was growing tomatoes and peppers because of what he taught me."

"How long did you work for Mr. Huang?"

"Eight years," Sofia replied.

"I didn't appreciate that when we first met. I'm sorry. I didn't ask. Mr. Huang wasn't just another client. He was like family."

Sofia was now weeping, quietly. Grace pushed the box of Kleenex toward her.

"How often did his nephew come to visit hm?" Grace asked.

"He was busy with his work," Sofia said. "His company is very demanding. Mr. Huang told me often how successful he was, how proud his sister would be of her son if she had lived longer."

"But that wasn't my question," Grace asked. "How often did the nephew come to see his uncle?"

"During the Chinese New Year. So, in January or early February?" Depends on the moon, the lunar cycle," Sofia answered. "Mr. Huang had some red clothing he wore just for New Year's. And we hung up lanterns in the trees in the back yard. Lin's wife and sons used to come also, but for the last three years it was just Lin."

"The nephew's name is Lin?"

"No, Lingyun," Sofia corrected. "Mr. Huang told me it means high goals? Exceptional aspirations? But he goes by Lin."

"And other visits were just whenever?"

"No, it was usually just the New Year's visit."

Grace took a moment to take this in. Lin lived in St. Louis, less than a five-hour drive. And he came *once* a *year*?

"How did Mr. Huang feel about Lin not visiting him more?"

"Mr. Huang never complained. He made excuses for him. I was more upset than he was."

"Did you ever talk to Lin about visiting more?"

"I did tell him, after I'd worked for Mr. Huang for about two years, that Mr. Huang looked forward to his visits, that seeing Lin made him happy."

"And Lin's reply?"

"Lin said it was very hard to get away from work. But I got the feeling that I'd overstepped."

"Are there other people in the will?"

"Not that I know. Mr. Huang and his wife had two baby girls, but they died very young. His sister had Lin. There are many other relatives, but in China."

Grace paused to consider.

"I think that Lin may be feeling guilty for not paying more attention to his uncle, but also discounted for not being the sole one to inherit. And not being consulted. Like the will is a rebuke."

Sofia sighed. "I had no idea that Mr. Huang was doing this. It is too much."

"Is Lin well off?"

"How do you mean?"

"Is he rich? Does it look like he has money?"

"He has very nice cars," Sofia said. "Mr. Huang always made a comment about Lin's car. And he had a new one every few years. There was an Audi, a BMW, and..."

"What do you drive?"

"A 2005 Corolla. They are very reliable cars."

"And did Mr. Huang have a car?"

Sofia looked confused as to why this focus on cars.

"Yes, a BMW also. He liked me to drive him around in it. But that was just two or three times a month."

"Who did he leave the car to?"

Sofia's face reddened.

"To me," she replied. "He would say that I was a good driver, that he liked watching me drive. That I was careful."

"And were you?"

"Or course. I was always afraid something could happen to his beautiful car."

Grace jotted down a few notes.

"Let me think about his for a few days, okay? And do you know Lin's full name? Maybe where he lives?"

"Yes, all his contact information was written down. I had it on the refrigerator. But I kept a business card in my purse." Sofia started digging through a pocket as she spoke.

"Here it is," she announced. "Why do you ask?"

"Just curious," Grace replied. "Can we meet in a week? I want to talk with a lawyer friend about options here. And do NOT talk to Lin, or impulsively say that you do not want the inheritance. Got that? And you can talk to an attorney yourself if you want."

"Of course," Sofia agreed, pulling out her planner. "What day and time?"

That evening, Grace asked Mickey to do a little research on Lin, just to get a better picture. Mickey managed to find where he lived, where he worked, and how much money he made, all by searching on LinkedIn, Zillow, Facebook, public records, and press coverage. As well as asking a buddy who did background checks.

Grace made a mental note to remove some details from her Facebook profile after that.

Lin was 55, married to a physician, with two sons in Ivy League schools. He was the CEO of a company that was maybe going public, with rumors of a buyout leaked on a Reddit thread. Assets of a few million. Pretty decent reputation.

So, he was *very, very* busy with his work. *This is not a man to go to war with,* Grace thought. He had the resources to make Sofia's life a living hell with the snap of a finger. Sofia couldn't afford to hire an attorney. Half the inheritance would go to a contingency lawyer if she could even find a decent one in the middle of a pandemic. Lin could drag this out for years.

But the real issue was with Sofia: she wouldn't lie, and she believed that she'd infected Mr. Huang. An attorney could easily argue against her claims that she didn't know Mr. Huang was leaving her anything.

Grace could just hear it: "So, Mrs. Dominguez, you state that you had no idea that your employer had put you in his will. And, also, that you cared deeply for Mr. Huang. But, nevertheless, in the middle of a highly infectious pandemic, knowing that you were Mr. Huang's lifeline, you concluded that you had not been exposed, despite having symptoms, and continued to care for Mr. Huang without even informing him that you had felt ill over the weekend? That sounds like he was worth more to you dead than alive..."

At which point a judge would cut him off, but Sofia's face would crumble into sobs that sounded like she was guilty. Because she felt she was.

A different tactic was needed.

By the time they met again, Grace had a strategy. Years ago, Grace had read, and thoughtfully absorbed, *The Art of War* by Sun Tzu. A Chinese classic written thousands of years ago, it was used in every intro class to military strategy. Core principles: diplomacy is best, but, if war is inevitable, then be strategic. Knowing your enemy, understanding psychologically what motivates him, how he thinks, matters more than weapon power.

In her work as a mediator with hurt and hostile divorcing couples, she'd found Sun Tzu helpful.

"Here's what I propose, Sofia," Grace started. "Lin has assets and power, and he will crush you in court. But if you take court off the table? Tell Lin about your relationship with Mr. Huang. Give him the power. He has it already."

Sofia nodded but did not speak.

"I don't know if this will help," Grace admitted, "but I don't think it can hurt. You can't cope with, or pay for, an extended litigation. This costs nothing. It may bring a good outcome. It may not. That all depends on Lin."

With that, Grace handed Sofia a letter.

Dear Lingyun:

Your uncle was very proud of you. He told me your name meant high goals and was a name for a man with exceptional aspirations. He often said that his sister, your mother, would be so proud of all you have achieved.

I understand that you are surprised and perhaps upset that your uncle put me into his will. I wish that there was a way to assure you that I knew nothing about this. I cared for Mr. Huang like he was my own father. He taught me more than my own father ever did.

We spent many hours together, usually 15-20 a week, for eight years. I would bring his groceries and he would sit at the kitchen table and tell me stories of his life as I cooked. When I folded his laundry, we would watch a TV program together, often National Geographic about far-away places. Your uncle liked to talk about China, growing up there, the seasons and connection to the earth. Each spring, I would take him to a nursery so he would pick out plants for his garden. He would inspect each plant to make sure the roots were strong. "Strong roots make the best food," he said. All spring and summer, he would sit in the shade of the big oak tree and direct me in his garden.

I've asked myself why he did such a thing. Why leave the house to me? I am not family. If my uncle did that with a stranger, I would feel as you do. Perhaps, though, it is because Mr. Huang had so much loss in his life. He told me that he and his wife had two baby girls but they both died. I do not know how or when, because it was too painful for him to talk about. He said that, in China, there are no places to send old people, and that old people are taken care of by their children, usually daughters or wives of sons. I told him that it made me happy to care for him, that he would never be a burden. And he was not.

But also, perhaps, is it because he wanted his home to be cherished, his garden to be cherished? He knows you are an important professional man and do not have the time to care for his home. You would probably sell the house. Did he teach me so much about gardening because he wanted me to keep doing it after he was gone? And the car? Did he see me driving the same old car to work every day? Did he know I took the bus when the car broke down? Mr. Huang really liked going out for drives. I drove him to all his doctor appointments, anywhere he wanted, to parks and out for ice cream.

I cannot fight you over Mr. Huang's will. I cannot afford an attorney, and I do not want to fight. I think his attorney may be able to explain more about the changes, and perhaps why, so you can ask him for more details.

I will say this: I will cherish Mr. Huang's home. I will care for it and live in it, will cut back the rose bushes in the fall, and tend to the garden in summer. My son will have a space in the basement for his friends to come over (and he will be excited to no longer share a bathroom with his parents). My family was poor. There was nothing to inherit but debts. This home is not just for myself but will give my son a future. We could sell our small home and use that money for his college.

I know that Mr. Huang's car is very expensive. I would not feel comfortable driving around in that kind of car. If you want that car, for your sons, that is fine with me.

I miss Mr. Huang so much. I realize that I probably infected him, that I did not know I had the virus and I brought it into his home. I would never, ever, have done anything to harm him intentionally. But I did. And he is dead.

So, whatever you decide, please just let me know.

I just wanted you to know that Mr. Huang was very proud of you, his nephew, of all you have built and created with your life. Do not have regrets. He was happy in his home, and I was very happy that I could care for him and that he was able to stay in his home until he died. It is just those last few days that break my heart, but the nurse told me he was in a coma and that here was nothing I could have done.

Sincerely,
Sofia Dominguez

Sofia looked up when she finished, eyes brimming with tears.

"How did you know I felt all of this?" she asked.

"Because you told me, with your words and eyes and grief. And this is what I saw when I imagined you and Mr. Huang," Grace explained. "I think Lin needs to feel that he can be gracious to you because he has so much more than you do, his sons are better off than your son. His sense of honor needs to silence his initial reaction that he is being cheated by you or disrespected by his uncle. Those were the only reasons he could see for why Mr. Huang would leave the house to you and not to him.

You give him other reasons, but respectfully, and you hand him back his power. There is no fight, only a choice. His choice."

"But that sounds like I'm—what? Manipulating Lin? I don't want to do that."

"Is telling the truth manipulative? This choice will make Lin feel good about himself and his uncle, rather than years of believing that he was a bad nephew, and his uncle was telling him so with the will. In his culture, that is a painful legacy. What do you think is better for Lin to live with?"

Sofia sat, thinking. Minutes passed.

"Yes, I see what you're saying. I know I can't fight Lin. But perhaps he would honor his uncle's decision."

Sofia left with the letter, saying she would talk with her husband.

Grace closed the folder on her desk. It was out of her hands now.

Max

The sauna had finally been delivered. Max found it all quite thrilling, to have a giant moving truck in the street in front of the house. It was complicated: a man in a forklift inside the truck would pick up a giant package, go to the end of the truck, press a button, lower the back of the truck, set the package where Mickey wanted it in the driveway, then do it over again. There were packages of lumber pieces that would make the barrel, and two big round end pieces, one for the back and the other the front where a glass door would go. Inside the barrel would be two benches. There was a heater, from Finland, and instructions that were in Finnish and English. Max had never seen Finnish before. It looked like a confusing language, and also very hard to pronounce.

Max did not quite understand what they would do with the sauna. He'd asked Mickey what it was for, and Mickey had said "To sweat. You sit inside and it gets very, very hot and you sweat all over your body. Then you stand under a cold shower. You feel great afterwards."

That did not sound like fun to Max. Sweating all over your body and then getting under an icy cold shower? That did not sound fun at all. But he figured Mickey would explain it more to him.

Mickey

After all of the prep work, the meticulous use of a level at each stage to ensure that the paver patio would work for the sauna, the actual assembly was—easy?

Mickey had asked his friend, who'd worked construction for years building high-end homes, to look at the "How To" video with him, and then come help assemble. He hired two college kids, for two hours, to carry the lumber and parts from the driveway to the work site. Since that was just across the lawn and to the side of the garage, they finished in 30 minutes.

"What else can we do, sir?" one asked, politely, obviously expecting two hours of pay since they'd dragged themselves out of bed at 8 a.m. but maybe hoping for the pay without more work. Mickey put them to work weeding and raking leaves, then digging two remaining post holes for the fence.

In the end, it took Mickey and Roger about four hours to assemble the sauna, and another hour to install the Finnish stove, placing hot rocks on the top that would produce a blast of even hotter air when Mickey poured water on them.

It was another week before Mickey finished the privacy fence sections and had the plumber hook up piping from the closest spigot to the cedar shower stall across the small patio from the sauna.

On a day when Grace was gone for the whole day, taking Max to the Kansas City Zoo, Mickey finished.

He'd ordered teal chaise lounges and outdoor string lights delivered to his house. He unwrapped them all and brought them over. Molly helped him string the lights up around what was now being referred to as the 'Sauna Garden.' They placed the new lounges out, with a small table between them.

When Grace and Max returned just after dark from their Kansas City adventure, Mickey and Molly staged a "Big Reveal." Molly put blindfolds on them both and escorted them across the small lawn and around the corner to the side yard. What had been, two months before, a neglected and barren space was now magical: twinkle lights lined the fence, chaise lounges were staged adjacent to the sauna, hooks for robes and towels were neatly lined by the shower. And it was all tucked behind a six-foot privacy fence.

When Molly took off Grace's blindfold, she stared, eyes widening, jaw dropping, and gasped. It was exactly the response Mickey had hoped for.

Max started waving his arms and jumping up and down. "It's a fairy land," he said. Then he wanted to sit in the sauna, with the door open, and smell the cedar. "It smells like a magical forest," he announced and demanded that Molly join him.

They took turns smelling the cedar and testing the chaise lounges. When Molly left with Max to quiet him down and get him to bed, Grace sat with Mickey on the lounges and just looked.

"Is this what you imagined when you proposed building a sauna?" she asked. "Because this is not what I envisioned..."

"Not really," Mickey said. "But it started to evolve, kind of take on a life of its own. I just started seeing it differently."

It was quite different from anything he'd ever done. And he knew he'd never have considered it, even thought of it, until COVID. He wondered how many other projects were being initiated and completed—because the completing part had eluded him in the past—inside yards and homes across the country. COVID had taken away so much, but had given some folks time to slow down, to get off the treadmill. To tackle a little dream and make it happen.

"Are you sure we're in the same yard?" she asked.

"Yeah, I'm sure."

"You did a swell job with your project, Mickey. I've never seen anything quite like this, at least not in suburban Kansas."

"No," Mickey agreed. "Definitely not mainstream."

Now, Mickey thought, all he had to do was get Gracie to *enjoy* sweating from every pore in 180 degrees and then standing under an icy cold shower. And doing it over and over and over.

Mickey & Grace

A few days later, Mickey was reading the paper and Grace was stirring soup as it heated up for supper.

"That makes three," he said.

"Three what?" asked Grace. They'd noticed they were each starting conversations in their heads, then verbalizing without a segue.

"You're doing it again," she told him.

"Doing what?" Mickey asked.

"You said 'three,' but 'three' of what?"

"Sorry. This obituary. Another teacher. She'd retired but was helping out early August before school opened. She died. COVID. Didn't your kids go to River Road Elementary?"

"Yeah, they both did, but that was a long, long time ago."

"Well, she taught there for 40 years."

"Damn, what's her name?"

"Mrs. Williams," he said. "Wanda Williams. Taught first grade. A celebration of life will be held at some point in the future. Donations to the school library can be sent..."

"I do know her. She taught Molly and Alex both," Grace replied. "But back then even the parents called her *Mrs.* Williams. I don't ever remember using her first name," Grace reflected. "She was a great teacher. Took Alex under her wing, put his desk right in front, not to keep tabs on him, more to steady him, reassure him. I remember Alex telling me that they had a 'secret wink.'"

"A secret *wink?*"

"Yeah. Who knows? Alex adored her and she helped him feel smart. He stopped wetting the bed. That was good enough for me."

Later, after supper, Grace picked up the paper. She didn't recognize the woman in the picture. *Oh hell*, she thought. *We all looked frickin' different 20-30 years ago.* But, yes, here it was. Wanda Williams.

Huh, she thought, and then let it go.

Pod-Potluck

Their Pod-Potlucks continued, with no predictable pattern. There were times when they fixated on what made a particular series binge-worthy, or why Brit Box was essential. But just as often they found themselves talking about race.

"When you said that your parents had *never* talked with you *directly* about race, it felt like you must have lived on another planet," Katrina told Grace. "Because, on my planet, every decision has a race component. It's always there, even if unspoken. If I try to explain the layers of how I learned about Blackness and whiteness? It would be a book."

"The total opposite of Mom?" Molly asked, gesturing at Grace who was slowly savoring a piece of Key lime pie. "Can you think of some specific examples?"

Kat paused to consider the options.

"What about being pulled over?" Mickey offered, as if he knew the selection process could take a while.

"Why do you say that?" Grace asked. "Isn't it making assumptions?"

"No," Mickey replied. "I've never met a Black person who has not been pulled over for 'driving while Black' even if under the umbrella of a 'failure to come to a complete stop' at a stop sign with no one in sight coming the other way."

Kat nodded agreement, something between a grimace and a smile rolling across her face.

"What have *you* felt when pulled over?" Kat asked Grace, but also gesturing to Molly.

"Pissed," Grace replied. "Maybe guilty because I was speeding." Molly nodded her agreement.

"But were you scared?"

"Not really scared. More nervous," Molly answered this time. "Trying to remember if the registration and insurance cards are in the glove compartment where they're supposed to be. Impatient for how long this will take because I don't want to be late for class or work or picking up Max."

"Not physically frightened? Not shaky?" Katrina persisted.

Kat felt shaky, now, just remembering times she'd been pulled over, ordered to exit the vehicle, to stand alongside the highway as people driving past stared at her, as the police took an inordinate amount of time checking her license and registration, her record, checking for outstanding warrants, her two Black sons, wide-eyed, in the backseat, looking both confused and scared.

Or when she was younger, alone, driving home late at night from the law school library. Being asked questions like, "Where are you going?" and "Where do you live?" Asked to produce documentation to prove she was a student. Explaining that the library was indeed open until 11 p.m., which might sound unusual, and, no, she was not lying to an officer. That the address on her driver's license was her home address, with her parents, but she lived in a student apartment. Being accused of "weaving lanes" when she'd had nothing but caffeine to drink for six hours. Told to walk a straight line. Waiting to be "released." Waiting for the unapologetic, abrupt, "You can get in your car." Scared of what else might come at her. Monitoring her tone, gestures, eye contact. Showing no feelings. No resentment.

Katrina felt violated, even in memory. It was too raw. So, she pivoted.

"Did you ever have 'the talk' with your kids?" Kat asked, abruptly turning to Grace. "And repeat it every six months from the time they were 12 or 13 until they were adults and told you to stuff it?"

"What talk exactly?" Grace asked. Across the table, Mickey audibly sighed.

"How to behave around cops, on the playground or street when they're just kids. But then much more detailed when they start to drive."

"I've never done that with Max," Molly joked. But Kat waved her away.

"We talked to the kids about following laws and being respectful," Grace said. "Like that?"

"When you get pulled over by a cop," Katrina replied, pointing a finger at Grace, "you don't have to question whether it's because you have a white face. If you're Black? You never know. And, if it is because you're Black, it can be dangerous not knowing how anything you do or say could be 'interpreted.'"

Kat paused. Her lungs felt tight, thinking about what dark mental cages she'd gone to, could still go to, if her sons were late coming home.

"I had to tell my boys, over and over, how critically essential it was to never, ever say or do anything disrespectful or even assertive, if stopped by a cop. Never argue. Just apologize, take the ticket, whatever. Just say 'Yes, sir' and 'No, sir,' and 'I'll remember that sir.' And 'May I reach for my wallet now, sir, to get my license out? It's in my jacket pocket." And 'May I open the glove compartment now to get my registration and proof of insurance?' No sudden moves. Explain whatever you are about to do before you do it. We practiced with them, like following a script, because one quick move could be 'misunderstood' and then it would be a hell of a lot worse than a ticket."

Grace considered. Had she ever talked to her kids in that detail? Had she ever feared for their safety with law enforcement? Or had she assumed that the police would treat them like kids, not see them as an armed threat?

Grace looked over at Molly and raised her eyebrows in a question. Molly's head swung side-to-side with an emphatic "no."

"No, Kat, I never had that kind of talk with my kids. Just told them that if they were respectful, the police would be respectful back."

Then Grace pushed back, but tentatively, regretfully.

"Why didn't you talk about this with me when it was happening?"

"Because... I don't know. Maybe I thought you might see me as over-anxious or over-protective. Or, if you didn't understand, I could have felt misunderstood, and that would have impacted our friendship," Katrina replied, slowly, thoughtfully. "Maybe because it's a Black thing to have to have the talk, and there is something—a shame—that we have to do that? That we have to put the fear of God into our kids, so they don't act like normal teenagers and accidentally mouth off?"

"So, what do you have to contribute, Mr. Ex-Cop?" Kat asked, turning her head to face Mickey.

"I think you covered the subject area rather well, Ms. Baptiste," Mickey replied. "Most cops do see Black kids as older than they are, potentially more dangerous, with no valid reason to think that. There are double standards for white kids and Black kids at every level. Double standards for adults as well."

Mickey stood up. "I'm running out to the car to get a DVD I rented—very old school, I admit—that we're all going to sit down together and watch. Maybe even cry. I have from a reliable source that Grace will certainly cry, and that Max has never seen it."

"What is it, Mickey? What haven't I seen?" Max was now on high alert.

"*The Black Stallion,*" Mickey said. "Your mom said she read you the book when you were younger..."

"Was it on a deserted island? And the boy was alone? That scared me, being alone on a deserted island."

"We're all here with you for the movie, kiddo. And the boy will be fine."

Grace

Over the past six weeks, Grace had been getting referrals for mediation cases over "COVID issues." It took her a while to sort out what that meant.

Any differences that divorced parents may have had before COVID were exacerbated. If exchanging the right pair of sneakers for soccer had previously resulted in a testy conversation, then communicating in detail about what each kid was doing in each class, what homework was due when, all the while navigating the demands of working remote?

But those were not the hardest cases.

The hardest cases were about COVID itself. Like, one parent believes that COVID-19 is a dangerous, communicable coronavirus, and follows every CDC protocol and guideline. But the other parent believes that COVID-19 is a hoax, "just like the flu," and refuses to mask or sanitize. So, one parent is trying to protect their pod (that often included grandparents) while the other parent took the kids to a Trump rally, or a weekend at a lake where everyone was behaving like college kids on spring break. Or had backyard cookouts with friends who shared their beliefs.

Meanwhile, their kids are caught in the middle. They're confused. They want to be loyal to a parent, to not make waves. And they'd feel *awful* if they infected or killed their grandparents. The courts are working remote, taking months to even get a Zoom hearing, and by then it would be too late anyway. And the "hoax" parent has no incentive to change behavior, if only to not place their former in-laws at risk, and just says, "Fine, then, the kids can stay with me until this flu thing is over."

These are not cases "appropriate" for mediation.

For mediation, it helped to have evidence-based data. Or at least agree on some facts.

Grace tried to mediate a few, mostly on Zoom as even being on the same patio felt too risky when you knew one of the clients was not taking precautions and didn't care.

But a few had been enough. Reason is futile when the basis for a position is a conspiracy theory.

She sent an email to the referring attorneys: "Please request a court order for conciliation as mediation will, in general, get us nowhere. With conciliation, there is a remote chance of reaching some sort of compromise. And, at the very least, conciliation saves the judge and court time by having the issues and positions defined."

The referrals dried up.

HISTORICAL CONTEXT: SEPTEMBER 2020

Sep. 9: U.S. death toll passes 190,000.

Sep. 10: "This is nobody's fault but China's," and "We have rounded the final turn," and, "I think we've probably done the best job of any country."
– *Donald Trump*

Sep. 14: "I'm on a stage, it's very far away, so I'm not at all concerned."
– *Donald Trump when asked if he's afraid of coronavirus risk at his rallies.*

Sep. 18: Supreme Court Associate Justice Ruth Bader Ginsburg dies from complications of metastatic pancreatic cancer. It is less than eight weeks away from the presidential election.

Sep. 19: U.S. death toll passes 200,000.

Sep. 21: "Take your hat off to the young because they have a hell of an immune system. But [the virus] affects virtually nobody. It's an amazing thing. By the way, open your schools everybody, open your schools." – *Donald Trump.*

Sep. 21: "We've done a phenomenal job. Not just a good job. A phenomenal job. Other than public relations, but that's because I have fake news. On public relations, I give myself a D. On the job itself, we take an A+."
– *Donald Trump*

Sep: 23: "We're going to have to see what happens," *Donald Trump in response to a reporter's question as to whether he would agree to a peaceful transfer of power.*

Sep. 24: "We have to be very careful of the ballots...The ballots. That's a whole big scam." – *Donald Trump*

Sep. 26: Donald Trump tests positive for COVID but keeps it a secret. He attends a ceremony for Amy Coney Barrett in the Rose Garden. Over a dozen White House staffers and GOP officials become ill.

Sep. 27: There is a press briefing and event for Gold Star families. Trump later blames this event for his COVID infection.

Sep. 27: Donald Trump goes golfing, the 291st time he has visited one of his 17 golf clubs while in office.

Sep. 29: The first presidential debate is held in Cleveland, Ohio. Despite prior agreements and requirements that all participants would be tested, Trump and his team arrive too late to be tested and are, instead, admitted under "an honor system."

October 2020

Grace

Grace picked up her phone and saw a text from Mickey: I need to talk to you. Something came up and I need your input.

An hour later, he was sitting in Grace's living room, a cup of coffee in his hand, and Grace seated across from him looking curious.

"Okay, Mickey, spit it out. What's up?"

"You know that I took care of Joanne in home hospice when she was at the end with her cancer, right?"

Joanne was Mickey's second wife, a teacher, who'd died some years back, when Grace was living in Alaska. Grace had never met Joanne, but Mickey had talked about her.

"Yeah," Grace replied. "You've shared some."

"Joanne has a sister, Jocelynn, about seven years older, so about 73 now."

"And?"

"Jocelynn and Joanne were close. Neither of them had kids. Jocelynn lives alone. She's been working remote and is in end-stage cancer. It's also spread to the liver. It's not curable."

"That's tough," Grace said.

"Yeah, it is. Jocelynn was always an introvert, but COVID shut her down. Her immune system was damaged after chemo. She was very scared of COVID. She knew it would kill her and she didn't want to die like that. So, she isolated herself."

"Where is she now?"

"At home. She's managed alone, with one home health aide, but she has to go into a nursing home or hospice. She can't walk. She's fallen three times in the last couple of weeks. I talked to her doctor, and he says it is a matter of weeks or maybe a few months."

"How did you get to talk to the doctor?"

"Jocelynn has me listed as her financial and medical power of attorney. I'm on her DNR form. I didn't know this until well into COVID, when she thought she'd better tell me so no surprises."

"Were you surprised?"

"Yes—and no. Jocelynn and I worked as a team caring for Joanne. She took a leave from work and moved in with us. It was for three months so we had a lot of late-night talks over honey whiskey and ginger beer. When one of us needed to vent, the other listened. No judgment."

"Why haven't I met Jocelynn? Where does she live?"

"In Ames, Iowa. She worked at the university. Admin positions. I've told her about you, selling the house, moving over here. Her cancer has been going on since before COVID, so she's been kind of 'in lockdown' for a few years. She knows she's dying. I think she's ready. But she's scared of being in pain and alone."

"So, do you want to go see her? Will she let you in if she is so scared of COVID?"

"I want to go get her and bring her to my place and take care of her the way she and I took care of Joanne," Mickey said, enunciating each word, speaking slowly, so there could be no confusion.

"Oh," Grace said, awareness sinking in.

"Jocelynn would never ask that, but that's what Joanne would want me to do. Jocelynn can't stay alone in her house. Her doctor recommended some nursing homes. But they're in lockdown, so no visitors. She'd die surrounded by overworked strangers in PPE."

"What do you want from me, Mickey? To say it's a good thing to do?"

"No, more," Mickey replied, looking her in the eyes. "I can't do it alone. Almost all of it, but maybe I need a partner. I want you to help me give Jocelynn a good death, like she and I did for Joanne."

Grace inhaled, held it, and exhaled slowly. She had never done this, never cared, hands on, for someone who was dying. But Mickey had, and he wouldn't ask her to do anything he didn't think she could manage.

"I'd still need to see some clients, and the grief group, and my time with Max," she said. "I can't be there all the time."

"I don't expect that. I just don't want to start something I can't finish, and this will require teamwork at the end."

Grace got up from her chair and sat down next to Mickey. She lay her hand against his cheek. It was quite scratchy.

"You're a good man, Mickey," she said. "But you gotta' remember to shave."

Four days later, Grace was at the front door of Mickey's ranch house waiting for him to return from fetching Jocelynn. He'd driven up to Ames rather than propose what he was proposing on the phone. It was too intense a conversation to have without being face-to-face.

"I just said what I wanted—for her to come back with me in my car," Mickey had reported. "That I'd take care of her like we did for her sister. That she wouldn't be in pain and no hospital. She just started crying, saying how scared she'd felt of being alone, with strangers, and not able to communicate."

"When are you bringing her back?" Grace had asked.

"We need to get all her papers in order," he'd said. "I've got a Zoom meeting with her attorney and doctor tomorrow, to make sure all the DNR's and power of attorney and such cover another state. I'll get them and make copies. And her doctor is going to talk to the top hospice doc here in Kaw Valley, plus give me multiple copies of prescriptions that we'll need. Just in case."

"So?"

"Day after tomorrow. Hospice will call you to arrange a time to meet you at my house and get it set up."

"What do you mean 'set up?'"

"They coordinate the arrangements: a hospital bed, wheelchair, commode, oxygen tanks, walker, pads, diapers, all of the necessary supplies."

Grace felt herself going a bit numb. It was intimidating for a newbie.

"Where does it all go?" she asked. "What's your plan?"

"I cleared out the family room before I left. Pushed the couch against a wall, moved chairs. So, have them put the bed by the picture window. But make up the bed? Okay? I left sheets and a comforter and extra pillows in a basket. Makes a difference to walk in and see a bed that doesn't look sterile."

"Got it, Mickey. Can do."

But Grace had not felt "can do" when they'd clicked off. She'd felt anxious that this might be more than she was prepared to handle. And, if she bailed or freaked, what would Mickey think of her?

Mickey had texted an hour ago that they were outside Kansas City, so it should be any minute. It was just under four hours from Ames to Kaw Valley, and they were not stopping.

"Maybe this is where the diapers come in handy," Grace muttered to herself. She was thinking that they might need a lot of dark humor in the coming weeks.

When Mickey pulled into the driveway, Grace did not see another person. But then she realized that the other front seat was almost all the way back down, and a small figure was curled up, covered by a blanket.

"She's asleep," Mickey whispered. "I gave her a few drops of morphine under her tongue when we started out. All the jostling with the car can be painful and she can't sit up that long."

"You're allowed to do that?" Grace whispered back incredulously. "Give *morphine*?"

"Yeah, I'm allowed to do that. It's what hospice is about: keeping people as lucid as possible, but not in pain. At this stage, ibuprofen is not going to cut it," he said. "Now, show me the set up."

When they walked into the family room, Mickey smiled.

Grace had made up the bed, draped the comforter, plumped up pillows. A white cubby in the corner was stocked with hospice supplies. The commode and wheelchair were parked in another corner. An overstuffed chair, with a small table and lamp, was facing the bed to make conversation easier. Fresh flowers were on the counter between the kitchen and family room.

"You got this, Gracie," he said. "Nice job."

Mickey unloaded the car, Jocelynn still asleep. He carried in a plastic bin of files and papers, and a Sprouts grocery bag of toiletries. Then another small plastic bin of pictures.

"Where are her clothes?" Grace asked, looking around for a large suitcase.

"In here," Mickey said, indicating a small floral carry-on bag. "Not like she's going anywhere. Just loose nighties."

Then it hit Grace, all over again. Jocelynn wasn't going *anywhere*, wasn't leaving this house, until she was *dead*.

Four hours later, Jocelynn was settled in her new bed, dozing. Mickey was cooking pasta, and the smell of garlic filled the room. Jocelynn wrinkled her nose, inhaling, then smiled.

"I haven't smelled anything that good in ages," she said.

Jocelynn had been shaky when she woke, and they'd needed the wheelchair, easing her from the car into the chair and into the house. Mickey had helped her to the bathroom, to change into a fresh nightie, and then into the bed.

Grace was impressed by how the bed, with a press of a button, lowered to make it easy to get on, then raised up, and they could elevate the head end if Jocelynn wanted to sit up.

"Yeah, Gracie, that's why they call it a hospital bed," Mickey said, with a trace of sarcasm. Grace rolled her eyes.

Mickey introduced Grace to Jocelynn. It could've been a little awkward, given that Jocelynn was his dead wife's sister and Grace was the woman he was not married to but in a relationship with. But Jocelynn eyed Grace up and down, turned to Mickey and said, "I think you got lucky. Don't screw it up."

They ate pasta drenched in olive oil, garlic, sausage, black olives, and artichokes. Jocelynn was propped up in her hospital bed, a tray table in front of her. But she was tired after just a few bites. "Maybe later," she said. "I wish I could. It's delicious."

Grace went home after supper, first giving Mickey a long hug.

"You did good, Mickey. I hope I can measure up."

The next day, a hospice nurse came over. She demonstrated the best ways to help Jocelynn into the wheelchair or onto the commode, to roll her body over to change her pads if she was too weak to move herself, to raise the bed to make it easier for Jocelynn to swallow, to strategically place pillows to prevent bedsores.

Grace thought all of this was premature, but within a few days it became clear that Jocelynn was never getting up again.

"Didn't she walk to get into the car in Ames?" Grace asked.

"Yes, but I was half-carrying her," Mickey replied. "I think she was holding herself together until she felt safe enough to let down."

Jocelynn's body was failing, almost imperceptibly but irreversibly. But her mind, despite having lapses, could be sharp. There were hours every day when she was fully present and aware.

The third morning, Jocelynn woke up and looked out the picture window. The sun was just rising, the Kansas sky layered with twenty shades of pink. Birds were gathering around the birdbath and feeder.

"Where am I?" she asked Mickey when he came over with her tea.

"In my family room, Jocelynn," he answered. "But in a different house. I sold the old house."

"This is better," she said, looking around as if seeing it for the first time. "That house felt so empty without Joanne. It was—what's that word? Desolate? It felt desolate."

"Yeah, it was that, and yet I felt like I was leaving her behind when I sold it."

"No, Mickey, you could never leave my sister behind. I bet she's hiding in a kitchen cupboard right now listening to every word. I bet she likes Grace too."

"I've thought that," Mickey said. "That they might have had some laughs together. Joanne would've liked Max too."

"Have I met Max?"

"No, not yet, but he's coming over tomorrow for supper and a movie. We do that every Tuesday evening. Gives his mom a break."

"And who is his mom?"

"Her name is Molly. She's Grace's daughter."

"You have a family now, don't you?" Jocelynn said wistfully. "That's a blessing, Mickey. You know that, right?"

"I know that, Jocelynn. Every day I realize that I have what I never imagined I could..."

"I can see that," Jocelynn said, adding, "I like it here, Mickey."

"Good," he replied, placing a hand on her arm, "Because you're staying here forever."

Mickey was a little concerned that Max might get upset around Jocelynn. She was, after all, dying. Hearing about death was one thing, experiencing it was another, especially for a kid.

But after 30 minutes of talking, it looked like Max and Jocelynn were going to get along just fine.

"My grammy says you're dying," Max said after a quick introduction. "Are you scared? What do you think will happen when you stop breathing?"

Jocelynn, who had fielded student questions for years, was unfazed.

"I'm a little scared, but mostly because I don't like surprises. I don't believe in a heaven like when I was a Catholic girl, but I think I believe that there is a restful place for our souls. Not just the Christian souls, but Muslim and Hindu and Jewish and Indigenous souls."

"What about really bad people? Will their souls be in the same restful place?" Max persisted. "Because that doesn't seem fair."

"Good point, Max," Jocelynn said. "What do you think? What would be fair?"

"That they're in a place where they can't rest. Like a movie is playing, over and over and over, of all the people they hurt, the mean things they did. And they're hot and sweaty and just want a shower and to go to bed, but they have to stay up and watch the movie. Forever."

"Wow," Jocelynn said. "That does sound icky. But you don't want to make them hurt? Like daggers or..."

"No," Max interrupted. "That would make me be like them. I think being trapped and hot and sweaty and watching the same thing over and over—that's like gym class for me. That's bad enough."

Max asked to visit Jocelynn almost every day.

"We talk about a lot of stuff," he told his mom. Max asked Jocelynn questions about her life and travels, but also how her body was changing.

"How is your body telling you that it's getting ready to die?" he asked her.

"Well, Max, it just stopped being hungry. I loved to eat, but now it's like that isn't important anymore. And my brain is not communicating well with my muscles. I used to be able to think 'move leg,' and it would move. Now it just lays there, maybe twitches."

"That's interesting," Max said. "What do you think will be the last part of your body to go?"

"I guess the lungs. There will be a moment when they simply stop, maybe very quietly. The brain will be flickering, like a lightbulb that is about to go out, and then just stop. And when the brain stops telling the lungs to breathe, then they will stop too."

"Were you a teacher?" Max wondered. "Mickey said you worked for a university. What did you teach?"

"No, I was mostly an administrator, for student services. There were times I was teaching students, but more one-on-one, like a mentor, not in a classroom."

"Like now? With me?"

"Maybe, but I usually taught them specific skills, like how to open meetings and how to work with a group when one student kept interrupting other students. They would ask me for ideas or help when they needed it."

"That's how I like to learn," Max sighed. "I wish you could have been my teacher. It's really sad that you're dying when I just met you."

Time is suspended in hospice.

Grace had felt cut off from the outside world during the first months of the pandemic, but this was different. Instead of being obsessed with the news, whatever was happening on the outside didn't seem to matter.

It reminded her of when she was first at home with a new baby, nursing every two hours, never even sure if she would get to shower, feeling accomplishment if she got dressed before lunch—or supper. The world had gone on without her and she'd been too tired to care.

And here they were: changing diapers, filling sippy cups with juice, organizing their days around naps.

Mickey was in charge of the medications, staying on top of the pain, balancing the increasing need for sleep with Jocelynn's desire to be awake and lucid.

Jocelynn ate regular food for the first two weeks or so, but in smaller and smaller quantities. She said it was hard to swallow, so Mickey continued to make the pasta dishes that she loved to smell, but pureed a cupful until it was a soup, richly flavored but no lumps.

There were hours of quiet, softly massaging her feet or hands with lotion, flute music playing in the background. Mickey kept a playlist of classics playing on the speaker: Simon and Garfunkel, Neil Young, blues, and reggae.

Each day here was a new mix, fostered by the arbitrary stuff of memories. They were never chronological. If Jocelynn mentioned something, Mickey found a way to weave it in.

One afternoon, trying to distract Jocelynn from a cramp that was not responding to a hot compress, Mickey asked her what she liked to dance to. He was surprised when she said, "Latin. I did a mean salsa in my day."

"I never learned to salsa," Grace said.

"Well, then it's about time," Jocelynn retorted.

So, Mickey made a pitcher of margaritas. Mickey and Grace got silly, laughing their way through a YouTube video on how to salsa, slipping in their socks on the hardwood floor as Jocelynn laughed along. Until she abruptly, in the middle of a song, fell asleep.

"She was happy tonight," Mickey said. "That music brought her back to a sweet spot."

Every afternoon, they watched TV reruns from the 70s: *Mary Tyler Moore, All in the Family, M*A*S*H*. Then the 80's: *Golden Girls, Hill St. Blues*. They started a *Cosby* episode but turned it off after ten minutes.

"I remember how much I liked Bill Cosby," Jocelynn said to Grace. "I'd wished I had a dad like that. And then he turned out to be swarmy."

"I felt the same way," Grace acknowledged. "It felt personal, like a betrayal. I would have trusted him with my kids."

"I'm trying to remember a movie, or maybe a show? It was about a priest and a woman, star-crossed, set in Australia?" Jocelynn asked, her mind going down a tangent that only made sense in her head.

"Yes, I can't remember the name. But who was the actor that played the priest? It was—Richard Chamberlain!" Grace sounded triumphant, like she'd beat the odds in a memory game.

"But what was the show?"

Grace realized that they could have the answer in seconds.

"Let me google it," she said, typing in Richard Chamberlain and Australia and TV in the 80s.

"*The Thorn Birds*," she read aloud. "1983. Four episodes. 467 minutes total. That's a big commitment."

"Damn, but he was one hottie of a priest," Jocelynn sighed.

"Wanna' watch it?" Grace asked.

"Sure," Jocelynn said. "No pressing plans for the next few evenings."

A few days later, chopping onions and peppers, Mickey played some old CDs, choir music with a Gregorian chant, as background to cooking. It was soothing. He noticed that Jocelynn, her eyes closed, was mouthing the words in Latin, her head sliding ever so slightly from side to side with the music.

"When did you learn Gregorian chant?" he asked her. "Not like that was a part of every Catholic service when you were growing up."

"I was in the convent for a while, Mickey. Didn't Joanne ever tell you that?"

"No, she did not. Is there a reason she did not? Or why *you* are just *now* telling me?"

"It never came up," Jocelynn replied. "Anyway, we were a very Italian-Catholic family. To go to a public school would have been heresy. Most generations, or so we were told, had one son who became a priest, thus scoring heaven points for the entire family."

"Heaven points?" Mickey asked. "There's a score card?"

"No, more than a family with a priest is more blessed. But our mom had a very rough delivery with Joanne, almost bled out, ended up with a hysterectomy. No son, only two daughters."

"So, you assumed the role?"

"Not really, I wasn't pushed or anything. I did feel a calling, but more I think because of what I imagined monastic or convent life to be. I liked consistency, predictability, quiet. Kind of the opposite of home."

This Mickey had heard about from Joanne, in bits and pieces, their father an alcoholic who tried to stay sober but got angry and blaming to justify drinking, like "You knew that would make me..." When he drank, he'd be alternately mushily sweet or enraged.

"I can see how all that would be appealing," Mickey pondered.

"Exactly. No wondering which dad would walk in the door. No yelling."

"What order were you in?"

"A very old Italian order, founded in 1692. The Sisters of St. Lucy Filippini. Just a very small presence in the United States. Mostly teaching, but also hospitals and orphanages. They were educating women back in Italy for centuries. Five nuns came over on a steamer, the St. Anne, in 1910 and their motherhouse is in Morristown, New Jersey."

"And didn't you live near there then, in New Jersey?"

"Yes. Made it convenient."

"So how old were you when..."

"Fourteen," Jocelynn replied. "They had a program for girls who were called to enter after 8th grade, complete high school there but live the convent life."

"Jesus," Mickey said. "Your parents let you make that kind of decision at fourteen? I could barely pick out my own clothes at that age."

"Well, it was a safe choice. The parish priest approved, the nuns at our school approved. And who were mere parents to interfere with a calling from God, a 'vocation?'"

"You wanted to?"

"I desperately wanted to, Mickey. Leaving Joanne alone at home was the only thing I regret."

"But you ended up leaving. When? Why?"

"That's complicated. It took me a year to stop being hyper-vigilant and anxious. The simplicity helped—my private space was just a bed, dresser, lamp, and bedside table. Yet the shared spaces were beautiful, especially the chapel, all high ceilings and old wood. It was so rich in community. There was structure: pray, school, work, pray, meals, outdoor recreation, homework, pray. No surprises."

"But you left?"

"Our father died of a stroke, or that's what we were told. Maybe he'd passed out one time too many and—it doesn't matter. I was 16, had been in the convent for two years. My mother was a mess. Joanne was only nine. I came home to help out, with the funeral and such, for what I thought would be a few weeks. And I never went back."

Mickey took a moment to process this. *There is so much we do not know about people we think we know*, he thought.

"That sounds like a no-choice situation," Mickey observed.

"It was. I guess I could have gone back. But the guilt would have done me in. How could I pretend to be a good person, do all that praying, while abandoning my sister and mom when they needed me?"

"What did you do?"

"It was summer, so I waited a month for things to calm down. Then I walked to the high school, got the papers, forged my mother's signature, enrolled myself, and found a part-time job. Mom clerked at a store, and she kept working. But it was all she could do. We never talked about whether I'd return. She'd been depressed before, but it got worse when I was gone, and I hadn't realized. And no Prozac back then."

"Did you feel guilty? Like you should have known?" Mickey

wondered.

"No," Jocelynn replied. "I'm glad I didn't. I'd have felt compelled to return earlier and that would have gutted me."

"But fifty years later, you still remember the Latin?"

Jocelynn grinned proudly. "Want me to sing something?"

"Yeah, I think I do."

Jocelynn started, slowly, softly, in what sounded like a dirge. *"Dies irae, dies illa, solvet saeclum in favilla..."* She continued for another minute, unintelligible consonants and vowels running together.

"What does it mean?" Mickey asked.

"It's about the day of wrath, judgment day, usually sung at a formal Requiem Mass. It's not uplifting, more judgmental, but the sound is comforting if you don't understand the lyrics."

"Is it something you would want?"

Jocelynn snorted and waved a hand. "God, no, Mickey. I'm not expecting a send-off, especially not with COVID, but I'd want something with rhythm and a strong beat. Dancing music."

Later that night, Mickey shared with Grace what Jocelynn had told him.

"How could I be married to Joanne and never know about that part of her life?" he asked. "I knew her dad died when she was young, but not the rest. When she talked, it sounded more like it was a relief, that life was better, easier, after he died."

"It probably was for her," Grace pointed out. "Her big sister was back, they got into a more normal family life. She was too young to appreciate what it took for her sister to make that happen."

"It makes sense then that she'd block a lot out," Mickey said.

"Who knows what 'makes sense?'" Grace concluded. "I sure as hell don't."

Jocelynn faded quickly. Mickey continued to cook meals that filled the room with aromas, even when Jocelynn could no longer eat. But she would inhale, sigh, and smile.

Breathing changes when someone is actively dying. There are often longer and longer pauses between breaths. The sound is different. Mickey did not know how or why, but, when he'd leaned over to say,

"Good morning, Jocelynn," he knew.

Jocelynn had been in a semi-comatose state for about a day, but he'd felt she could still hear, and he'd kept talking to her, kept playing music. He thought he saw her eyes moving beneath closed eyelids when music started. Later he'd wonder if he'd imagined it.

Grace had a small sponge with cool water, and she moved it gently over Jocelynn's dry lips, inside her open mouth. Her mouth was in a fixed rictus.

"It's all okay, Jocelynn. You can let go." Mickey said. "Your body has done a great job holding together but it's wrapping up. You're going to have a great adventure, a journey. Soon you'll be walking through a beautiful forest, with ferns and tall trees. Sunshine is filtering down through the branches. And there's a lake, so clear, like glass, and every tree is mirrored in it. The water is cool, but not too cold. Joanne is waiting for you. She has been hoping you'd come find her."

Grace didn't remember everything Mickey said, but he just kept talking, reassuring, gently painting a picture of somewhere beautiful. Telling Jocelynn that she was almost there.

And then there was no more breathing.

Mickey leaned in, cheek to cheek, to listen.

Grace stood next to the bed, her hand resting on Jocelynn's arm, which she'd been, ever so softly, massaging.

Could this be death?

Grace had never witnessed human death before. Not her parents. Not her husband. She felt humbled, honored, to be included. It was—sacred? A sacred transition?

And then Mickey took his hand off Jocelynn's head, and Grace lifted her hand from Jocelynn's arm. They let go.

Mickey made them coffee. They sat on the couch, across from Jocelynn, hands encircling the hot mugs. Grace slid closer to Mickey and rested her head on his shoulder.

"Now I know what a good death looks like," Grace said. "I'd kill for one this good."

When they finished their coffee, Mickey called Molly, explained, and asked if she thought Max would want to come over to say goodbye. Ten minutes later, Molly and Max were at the front door. Max looked teary but determined. He walked over to Jocelynn's bed and looked at her.

"Why is her mouth like that?" he asked Mickey.

"It's what happens sometimes at the end, but she wasn't in pain. It does look a little scary though," Mickey explained.

Max lifted his hand and put it on Jocelynn's arm, then reached up and stroked the side of her head. "I really liked you. You would have made a great Grammy for someone. Maybe next time?" Then he stepped back.

"She's not really here, is she?" he asked, to no one specifically.

"Just her body. Her spirit is flying somewhere," Molly answered.

Max turned to face them. Tears were sliding down his cheeks, but he didn't wipe them. "Thank you for letting me come," he said to Mickey and Grace. "I'm glad I got to say goodbye even if her mouth does look a little scary."

After Max and Molly left, Mickey called hospice. A nurse came over, took nonexistent vitals, and declared Jocelynn dead. Then Grace and the nurse washed Jocelynn's body and dressed her in a soft oversized sweater and long flowy skirt. After an hour or so, the funeral home came, and with a reserved, respectful solemnity, put her body on a gurney and wheeled her out.

Her body would be cremated by evening, her ashes in a box.

Grace looked at Mickey, seeing the lines of exhaustion in his face, the emptiness of his eyes. He had been on call, 24/7, for a month.

"C'mon Mickey," she said. "It's time for a little nap."

Mickey napped for five hours.

Later that night, after Mickey called Jocelynn's friends, they put the hospice supplies in the garage. Then they collapsed on the couch in the living room.

"So, how are you doing?" Mickey asked. "What are you thinking about? You're— pensive?"

Grace took a moment to collect her thoughts. "First, I'm really glad that I could do this with you. I wasn't sure at first how I'd be, and I didn't want to let you down. But, more, I'm realizing how little I understand of the specific grief process that everyone in the group that I supposedly facilitate is going through."

"What do you mean?"

"They each have someone they loved who's dead. But their pain is so much worse because of *how* their mom or son or wife or husband died. They couldn't do what you just did, what we did, for Jocelynn. They were cheated of a good death. And COVID is a horrible death. And every day there are images plastered all over the media to remind them of just *how* horrible..." Grace's voice stopped mid-sentence.

She paused, then continued. "I haven't told the group about Jocelynn and hospice. On some gut level it feels cruel, even sadistic, to tell them what I was doing—what I got to do, to give—that they never could..."

Mickey said nothing. He just reached for her, pulling her to him, holding her in the darkness.

Zed

Zed was working—volunteering—on the campaign to re-elect Donald Trump. It had started with a phone call on a Saturday morning in September.

He'd never received a personal call like that: "Hi, Zed, my name is Nick Watkins and I see here that you are a loyal supporter of Donald Trump. I'm asking for your help with this re-election campaign on his behalf. We need citizens to bring out the vote, and so we're reaching out to you..."

Now Zed called people, asking for their financial support to help Make America Great Again. Because of COVID, he mostly did it from home. He and Cherry would each take an hour making calls while the other one watched the kids.

Zed believed that Donald Trump understood what most people could not see. He and Cherry had watched YouTube videos about how Trump was secretly rounding up Satanists. He was going to put a stop to child trafficking and destroy the Democrat's cabal. But Trump wasn't bragging about it. He knew that to get them all, he had to keep it under wraps. But he could let out clues, like drops, in his speeches at his rallies, so they all would know he understood and was working on it.

Trump was shrewd. He could communicate with a wink and a "Well, we'll see how it turns out." His whole life he'd made deals and come out ahead, which was why he had mega-millions. And he cared about working families. His own kids were working in the White House with him, so he must be a good dad. Most kids can't wait to get away from their parents.

Molly

Molly and Mike had not missed a Tuesday night Zoom in two months. Their calls lasted at least two hours. And they texted almost every day.

It was hard to avoid politics when they were bombarded with political ads every moment of every day. The outcome felt bigger than which political party would "rule." *Democracy* was at stake.

"Trump was as surprised as the rest of us when he got elected," Molly argued. "He likes power, but responsibility? Accountability? Not in his wheelhouse. It was like some TV show to him. He wants to be president for the title, the image, to satisfy his narcissism."

Mike grinned. "You are one harsh woman, Molly McDonald."

"No, I'm rather restrained," Molly countered. "I haven't used the f-bomb since Max called me out. And I miss using it. Not as a verb, but more as a preferred adverb and adjective."

"For the record, David called me out as well," Mike added. "But I was ranting on DeSantis at the time. He acts like he has the entire state of Florida in his pocket when he won by a quarter of a percentage point last year. The man looks so damn good on paper: Yale, JAG, blah-blah-blah. But he rejects global warming, medicine, science in general. If he keeps basing every decision on how it appeals to Trump's base, not science, we're going to end up with more and more people dying."

"Oh, shit, Mike. We're doing it again," Molly interrupted. "We go down this rabbit hole every time. The same dark, stinky, dead-end rabbit hole. No cute bunnies in this hole."

They both laughed for a moment, looking at each other through their screens.

"If we have to run away from the President of the United States, what would be your preferred destination?" Mike mused. "Let's do some pretend vacation planning. I like the idea of Canada but maybe someplace warmer."

"I told you my brother lives in Panama, right? So, we'd have family there to help us acclimate. But they shut their borders, and no one can get in. They enforce strict curfews with big fines. No 'I have a right to not mask' down there.'"

"So, what countries are open? That will take Americans?"

"We're not popular. Maybe google it and go from there. Okay?"

Grace & Theo

"**Can you give me** a quick overview?" Grace asked Theo at the start of their next session.

"It's been a blur," Theo said. "We're all strung out. But the kids are okay, better now that they are back in school. We're all together. Work is still insane. But I've been told that I have an anger problem."

She scribbled something in her notes. "So, can you tell me about this anger problem?"

"Medical treatment is not supposed to discriminate in any way," he said. "The guy who shot the gun gets the same quality of care as the guy he shot. At least that's the theory."

Grace could sense that there was more he wanted to say. She raised her eyebrow. "But?"

"It isn't fair," he sighed. "I never really questioned it before, but now? Why should people who refused to mask or distance, who've infected others and spread the virus, go to the front of the line in the hospital over people who've been respecting all the protocols? Just because they're 'sickest?' And why do I have to risk my life—and the lives or health of my family and co-workers—to provide care for people who are meanwhile telling me that it's all a conspiracy?" Theo's voice was tight and clipped.

"Is this happening a lot?"

"Every damn day," he replied. "Some patients are really scared, finally realizing they were duped by all the Fox News bullshit. But others are still arguing. They're telling doctors and nurses what to do, demanding hydroxychloroquine, or whatever bogus treatment is plastered all over the internet that week, while we waste precious time explaining what they're demanding isn't worth shit."

"Which means you're angry every day?"

"My job description never included, 'persuade assholes to let you save their lives.' Not when there are people lined up who need and want medical treatment."

Theo's voice had gotten louder as he spoke. He stopped abruptly, shook himself like a dog after a bath, and then resumed in a lower volume.

"We all feel angry every day. But I've had a hard time containing it. I told a man last week, 'Fine by me if you want to be an idiot. Just sign this form that you're refusing treatment, that way we have space for someone who wants to stay alive.'"

Grace paused, wrote something down, then looked up. "And that did not go over well?"

"He started yelling at me, and I yelled back."

"Did you get in trouble?"

"If they didn't need RTs so bad, it would have been a censure. But they just pulled me aside, told me to go for a walk and calm down."

"What happened to the patient?"

He shrugged. "I have no idea. He wasn't in the ER when I got back. He was either admitted or sent home. I don't care which one."

Theo kind of shut down after that.

Grace ended up talking about how he had a right to be angry, that it was legitimate, but exploding was not sustainable. He could lose his job, but he could also lose the respect of his colleagues.

She recommended a book on anger, with tools for diffusing anger before exploding. But the tools generally involved interrupting the anger build, separating yourself from the engagement, and then reflecting, looking at the short-term gratification versus the long-term consequences.

There was no time for self-reflection in the ER, or on any COVID unit. It was like telling a soldier to take a break and think it through before he returned fire.

"I know you don't have time to read, but if you keep the book next to your bed, and just read a few lines, maybe a page before passing out, the content will settle in your brain overnight and may impact your behavior."

Theo chuckled. "Do you have evidence-based data on that?"

"Nope," Grace deadpanned. "Nada. But it works."

Grace & Alex

Alex had been calling Grace more frequently, spontaneously, not scheduled. On WhatsApp or something like that. Molly had downloaded it for her.

Grace remembered the days when a long-distance call was something special and an international call was reserved for a crisis. Now there were options for calling that were instantaneous and free. When she'd done rotations on military bases overseas, she'd used Skype. She could still hear the doo-doo-doo the computer would make when she got a call.

Damn, she thought, *this technology-shit makes me feel old.*

It was fun to hear the WhatsApp alert and know that when she picked up, her son would be waiting. It had been many years since they had had any kind of easy communication.

Alex talked about what life was like in Panama, how they were coping with quarantines and lockdowns, what was opening and what remained closed. He and Graciella had started a home garden, which had never been worth the work when they had abundant produce fresh daily—and cheap—at the local market. But now it gave them a shared project.

Grace envied their access to the ocean. To be able to walk at sunset or sunrise on a beach, to cool off in the waves? That seemed heavenly.

So, when she heard the ringtone on this crisp October afternoon, she was expecting a light conversation about what they were doing, and then she would share the latest Max anecdote, or what they were cooking.

"Mom," Alex said as soon as she picked up, "Bad news. Really bad. Graciella's father died last night. Heart attack. Graciella is broken up."

Grace's demeanor shifted. "Oh, Alex, I am so sorry. And didn't he just make it through COVID in July?"

"It was COVID that damaged his heart," Alex said. "He got through

COVID after a month but never got his strength back. When they did tests, his heart was damaged. But they were still in 'wait-and-see' because surgery was..." Alex's voice cracked, and he could not finish the sentence.

Grace heard her son weeping, realizing how attached he'd become to his father-in-law. In a momentary flash, she also realized she'd never grieved *with* her son when *his* father had been killed. So much had happened so quickly that there had not been time. And then...

"You loved him a lot," she said softly. "This is going to be really hard for you and Graciella both."

"You never met him," Alex said. "I wish you'd known him."

Her heart sank. "I really wish that too," she said. "Do you want me to tell Molly?"

"Yeah, please. Look, I have to go. I'll call in a few days."

Covid Grief Group

Grace was getting ready to head over to the weekly grief group. Over the weeks it had become something she found herself looking forward to. It mattered to everyone that they meet in person even if they had to sit in a circle with distance between each chair. For each of them, this was now a safe place to vent in what felt more and more like an unsafe and hostile world. Or to just listen and recognize that they were not alone. Even better, they often went out for supper or a drink afterwards. Someplace with a big deck or patio, of course. Grace never joined them. This was their time to just be friends.

She parked her car and began walking to the garden. There was, if the raised voices were any sign, an animated discussion already in place. She slipped into the remaining chair.

"I miss her so damn much," Larry was saying. "I think of every time she wanted me to do something, like go to the farmer's market or shopping or a movie. And I was too busy, or lazy. Or I just wanted to watch whatever stupid game was on the TV. I'd give anything to make it up to her, to just feel her touch."

"You don't think she knows that?" Cheryl abruptly interjected.

"Jasmine knows that you loved her even when you were being a lazy ass. She probably even loved the lazy ass parts of you. I loved Robert and he could be a pain in the tushie. I still pat his side of the bed in the middle of the night, when I'm mostly asleep, and think he must be talking a whiz. I forget he's really gone."

The group all turned to face Cheryl. She was generally the quietest of all of them. She listened and nodded but didn't talk much. Supportive, yes, but little disclosure. She had yet to come to the weekly potluck.

"Why, Cheryl, I do believe that was the first time you said your husband's name," Grace speculated. "So, it's Robert. Did folks call him Bob?"

"No," Cheryl said. "It was always Robert. He was a little stuffy and the Robert fit." Then Cheryl made a sound, something between a snort and a laugh. "The hardest thing about being in this group is that I'm not sure I'm entitled to be here, although you're the only people I talk to, ever, and I like to listen. But I'm not grieving like you are."

"Everyone grieves differently," Grace said. "There are so many different time-lines and..."

"No," Cheryl interrupted Grace, her arm raised, waving away whatever she'd been about to say. "I understand all of that. But I'm not *grieving* Robert. Robert was a pretty rigid man, and he liked control. He controlled most everything in our lives: the money, what we bought, where we went on vacation, what he thought I should wear..."

Grace noted that Kayla's eyebrows wrinkled at those last words, and she wiggled her nose, like she'd suddenly smelled something unpleasant.

"Yet you say you loved him?" Grace asked softly.

"I always thought I did, but maybe that was because we were married, and good Christian women say that," Cheryl answered. "But listening to all of you, I'm not sure. I was mostly scared after he died, scared that I couldn't make it alone. He always told me I'd never manage without him. I knew nothing about our finances. We never talked about any of it."

"Are you still scared?" Grace asked.

"Not as much. I'm learning something new every day. I paid the bills online last week for the first time. A woman at the bank helped me. She said I can come back next month, and we'll do it together."

Cheryl paused, as if bracing herself to admit what she did not want to admit.

"I feel guilty saying this, but I feel relief. I used to get anxious when I'd hear the garage door opening. He was always looking at what I was doing and telling me how I was doing it wrong," Cheryl hesitated, a hint of a smile showing in the corners of her mouth. "I ordered out Chinese to be delivered last week, whatever I wanted from a menu on a website, and the world didn't end. Robert was a tightwad. I'd never ordered out before."

The group seemed to take a slow collective inhale to consider the far-reaching implications of that innocuous admission.

"Do you feel lonely?" Debra asked.

"I've been lonely my whole life. I'm like a turtle. Stay inside my shell most of the time. It's safer in the shell."

"Well, sounds to me like you have a lot to work through," Beth said. "Maybe your 'grief process' is learning who you are without Robert in charge."

They nodded as one. Grace sent a quick glance of appreciation to Beth, who acknowledged it with a wink.

"Cheryl, I appreciate you speaking up," Grace concluded. Then she gestured to the circle, asking, "So, how have the rest of you been doing this week?"

A few days later, Grace was googling "COVID grief" when an article popped up with a big cover photo. At first, Grace thought she was looking at a picture of Arlington National Cemetery, but then realized it was not headstones but flags. Hundreds? No. It was thousands. *Thousands of flags.* They covered the entire D.C. Armory Parade Ground, in front of the RFK Memorial Stadium in Washington, D.C.

In America: How Could This Happen? was the name of the installation.

An artist had gotten permission to use the parade grounds, enlisted the support of a landscape company, solicited volunteers. The plan was to have one flag for every life lost to the pandemic, but the number now exceeded all predictions. When initially planned, it was anticipated to be about 170,000 flags. That was felt, at that time, to be an unthinkable number. By the end of the exhibit, there were 267,000.

Grace had never heard of the artist. Suzanne Brennan Firstenburg had come to art later in life. She'd worked years in a corporate setting, more years at the U.S. Senate. For two decades, she was also a hospice volunteer. It was when she took a sculpting class that her life shifted and began to move in a totally different direction. At 61, she was still emerging as an artist.

That's me, too, Grace thought. *Emerging. Just not sure how.*

For Firstenburg, art was a means to illustrate social justice. In the interview, she explained that when she realized that the casualties of the pandemic were being dismissed as mere statistics, and individual lives lost in the sheer numbers, she had to do *something.* Something that would make *each* life visible. *Each* life *real.* In one place.

"Every flag has a soul," she was quoted as saying. And every flag was the same size, each life valued and represented equally.

Grace had no answer to the query: *In America: How Could This Happen?* It took hours to deconstruct all of the reasons—the failures, denial, ego, indifference—that had contributed. Any answer was incomplete.

The question itself? That was for history to explain.

Grace made copies of the article, with the photos, to bring to the group. They couldn't fly to D.C., but she wanted them to be aware that there was a flag, however temporary, for Jasmine and Mariana and Dean, for Kayla's mom, Beth's parents, and Cheryl's Robert, for all the relatives that Shawnee would never see again. She wanted them to know that their losses were not invisible.

Grace wished they all could go, put a name and words on *their* flag and plant it among the over 250,000 flags.

That number was so insane. Who would have believed…

Grace & Katrina

Grace and Katrina were having a late lunch on the outdoor patio of Zen Zero, a local restaurant. It was the first time that Kat had been in a restaurant since before COVID. She was masked and had a bottle of sanitizer handy. And so did Grace.

Grace had requested a table at the far end of the patio, and they arrived at 2 p.m., after the lunch crowd had left. There were only four other people, and they were at least 15 feet away.

It still felt risky. Grace didn't want to be seen eating out, even on the patio. There was a hierarchy of cautiousness. She knew people who'd judge, who'd see this as irresponsible. But she was so ready for a lunch out.

"Are you okay with this?" Grace asked Katrina as they were seated. "We can get something to go if not."

"No, let's stay. My life sucks so bad right now that I'm not as anxious as if I hadn't had COVID. It's like, how much worse could it get?"

It was a rhetorical question that did not require a response.

When the waiter came, masked, standing five feet away, they ordered.

Grace went for her staple: a salad with both shrimp and chicken, called, for some reason, the Vietnamese Spring Roll Salad.

Katrina asked the waiter, "What is the spiciest dish you have?"

"The spiciness is rated next to the dish, ma'am. But the spiciest ones can be really intense."

Kat looked down again at the menu. "I'll try the pad prik."

The waiter looked like he wanted to offer alternatives, that this nice lady was making a big mistake, but Kat's tone was final.

"What's that about?" Grace asked.

"There is some anecdotal research that intense, over-the-top spiciness, might arouse dead taste buds."

"So, I guess we won't be sharing, huh?"

"Nope," Kat replied, then peered across the table at Grace. "You look like you're waiting to say something? Just spit it out."

"Okay," Grace replied. "I keep thinking about what you said, monitoring *how* you say something more than what you say. Like how it is for girls and women? That it's not feminine to show anger. If men get angry, that's masculine and strong. But women show anger, and they're bitches." By the time Grace finished, Kat's head was nodding *no-no-no*.

"It's way more than gender. White anger is righteous, Black anger is dangerous," she corrected. "Black male anger is never just masculine and strong. It's threatening. Black words are never just words. A Black kid talking back must be shut down *before* he gets *aggressive*."

"So, regardless of whether the anger is appropriate or justified, we're back to the focus on *how* something is being said and not the content?"

"We're talking about 'tone policing' here," Katrina said. "Whites do it unconsciously, trying to shut Black people down, but we do it to ourselves too. My mama was on me about 'attitude' a lot. I learned early to tone myself down around some white teacher or even friend. It was a tightrope: 'How am I coming across?' This constant inner judgmental voice. Like if I find the perfect mix of language and affect, words and tone, the fragile white people might actually hear my content for itself?"

"That sounds exhausting," Grace said.

"And it never stops. I heard it as a kid, then in college, then law school, then when working, even in court."

"What exactly did you hear?"

"Well, I told you one example. That history class? Education is no protection against feeling white fragility. If a person has a Ph.D.? Or a law degree? I used to think education would override bias. Now I think it can entrench it."

"What have you been told? To shut you down?"

"I've been told that my language was divisive, or my tone was not engaging. That I didn't need to sound upset or angry to make a point. Just be nice. Smile more. Be more thoughtful about how you talk to white people if you want them to join your cause."

"What cause?" Grace asked.

"Darned if I know. Don't all Black people have some agenda? Don't we need white approval and support to be treated as equal?"

Katrina had stopped talking, lost in her head. Remembering?

"In my first year of practicing law, I did some Legal Aid work. I was representing a Black woman in a shoplifting case. Just a judge, no jury. Yes, she'd lifted several items and stupidly put them in a grocery bag. But the total value was about $75, and it was kids' shoes, two kids' backpacks, and school supplies. The prosecution was talking jail time. When was the last time you heard of a white mom going to jail for taking shoes and school supplies? Huh? So, I was asserting that the case should never have made it to a courtroom, that it wasted taxpayer money, and that race was the sole determining factor for it becoming more than a warning or a fine. This was in a rural town with only white male district attorneys, white male judges, white cops."

"What happened?"

"The judge said that I would never make it as a lawyer if I continued to display such unwarranted racial bias. That my client was guilty, a thief. That I was making this about race when race was irrelevant."

"What happened?"

"Guilty. Sentenced to 30 days in jail, but she'd already done 36 because she couldn't pay bail. Her kids almost ended up in foster care, which would have been a nightmare, because then she would have been an 'unfit' mother who'd been in jail. But she'd reached a cousin who'd picked the kids up and took them home—for what turned into 36 days. Oh, and the mom lost her minimum wage job."

"That sounds so unfair." As soon as she said the words, Grace heard how empty they were. How pathetically empty.

"I felt horrible," Kat continued. "Like puke-in-the-courthouse-bathroom horrible. I screwed my client with my agenda, my 'defense strategy,' of showing how this was a case of racial injustice."

"But it was," Grace retorted.

"No, Grace, listen to me. Sure, it was racist, in so many ways. But they already knew that. All the white judges, prosecutors, cops. Pointing it out just made them have to refute it. To vehemently deny any such false allegation against their system. They had to teach me, this young, uppity, Black woman lawyer, to appreciate how much power they had should I ever make this same accusation again."

"And did it teach you?"

"Yeah, it did. I practiced keeping my voice soft, a gentle cadence, and to exploit their bias." Kat's voice took on a fake Cockney accent as she said, "Yes, my lord, my client did take the items, but nothing for herself. Just for her children. Their father has abandoned them all. She works a minimum wage job, trying to hold her family together. School was starting, and she wanted her children to have backpacks and shoes that didn't have holes. But she knows she made a poor choice. Just being in the courtroom has been frightening enough, and the state has now provided her a social worker, for which she is grateful, so she is now aware of resources and how to ask for help for indigent mothers like herself. This will never happen again. She is deeply sorry for taking up the court's valuable time."

"But none of that is..."

"True? Hah! That fairy tale? First off, Dad didn't *abandon* anyone. He was serving 14 months for a stupid bar fight. A white guy would *never* have done time. No weapons, just fists. White kids told the same story, that he jumped them—as if a Black man would pick a fight with three white frat boys? He was a 6'3" Black man who stopped at the wrong bar in the wrong neighborhood. In Louisiana, decades ago. But my version—abandonment—elicits judicial mercy. I learned to create a narrative that reinforces stereotypes, that does nothing to challenge the system. I learned, my friend, to do what my mother had taught me: 'Talk nice to the white folks. Don't give them anything to use against you.'"

They paused to appreciate the bowls and plates that were being placed in front of them.

Why is it that food someone else cooks, someone else serves, and someone else will clean up, is more appealing? Grace wondered.

The sun was shining, the air crisp. It was, in so many ways, a beautiful autumn day. They ate, quietly, slowly. Racism wasn't going anywhere, and nothing had to be resolved today.

Max

Max was thinking about *normal* again.

"Do you remember when we could go to a store or school or anywhere and not wear a mask?" he asked his mom.

"Yes, but that feels like a lifetime ago," Molly replied.

"It wasn't a lifetime. It was just five months ago. We didn't start wearing masks until May or June," Max corrected. "Because they didn't know before then that people could infect other people when they didn't seem sick. But also, because there were not enough masks for the nurses and doctors in the hospitals, so every mask needed to go to them first because they were stuck all day and night with sick people."

"I forgot that, Max," Molly said. "Were we really not wearing masks? What did we do?"

"Washed our hands a lot and used sanitizer and didn't get close to other people. You even sprayed the outside of the milk and juice containers and all the food that came in packages. Remember when we went to five different stores to get sanitizer, but they were sold out and when you found it you bought twenty bottles? But it was the Dollar Tree so they were just $1 each."

"You remember all that?" Molly asked, laughing.

"Yes. And you found some songs that lasted twenty seconds, so I didn't have to count when I washed my hands," Max continued. "I could just sing or hum."

"Yeah, we did sing washing our hands," Molly mused.

"Now it feels weird to go into a store without a mask. And we wear masks in school. And our desks are more separated."

"What else is different, Max?" Molly asked.

"We're a lot more afraid of people," Max replied. "Even nice people, people we know, could be dangerous. No hugging. No touching."

"That's sad for me," Molly said.

"It's a whole different normal," Max added. "Do you think we will ever go back to the old normal?"

"I don't know, Max. I hope so. But I really don't know."

HISTORICAL CONTEXT: OCTOBER 2020

Oct. 2: President Trump announces he and First Lady Melania Trump have tested positive for COVID-19. More than a dozen White House staff and aides test positive shortly after. Trump leaves the White House for treatment at Walter Reed National Military Medical Center.

Oct. 3: In a virtual campaign event, Biden admits that he has advised some governors to not publicly endorse him, fearing that the Trump administration would retaliate by withholding federal resources to their respective states.

Oct. 4: The *New York Times* quotes Trump Chief of Staff Mark Meadows: "The president's vitals over the last 24 hours were very concerning, and the next 48 hours will be critical in terms of his care. We're still not on a clear path to a full recovery."

Oct. 5: "Don't be afraid of COVID." – *Donald Trump.*

Oct. 9: The Presidential Debate Committee cancels the second debate as Trump refused to participate virtually.

Oct. 12: "I went through it. Now they say I'm immune. I can feel—I feel so powerful." – *Donald Trump.*

Oct. 18: "If I'd listened to the scientists, we would right now have a country that would be in a massive depression. Instead—we're like a rocket ship. Take a look at the numbers." – *Donald Trump*

Oct. 19: U.S. death toll passes 220,000.

Oct. 19: White House senior advisor Jared Kushner says Black Americans must "want to be successful." Kushner told Fox News that while Donald Trump's policies can help Black people, "he can't want them to be successful more than they want to be successful."

Oct. 19: "They're getting tired of the pandemic, aren't they? You turn on CNN that's all they cover. COVID. COVID. Pandemic. COVID. COVID. They're trying to talk everybody out of voting. People aren't buying it, CNN, you dumb bastards." – *Donald Trump*

Oct. 23: The United States has (at least) 82,600 new cases of coronavirus, the highest daily level of cases in a single day.

Oct. 27: "Well, we have a spike in cases. You ever notice, they don't use the word death. They use the word cases... Like, Barron Trump is a case. He has sniffles. He was sniffling. One Kleenex, that's all he needed... But he's a case." – *Donald Trump*

Oct. 30: "Our doctors get more money if someone dies of COVID...and so, 'When in doubt, choose COVID.'" – *Donald Trump*

November 2020

Katrina

It was on November 1st that Katrina maybe, possibly, actually, smelled something. At first, she thought she was imagining, but she was able to sniff, sniff some more, nostrils widening and closing as she pointed her head in different directions like a bird dog, and detect where it was coming from. A neighbor was burning leaves, and she knew that because she could *smell* it.

Over the next few days, her sense of smell started to return. At first it was heavier smells, a car discharge, smoke. She wore the same socks for two days and then held them up to her nose and inhaled. *Yes, yes*, she thought, *I am not imagining this. There is something.* And then she smelled her cooking, although she did cheat by putting in an insane amount of garlic and spices into a tomato sauce. Lastly were flowers, freshly mowed grass, more amorphous, lighter, not contained in a sock or a pot.

To Katrina, the smells felt like colors, dark to pastel, each level, each intensity, on a spectrum of smells. She did not want to tell anyone, not yet, until she felt that this was not a sensory mirage that could disappear as she got closer.

And then, one morning, she woke up wanting breakfast. She had not eaten her favorite kind of breakfast—eggs over-easy, crispy hash-browns, even crispier bacon, sourdough toast, raspberry jam—in eight months. When she'd tried, only once, she'd choked on the eggs, too slimy, and the hash browns and bacon had felt like chewing dirt. She'd never tried again. But now she felt desire.

She didn't make breakfast, but that morning she did feel a frisson of taste from the protein-packed smoothie that had become her morning routine. It had been, for months, something to simply swallow as quickly as possible. But now she detected—something. She rolled her tongue

210

against the roof of her mouth, along the tops of her teeth, against her gums. Then she had an idea.

It took ten minutes to find the decadent chocolate truffles she'd hidden away in a bedroom drawer. They'd been sitting there since March, when a well-intentioned friend had dropped them off in a care package. After a few attempts, which had felt like gooey sludge filling her mouth—not at all like chocolate melting—she'd put them away.

She unwrapped a truffle and delicately bit off a piece. She let it sit on her tongue, which, she had learned when researching one frustrating and depressing night when she couldn't sleep, had over two thousand tastebuds.

Not yet, she realized. But someday. Soon?

Mike

Mike was trying to keep up a good face for David. But they were all wearing thin.

David was back in school, but with masks and social distancing. It was better than trying to manage classes online at home, but it was school without the perks of school. Like the fun of hanging out, jostling up against one another in the lunchroom, shooting some hoops, laughing and poking at each other, and being kids. They had social distancing, masks, sanitizing.

The kids were all looking like small, tired adults.

And it was looking to be a shitty few months: Election, Thanksgiving. Christmas. So much to *not* look forward to.

Of course, Mike was deeply grateful that his parents had not contracted COVID. They were older and Hispanic. He was also deeply grateful that they were each other's "pod" even though it limited any contacts he had with other people. He felt that their lives depended upon him being scrupulous and diligent, taking every possible measure to avoid getting infected.

The highlight of each week was his Zoom call with Molly. Yeah, they texted back and forth, snippets, and had "venting" calls, but the Tuesday Zoom? It was when he could really let down, not keep up a front.

Mike had never felt this anxious about an election. In his mind, the Democrats won some and then the Republicans won some, and the people in each party who understood the word *compromise* made it work.

Mike often thought of a comment Trump had made about men in the military, that they were suckers or stupid. Like "What do they get out of it?" Because, to Trump, what *he* got out of it was all that mattered. He had no idea what "serving his country" even meant. And he was the Commander in Chief? All he wanted was a parade. He'd shit his pants walking the perimeter of a FOB.

Hell, Mike thought, *Trump probably didn't know that FOB meant Forward Operating Base and not just some gizmo to open doors.*

Today, November 3rd, the first Tuesday in November, was Election Day.

Mike had voted in person during the early voting period. He'd been worried that he'd get sick, or David would get sick, or his parents would get sick, or a hurricane would be used as an excuse to shut down the polls or make getting to the polls difficult. He'd imagined all the possible ways that his need to vote against Donald Trump could be thwarted. So, he'd been in line ten minutes early on the first day the polls had opened for early voting.

He could have done a mail-in ballot, the sensible COVID choice, but Trump and DeSantis had been posturing for months that mail-in ballots were compromised, and if they lost, then it was because of voter fraud.

Mike had not wanted his ballot invalidated by insane accusations.

This evening, David would be with Abuela. And Max with Uncle Mickey.

And Mike would have uninterrupted time to talk with Molly.

But considering that Molly found Trump more reprehensible than he did, Mike did not anticipate a relaxing conversation. They were both wound way too tight. This election was going to be close. And Donald despised "losers." He'd been setting up any loss as a failure of the electoral process. Because it sure as hell couldn't be him.

Cheat? Sure. Lie? No problem. But lose?

If he won, then the election was fair and secure. "Perfect.". Everyone who voted was an American patriot.

If he lost, then it was fraudulent and stolen. Exactly what every autocrat and dictator said. But they were in Africa, the Middle East, Russia, South America, Asia.

Not the U.S.A. Not until now.

No orderly, respectful transition of power this time, Mike thought. *It's going to get ugly.*

Mike needed bourbon. 80 proof. No mixer. It was going to be a long, long night.

Zed & Cherry

In the weeks leading up to the election, Zed and Cherry continued to volunteer. It felt good to be part of a winning team.

They knew that Donald Trump would be reelected. Every time they opened the computer, it was all about Trump and what he was doing and how the Dems would go to any lengths to block him. Zed sometimes felt ashamed that he'd been so ignorant, so oblivious, for so long.

It was tense because the Dems were changing the rules so that anyone could vote early, and by mail, and everybody knew that mail ballots could be forged. The only safe voting was in person, with current photo IDs that could be validated. Heck, changing things like the Dems wanted was just so illegals and even dead people could vote. They'd stuff the boxes so you couldn't separate out what was legitimate from the fakes. Then they'd roll out a few bins of "overlooked ballots" when it came down to the wire and they realized they were losing.

But there was no way that Donald Trump could lose unless the election was rigged. No damn way. And Trump was smart enough to see how they were trying to rig the election and he was preparing them that it could happen. He was letting them know he knew how corrupt things had gotten.

On election night, Cherry and Zed believed it was obvious that Trump had won. Every polling place was showing higher counts for him from the in-person legitimate votes. But, by the next morning, the totals started shifting. Days passed while they kept saying that mail-in ballots were being counted, to be patient, that this was just the process. But it wasn't "the process," it was a fix. It was obvious that ballots were being "found" because there couldn't be more mail-in than in-person voters. That had never happened.

When Biden was declared the winner, Zed and Cherry felt stunned. This could not be happening in America. How could the world not see and do *something*?

Day after day, as foreign leaders capitulated, as judges and election officials around the country also caved, they realized just how powerful and insidious the "Deep State" could be. It had not been exaggeration or hype. This cover-up, the collusion of so many "officials" was massive.

But they held together. Even discouraged, disbelieving, they kept the faith. "Where we go one, we go all," was their mantra.

Grace & Theo

Grace's "office" had moved from the gazebo, which was, in late autumn, too open to the wind and cold. Now she was meeting with clients on her small back patio, under a large restaurant-style space heater that Mickey had found on Amazon, sitting on opposite ends of a six-foot table.

Or they could Zoom.

Theo preferred being outside no matter how cold it was.

"Do you remember about ten years ago, maybe more," Theo asked, "when people would go up to someone in uniform, a lot of time in airports, and say 'Thank you for your service?'"

"Yeah, I do. It was a patriotic gesture or maybe...they were just trying to..."

"But it was more for the person saying it to feel good about themselves than anything for the serviceman—or woman. Strangers have no idea what combat is like..."

"What is your point here?" Grace interjected.

"Those 'patriotic' people, the flag-wavers, MAGA, are often the ones who are making our lives hell. We're putting *our* lives on the line for *them*. But they say COVID is a hoax, and spout conspiracy theories. Which means docs, nurses, RTs—in every damn hospital—are in on it?

Getting bribes for saying that the bodies piling up in morgues died of COVID? And then they want to 'thank me' for my service?"

"Is this happening a lot?" Grace asked.

"No," Theo replied. "I avoid going out in scrubs. But I was walking across the hospital parking lot yesterday, and this guy is getting out of a car, and he says, 'Hey, bud, thank you for your service.'"

Grace raised an eyebrow. "I'm not sure how you knew..."

"He was wearing a MAGA ball cap. His truck had Trump bumper stickers."

Oh. Grace inhaled. "And you commented on that?"

"Yeah, I asked him, 'Do you watch Fox News? You follow Donald Trump?' And he kind of pulled himself up a few inches, like hitched up his pants and shoulders in one move, and says, 'Yes, I do.'"

"I said, 'In that case, buddy, you're killing my patients and hurting my friends. You make my job a hundred times harder and more dangerous.' And then I turned and walked off. I expected him to yell out, say something, but—nothing."

Grace listened to the pent-up grief, anger, and pain. She had nothing to add.

"Do you understand what a DNR means?" Theo asked, abruptly redirecting their conversation.

"Yes," Grace replied. "Do Not Resuscitate."

"Here's the thing," he continued. "Unless there's a DNR in a patient's hospital file, we're *required* to *try* to resuscitate a person whose heart has stopped. But most ER patients don't show up with a document they keep with their wills in a safe deposit box. And that's if they'd ever signed one in the first place."

"Right," Grace said, nodding.

"COVID patients whose hearts stop do not just have heart issues. Getting it beating will not fix lungs that will never recover. So, all the extreme measures that might make a difference for someone with a heart attack, or with a different disease trajectory, are mostly hopeless with end-stage COVID. Yet every damn day we have a Code Blue where we're risking our own lives to fulfill a law that makes no sense. Because when we pound and push, like they do on TV, more virus is expelled. We are blanketed, like a mist, with the virus that has killed our patient. It is insanely dangerous."

"What is the alternative?" Grace asked.

"Just let the patient die in peace, or at least without more suffering. And set some new protocols because now," Theo said, "if we do not pound the crap out of someone who is actively dying? We're breaking the law and could get sued and lose our licenses."

"Is that happening?" Grace asked.

"Which one?" Theo asked. "Getting sued? Losing our licenses?"

"No, just letting patients die in peace, no more suffering."

"Every day," Theo answered. "Isn't that what you would want?"

Pod-Potluck

Kat was feeling, overall, very, very cranky.

Language was still crosscutting in her brain, which made her want to scream. *This damn COVID fog.* It had been months, but she still had hours, even days, when finding even basic words could be a challenge. It was embarrassing.

Kat didn't care how many times Grace or Mickey or Molly reassured her that COVID memory lapses were temporary. They weren't raised with the expectation to "be the best" if they wanted to "make it." But not "best" in a splashy or obvious way because that could make people jealous.

Simply, quietly, methodically—non-threateningly but inarguably—better.

It had taken until law school for Katrina's confidence to blossom. Until then, she'd discounted the little voice telling her that, maybe, just maybe, she was one of the smarter girls in the room. She'd always tempered the voice by reminding herself that the Ursuline Academy, and then, her fellow undergraduate students, were not the same level she'd have to face when she got to law school.

Law school was the test. She'd always feared that law school would be the "sink-or-swim." But she didn't sink. She swam. And, some days, she sailed.

And now, however, she missed working. Missed the challenges, the routines, the small but consistent feelings of accomplishment.

Mickey was picking her up any minute to go to Molly's for supper. She wanted to bail, to hole up under the covers and not come out. But then she'd have to explain, which would, ultimately, be much harder than just going.

When they got to Molly's, Grace was in the kitchen. She had a pot of decaf and a bottle of whiskey on the counter.

"You are gonna' love this," she announced, raising a tall, narrow can above her head.

"What is it?" Katrina asked.

"The best whipped cream on the planet," Grace replied. "Isigny Sainte-Mére."

"Where did you get it?" Kat's voice sounded excited. "I've never seen it for sale here. And, FYI, your pronunciation was almost okay."

"Great, as I've never heard anyone say the name. So, want some decaf with Irish whiskey and Isigny Sainte-Mere?

"Bring it on. Get the chill out of my bones."

"After supper, okay? The food is already on the table."

After a "light supper" of clam chowder, salad, and French bread toasted with gruyere, they cleared the table and moved to the living room.

Five minutes later, when all five of them were seated, four mugs of Irish coffee and one of hot cocoa in front of them, Grace ceremoniously opened the top of the can, shook it vigorously, and spiraled Isigny Sainte-Mere whipped cream in each mug.

"So, I've been thinking how white kids are *taught* to feel superior," Grace plunged in. "Like, how can they not when everything around them reinforces that the 'white way' is the 'right way?' They'd have to be blind and deaf when the books in school are by white people, most professionals they encounter are white, neighborhoods are segregated..."

"You're preaching, Gracie," Katrina interrupted.

"I looked at Max's textbooks," Grace continued, ignoring the comment. "They're a little more balanced than the total whitewash of when I was in school, but it feels like an afterthought—for bonus diversity points? *Everything* taught—history, literature, music, art, movies, science—is edited through a white lens."

"Where are you going with this?" Katrina queried, but without affect.

"It just feels so overwhelming. So lopsided. And..."

Kat realized that Grace was almost in tears. *Yup,* she thought, *when empathy hurts.*

And then Katrina thought, *I don't want to do this now. It's too hard when I feel so lousy...*

"I don't want to do this tonight," she heard herself saying. "Just not up for it."

Kat braced for the blowback: trying to persuade her, asking what was the matter, why didn't she feel up to it. But the blowback didn't come.

"What could you be up for besides more whipped cream on your coffee?" Grace asked, holding out the can.

"Can we watch *Schitt's Creek?*" Molly suggested.

"Absolutely," Kat replied.

So, they did, Molly and Max and Grace snuggled on the sofa, Katrina in the armchair with the ottoman to put her feet up, Mickey on the floor, his back against the couch.

Covid Grief Group

They were still meeting outside, huddling around large heaters with their coats on. Grace planned on moving the meetings inside once it snowed.

Grace hadn't mentioned Jocelynn or her good death. It seemed cruel to bring it up. Not just what they had not been able to do but also pushing in their faces what awful deaths the person they loved had experienced. A COVID death was the stuff of nightmares.

I'll wait, she thought. *It'll come up.*

Election Day had passed with barely a mention. The group did not talk politics, not with labels like Democrat or Republican. Grace suspected that some of them had been traditional Republicans (this was, after all, Kansas—the land of Bob Dole and Dwight Eisenhower) but they were now too wounded, too angry, to identify with a party that had turned its back on medicine.

They did agree that their parents, spouses, kids, and relatives had not died of "natural causes" but from the unnatural and malignant disregard of their fellow citizens. While some people respected CDC protocols, others didn't care enough to be bothered.

They didn't have to say it. They were faced with it every day.

When Grace asked what was on their minds, Beth jumped in. But it had nothing to do with grief.

"Do you remember that movie set in the south, where the Black housekeepers got revenge on the hoity-toity White ladies who treated them like they were invisible? What was it called?" Beth asked.

"*The Help*," interjected Kayla.

"Yeah, that's the one," Beth replied. "Well, that's how I feel at work. Invisible. They make racist and put-down-women-locker-room 'jokes.' They mock the governor's mask mandate and get mad about how this 'hoax' is hurting business. They must assume I agree with them or how could they ever talk as openly as they do?"

Beth worked at the state capitol building, in the office of the Secretary of State.

"They know they're supposed to wear masks inside, and socially distance, but they keep making a joke out of it, like wearing the masks below their noses because their glasses fog up. Like adolescent kids proving that they're cool. Some come right up to my desk and lean over to ask a question. I want to..."

"Do you tell them to go shove it up their..." Kayla interrupted.

"I say nothing. Nada. Zilch," Beth rebutted. "If I let them know that they're getting to me? I'm the bitch with no sense of humor. Then the complaints would start..."

"So, what do you want to do?" Kayla asked.

"What can I do? They have the power. And they hold grudges..."

"If you made a complaint with HR? This is a safety issue," Kayla persisted.

"And risk losing my job? Health insurance? Retirement? No thank you. I've had enough loss for one decade."

There was a collective silence as they each let that last line sink in.

"Anyone else having issues with work?" Grace asked, gesturing at the members.

After the meeting, some of the group headed over to La Parilla, a

Mexican restaurant with big outdoor heaters. Many local restaurants downtown had creatively developed outdoor seating in what used to be parking spots, with heaters, so customers didn't have to crowd inside. Beth, Larry, Kayla, Cheryl, Bill, and Debra sat at a big round table. Shawnee did not come as she had a family conference call. Luis had to go back to work.

"What are you thinking about?" Cheryl asked Kayla after they'd ordered a pitcher of margaritas and nachos. "You haven't said a word in fifteen minutes."

"Ashes," Kayla said. "That's what I'm thinking. Just ashes."

"Like ashes in a fireplace or the other kind?"

"The other kind."

"I have Jasmine's ashes in our family room," Larry volunteered. "On the sideboard, facing the window to the backyard but also where she can see the TV. I talk to her sometimes about what I'm watching."

"Mom is in the kitchen," Kayla added. "That was her favorite room. I talk to her too, more when I'm cooking. Like 'So, you think it needs more basil? Yes, definitely, more garlic as well. Good point. Can never have too much garlic.'"

"Robert's out in the garage," Cheryl said. "I had him in the living room when I first brought him home, but I kept feeling like he was staring at me, pissed-off. Like I should have been the one who died first."

"That sounds like Robert," Beth said. "So, when did you move him?"

"That night I first ordered out Chinese. I couldn't enjoy it with him watching. So, I put him in the garage. It was just going to be for a few hours, but I never brought him back in the house."

Bill and Debra just listened. Their son's body had been shipped home to them, but they were not allowed to open the coffin because his body could still be infectious. And it had taken weeks, because his body had been piled with thousands of others in makeshift morgues in NYC. They could not have a public funeral, so there had been a private graveside reading and burial. They could not face a Zoom celebration of life. They didn't know if they ever would.

"What about you, Beth?" asked Kayla.

"Mama is in the living room. Dad is in the attic. I could not have them together. Not after what he did to us."

It was the kind of conversation that was safe to have with each other, but that other people might not understand.

They talked for two hours about everything and nothing. If asked later, none of them would be able to identify exactly who or what moved them from joking around, all of them loosened up by the second pitcher of margaritas they'd shared, to an 'action plan.'

The idea that had sparked in Kayla's mind when she'd said *The Help* a few hours prior was just a wicked idea. Probably dumb. Maybe illegal? But, definitely wicked.

Which was why she couldn't drop it.

"What if we did something like *The Help*?" Kayla asked, her voice an exaggerated whisper, and a bit slurred. "We don't have to tell anybody, just know it for ourselves? A secret revenge?"

"Like do what?" Beth snorted. "Make brownies with a spooky hex?"

"Yeah, maybe. Or cookies with an invisible message."

The group met again on the Tuesday before Thanksgiving, although Grace had suggested that they could skip the holiday week. But it was their first Thanksgiving without…everyone.

Bill and Debra unexpectedly invited them, all of them, for Thanksgiving Dinner.

"Thursday at 3 p.m.? Will that work?" Debra asked brightly.

Cheryl and Kayla chimed in with, "Oh, you don't have to do that, we'll be fine." But it was immediately clear, in the sudden wetness of Bill's eyes, the fake smile on Debra's face as she looked away, that they were not asking to be polite. They were asking out of a desperate need to not have to go it alone, not sit across from each other in pandemic isolation and face the raw emptiness that was now their family.

In just moments, Cheryl and Kayla and Larry spouted versions of, "Gee, that is so nice of you to offer. What can I bring?"

Luis explained that he was visiting Mariana's cousin in Topeka. Shawnee was driving to Georgia, leaving at the crack of dawn the next morning, a whirlwind trip. She promised them that she'd only stop for gas and to pee, pack her food, wear two masks, and sanitize after every stop.

Beth said nothing. Thanksgiving was a day she'd intended, at least since last week, to ignore. Her son was working remotely from a rented Airbnb in Arizona with his girlfriend—and they had no intention of traveling. Her daughter, the one with the purple hair and multiple piercings, had made a 90-degree turn two months back, probably born from 'Anything would be better than being stuck here,' and enlisted in the Army. Beth was still in a state of shock. No more purple hair, and the ear holes were closing up. She'd finish basic training at Fort Sill in December.

Beth's parents had always hosted the holidays, and she and her three brothers had come with their kids to the farm outside Abilene. All the grandkids, nine cousins, had gone wild, chasing chickens and playing games in the barn. One year, the grandparents produced a pony, with a little cart. Another year there were three baby goats. It was the quintessential midwestern farm holiday.

But no more. The family farm was sold in September. The siblings had voted, and it had been three against one. Beth had just wanted a little more time. But it made economic sense: the pandemic had made rural property more appealing as urban people looked for where they could be safe, have space, yet work remotely.

It had sold in two weeks. Beth was socking her share, her one-quarter of the inheritance, with a financial manager, with instructions to keep it low risk.

A younger brother, who ran a business in Hutchinson, had offered to host, but each family would have to find their own lodging. His kids were still in junior high and high school, and their four-bedroom house was full up. Beth had assumed she would go, of course, but share an Airbnb.

When she'd phoned about coming down a day early to help with the cooking, she'd asked if they'd all be masking. When her brother said, "Hell, no," she'd lost it. "That's how Daddy killed Mama," she'd choked out. Then she'd called him a litany of names that would have horrified her mother. Within an hour, he'd ratted her out to the other two brothers.

So, Beth was, temporarily at least, not on speaking terms with her siblings.

Beth felt relieved, just a bit, that her mom was not telling her to "make nice." How her brothers were "just like that." That being together was what mattered, so don't say anything to provoke them.

Holidays had always been on Beth—as the oldest sibling and only girl—and her mother. They'd baked pies *all* day on the day before a holiday. Then they were up at dawn stuffing turkeys or baking hams, making a sheet-cake size sweet potato casserole, mashing Yukon Golds with chunks of melting butter and just the right amount of sweet cream, baking green beans they'd frozen from their summer garden with fried onion topping.

Hearing her mother's voice in her head made Beth weepy and deeply sad. Being "together as a family" had always been what mattered most to her mom. And to Beth. It had mattered enough that they never spoke up, never told the boys or their dad that every other word out of their mouths was stupid, bigoted bunk.

"I'm sorry, Mama, not this year," Beth had whispered in her bed the night after yelling at her brother. "Don't be disappointed. Please?"

Lost in her racing thoughts, Beth had not realized that no one was talking, that the group was quietly, kindly, waiting for her to return.

"This is really *hard* for you," Grace said softly.

"*Hard* does not even begin to touch what this is," Beth answered, in a monotone.

She looked over at Debra, twisting the corners of her mouth upward into a smile. "I make a mean sweet potato casserole and a fabulous pecan pie. So, what time do you want us again?"

Grace

Grace was cooking a turkey, stuffing, gravy, cranberry sauce, and sweet potatoes. Molly was making two pies. Mickey was contributing mashed potatoes and a salad. Grace had reggae music playing loud.

This was the first time in years that Katrina would not be with them. Malcolm was staying in New Orleans, and MJ had asked her if she'd come with him to Crystal's home. It was the first Thanksgiving without his father, and he wanted to be with his stepmom and the younger kids, his "halfsies" as he called them.

"It's harder on them," he'd told Kat. "They really miss their daddy."

Kat thought that being distracted, focusing on entertaining the "halfsies," would make it less hard for MJ as well. And the holiday was going to be damn hard for Crystal. Since her father or brothers had infected her husband, Crystal had, at some point in her grief, gone off on them. Relations were strained. If MJ and Kat did not come, Crystal would be alone with two kids and her mother.

No one was having expansive gatherings. Without COVID, Crystal could have gone to a dozen friends' homes. She'd have had lots of invitations and support.

But then, without COVID, she'd still have a husband.

Grace, Mickey, and Max sat at the table in Molly's living room.

They had a monitor and computer set up on a side table. Alex and Graciella were joining them to chat for a bit before eating. It was their first Zoom holiday. Max kept looking at the screen and waiting for them to appear.

"Almost time," Mickey said. "See? They're in the waiting room. We just push this and..."

"You're here, you're here!" Max yelled. "My uncle and auntie are here!"

There was a flurry of talking. Max asked lots of questions. Graciella carried her laptop around to give Max a tour of their house. Alex explained that they didn't have Thanksgiving in Panama, so they would be cooking some fish later that he'd caught that morning in the ocean. It was just another Thursday in Panama.

"I love the ocean," Max gushed. "When I'm grown up, I want to live by the ocean."

"Well, if your mom gets you a passport, maybe you both can visit us here," Alex said.

"That's a great idea," Max replied. "My own passport!"

"What kind of fish?" Mickey asked. "Do you fish from a pier or beach or take out a boat?"

Grace was happy to just listen and watch Alex and Graciella talking with Molly, Max, and Mickey. It was a first for her. She didn't ask if they'd Zoomed—or Skyped?—before. She was just happy to be included, have her family together, with Mickey as well.

After they closed the chat, Mickey started to carve the turkey. Molly and Grace carried in bowls of potatoes and gravy.

Their tradition was to share what they were grateful for before diving in.

"We're not dead like a lot of people," Max said.

"Ditto," Mickey said. "That about sums it up."

"We have each other," Molly said. "I could not have managed this year without each of you."

"Ditto," Grace said. "Let's eat."

"What possessed you to get a 24-pound turkey, Mom?" Molly asked, grabbing a hunk of white meat as Mickey carved. "It's big enough for a dozen people."

"Because they didn't have small turkeys. The entire country is having smaller gatherings. The 12-14 pound ones were apparently gone as soon as they hit the store. Big run on small turkeys."

"I never thought of that," Mickey reflected. "But it makes sense."

"They cut the price on the big ones to 49 cents a pound just to get them out of the store," Grace added. "We'll have turkey sandwiches, turkey soup, turkey salad..."

"Pass the sweet potatoes, please," Max asked. "I'm *hungry*."

Mickey & Grace

Grace walked in the door to her casita to what she'd expected would be the quiet of her own home after several hours at the office, but Mickey was waiting in the living room.

"Hurry up and sit down," Mickey told Grace. He was waving a few pages of something that looked official.

"What is so damn important that it can't wait until I take my coat off?"

"Okay, take off the coat and then sit down."

"Can I get something to drink first?"

"Way ahead of you. Look at the coffee table."

The coffee table looked "Instagram worthy," as Molly would say, neatly arranged, a bottle of Pinot Noir, a small bowl of kalamata olives, some smelly cheeses, and two round French rolls. Grace's nose picked up a whiff of yeasty-bakery rolls.

"Are the rolls warm?" Grace asked, her interest heightened.

"Probably," Mickey replied. "So, would you please sit down?"

Grace sat, reaching for a warm-ish roll. She grunted just a bit as she ripped it in half, then cut a piece of cheese to slather on the bread.

"Oh, Mickey, this is *quite* good. Why the splurge?"

"Because four hours ago I received a letter from Jocelynn's attorney. And it turns out that she has a solid estate after living frugally for decades and investing early and wisely. She was giving it to the university, which makes sense since she worked there for so many years but changed her mind. She now wants it to go to different 'good causes' that directly help people. It's in a trust, and there's a trustee to manage the process, manage the distributions, keep it legal, all of that. But here's the kicker: Jocelynn wants Max to choose the recipients."

Grace was slack-jawed. She'd stopped chewing. She stared at Mickey.

"Huh?" she asked. "Can you say that again more slowly?"

Mickey did, with interruptions every five words.

"Jocelynn wants *Max* to choose what causes to support with her life savings?"

"Yes, with guidance from the trustee. So he doesn't get sucked into some shady..."

"But she just met the kid? What makes her think..."

"You know how Max gets fixated on something and can talk about it for hours? So, Max was talking to her about how very small things can change people's lives when they have almost nothing. What is little in one country is huge in another. How $1,000 can mean little in the U.S. but is enough to start a business or a farm in developing countries. It's all summarized in the addendum. Programs that provide women with mini-grants and sewing machines. And something called the 222 Foundation, where every cent donated goes to one specific project each year to benefit women and kids."

"That does sound like Max. In fact, I think I heard some of this from him last month," Grace reflected.

"The attorney wrote that Jocelynn 'reconsidered' her $500,000-plus that would have ended up as some building renovation, with her name on a plaque that nobody cares about or remembers."

"I agree with that," Grace said. "Not that I'd ever have a half-mil to donate."

"It's quite specific: Jocelynn wants $5,000-$10,000 in mini-grants to go to five to ten 'good causes.' Every damn year. Max gets to decide where $50,000 a year will go, for ten years. Maybe longer."

"He'll love being able to do that. He'll research his little tushie off. Does it have to be established agencies?" Grace asked, her mind spinning.

"No, just so it goes right into people's hands. Not support admin," Mickey said, then paused. "And there's more."

"What?" Grace asked. "What could there possibly be?"

"She left a trust to pay for Max's college and even grad school. She wrote that, and I quote, 'I do not believe that his curiosity will be satisfied with just an undergraduate education.'"

Grace was speechless.

"Damn," Grace said. "I am truly, truly blindsided."

"I want to wait until this is all finalized before saying anything to Molly, okay?" Mickey asked. "It seems too…too…like a COVID fairy tale?"

Grace & Betty

Grace did not like Zoom sessions, and she definitely disliked starting with a new client on Zoom. It was too hard to get a sense of a person, to read body language, or connect. Zoom was so "in your face." Grace never knew when a leg was jiggling, a foot tapping, or a hand anxiously rubbing a leg.

But a local priest had referred a parishioner he was concerned about. The parishioner, a woman, was COVID anxious, with good reason. Her husband had died in the ICU six weeks ago. Grace was not going to push her to come to some strange therapist's back patio. And it was damn cold on the patio anyway these days.

Also, while a lapsed Catholic herself, Grace felt it was bad karma to turn down a request from a priest.

She'd emailed the woman intake paperwork and asked her to scan it back or put in the mail. She expected that USPS would be the preferred option.

Grace clicked on the link, and, within two minutes, they were both on their respective screens. The woman, Betty Miller, looked about 50. She was sitting up straight, dressed for a business meeting, and staring at the screen. Grace felt under-dressed, and that was just from the waist up. The lower half was still in PJs.

"I know this may feel awkward, Betty, but once we start talking it gets easier," Grace assured her. "Can I get a little background info first?"

After covering the basics—married after high school, three kids, worked for years until COVID doing the books for a roofing company, planned to return to that but having a hard time since Eddie had passed— Betty seemed a little less tense.

"I've never been alone," she shared. "I don't think I ever spent a single night alone in this house. Maybe once when Eddie went to get the kids from camp in Colorado and I had the flu. But then I was too sick to notice I was alone. And a friend was checking on me."

Yes, Grace thought, *lots of adjustments. You could use a grief group.*

"What is the number one thing that's hardest for you now?" Grace asked. "I don't want to focus on something minor and then realize we didn't get to what concerns you the most."

"Well, that would be Donald Trump," Betty said.

Grace's head jerked up. She'd expected Betty to talk about grief and losing her husband. *What the hell?*

"Your number one concern is Donald Trump?" Grace repeated, buying time.

"Yes, he is my number one concern," Betty reiterated. "And no one will believe me."

"Believe what?" Grace asked.

"That Donald Trump is Satan. I know it. I can prove he is, but nobody is paying attention."

"I can understand you feeling that way." Grace shifted in her seat. "He doesn't appear to make moral choices."

"Now you're sounding like all the others," Betty said, throwing her hands in the air. "I'm not saying that Donald Trump is an immoral man, a sinner, or a toxic narcissist. I'm saying that he is Satan. Not just doing bad things." Her voice rose in frustration. "Our President is Satan, dammit. He's walking the earth, drawing millions of people away from

God, seducing them away from the Commandments and Beatitudes."

Grace was speechless. It had been a long time since she'd been blindsided as badly as this. Was Betty schizophrenic? Delusional? Experiencing a grief psychosis?

"I don't want to sound like all the others, Betty, but what you're saying is troubling. Can you explain how you've come to know this?"

"It does sound kind of nuts," Betty admitted. "I mean, I'm just an ordinary mom and wife in Kansas. Not like Fatima, or Lourdes. No Blessed Virgin appearing in a cloud to show me the way. It started a month ago. I usually have the TV on when I'm cooking, like for company? So, I was cooking soup, and some TV show about rich people's homes popped up. Not like I looked for it. It was a rerun about Donald Trump's apartment in Trump Towers in New York City. They were giving a tour. And all of a sudden, I felt all trembly, shaky, like I was about to faint."

"What did you do?" Grace asked, leaning in.

"Well, I turned off the stove so I wouldn't burn the house down if I did faint, then sat on the couch. I watched the whole show. This apartment was, like, gold-plated. Everything was gold. The damn toilet seat was gold. It was disgusting. Who would want to live with that? And then I had a ringing in my head and heard a voice, *He is the father of lies* and, *When he lies, he speaks his native tongue, for he is the father of lies.*"

"How long did the voice last?" Grace asked, keeping her voice neutral.

"Just a few minutes. But then the voice came back. It says different things each time. I didn't recognize any of it, but when I told a friend she said, 'Why, Betty, that's in the Bible. Don't you know your Bible?'"

"What was your response?"

"No, I don't know the Bible," Betty explained. "I was raised Catholic. We studied our catechism. We weren't encouraged to read the Bible back then. It needed to be interpreted. And not like the voice is telling me what chapter and verse."

"I was raised with the catechism too," Grace reassured her. "So how do you know that they're from the Bible?"

"There's Scripture Search Engines, where you type in words, and it identifies what chapter and verse it is. Very helpful."

"You did that? Is that how you made the connections?"

"When I remember the words and don't mess it up, yes."

"Could you tell me some examples?" Grace had her pen ready to take notes.

"Okay. First came Deuteronomy 17:17: 'And he shall not acquire many wives for himself, lest his heart turn away, nor shall he acquire for himself excessive silver and gold.' That was more what Trump already did, how this has been going on a long time."

"But does that connect Trump to Satan?" Grace asked.

"No, but then came Thessalonians 2: 9-12: 'The coming of the lawless one will be in accordance with how Satan works. He will use all sorts of displays of power through signs and wonders that serve the lie. And all the ways that wickedness deceives those who are perishing. They perish because they refused to love the truth and so be saved. For this reason, God sends them a powerful delusion so that they will believe the lie. All will be condemned who have not believed the truth but delighted in wickedness.'"

"And what do you think it means?"

"That Trump is Satan," Betty said, exasperated.

"Have you memorized these? How can you remember..."

"No," Betty interrupted. "I try to write down what I hear. Sometimes it takes looking at different translations and versions of the Bible to find the best fit. But by now I've gone over them so many times that they're stuck in my brain."

"That's a lot of work," Grace said. "Do you have any more?"

"Yes. John 3:8: 'The one who does what is sinful is of the devil, because the devil has been sinning from the beginning.' And Corinthians 11:3: 'Just as Eve was deceived by the serpent's cunning, your minds may somehow be led astray from your sincere and pure devotion to Christ.' And John 8:44: 'He was a murderer from the beginning, not holding to the truth for there is no truth in him.' And James 4:7: 'Resist the devil and he will flee from you.'"

"Is there any verse that seemed to make the most sense?" Grace was digging here as she wasn't sure how it all connected.

"Peter 5: 8-9: 'Be alert and of sober mind. Your enemy the devil prowls about like a roaring lion looking for someone to devour. Resist him, standing firm in the faith, because you know that the family of believers is undergoing the same kinds of sufferings.'" Betty paused, cocking her head to look Grace straight in the eyes through her screen.

"Really, could it be any more obvious?" Betty questioned. "I'm trying to warn people," she continued, "but they have been seduced and deceived. Ephesians 6: 11-16: 'Put on the full armor of God so that you can take your stand against the devil's schemes. For our struggle is not against flesh and blood, but against the rulers, against the authorities, against the powers of this dark world and against the spiritual forces of evil in heavenly realms.'"

"How do you try to warn them?" Grace asked, keeping her voice measured and calm.

"I've written letters to the editor of the paper. I stood up in church and said that I have critical information about Donald Trump. But Satan is so strong—he's turning people away before I even start. There was this one verse about how Satan can outwit us. How we must be aware of his schemes?"

"And no one is listening to you?"

"I told them: 'He will oppose and will exalt himself over everything that is called God or is worshipped, so that he sets himself up in God's temple proclaiming himself to be God.' I mean, who does that sound like? Huh? 'I alone can do it.' All the bragging about how he is smarter than anyone else, how the crowds at his rallies are the biggest ever recorded. It never ends."

"But couldn't that just be an evil man bragging?"

"No, Donald Trump is the *'god of this world.'* His words twist truth and sow distrust. He is *'the lawless one,'* with a power to make people abandon their principles. He offers them power and they are seduced. Look at what has happened in our country. A man who lived by the flesh, who could not control his impulses, whether for sex or food? How could a mere man, who delighted in inflicting emotional pain on television, who said many years ago in interviews that he lusts for revenge—how could this man rise to power on the backs of the very workers he cheated of their due? A *man* could not do this, not so fast. But Satan? *Come to turn us into raging beasts, so we turn on each other. He fears and detests truth..."*

Betty had been speaking, not loud, but steadily, her voice insistent. It was as if she knew that she sounded crazy but did not know how to stop.

"They're worshipping the beast," Betty said, defeated. "They're worshipping a beast who has rejected the teachings of Christ, who pushes those who follow him to commit sins. Satan is delighting in wickedness, and millions of people are also. He doesn't even hide what he's doing."

"What do you mean?"

"Have you seen his email campaigns? To raise money? I signed up to be able to see what he was saying. 'Gold is my favorite color—and you're my favorite supporter.' He tells people over and over that he has 'a golden opportunity' for them. It's gold-gold-gold. Money-money-money."

"But isn't that like a lot of people with wealth and power?" Grace persisted.

"No. Donald Trump can't resist bragging. He craves adulation and will destroy anyone he feels betrays him. His need to be adored is insatiable. He needs us all to follow him to hell. That's how he'll win."

Grace tapped her pen against her desk. "What can I do that would be helpful for you, Betty?" she asked. "Because I'm not sure where to go with this."

"I don't know," Betty admitted. "I just wish the voice would stop but, every time I hear it, I feel a compulsion to act. It's exhausting. I open my computer and with every picture of Trump I see that daemonic smirk."

With that Betty covered her face with her hands, then began to rub small circles on her temples.

"Does this give you a headache?" Grace asked.

Betty flapped her hand at the question, as if that was the least of it.

"Trump hates losing more than anything. He'll do anything—cheat, lie, steal—to win. That's how he's lived his entire life. But the forces for good do not play dirty. They trust the good will of people to choose what is right and moral. Satan could destroy the world. But no one will notice until it's too late."

"Can we schedule for two weeks from now? I'd like a consult on some of what you're sharing. I don't want to make assumptions."

"Okay," Betty answered. "Thank you for not laughing or calling me a mental case."

Grace felt instantly guilty. She hadn't said it out loud, but it was in her notes.

HISTORICAL CONTEXT: NOVEMBER 2020

Nov. 1: U.S. death toll passes 230,000.

Nov. 2: "Joe Biden is promising to delay the vaccine and turn America into a prison state—locking you in your home while far-left rioters roam free. The Biden Lockdown will mean no school, no graduations, no weddings, no Thanksgiving, no Christmas, no 4th of July." – *Donald Trump*

Nov. 2: Election Day. By midnight, the news networks were unable to call the results from Wisconsin, Pennsylvania, Michigan, and North Carolina.

Nov. 4: "We were getting ready to win this election… Frankly we did win this election." – *Donald Trump*

Nov. 4: Donald Trump declares victory in the election despite many states still counting ballots and alleges voter fraud that he promises to fight all the way to the Supreme Court.

Nov. 7: Multiple media outlets confirm President Joe Biden as the winner of the 2020 election

Nov. 9: Biden named 13 scientists and public health specialists to his COVID-19 advisory board. The board will "help shape my approach to managing the surge in reported infections; ensuring vaccines are safe, effective, and distributed efficiently, equitably, and free; and protecting at-risk populations," the president-elect says in a statement.

Nov. 11: Texas is the first state to surpass 1 million confirmed cases of COVID-19.

Nov. 13: "The Nov. 3rd election was the most secure in American history… Right now, across the country, election officials are reviewing and double-checking the entire election process prior to finalizing the result…. There is no evidence that any voting system deleted or lost votes, changed votes, or was in any way compromised." *Department of Homeland Security's Cybersecurity and Infrastructure Security Agency (CISA)*

Nov. 17: Donald Trump fires the CISA director, Christopher Krebs. Krebs responds on Twitter: "Honored to serve… We did it right. Defend Today. Secure Tomorrow."

Nov. 16: Moderna announces that their COVID-19 vaccine is 94.5% effective at preventing the virus.

Nov. 19: The last Coronavirus Task Force press briefing under the Trump Administration.

December 2020

Theo

The bootie was lying on the floor of the ER waiting room, half hidden under a chair. It was about the right size for a toddler, made of overlapping, interwoven bright colors: green, orange, yellow, purple, pink, and blue. It had a top like a sock so it wouldn't slide off.

Theo was searching for his favorite pen, which he was sure had slid out of his pocket just ten minutes ago, in this very spot, when he'd been looking for the wife of a man being assessed in the ER. They'd needed his medication list. ASAP. But no luck.

Theo picked up the bootie and brought it over to the desk.

"Just found this," he told the receptionist. "On the floor." He gestured toward the back of the waiting room.

"Shoot," the receptionist said. "A girl was asking if we'd seen it. She was taking care of her little brother and she held up his other foot to show me what it looked like. They'd come in with their mother."

"Do you know where they are?" Theo asked. "I could bring it. A kid needs two booties."

"No, the mom was admitted, and it took us a while to realize that the kids were hanging out here alone. Social work checked with the mom, but there are no relatives, nobody to take care of them. So social work called social services, and someone came and picked them up. The baby was crying for his mama, and the big sister—she couldn't have been more than ten or eleven—was trying to calm him down and telling the social services worker they could not leave without their mother, that she'd told them to wait right there. That kid was hanging onto the baby and refusing to move without her mom telling her. She spoke some English but was talking to her brother in Spanish."

"What happened to them?" Theo asked.

"Social services took the contact info on the mom from us, left

235

contact info for the mom on how to reach them, then bundled up the kids and took them. I'm hoping they won't be separated but there are hardly any emergency foster care placements available, so they could be put in different homes."

Theo felt his gut turn over. He thought of his kids, and what it would be like for them to be hauled away by total strangers and separated from their mom. And then separated from each other? In a strange place? Without anything familiar to comfort them?

Somehow, in all the chaos of this pandemic, he had not been exposed to this small corner of hell.

"Does this happen often?" he asked.

"Yeah, once or twice a week. Sometimes it's just for a few days until out-of-state relatives can get here to take over. Or until a neighbor or friend finds out and contacts social services to volunteer care. But then the parent needs to designate them, and if the parent is on a ventilator..."

"The kids can't be taken care of in their own home?"

"You don't get it," the receptionist said. "A lot of single parents are alone. No support systems. Some are 'illegals' even if they've been here for years working and paying taxes. They wait until they're half-dead to get medical help because they're terrified of the system. And they keep working, no matter what the conditions, what the government says, because they have to."

Theo thought of his kids, tucked into their beds, their own rooms, with parents and grandparents and resources.

For the first time in a long time, he felt blessed.

But then Theo felt the slow burn of impotent rage. It didn't have to be this way.

Katrina & Grace

"I just remembered something, and I wanted to tell you before I forgot it again," Kat said when Grace picked up her cell. "Because my memory is for shit."

"I'm listening," Grace said.

"When I was little, there were times I'd be somewhere and some little white kids would point, or say 'Look, she's Black.' But parents never just said, 'You're right, Billy.' They'd get all flustered, and say, 'She's not Black, she's a kid, just like you.' Like even saying the word 'Black' was bad, or don't call anyone that. Which translates to 'What's so shameful about being called Black? I am Black.' And what kind of reaction should I have? As a kid? As an adult even? Is it my responsibility to make the parents feel okay because they were trying, in a screwed-up way, to not express bias? Or do I have to educate them on the mixed message?"

"I may have done that myself," Grace admitted. "Being embarrassed when a kid starts to point or yell? I probably said all kinds of things. Mostly 'It's not polite to point' or some such drivel."

"No biggie," Kat continued. "Just something that happened at least once or twice a year."

"Can I tell you about a Max encounter?" Grace asked. "Before I forget it?"

"Sure."

"So, I was reading *Caste* by Isabel Wilkerson and Max came over and asked me what it was about. I tried to explain how when one group of people consider themselves superior, they need to justify that by making other people inferior. And how, over time, everyone just accepts it because it can feel like 'That's just the way it is.'"

"And what did Max say?"

"He absorbed it for a minute, then said, 'Yeah, that's what neurotypicals do.' And he walked off."

"Good point," Kat said.

"There are times when I feel blind to what is inside that kid," Grace said. "And then I wonder what else I've been blind to."

"Do you want me to answer that? Seriously?" Kat replied.

Grace & Betty

Grace was having a brief Zoom session with Betty.

"I've been thinking about everything you said," Grace started in. "And I'm not sure where to go with this. I think the priest referred you because he may think that you're delusional. And everything you're saying could sound that way, especially when you discuss the voice in your head."

"It's just what happens." Betty protested. "I'm not making things up."

"I'm not saying that you are, Betty. But people may think that."

"So, what do I do? I can't just ignore what I'm hearing. And I have no idea why this was dumped in my lap."

"Yet, here you are, talking to a therapist because a priest thinks you may be bat-shit looney."

With that, Betty hooted. "Oh, hell," she said, once she caught her breath. "I even think I may be bat-shit looney. I tried to shut it down. Hoped, if I ignored it, maybe it would fade away?"

"But that didn't work, huh?" Grace asked.

"No. It's gotten more insistent."

"Well, Betty, if this helps, I do not experience you as bat-shit looney. But you may want to be more strategic in how you tell people. Leave the voice in your head out of it. Just lay out the Biblical citations and how they need to be studied because the Bible has told us that Satan is coming. And maybe Satan is here now, on Earth, to weed out who will remain faithful to Jesus, who will not be seduced by Satan before the Second Coming. Anyone who follows him is rejecting Jesus Christ."

"Do you believe that?"

"Doesn't matter what I believe. It's how you can hold up the teachings of Jesus, Christian values, and compare them to a man who embodies the antithesis of Christian values yet is endorsed and admired by almost all Evangelical churches and lots of Catholics too. Could that happen if he's only a man? Or is his pull so powerful, so seductive, so manipulative, because he is *more*? Because he is Satan come to test us?"

"Why would anyone believe me?" Betty asked.

"You're just the messenger, Betty," Grace replied. "They're believing the Bible, the warnings of the Bible. Just write it all out: 'The Biblical Case that Donald Trump is Satan.' Share the message. The rest is up to the people."

"Okay, I can do that."

"Newspapers won't take it as an op-ed. I'd suggest you look for Christian and right-wing websites and send to them. If even one posts it, it could go viral. Treat it all seriously, more like you are a Biblical scholar and this is what you've connected. Don't yell at people that they're being idiots."

"Yeah," Betty concluded. "Been there, done that."

"Email or call if you want to talk, but this is not a mental health issue. It's a faith issue."

Grace & Mickey

Grace was emotionally on an upswing. The election was still being "contested" and every day more fabrications were being shouted from Fox News and the White House: the voting machines had been rigged, thousands of people had voted twice, boxes of ballots had been tossed out or boxes of ballots had been discovered.

What it came down to was Donald Trump did not like to lose. He insulted and demeaned anyone he saw as a loser, and he'd cheated his way through life (or so shared former classmates and anyone he played golf with). He'd never been a team player. He needed to be the star, whether legitimate or rigged. And he didn't care which. Rigged might even be better. Rigged proved he had power.

But Grace was sure that, given a few weeks, it would all settle down. It wasn't like any president in the history of the country had refused to leave the White House. Biden had been elected, and as far as Grace was concerned, people would soon forget the reality TV star who had been pretending to be a real president for the last four years. And then Congress could lick their wounds, make nice-nice, and get down to the hard work of getting the country back on track. It was going to be time for a New Deal, something sweeping, after the cracks in the system had turned into chasms under pressure.

Grace knew that this Christmas would not be like the past. Last Christmas was in a different universe. But Mickey, Grace, Molly, and Max had a surprise. They were going to drive around and show up at their friends' front doors, maybe even go to the hospital at shift change time.

They were going to try caroling—outside, socially distant, even masked—but caroling.

They did not have good voices, so the choice of songs was limited. And they needed new lyrics to better fit the new world order.

How's this?" Mickey asked from the couch as Grace prepped salmon for supper.

We wish you a Merry Christmas, blah-blah, but then a rousing chorus of: *Please keep on your mask—And safely distance—If you want another holiday and more Happy New Years'.*"

"Good start, Mickey. But it does sound like a public service announcement, like 'do what we say, or you could die.'"

"Isn't that the message? Better follow the rules if you want *more* holidays?" he retorted.

"Could the next stanza be more personal? More friendly?" she asked, sliding the tray into the oven.

"Okay, okay. More personal and friendly coming up."

Before the salmon came out of the oven, Mickey had more.

"Gracie, listen. I think this might nail it. Ready? Here goes." He stood, swaying side-to-side as he sang. *"This really is hard—We miss you a bunch—We want to have you over—To drink wine and munch.* Then we segue back to *We wish you a Merry Christmas—We know that you won't miss this*—With this line, his voice slowed to enunciate every word and, as he sang '*this,*' he waved a mask with his right hand. "Then a finale of: '*Next year, we're gonna' kiss-kiss*" punctuated by smooch-y noises and pursed lips—"*Cause we love you so much!!!*"

With that Mickey grinned and feigned a curtsey.

Grace started to giggle, then laugh. There was something about his earnestness, his willingness to not give a shit about how he might appear, to fully engage with this ridiculous idea just to give their friends a laugh.

"I do love you, Mickey Donahue," she said,

"That's the only reason I'm doing this, Gracie."

After curried squash soup, salmon with lemon butter and herbs, roasted red potatoes, garlic bread, and a few glasses of Bordeaux, they ended up on the couch. Like so many people who were spending far more time in a kitchen, COVID had pushed her to be a better cook.

"Okay Mickey, would you do the whole song, again, with the gestures and sound effects?" she requested.

And he did.

Ian

On December 14thth, Ian woke up feeling as if his oversized Labrador was asleep on his chest. Even when he sat up, went to the bathroom to piss, the weight, the pressure, did not shift.

"Nell," he called, trying to sound calm. "Something is wrong."

Nell was downstairs making coffee. She hurried up the stairs bringing Ian coffee in his favorite green mug, with a moose on it. As she walked through the doorway, Ian remembered, in that microsecond, the gift shop in Denali, and Nell's wide grin of delight as she turned to show him her find. Ian had always had a soft spot for moose. No moose in Texas.

Nell knew, in that same microsecond, that something was very wrong. Ian's face was strained, jaw clenched. He was breathing through his nose; short, tight, panting. His eyes looked afraid.

Ian never looked afraid.

"Let's get you dressed, baby, and to the doctor," Nell said.

"Get the pulse oximeter," Ian said. "Top drawer, bathroom cabinet."

Nell put the mug down and got the oximeter. She gently put it over his index finger. In seconds it read 90.

"Call 911," Ian said. "That can't be right. Something's wrong here.

Thirty minutes later, the EMTs were strapping Ian onto a stretcher and sliding it into the back of their ambulance. They'd taken vitals, started him on oxygen, made reassuring noises at Nell, and told her where to call for more info as she would not be allowed into the ambulance nor the hospital.

Nell leaned over the stretcher on the front walk as they were opening the back of the ambulance. She put her cheek against Ian's cheek and whispered in his ear. "You'll make it through this. You're the strongest person I know. You got that?"

When the ambulance pulled out of the driveway, the siren started up. Listening, Nell felt a shaking chill, trembling, as if every fear she'd ever had in her life had been leading to this, to this day, this hour, when the words that all parents say to reassure their children—*Don't worry, it will all be okay,* or *There's nothing to be afraid of* became the lies they'd always been.

Eight hours later, a doctor phoned. "I'm sorry, but your husband needs to be on a ventilator. It's better to do it earlier rather than wait," he explained. "We've learned a lot in the last nine months."

"What does Ian want?" Nell asked.

"I think Ian just wants to breathe," the doctor said. "Would you like to speak with him?"

She heard some muffled noises as the phone passed to Ian.

"Nell, honey, I am so sorry," Ian said, his voice hoarse. "But this is our best shot. I love you so much. I love you. You know that, right?"

"I'm holding you, baby. I got you." Nell replied, her voice choking. "Feel my arms? Feel the hug? I will not let you go. I got you."

It was a blood clot nine days later that killed him. The ventilator was doing its job as far as the lungs, and the medical team had felt cautiously hopeful. But this coronavirus could affect so many different body systems. It was sneaky.

"Patients have venous or arterial thromboembolisms with COVID," the physician told Nell. "Over 30 percent of COVID patients in the ICU develop clots. Sometimes they settle or get stuck, others make it to the lungs. Pulmonary embolism. Clots can cause strokes…"

"Are you saying that my husband did not die from COVID?" Nell interrupted his lecture.

"A stroke is a secondary, a side-effect or consequence of COVID," the doctor said. "COVID kills people a dozen different ways. I am so sorry for your loss. Your husband was a fighter. We thought…"

But Nell could not hear anything. A roaring was rising in her head. A wailing, primitive and deep. The phone fell from her hand, and she heard it crack as it hit the tile floor.

How do I tell my in-laws that the next body is their son? was Nell's last thought before the wail erupted. *Are there words for that?*

Katrina & Grace

Grace and Katrina were walking downtown on Main Street. It was cold, but not windy, which made it a decent evening to window shop and stroll.

The holiday lights were up, on every tree that lined Main Street, for blocks.

Tonight, she and Kat were following that tradition. They would walk, look, chat, and maybe come across something for their children (or, in Grace's case, grandson).

They settled in at the Fish House, ordering bowls of chowder and hot toddies.

"Are Malcolm or MJ in relationships?" Grace asked as they sipped their drinks. "Do they ever talk about wanting to have children?"

Kat looked up at Grace, amused. "Where did that come from?"

"I don't know. Just looking in the toy store window, I think. I've been thinking about how much harder it is to be the parent of a Black child," Grace answered. "To have to be so vigilant, not trust that other adults will protect your kid if something happens. If I had a Black kid, I don't think I'd let them out of my sight."

"You learn to be a parent of a Black kid by being a Black kid." Kat's voice was quiet, reflective. "For me it started when I was little. I never assumed that adults would protect me or that I could turn to them. Certainly not white adults. It's a different world for many Black kids, a world that many white kids have never stepped foot in."

"That's hard for me to imagine," Grace said. "I think I saw most adults as possible resources. Like 'Of course they would help me if I asked nicely.' And assumed that for my kids as well."

Kat nodded. "That sounds about right. Black kids have never been as protected as white kids in almost any system. Especially teenagers. And they're perceived as less goal-directed, even less intelligent, so not encouraged as much academically. I want to believe that's changed, but..." Kat's eyebrows and mouth lifted, more dismissive, less questioning.

"How was it when Malcolm and MJ were little?" Grace asked.

"Less blatant, but—ubiquitous? They were in majority white schools, so more micro-aggressions than 'in your face' shit."

"Tell me," Grace's voice was insistent. She wanted Katrina to share her own experiences, not generalities.

Katrina took a sip of her drink.

"When Malcolm was in the third grade, they were doing some little kid play, based on Cinderella. Malcolm wanted to be the prince, and they had informal 'auditions.' He came home deflated. Told me 'I was better, Mom. I memorized the lines. The other kids read from the sheet. And I used inflection, like you said.' I asked who got the part. It was a white boy and Cinderella was blonde."

"What did you do?"

She sighed. "It was tricky. I dropped by the classroom the next afternoon and chatted with the teacher. She told me straight out that Malcolm was great, but having a Black prince rescue a white girl might upset some parents. 'I wouldn't want him getting caught up in some backlash and then get teased,' she told me.

"What the hell?" Grace interrupted. "These are third grade kids? And the teacher is worried about blowback of an eight-year-old..."

"This teacher *liked* Malcolm," Kat interrupted. "That's what confused him. He was the best, so he didn't understand why the other kid was picked. It was his first experience of racism stomping on his goals."

The waitress brought out their chowder, the bowls hot to the touch. She put a basket of warm rolls in the middle of the table. Grace took one, slathering on butter.

"What did you say to the teacher?" she asked Kat, her mouth full.

"That Malcolm was disappointed. I could see that she was trying to protect Malcolm but maybe..."

"You were that civil? Did you believe it?"

"She was trying to protect him, but in a backward way. Then she said, 'Malcolm is a strong young man. He'll be fine. It's a learning experience.'"

Grace snorted. "Learning what? That the teacher you adore will betray your trust?"

"No, I think she genuinely thought that he was 'strong' and would survive," Kat explained. "And that he would need these 'learning experiences' to help him navigate living in a white world."

"I'm confused. How does not getting a role in the third grade prepare a boy..."

"You asked for examples. This was one. I think it covers a lot of how Black kids are perceived, what assumptions are made."

Grace looked at Katrina over the table. "This sounds so damn confusing. And anything you could do as a mom could have made it worse."

"Yeah, I did feel caught. Complain to the administration and he loses a teacher who really likes him. I would've been labeled the angry Black mom who didn't understand the larger issues."

"But you weren't just an angry..."

"That never matters. One confrontation and I'd be locked into that box. They were already a little edgy because I was a lawyer."

Kat paused to slurp her chowder.

"Did you do anything?" Grace wondered, reaching for another roll.

"I wrote a card to the teacher that maybe next time we could talk first? That I understood she had good intentions. How having a teacher who genuinely respected his intelligence and spirit was more important than being the prince."

"Did you believe that?"

"Yes. And, by giving her the benefit of the doubt, I made her an ally. I think she gave Malcolm even more attention and encouragement after that. And then, a few years later, she taught MJ. He had a really good year too."

"Is this shit still happening?" Grace asked, as if Kat could speak for all Black families.

"Yes, Gracie, it's still happening," Kat said, with a touch of impatience. "Depends on the school, area, and the district. In Kaw Valley, if a Black kid wasn't picked but the other kids could see he or she was the best choice, the kids would know something was fishy. But parents? They wouldn't complain because that's too racist. But might they assume that the teacher had to pick the Black kid for optics? Maybe. Way too many white folks cannot accept that a Black kid could really be the top choice."

She leaned back in her chair, reflecting on her words.

"Like when Barack was elected?" Grace posed.

"Yeah. And now we're living with what that blowback uncovered."

Grace & Sofia

Sofia emailed again, asking for a short session.

It felt like a year had passed since they last met, but it had only been—what? Weeks? Months? Grace explained that she was no longer in the gazebo, that she could Zoom or meet on her back patio. With a heater.

Sofia said Zoom was okay.

Three days later, after some initial fussing with the sound, Zoom was ready to go. "So, what happened, Sofia?" Grace asked. "I didn't hear back so I assumed it was not productive. I'm sorry. I thought..."

"No," Sofia interrupted. "I signed papers two days ago, transfer of the deed, for the house."

"You got the house? Seriously?" Grace exclaimed. Her face on the screen was one big smile. "I'm so happy for you and your family. So, please, tell me what happened."

"I mailed the letter to Lin at his office after talking with my husband," Sofia reported. "Lin replied in an email that he received it, thanked me, and wrote that he needed to think. Then nothing, *nothing* from him, but also nothing from the attorney about the will. It was not being contested."

"And then?"

"I got a letter, that I had to sign for, right after Thanksgiving. Lin said he'd wanted to speak with his sons, face-to-face, as this was also their inheritance. And they had not come home until Thanksgiving."

"It would have been nice to know..."

"Doesn't matter," Sofia said, waving a white paper. "Let me read it to you, okay? Just a part?"

"Sure, go ahead."

"Here it goes:

Dear Sofia,

My wife and I spoke with our sons and gave them copies of your letter. They talked between themselves, and then told us that they wanted to respect their great-uncle's choice, and that he was a kind and generous man. They said that if I were to make such a decision, that they would respect my wishes. My uncle would be proud of his great-nephews, as I am. I have spoken with the attorney and all of the papers are ready to sign at his office. The car as well. You can sell it and buy a new car, and for your son also..."

"No way!" Grace exclaimed. "The car too?"

"Yes. Here, let me show you something," Sofia replied. She turned the screen around to face the room. It was a small living room, with worn furniture. There were bookshelves against a wall, but empty. Boxes were piled next to them, and more boxes could be seen through a door into what Grace expected was the kitchen.

"You're packing?"

"Yes. I asked the attorney if we could delay the inheritance until 2021, so we don't have to come up with the taxes until 2022. I signed the deed transfer to be processed on January 5th. But he wrote an agreement so we can move in now. We will be in our new home by Christmas."

"That's wonderful. It's what Mr. Huang wanted. What about the car?"

"The attorney sold it to a BMW dealer in Kansas City. In one day! I could not believe how much it was worth. We received a check, enough to buy two new Corollas, but I'm waiting until I'm less busy to think about that. And I want money in the bank. To have money in savings? That has been our goal for many years, but every time we saved, something else would break down."

"If you put half of it in a retirement account with a financial planner, it will be so much more in 20 to 30 years. You are how old?"

"I was thinking that too. I'm 42. I expected to work all my life. But in thirty years? Then I might like the idea of retiring, especially now that we have no mortgage and a beautiful garden. Such a blessing, one I never dreamed of. Security. We can feel secure."

"Will you sell your house?"

"That is not decided. My husband wants to keep it and make it a rental. The rent will pay the mortgage and a little extra. See how that goes. It would be paid off in nine years, so then we'd have what my son calls an 'income stream.'"

"Good planning. Would you call me in May, if not before? I want to come see your garden."

"That would be lovely, Mrs. McDonald," Sofia said. "It would make Mr. Huang smile also."

When they ended, Grace reflected on how Sofia had never used her name, her first name, and how rare it was to be called Mrs. McDonald.

She also reflected that what she'd just heard was a lesson in how *owning* property, how *inheritance*, dramatically impacts security, socio-economic class, options like education. Choices.

Grace imagined Mr. Huang smiling. His legacy mattered. He would be a hero in the Dominguez family story. It would extend for generations.

And his garden would be cherished.

Zed & Cherry

It was mid-December when Zed started to notice all the stirrings about something that might happen on January 6th in Washington D.C. Cherry told him he must have taken a civics class in junior high, or maybe high school, but he didn't remember any of it. So, to learn that a president was not *really* elected until the citizens in this Electoral College voted based on the ballots? And until the Congress accepted and approved all of the ballots, state-by-state? And that they didn't finish that process until January 6th? In the Capitol?

That was all news to him.

And the whole Electoral College thing was a way to rig an election. A candidate could win the popular vote nationally but lose the election because each state gave *all* their Electoral College votes to whoever won in their state, not divided them by percentages.

Zed wasn't even sure if he had it right because it sounded so unfair.

All Zed knew was that Donald Trump had to have won the popular vote, and then some states rigged the process to tip the scales for the Dem.

Donald Trump was asking for patriots to come to Washington, D.C., and show the Congress that they knew the election had been rigged and that they wanted their sitting President, Donald Trump, to remain in office.

Zed and Cherry talked about what it would take for them to make that happen. First would be childcare for at least 4-5 days because they had to drive from Kansas to D.C. Plus, the costs—a hotel, meals, get the car in shape for a long drive. After talking for three hours, they agreed that it did not look workable.

But Zed kept chewing on it. He had vacation time saved because they hadn't done anything during COVID. And this was not just a vacation, like taking the kids to Branson. This was a once-in-a-lifetime opportunity to be part of something bigger than themselves, to take action for their beliefs, to be patriots.

Just thinking about it gave Zed a jolt of excitement. Damn, to be able to say, years and years from now, to tell their kids, that they had been part of the biggest march on Washington? That they'd actually been there when history was made?

The next morning, he rolled over and stared at Cherry, staring until she opened her eyes.

"What?' she asked, her mouth gummy from sleep.

"We're doing this," he said. "We're going to Washington, D.C. We can make this happen and we will. Are you with me?"

"Yeah, we're in this together," she said, almost giggling. "No way you're leaving me home with the kids." She paused, then poked Zed in the arm. "But that stare thing creeps me out."

Mike

Mike was having a hard time with time. He kept losing track. Had something happened a few days ago? Two weeks ago? Entire weeks, even months, had floated away like clouds.

Had something happened last week? Or was it in September? And what day was it anyway?

There had been about two minutes of relief and joy when Biden had won. Then the Big Lie—that Trump and the GOP had been marketing for months as the *only* possible explanation for Donald not winning— became front and center of every Fox newscast, every Trump speech.

It was almost Christmas and Donald had not conceded the election. He kept hammering away that it had been stolen. The election officials were in on it. The machines had been messed with. *His* votes had disappeared. That every vote was matched with a person, and the rolls showed not just who voted but who had not bothered to show up to vote, that every vote was tabulated and traceable, that this was a process with strict protocols that had functioned fairly for decades—none of that mattered. Because, if Donald didn't win, then it wasn't *fair*.

He'd lost on the same ticket, ballots, and voting machines that had elected GOP governors, senators, and representatives. Were the ballots for all the other Republicans fraudulent? Or did the ballots just get Donald wrong?

Mike and Molly were talking themselves hoarse dissecting Trump. They wished they could ignore him, not make him the focus of their diatribes. But they couldn't stop.

"He's a toxic addiction," Molly told Mike. "We need to include it in the DSM."

They made lists of things they could talk about other than the election. Like the vaccines. Or what countries they wanted to visit next summer when they would be vaccinated, and the world would open back up like a beautiful flower and everyone would be happy.

They were cautiously optimistic that once Trump conceded, and retired to eat burgers, play golf, and lick his wounded ego, that sanity and compromise would return to the Legislative and Executive branches of government. While they did not love Joe Biden, he was a huge, huge improvement on Donald.

Starting with being sane.

But they each confessed to longing for someone younger, someone that looked like and talked like them. Someone with fire in their belly.

December 25th was a Friday. Molly and Mike had their regular Tuesday evening Zoom on the 22nd. Each made a special holiday drink.

Molly made Godiva hot cocoa in a clear glass mug with Irish whiskey, piled with whipped cream and a dusting of grated chocolate. Mike made a green colored vodka concoction, with ginger ale. The red straw did not redeem it.

"Green is not a good look for alcohol," Molly commented. "Mine's better."

"You're in the cold. It's harder to get into Santa when there are palm trees. But you win the drink contest. It does look fabulous."

They had resolved to not mention Donald Trump, or politics, and whoever did would owe the other one $25. They needed a consequence to stick to the resolution.

"So, what have you been doing to foster holiday cheer," Mike asked.

"We went caroling," she replied. "Mom, Mickey, Max, and me. We drove around to a dozen different homes of friends and sang on their front walk. And brought cookies. It was mostly one song: a COVID Christmas Carol."

Mike grinned. "That tops whatever I've done. Will you sing it for me?"

She laughed, waving a hand. "Seriously? No. I can't sing. I had a mug of this with me the whole time."

"Maybe next year?" Mike teased.

"Next year? We won't need a COVID Carol next year. The vaccine is coming, remember? Soon. That's the B-E-S-T Christmas Present Ever!"

Christmas came, and, for their kids, their parents, Mike and Molly tried to keep up traditions and make it fun. But it was a Christmas—the first Christmas ever—where to celebrate with extended family, or cherished friends, could be dangerous. Lethal even. They felt so cut off. At the same time, they felt a responsibility to keep their pod safe. Just a little longer.

There was fear in the air, an edge of desperation. They could not keep this up. People could not keep this up. They needed it to be over.

HISTORICAL CONTEXT: DECEMBER 2020

Dec. 8: White House Holiday parties continue, unmasked, despite all CDC directives.

Dec. 10: Vaccine advisers to the FDA vote to recommend the agency grant emergency use authorization to Pfizer's coronavirus vaccine.

Dec. 11: The Supreme Court rejects a suit brought by Texas and supported by GOP state attorneys general seeking to overturn the election results in several states.

Dec. 14: Presidential electors cast their ballots to make Joe Biden the president-elect.

Dec. 14: U.S. officials announce the first doses of the FDA authorized Pfizer vaccine have been delivered to all 50 states, the District of Columbia, and Puerto Rico.

Dec. 14: UK reports it has identified a new variant of the coronavirus. Alpha was the first of the highly publicized variants. It would become the dominant variant in the U.S. until the rise of the more aggressive Delta variant.

Dec. 15: Sandra Lindsay, a nurse and director of patient services in the Long Island Jewish Medical Center's Intensive Care Unit, is the first person in the US to get a COVID vaccine.

Dec. 18: The FDA authorizes a second coronavirus vaccine made by Moderna for emergency use.

Dec. 25: U.S. death toll passes 330,000.

Dec. 30: Trump Administration promised 20 million vaccinations by year's end, but only about 2 million people have been vaccinated.

Dec. 31: "The Federal Government has distributed the vaccines to the sites. Now it is up to the states to administer. Get moving!" – *Donald Trump*

January 2021

Zed & Cherry

Zed and Cherry did not have to drive to Washington, D.C., because it turned out that there was a busload of like-minded patriots who also wanted to go. Someone in Wichita did a shout-out and within a few days the bus was filled. It would start in Wichita, swing by Hays, then Topeka, then drive straight through to D.C. They'd arrive in D.C. the morning of the 5th, stay in a hotel where they'd scored a group rate, and wake up on the 6th ready to make history.

Neither of them had ever been to Washington, D.C. Cherry got maps from AAA and planned a walking tour—with a few Ubers in the middle—for when they arrived.

"We can sleep on the bus," she said, "but I want to see it all, as much as we can cram in, even if the museums are still closed."

The bus ride reminded them of being back in high school, going to an away game or an end-of-the-year field trip. Everyone started out talking, excited. They didn't know anyone, but it felt like they'd known each other for years after just a few hours. Around 10 p.m., everyone quieted down and curled up to try to sleep. Cherry had brought a few Benadryl to help them sleep and they drifted off, her head on Zed's shoulder. They actually slept, rocked to sleep like little kids by the movement and the background noise of the wheels on the road. They woke to a woman from Salina, who had a really pretty voice, softly singing "America the Beautiful" as the sun was rising, layers and layers of pink on the horizon.

By 10 a.m. they'd stashed their luggage in the room, taken two-minute showers, and were ready to set off with their maps to explore.

"Eleven Smithsonian Museums span 3rd to 14th Streets and Constitution Avenue to Independence Avenue," Cherry read aloud from her guidebook. "But they line the National Mall," she added, looking up.

"So, we're gonna' walk from the Washington Monument at one end to the Capitol at the other end and then back down, with the mall and the reflecting pool in the middle."

Zed just grinned at her. "Lead the way," he intoned. "I'll try to keep up."

There were so many buildings, and they were all very, very big: American History, Natural History, National Gallery of Art, Air and Space, the Holocaust, more art, Arts and Industry, African American History and Culture.

"Why is there a separate one for African American History and Culture?" Zed asked.

"How am I supposed to know?" Cherry replied. "But the guidebook says it's a new museum that opened in 2016."

They walked through the sculpture garden and saw an antique carousel.

"The boys would love that," Cherry gushed.

"We're coming back," Zed said, his voice suddenly serious. "When everything opens up, and Covid is over, we're all coming here, and we'll see *everything.*"

"Promise?" Cherry asked, looking across the Mall. *Everything* would take a while.

"Promise. I want the kids to know their history," Zed answered.

They walked and walked. To the National Cathedral and Union Station, up Connecticut Avenue to DuPont Circle. They saw the Vietnam Memorial. There were restaurants and coffee shops open with outdoor seating and big heaters, and they stopped for lunch.

It was dark when they got to their final stop, the Lincoln Memorial, but Cherry had timed it that way. The guidebook said it was more magnificent at night when the lighting reflected the magnitude of the statue itself. And it was. They read portions of the Gettysburg Address and the Second Inaugural Address, both etched in stone.

"Damn, Cherry, this is so amazing," Zed whispered, awestruck, reaching for her hand. "We're sitting in front of history and we're gonna' be making history. We are so damn lucky."

The next morning, they were up early. Some in the group were going to stay together, being in an unfamiliar city and worried about getting lost. But after their adventure, Cherry and Zed didn't feel anxious about navigating the city alone. They could walk anywhere and never *really* get lost because all they had to do was look at the street signs, call an Uber, and then say, "The Capitol, please."

This was a day that could change history. They were taking back their country.

The rally was on the Ellipse? Called "President's Park, 52 acres, just south of the White House?

There would be many speakers, but President Trump was scheduled for noon.

As they approached, they realized that there were thousands of people. It was overwhelming. They kept walking around the perimeter of the crowd, circling, until there was an opening to slide through. Zed held Cherry's hand as she somehow managed to navigate, saying "Excuse me, please," and smiling. People made space for them to move through, like the parting of the damn Red Sea.

And then they could see the stage, from the side. The music was pumping, the flags waving.

"Look. Zed! There he is. It's really happening—look-look-look!" Cherry said.

Zed was speechless. He was just staring at the stage, the music pumping up the crowd even more, and there was Donald Trump, President of the United States, smiling and waving at them.

They could see the president so clearly, in profile. And then he turned to his left, almost 90 degrees, looked right at them and gave them a thumbs up before turning back to face the crowd.

"Did that just happen?" Zed asked.

"I think so, Zed. I felt like he was looking me right in the eye, that he saw me. And then looked at you. Like he saw *us* and gave us a thumbs-up. It happened. That happened."

"Damn," Zed said. "That was better than a blessing from the Pope."

Later they would have a hard time remembering all the details.

When Donald Trump started speaking, they knew this was where they belonged.

"It's just a great honor to have this kind of crowd and be before you and hundreds of thousands of American patriots who are committed to the honesty of our elections and the integrity of our glorious republic." President Trump presented so much evidence of how the election had

been stolen, state after state. How he was ahead in so many places when the polls closed, but then ballots kept coming in late, and the totals would shift. *"We're gathered here together in our nation's capital for one very, very basic and simple reason: To save our democracy."* How could everyone not see how rigged the whole system was? *"We will never give up, we will never concede... You don't concede when there's theft involved."* How could he suddenly be behind by thousands when he'd been winning? *"At 1 p.m. we will march to the Capitol Building and call on..."* But the rest was lost in a roar.

Then it was over, and, like a tide turning in the ocean, the crowd shifted. They started moving, thousands of people, carrying signs, chanting, moving down Pennsylvania Avenue toward the Capitol. There was a force of people moving all around them and they had to quicken their steps, then almost jog.

Cherry saw men in camouflage, or all in black, with gear hanging from their bodies, talking on walkie-talkies, walking with steady purpose. There were flags, lots of flags: the American flag and MAGA flags and Confederate flags and Q.

Where We Go One, We Go All-signs were everywhere.

"Cherry, look, see the Q flags," he said, grabbing at her shoulder to turn her to see. "It's like Q is here too."

"I bet he is, Zed. We don't know who, but I can feel it. He's here. Like the 'Q Shaman?' I'd only heard stories about him, seen pictures, but here he is, right in the middle of it."

Later, when they tried to describe what happened that afternoon, it was a blur. Time both expanded and compressed, some moments vivid and others buried. They were off to one side as the crowd pressed forward, then engaged with Capitol police who were behind flimsy metal barriers. It was hard to see from where they were what was happening, but the Capitol steps were covered with people. Others were—climbing? Could they be climbing? Yes, climbing up. Then there were hundreds— thousands—a sea of red and blue, MAGA hats and flags. And through the red and blue, like twisting streamers, lines of brown and black.

By the time they got to the front, massive wooden doors were propped open, and people were just walking in. The police seemed to have disappeared but there were signs of a fight, broken windows and doors, debris strewn around, tables overturned.

Despite that, what they felt when they entered the rotunda of the Capitol was that same awe as they had at the Lincoln Memorial. They stood in the middle, people streaming past on either side of them, and put their heads back to take it all in. They were in the middle of what they'd only seen in textbooks or magazines.

They looked into the Senate Chambers but did not go in. People were riffling through desks, taking photos of papers, some stuffing documents in backpacks, others throwing files on the floor like trash.

"This doesn't feel right, Zed," Cherry said, grabbing his wrist. "We need to leave."

But Zed wanted to walk around some more, not to *do* anything but to watch what was happening. Cherry was too unnerved to leave him. In her gut she felt a spreading, unsettling, anxiety. There were so many halls, so many staircases, like a maze. Some offices had been broken into, and from the hallways, they looked ransacked. People in MAGA hats were sitting with their feet propped up on desks. This was not—right.

They came around a corner and stopped, pulling back behind a statue. At the other end of a long corridor, men in uniforms were carrying out stretchers.

Were the bodies on the stretchers also in uniforms?

Two of the men, who were leaning over a stretcher and talking in low tones to the person on it, looked up and saw them. But neither did anything, didn't even yell or tell them to move along. They just kept doing whatever they'd been doing for the guy on the stretcher. It was like she and Zed were invisible.

"Zed, we gotta' get out. Those are cops. We can't be in here. Bad stuff is going on."

This time, Zed did not argue. They backed up and headed down the first staircase they came to and started following any exit signs they saw. It felt like forever before that reached a door that led outside.

As they exited, police and National Guard were telling people to move along. They were not stopping them, not arresting them, just standing back and letting them leave.

It was like after a movie or a concert, and the theater crowd was emptying out.

They walked for thirty minutes, putting distance between

themselves and the Capitol. They stopped at a café, drank a gallon of water, and ate. They were parched and famished. Then they continued to their hotel, took an elevator up to the 6th floor to their room.

It felt like a lifetime since they'd left that morning.

They took off their sneakers, lay down on the bed and spooned, not speaking, numb, until they fell asleep. They did not even turn on the TV.

The next morning, boarding the bus, the group was subdued. No excited chatter, no high fives, no thumbs up. Congress had returned the night before, walking past broken windows, desecrated statuary, and vandalized offices, and stayed up half the night to do what they'd started to do: certify the election.

There had been so many hopes pinned on January 6th, and they had not materialized. Many thought that that was the day when thousands within the cabal would be rounded up by the military. The military, which mostly had not been corrupted, would ensure that the rightful president stayed in the White House. It was the Storm. There would be violence, but it was necessary. All of it was to make way for the peace to follow.

Zed and Cherry were disappointed. None of that had happened. But they trusted that the Storm was coming, and, when it did, the stolen election would be overthrown, and President Trump restored to his rightful place. They knew it would be difficult, but the purge was essential to rid the world of their evil. It was how America would be restored to greatness. Zed and Cherry were prepared to be patient.

They knew that there would be a reckoning. It was maybe the same thing, but Zed thought different groups called it by different names. There would be mass surprise arrests of members of the cabal, starting with Hilary Clinton and George Soros and the puppet Joe Biden. They would be imprisoned at Guantanamo Bay and executed for their crimes against the people and the terrible harm that had been done to children.

Zed was never clear on who George Soros was, but the name kept coming up so he must be someone who pulled the strings.

Molly & Mike

"Mike, call me now," Molly texted, her fingers missing keys, so she had to start over: Turn on the TV if you haven't yet. Something horrible is happening. It was 7 p.m. on January 6th when she'd turned on the TV. It was insane that this had been happening all day and she'd been oblivious. It was like watching an insurrection in a third world country.

Who stormed the Capitol with spears?

The newscasters reiterated every twenty minutes that today, January 6th, was a routine if ceremonial day for Congress, as the verified and certified vote tallies for every state were spoken aloud, state by state, and both houses of Congress certified the election results. It was the kind of day that some legislators brought their kids to watch from the gallery.

But, instead of tradition and ceremony, the Capitol itself had been "breached." Thousands of Trump supporters had come to Washington, D.C., at the urging of the incumbent. And, after a rally at which Donald Trump spoke and urged them to march to the Capitol, a shitstorm had exploded.

Capitol police had been mowed down. Hand-to-hand combat in the Capitol? Senators and Representatives being hurried down back staircases to safety? Hadn't Homeland Security been able to predict this? Where was the National Guard? Where were the D.C. police?

Later that night, and through the next day, Grace and Mickey—and Molly and Mike—watched, in horror, as the video coverage re-looped, over and over.

Throngs of people draped in MAGA regalia, or camouflage, waving flags—Was that a Confederate flag? A QAnon flag? A MAGA flag?—broke through police barriers, attacked Capitol police, broke windows and doors, surged into the Capitol, ransacked the Senate, desecrated statues and art, roamed halls calling out their intent to find Nancy Pelosi, to hang Mike Pence, to...

It was a mob, self-justifying, rabid, and terrifying. The hastily built gallows would have been used if they'd caught some of the hunted.

It was visible for all to see. *Incontrovertible*, Molly thought. *Mob violence.*

What else could anyone call it?

Covid Grief Group

On January 11ᵗʰ, the date that the Kansas Legislature reconvened, a table covered with "Welcome Back" treats was set up by 8 a.m. in the hallway outside the Secretary of State's office. All morning and into the afternoon, legislators strolled past to drop off papers, or simply to be noticed, as if to demonstrate, "See, I'm here, doing my job."

The Republican legislators were not a happy bunch, deeply unsettled by the election that had put "Sleepy Joe" in the White House. They unequivocally supported all of the demands in other states for vote recounts, and nodded solemnly whenever anyone said, "It was stolen."

In Kansas, of course, Trump had won—significantly—so they had nothing to contest. Unless they wanted to argue that the Dems had somehow manipulated voting so that *mostly* Republicans won but a *few* Dems had slipped in also.

They felt secure. Kansas was red and staying red, except for that liberal blue holdout that surrounded the university. But redistricting would soon fix that. Plus, the movement to pass regulations to "secure safe elections": limiting times when low-income people could vote, like evenings; limiting advance voting and mail-in ballots; limiting or removing drop-off boxes for ballots. All of those measures would "secure" the elections. For Republicans. At least that was the goal.

One legislator summed it up succinctly: "The regulations are to weed out people who should not be voting. They are not designed to affect Republicans."

There was a sign over the table: "A Gesture of Appreciation for All of Your Work from Your Grateful Constituents." The tablecloths were red-white-and-blue-stripes—a loan from Beth's parent's linen closet as they'd been big on 4ᵗʰ of July festivities. Several tiny American flags were laid out as well.

The MAGA messaging was clear. Democratic legislators avoided the corridor. Joe Biden may have won—but their position in Kansas, despite a Democratic governor, remained precarious.

Beth was working, industriously, her eyes on her computer screen. But she could see the table from her desk, could see the plates with neat little hand-printed signs in front: "Devilishly Delicious Walnut Chocolate

Chip," and "Heavenly Molasses Crisps," and "Once in a Lifetime Luscious Lemon Bars," and "To Die for Chocolate Caramel Brownies."

"Who brought the treats?" a representative asked her, one paw of a hand holding a blue napkin with four cookies.

"No idea, sir," Beth replied. "Some women swooped in and laid it all out and then left. I think the sign says it all: 'A Gesture of Appreciation.'"

"Damn," he mumbled, his mouth full of a chocolate caramel brownie. "I wish my wife could bake like this."

Beth watched as the piles dwindled down, until crumbs were all that remained. She kept working at her desk until the corridor was deserted, until a single step would echo, then took a big plastic garbage bag and quickly cleared the table. She'd told the others to not come back, better not to be noticed, and that she would clean up.

Beth, Larry, Kayla, and Cheryl had baked the treats together while drinking a bottomless rum punch. They'd gathered in Beth's kitchen, because she had a KitchenAid Stand Mixer and Kayla's kitchen was the size of a closet.

Bill and Debra had opted out as they had no ashes and, well, it all felt kind of creepy and probably illegal. Shawnee and Luis had not been at the post-group margarita table, and if they brought them in, they thought they'd have to tell Grace as well.

"If we tell Grace then we may put her in a position where she has to put a lid on it, right?" Kayla had asked. "Better to leave her out of it."

Each of the four had brought a recipe of a sweet that their loved one had adored. And, once all the ingredients of each recipe were thoroughly mixed, they each took out a baggie of the ashes of their dead parents, wife, and husband and sprinkled, ever so carefully, some ashes into the mix.

The lemon bar mix had initially had them worried. Ashes might be visible. But making it lemon-poppy seed resolved that concern.

"Can someone remind me why we're doing this?" Larry had asked in the middle of measuring chocolate chips into a bowl. "Isn't this illegal?"

Kayla had stepped back, put both her hands on her hips and hooted.

"Seriously, Larry?" Kayla asked. "I've never heard of a law that addresses baked treats directly, but I'm sure there's a statute somewhere."

"Well, actually," Cheryl added. "I googled it. There are lots with guidelines about where you can spread human ashes, how to store them and such. Not much on baking. But I did find an article that said—and let me loosely paraphrase—There is no medical reason not to bake your grandpa's ashes into a sugar cookie and eat it—and then described how a high school student in California did just that in October of 2018 and gave the cookies out in school."

"And here I thought we were being so original," Beth sighed.

"Cremated remains are a natural substance," Cheryl continued. "There are many cultures where ashes, not necessarily human, just ashes, are a part of the cuisine. The Navaho Nation uses ground juniper ash in their flour. And the Onondaga Nation is big on 'nixtamalization,' which I think is cooking corn in wood ash to break down the outer shells."

"Did the kid get in big trouble?" asked Larry, less interested in Navaho cooking and cuisine than legal consequences.

"Suspended from school? Maybe? But not 'big' trouble," Cheryl replied. "Larry, this is an *invisible* political act *unless* and *until* we go public. And, if and when we did tell someone, I cannot see GOP politicians wanting to go after us when they know they'd be the butt of every joke, newscast, and late-night TV show commentary. I bet we'd even get a *Saturday Night Live* skit."

"All of that makes me nervous," Larry said.

"These are the politicians that fought against mask mandates," Beth cut in. "Most follow Donald Trump. They've sold their souls to Satan. If you'd died, and Jasmine was here, what would she do? Or say? Huh?"

Larry paused, taking the question seriously.

"Feed the bastards some cookies, honey. Do it for me," he said, slowly, the words flavored with a Caribbean accent so perfect it was like he was channeling Jasmine.

And, until that very moment, no one in the group had envisioned Jasmine as Jamaican.

Katrina & Grace

Katrina and Grace were at Grace's casita, sitting across from one another, inside and toasty warm, while the cold winds of January in Kansas shook the windows. They were sipping tea. Two cranberry scones waited on the coffee table. They'd intended to go for an invigorating walk, but, once the wind had picked up, beat a hasty retreat back.

They'd covered the latest updates on what they were watching, how they were holding their breath until they could get vaccinated, what the hell was going on in the damn country as far as Trump and the GOP and more.

Then Grace segued, "Remember how I said that on the playground, when I first met you, that you felt Black—but also white?" Grace asked Katrina.

"Yes, I do recall that," Kat answered.

"So, how is that for you? Do you *feel* Black but *also* white?" This was an intimate question, and Grace's voice was tentative.

It was a question that Katrina had wrestled with her entire life. It ebbed and flowed, depending on the situation, the circumstance. Both her parents were 'Black' but lighter-skinned. They'd never tried to pass. But they'd recognized that doors had opened a bit more easily for them. And they'd been keenly aware of what was required of them to succeed professionally, to be accepted and respected by whites.

Katrina remembered her mother admonishing her for coming home after playing with kids in the neighborhood and using slang, different pronunciation, or even a tone, that she'd heard from other kids.

"Katrina Baptiste, you do not talk trashy in this house," her mother would say. "You use *proper* English. *Enunciate.* You have to show the world that you have manners. You're getting a good education, so act like it."

And Katrina had complied. She had not questioned why *proper* English was the only acceptable way to talk, or why it was up to her to always show the world—anything? She'd just ducked her head when other Black kids had mocked her for talking white, for having a funny name, even for how she dressed.

She was just wearing what her mother told her to wear.

But there had been a divide between Katrina and other Black children. She talked different, looked different, and went to a different school.

New Orleans then had been very segregated—although New Orleans *now* was not much better. There was never any real "separate but equal."

Katrina's parents wanted more for her, wanted her to have a *good* education.

Her mom, like many Blacks in southern Louisiana, was Creole and Catholic. The best Catholic girl's school in New Orleans was the Ursuline Academy. It had integrated in 1962, and her mother had talked with the nuns when she was a toddler.

Katrina's mother had appreciated its history

"It's the oldest continually operating school for girls, and oldest Catholic school, in the United States," Kat remembers her mother telling people, explaining why her daughter was going there. "It was founded in 1727 and provided the first classes for free women of color, for Native Americans, for African American slaves."

"And the Ursuline nuns," she'd continue, "they expect excellence. All the girls are treated exactly the same."

The school tuition was their biggest expense besides their mortgage. But they believed that any sacrifice was worth a good education, and a good education was where white kids went.

The Ursuline Academy was a half-hour bus ride away, on State Street, just outside the old Historic District. It was an imposing building, behind tall wrought-iron fences.

Katrina attended the Ursuline Academy from first grade through high school. She took a bus to school every day, which meant getting up a lot earlier than some of her classmates. The bus regulars got used to her, but, when new people got on? A Black girl wearing a uniform? What was *that* about?

"You went to a parochial school, right?" Kat asked, shaking herself out of that jog along memory lane. "For elementary?"

"Yeah, I did. St. Mary's."

"Any Black kids?"

"No," Grace replied.

"But you wore a uniform, right?"

"Sure," Grace said. "Where are you going with this?"

"My parents sacrificed to get me a good education. For twelve years, I went to the Ursuline Academy. The uniform was a wool skirt—gray and navy, houndstooth print, princess style—with a white blouse with a Peter Pan collar, and a grosgrain navy tie that actually had to be tied. Then a navy-blue wool blazer and a beanie of the skirt material. Plus, a wool felt hat for special occasions."

"Lordy, you can remember all that? That's a lot of wool for New Orleans. Better for Nebraska."

"Does it sound like what you think a Black kid in New Orleans would be wearing?"

"No, it does not."

"People would ask me, 'What school do you go to?' and 'What are you doing in that uniform?' Like I had no business wearing it," Katrina said. "And I did not have the right, as a Black girl, to ignore them, or tell them it was none of their damn business. Because, 45 or 50 years ago, if a white adult asked a question, you answered. And you were respectful and polite no matter how much you were screaming on the inside."

"I don't think that an adult ever questioned me about my uniform, ever. But I lived in a small town, not a city, and there was only one parochial school."

"You're missing the point, Gracie." Kat leaned forward in her chair. "It's not about the number of parochial schools. I was a Black girl in a uniform intended for white girls. And any white person felt they had a right to ask me whatever came into their head. And I never knew where it could lead, like if somebody would get angry. I rode the public bus to school, and I sat in the back of the bus, or front row by the driver. I took off my beanie and tie. I tried to blend in, hide behind a book."

"Did it work? Did you talk to your parents? Or the teachers?"

"I tried with my parents, but they had enough to deal with," Kat replied. "And what could they do? Ride the bus with me? Run interference with white people?"

"What about the nuns?"

"Nope. But you know how we talked about color blind? That was how it was inside the school. Every girl was treated exactly the same. The nuns were determined to make it a safe environment, no discrimination. But that meant that we had to be color blind to ourselves. Nobody asked what it was like outside the school gates. We didn't talk about being Black in New Orleans. Or how being in a white school affected our relationships with Black friends, how we didn't really belong."

"Belong as fitting in with Black friends? What about the other students?"

"We were friends with white girls, even really good friends. But it was limited to *school*. Once we walked outside those towering gates, we were Black again. We didn't go to the white kids' homes. They did not come to our homes."

"And this was never directly addressed?"

"A few nuns approached me, said something like, 'I expect it is hard being a minority here, and, if you ever want to talk, I'm here to listen.' They were well-intentioned and kind. But how do you tell them that school is not the problem, being Black in a racist world is. Like 'Can you fix that, Sister Francis?'"

"Did you want to go to a public school?"

"It wasn't my decision. And you've seen what inner-city, low-income schools can look like, smell like? You want your child to go to one of those? Not enough staff, dated textbooks, no arts or music," Katrina said. "My school was beautiful: tall ceilings, wood, big windows. And, oh my God, the chapel. I loved singing in that chapel. I was getting a white girl education and I knew that whatever shit I had to put up with—on a bus, or anywhere—it was worth it. But I also felt guilty that I was escaping what other Black kids could not escape. I was learning how to work the keys that would unlock the cage."

Grace was listening intently. This was the most that Kat had ever shared about her school, growing up in New Orleans. She did not want Kat to stop talking.

"So, Gracie, now you tell me about your parochial school," Katrina segued.

"It was boring, sometimes 50 kids in a classroom. Brick and cement building, eight classrooms on the top floor, cafeteria that doubled as a gym on the ground floor. It echoed a lot but not in a good way, just noise. A building with no soul. I was a good kid. Never caused trouble. I really believed, had faith." Grace paused to refocus. "But race? Race was not a part of my daily life. It never came up. We didn't think about being white. White was a given, a norm. I was color blind to my whiteness."

Grace realized that Kat had abruptly checked out, that she hadn't heard a word she'd said.

"Katrina? Are you okay?"

"I just realized something about meeting you on that playground, what made you different from other white girls."

"I wasn't exactly a 'girl,' but go on."

"*You invited me to your home.* With my kids. Right off. Open door."

"And that made a difference how?"

"Remember how you told me that I did not clam up and freeze you out like the college Black girls, right?"

"Yeah, I said that."

"Well, you didn't put up walls. *You invited me into your home.* The entire time I was at the Ursuline Academy, I did not go to a white girl's home. I think there may have been some all-class holiday things, but never *me* being invited."

They were quiet then, thinking about themselves, as girls, hungry for acceptance and still yearning now.

Theo & Grace

Sessions were still on the back patio, although Grace had offered to Zoom if Theo preferred. He'd asked if she was offering because he was too high a risk to meet with, even if outdoors. She said he was high risk, but that an hour outdoors, distanced, mostly masked, every three or four weeks, was nothing compared to what he did every damn day.

The heater was working well, and they both wore hats and gloves. Their hands were wrapped around hot mugs of tea.

Grace started by asking about work, kids, his wife. Theo gave a quick update.

"I've decided that when COVID is over, I want to enroll in a grad program in bioethics," Theo said when Grace asked what was on his mind. "I found a program for working professionals, with classes just one day a week, and I could schedule around it."

"What degree would that be? And what kind of work?" Grace asked.

"I'm not sure. I can start as a special student. And, while this is long-term, maybe a Ph.D. down the road. It's a growing field, and bioethicists don't just teach but do research and consult a lot on complicated issues."

Grace had taken a few seminars, mostly online classes, on ethics and bioethics when she'd started working rotations for the military, working with combat troops returning from deployments. Now *that* had been ethical quicksand.

"What grabs you about it?"

"I'm living it. Bioethics has only been around as a field since the 70s and 80s. It's still emerging, and this global pandemic is making it clear that we lack pragmatic and flexible policies."

"How do you mean?" Grace asked.

"Bioethics needs to be an essential part of medical decision-making and protocols. When medical care has to be triaged, we need guidelines."

"Such as?"

"I've been thinking about this a lot," Theo explained, smiling. "So please stop me if I get into a rant."

Grace nodded.

"Well, *every* action is informed by ethical principles or lack of ethical principles," Theo said, as if launching into a lecture on Ethics 101. "Emmanuel Kant believed that right or wrong is not based on consequences, but more if our choices or actions fulfill a moral imperative. Moral imperatives trump 'rules' that do not adhere to a moral imperative."

Theo looked at Grace. She waved her hand to continue.

"But some ethicists focus on the consequences of a decision, usually the greatest good. With limited resources, is it more ethical to dedicate a million dollars to kids' health—screenings, vaccines, healthy food supplements for a million kids—or to allocate that money for extreme end-of-life measures to preserve a few individual lives?"

"And that would be...?"

"Utilitarianism. An unethical person can make a decision with an outcome that fits utilitarianism because it benefits the greater good even if made for a selfish reason."

"So, by that standard, Trump would have been ethical if he'd modeled and mandated masking, and ordered factories to produce PPE, even if he did it to improve his approval ratings and not to save lives?" Grace asked.

"I hate to say yes but—*yes*," Theo answered.

"So narcissistic, self-serving choices can ultimately be ethical? That's disturbing."

"I asked you to stop me if I went into a rant," Theo said. "I'm ranting..."

But Grace ignored him, asking another question. "So, tell me about bioethics during COVID?"

"With COVID-19, it's a shitshow," Theo said, smiling, something Grace had rarely seen. Theo had a great smile.

"In a crisis, without ethics-based protocols, life-and-death decisions get kicked down the road," he continued. "The Federal Government abandoned its role to lead, direct, coordinate. Donald Trump modeled defiance..."

"And you see a different outcome with ethics-informed decisions?" Grace interrupted.

"Absolutely. What happened in the United States during COVID, and continues to happen every day, defies *every* tenet of *every* school of ethics."

"But aren't ethics different in war?"

"When POTUS ignored his ethical responsibility to 'lead' the country, to guide if not compel citizens to do some things that were inconvenient or difficult but essential for the *greater* good, the moral imperative was destroyed."

*Now **this** is what I call a rant*, thought Grace. *A damn good rant at that.*

"Do you remember when Trump read a half-decent speech off a teleprompter on national TV? We had hope for about twenty seconds. Then he back-pedaled and tossed the COVID war into the laps of the governors. They scrambled, bidding against each other for ventilators and PPE, often from China, with everything ten times, a hundred times, more expensive than if the feds had managed procurement and distribution. We're fighting the same war, but state by state..."

Theo paused, thoughts running ahead of words.

"From there, it all slides downhill—dumped on to frontline medical workers. From 'Make your own PPE out of garbage bags and duct tape,' to 'Figure out how to have two patients share a ventilator,' to 'Make split-second life-or-death decisions.'

When the president flaunted not wearing a mask, as if any discomfort or inconvenience was an affront to his ego and privilege, he modeled not just non-compliance but a *basis* for that noncompliance. *'Feelings' became a basis for non-compliance.* Science became suspect."

Grace watched as Theo's face tightened in concentration.

"We're the only country on the planet with this degree of conflict over blocking the spread of a highly contagious infection. Nations who looked to the United States for ethical leadership, for guidance, have turned away in disgust. They blame the U.S.—and Facebook and Twitter—for fringe groups surfacing in their own countries."

Theo stopped, as if a tape that had been playing in his head had just broken. A switch flipped off. He took a few breaths and then spoke again, but his voice was no longer strident, but halting, discouraged.

"My country, that I trusted to be ethical, to protect its citizens, abandoned us. So, it's been up to frontline workers, with no power, to cope with this hell, to face patients in excruciating pain and not have what we need to do our jobs, pushed to an exhaustion that words cannot..."

No, Grace thought, *you are absolutely correct. Words cannot...*

Zed & Cherry

Zed traded shifts at work so he could watch the inauguration with Cherry. It was more to console each other but, also, with the slim, slim hope that *someone* would intervene. And *that* they did want to witness.

It was a strange inauguration, so few people, all masked and distanced. Nothing like the wild celebration and crowds after Trump had been inaugurated, the biggest in history. No parties and celebrations in the street. It was just that upper crust who knew that they had stolen the election. Like they knew it and were ashamed, so no parties planned.

The fake news was spouting the party line: "No parties are being held due to COVID."

But that was just an excuse. Zed knew they were all gathering whenever they wanted. The "rules" were for the people without the power, to keep them from talking to each other. It was just a means of control, and the virus was to keep them down, to make them afraid, to distract them from what was really happening behind the scenes.

But Zed and Cherry were tracking the undercurrents. One was that today, Inauguration Day, while so many of the Deep State were gathered in one place, that the round up would take place. The entire mall would be surrounded by military, and by night everyone would be jailed, and Donald Trump would remain in the White House. There were posts from people inside the White House that the president had not started packing. Like he knew he was not moving out. And no way would he be showing Biden and his Dem wife around the White House. The election had been stolen and he was not about to pretend that this was some normal "transfer of power."

For a week or so after the inauguration, there was little to track. They wondered if something had happened to Q, if the Deep State had silenced him. Because that would be the only reason he would disappear.

But then they read that the dates were mixed up. It was not the Inauguration Day in January but the *original* Inauguration Day, the date set by the founding fathers in the Constitution. That was March 4th, and it hadn't been changed until 1933 with the 20th Amendment. The 20th Amendment was called the "Lame Duck Amendment" and it shortened the period of time between election in November and when new president and members of Congress are installed. So perhaps that was when the reckoning would take place.

Zed needed to do more research.

Katrina

Katrina was getting vaccinated at 11 a.m. Her first shot. Pfizer required two shots given three weeks apart.

She had had to fight to get it because she was not yet over 65 and not an essential worker. She'd never had a positive COVID test. But she did not back down when told that "You will get a call when your age group is up." She'd gotten a letter from her physician and hand-delivered it to the hospital.

She was frightened, but also excited. Several people in her online support group, and Survivor Corps, a national group, had already been vaccinated. Some had been part of a test group to get the vaccine when in development, to see if people who were previously infected with COVID reacted differently.

Some people shared that their long-haul symptoms had dissipated after their second shot. Nobody could explain why, but conjecture was that the first vaccine promoted an immune response that was then triggered by the second vaccine which then reached "pockets" of the virus that were lingering, in hiding, and had not been defeated. But nobody knew anything for sure. Not yet.

That is how Katrina now visualized her condition. Her body was engaged in a war with a virus, and she—the bodily *person* of Katrina Baptiste—was simply the property, the land, over which they were fighting to control. Her injuries were not the result of an intentional attack against her. She was collateral damage. Like "Hey, so sorry you got caught up in this, nothing personal—didn't mean for the bombs to drop on your house."

She looked at the clock. Nine a.m. She needed to get moving. It would take her at least an hour to get showered and dressed since even that much activity left her winded. She needed to sit down, draped in a towel, for ten minutes after her shower before drying her hair, and another ten after putting on her clothes. Driving to the hospital would require stamina. But she was motivated.

Katrina would not allow herself to hope that the vaccine would heal her body. She was more afraid she might be one of the small minority of long-haulers who felt worse after the vaccine.

But she knew that being vaccinated would protect her from a devastating reinfection. And, with everything she was hearing about more surges coming—something called variants—any protection was better than none.

Nell

When Ian died, a part of Nell died too. She did not return to teaching. The holiday break started while Ian was on a ventilator, and, when she was supposed to return, just a few weeks ago, she could not get out of bed. She simply laid there, the comforter clutched in her hands under her chin, staring at the clock and doing the *unthinkable*. How could she not go to work? How could she let down the people who depended on her? The children waiting in the classroom?

But Nell did just that. When the school called, sounding worried as she hadn't missed a day of work in years, Nell apologized. Then she said she needed a leave-of-absence, and, no, she did not know when she might be well enough to return.

Instead, two days later, Nell was back at the funeral home. She sat at the desk and answered the phone. She listened to grieving and frightened people, explained what could be provided, expressed empathy. She again organized the ever-growing inventory of black boxes of ashes. Although her system had worked well in her absence, they needed another four shelves to accommodate more boxes, and that required finishing the alphabet of shelves and starting over with "A-2, B-2, C-2…"

Nell had married into this family. She had not grown up with death so visible and omnipresent. But it felt comforting to her now to be surrounded by death and grief. She appreciated the concerns of some friends, when they asked, in a worried tone, "Isn't it more painful to be in the middle of so much death, like a constant reminder?"

How could she explain that still being alive was the reminder? That dealing with death, so much death, made her loss more normal, even bearable. And, if she started sobbing, in a corner behind the caskets, her in-laws just pulled her into a hug and murmured, "Hush, hush, now," and patted her back until she cried herself out.

In late January, a letter arrived from the state that Ian and Nell Thomas had been approved to adopt, and to schedule their home study, a final step. Nell wrote back explaining that Ian had died of COVID in December. She thought that would be the end of it. But another letter came asking if she wished to proceed as a single parent adoption.

But being a single parent had never been part of their plan. It had always been the two of them, relying on each other, tag-teaming, sharing. Two parents, not one. She put the letter in the file labeled "Adoption" and did not reply.

HISTORICAL CONTEXT: JANUARY 2021

Jan. 3: "...Dr. Fauci is revered by the Lame Stream Media as...having done...such an incredible job, yet he works for me and the Trump Administration, and I am in no way given any credit for my work. Gee, could this just be Fake News?" – *Donald Trump*

Jan. 3: "The number of cases and deaths of the China Virus is far exaggerated... When in doubt, call it COVID." – *Donald Trump*

Jan. 4: "The deaths are real deaths. All you need to do is go out into the trenches." – *Dr. Anthony Fauci in response to Donald Trump.*

Jan. 6: Trump supporters march from a rally to the Capitol in Washington, D.C. Police officers are attacked, a rioter is shot, and three others die during the rampage. Capitol Police report that 140 officers were injured.

Jan. 7: U.S. Congress certifies Joe Biden and Kamala Harris' victory in the 2020 election.

Jan. 8: Twitter permanently suspends Donald Trump's account, @realdonaldtrump, "due to the risk of further incitement of violence" after the January 6th insurrection.

Jan. 12: Judge Peter Cahill rules that Officer Derek Chauvin will be tried alone in the murder of George Floyd. Three other officers will be tried later.

Jan. 13: The U.S. House of Representatives votes in favor of impeaching President Trump, making him the first U.S. president to be impeached twice.

Jan. 19: President-elect Joe Biden and Vice-President-elect Kamala Harris lead a lighting ceremony at the Reflecting Pool at the Lincoln Memorial, honoring the nearly 400,000 Americans who have died from COVID-19.

Jan. 20: Biden's Inauguration takes place in Washington, D.C. In his first action as president, he imposes a mask mandate on federal property, installs a coronavirus response coordinator to oversee the White House's efforts to distribute vaccines, and halts the United States' withdrawal from the World Health Organization.

Jan. 22: "A lot of America is hurting. The virus is surging. We're 400,000 dead expected to reach well over 600,000. It will take months to turn around the pandemic's trajectory." – *Joe Biden*

February 2020

Covid Grief Group

Everyone in the grief group was counting the days until they would be eligible to get vaccinated. But their survivor syndrome guilt was escalating.

"If only..." consumed their minds. Not just about the vaccine, but the medical knowledge that had emerged, over months, incrementally, from trial and error, as physicians discovered what small things could make a difference. Like how proning, flipping people over on their stomachs, helped breathing. And how ventilators used much earlier were more effective because the lungs were not too far gone to recover.

While different in specifics, they felt a shared despair, deeply embedded with self-recrimination.

And rage. Now that there were vaccines, it felt, somehow, that the deaths had been even more arbitrary.

"My mom would be alive to get vaccinated if the assholes had worn their masks like the CDC told them to," Kayla vented. "But, no, they have their 'rights' to whatever they want with their bodies," she said, making air quotes with her fingers. "Nobody is gonna' boss them around. They don't like the way a mask *feels*? Seriously? So maybe they should get to see what *dying* feels like instead? Huh?"

The group was quiet, recognizing that Kayla was mired in fear and loneliness, missing her mom every day and every night.

"I don't get how so many of the anti-maskers, who followed Trump's lead, bought his macho bullshit that masks were a choice and not necessary. So how come those same people aren't questioning *everything* he said about the 'hoax' when they see him first in line for the vaccine?" Larry added. "I bet his pretty young wife isn't waiting for her turn in line. No way his kids will be waiting months for their turn."

"What are your ages again?" Grace asked. "And what are the

breakdowns by age for the tiers?" She was trying to back away from going down the Trump rabbit hole. Or was it Trump quicksand?

It was a harsh moment when they did the numbers. For some it would be a few months. For Kayla, the youngest in the group, it could be as late as summer.

They *knew* that every damn day until then, any one of them could get infected, suffer, and even die while protection was *almost* within reach, *almost*, just around the corner. Like drowning when you could see the Coast Guard coming. Just not soon enough.

"I cannot do this right now," said Luis softly. "I cannot think that I could have had my Mariana, *y mi hija*, her name is Isabella—she would be five months now—have them *alive*? We could be in our home, cuddling our baby together, in our bed? That their dying was not an act of God, but could have been prevented? Not even an accident? If I think that, I will fall down and never get up. If I think that, I must hate God."

"Oh, damn, Luis, I didn't mean for it to... I don't know what I meant, just that I feel like my gut is burning and my head will explode," Larry said. "I miss Jasmine. But when I think about you losing Mariana and your baby as well?"

There are times when any words would be tools to pacify, minimize, deflect. Others, when words are useless.

So, they sat, with tears falling or eyes clenched tight as fists. They sat as Grace stood up and walked to Luis, knelt by his chair, and put her hand on his knee.

They sat, simply breathing together. Even if some of them longed to not have to keep breathing, to give up, they had, in this moment, no other option.

Theo & Grace

Theo was late, which was unusual. He was scrupulously punctual due to working in hospitals, especially this past year, when doctors, nurses and RTs depended on their relief showing up. How they counted down the minutes.

He must have gotten held up at work, Grace conjectured.

It was a 9 a.m. appointment. Theo preferred the morning because he was often wired after work and couldn't go to sleep anyway. When he did show, just 20 minutes late, he was still in his scrubs and appeared distracted.

"What's going on?" Grace asked.

"A patient died toward the end of my shift, and I had to complete the paperwork."

"COVID?" Grace asked.

"Yeah, end stage. Lungs kaput. He was 72, just came in yesterday. His doctor was ready to put him on a ventilator later today if he didn't improve. But then his heart stopped. He had a DNR, so we didn't have to make futile attempts to resuscitate. But his doctor was upset. Like he'd wanted us to bypass the DNR, get the paddles, shock him, everything we'd do if he didn't have COVID. Except he *did* have COVID."

"And this fell into your lap because?"

"I was the RT who was working with him, managing supplemental oxygen, all the steps that we try before a ventilator. I'd just upped his oxygen levels, ran to the bathroom, then checked on one other patient. He coded while I was gone.

"Anyway, it is what it is," Theo concluded. "So, have you gotten vaccinated yet? Josie and I both got our first shots in early January, the *only* benefit for being frontline. They had us in a waiting room afterward for 15 minutes to make sure no one had an allergic reaction. All these people in scrubs were sitting in their socially-distanced chairs and crying. That's what a relief it was. And anyone who walked into the waiting room took one look and their eyes would instantly fill. We've all been trying for so long to be stoic."

"Did you cry?"

"Of course. Then this nurse from the oncology unit sang *Amazing Grace*. She started out really soft, but then we all joined in, just the same stanzas that everybody knew, over and over. It felt like a lament, so much pain in one damn song. We've all been feeling so lost, so blind."

"That sounds intense."

"It was. Then a doctor from obstetrics said, out loud, to the room, 'I haven't held the babies in a year. I deliver them and then hand them off. But I used to always take time after the delivery to cuddle them, look in their newborn-baby eyes and say, 'Welcome to the world, peanut.' But

I've been so scared of infecting them. And their parents too. So afraid I'd hurt them.'

We were all crying, but we all understood. So much of medical care is intimate. We can't really care, or heal, without touching."

Mickey & Grace

Mickey had a text from Grace: I just got an email, so check your inbox NOW. Health Dept got shipment of vaccines. They're booking slots. I grabbed one for Friday.

Thanks. On it, he replied.

An hour later, over coffee in Grace's living room, with almond croissants from Wheatfields that Mickey had picked up to celebrate their scoring appointment slots to get vaccinated, they felt giddy. Grace was at 9:45 a.m. Mickey at 11 a.m. Then, in three weeks, the second dose. And then...

Could this really be over? Could a one-second shot in the arm protect them from a horrible illness and death?

The scientists, doctors, and researchers all said yes. They'd worked for years to finally have the breakthroughs that made it possible.

"Let's celebrate," Mickey said. "Drive to Kansas City and find the biggest outdoor patio we can and be carnivores. Expensive-steak-kind-of-carnivores. Polish off a bottle of overpriced wine."

"And then who drives back?" Grace asked, her practical side surfacing. "After a bottle?"

"Okay, then let's celebrate here. Eat whatever. I don't care. And we Uber home if we're buzzed."

"Whatever happened to *tipsy*?" Grace asked. "I liked '*tipsy*.' I could say I was tipsy, and it was almost cute, affectionate. But 'buzzed?' That's harsh."

"We can cover linguistics when we're drinking. Get your coat. I feel..."

"Hopeful?" Grace interrupted. "Cautiously optimistic?"

"I'll be in the car," Mickey replied.

Mike & Molly

When Molly checked her phone, she saw a missed call and a text from Mike. She called him back immediately.

"My dad has COVID," Mike said. "He took a test, and it came back positive yesterday."

Molly felt her heart sink. "But he's vaccinated, right? Didn't both your parents get their shots?"

"Yeah, but they've just had one dose," Mike explained. "Pfizer. Got it as soon as they were available. They're scheduled for the second one next week."

"So how did he get it?"

"Being vaccinated doesn't mean you can't catch the virus, just that it will probably be a lot less serious," he sighed. "Oh, hell, Molly, I don't understand the medicine. But without the vaccine people can die and that's a lot less likely if you're vaccinated."

"How is he feeling? Are the symptoms bad?"

Mike's voice sounded shaky. "He feels like shit, but he's being stoic about it. He's feverish, but not too bad. Achy, tired, says his joints hurt. Staying in bed. Gets exhausted walking to the bathroom. I've never seen him like this. Not ever."

"You're scared, aren't you?"

"Yes, but not nearly as crazy-scared as I'd be without him being partially vaccinated. That would have been a death sentence. He's an older Hispanic man. And did I ever mention the cigar he smoked on the back patio every evening when I was a kid? His one pleasure. One cigar a day."

"Does he have any idea where he caught it?"

"That's also hard on him. Since they got vaccinated, they started going out some. Not dining inside, but an outdoor restaurant or doing some shopping. But he was in a restaurant bathroom and four young guys came in at once, crowding, no masks, and loud, laughing, poking at each other, talking about how many bars they'd cruised, who scored. And he says he felt a shiver of apprehension, of danger. So, it could have been in the deli, or anywhere, but he's convinced it was in that bathroom. He wasn't dining indoors, he just had to piss really bad. And he had a mask on."

"Well, your parents do have some highly developed intuition, so maybe it was. Does he need to go to the hospital?"

"Not yet. Maybe never."

"Do you want company? Can I come down and help?" Molly asked.

Mike snorted. "Think about what you just said. You're unvaccinated, so travel across many states or fly, show up here, just to quarantine for two weeks?"

She flushed. "Okay, I get it, it was a dumb thing to say."

"But your heart is in the right place. And I appreciate the sentiment."

Abuelo was stoic, weathering the virus with few complaints. He was more worried about his wife, Marta. He did not want her taking care of him, being further exposed. Mike put box fans in the windows, pulling the air out.

Marta sat on a dining room chair in the doorway to their room, wearing a mask, with a face shield over the mask. She had Mike hook up a computer to a monitor in their bedroom so they could—at a distance—binge watch old TV shows and movies. She cooked every favorite dish he'd ever had even though he had no appetite. She knew he would take a few bites just to make her feel better.

Mike was anxious about David being over, but David argued. What if he promised to stay in the living room and kitchen, to only use the bathroom in the basement? And if Mike was doing the caretaking, but still going between the two houses, their house was part of the quarantine group, and David would be exposed anyway.

The kid might turn out to be a lawyer.

Mike knew that this was scary for David. He had endured so much loss in his life, that *any* loss, especially the grandfather he had come to deeply love, would be traumatic.

It took two weeks, but Abuelo started to recover. He finally tested negative. He got his appetite back. Abuela did not get sick. Mike and David didn't take tests, but they didn't have symptoms, either.

They felt as if a tornado had been heading directly toward their home but had changed course at the last minute. It was so arbitrary.

Max

"**Some people on TV** say that COVID was completely unpredictable, and that no one could have imagined it," Max was telling Mickey. "But that's not true at all."

"Why do you say that?" Mickey asked.

"The movie *Contagion* imagined it. It even had the virus starting in China and spreading all over the world. And all the stuff we have to do, like masks and social distancing? It was all in the movie. It had a vaccine. But they had a different way to give out the vaccine in the movie. It was a lottery, like lotteries for who had to be soldiers in wars, or bingo but the balls all had birthdates. So, it wasn't exactly right. But..."

"That's interesting," Mickey nodded. "We'll have to watch it together."

Mickey didn't have to engage much for Max to keep talking.

Max then explained all the ways that the world could have anticipated a pandemic. Then why they had not. Then he compared COVID-19 to Ebola and polio and AIDS and listed how COVID was different than the flu. It was a 17-minute monologue.

Then Max made a quick segue.

"Did you know that doctors in the Middle Ages with the plague wore masks? That looked like giant beaks?" Max asked Mickey. "They had long beaks, and sometimes goggles too."

"Really?" Mickey asked. "Why the beaks?"

"To put in herbs and stuff so that smelly air could get purified before it got to their noses or lungs."

"Did that work? What about this smelly air?"

"They believed that bad smelly air caused disease. But everything smelled a lot in the Middle Ages. They didn't have plumbing or electricity," Max explained. "They thought that if they could block the smelly air then they wouldn't catch it. They also never touched the sick people and had sticks to keep them away. Is that like social distancing now?"

"The doctors wouldn't touch sick people?"

"No, just leave them herbs and stuff, I think," Max replied.

"Herbs and stuff? Not so farfetched from what's all over the internet now," Mickey said.

"Wanna' see a picture of the masks?" Max asked. "People still wear them for Mardi Gras."

"Absolutely," Mickey answered, smiling at Max's enthusiasm. "Bring 'em on."

Grace & Katrina

Katrina didn't look at the time before she punched-in Grace's number.

"I just remembered something that I hadn't remembered in decades," Katrina said as soon as Grace picked up the phone.

"What?" Grace asked, swallowing a yawn. "You do know this is past my bedtime, right?" It was only 10 p.m. but the ring had jerked her awake. She'd dozed off in her chair with the TV on.

"I had an auntie who was darker, more African-black. She used to take my face in her hands and tell me how pretty I was. How blessed I was to be pretty," Kat blurted out. "How I would have such beautiful children."

"What's wrong with being pretty?" Grace asked.

"I didn't understand it at first. She was so tender, sincere. But there was a wistfulness sometimes in her face, looking at her own daughters, my cousins, who have more Black features and darker skin. Like she knew they were going to have a harder time in life and there was nothing she could do to change that. She couldn't protect them."

"Ohhhh... How did your cousins feel?"

"More 'It is what it is.' But I believe that every one of them, at some point, wished they looked less Black, more Creole, more mixed-race. Because it is easier."

"Even as kids? It was that much harder?"

"By the time they were seven or eight? One told me how a group of white boys on a city bus circled her seat and started jumping up and down and making monkey noises. Another one had a car full of white boys yell out, 'Go back to Africa' and 'Hey, coon girl, wanna' eat my banana?' It was freaky scary."

"But that didn't happen to you?"

"Not that. More how white adults felt they had the right to question me, like 'Where are you from, girl?' Because, maybe, I wasn't Black. Maybe Greek or Portuguese. And being able to put me in a 'category' mattered a lot."

Grace was silent. Sometimes she had no idea what a decent response would be. 'I'm sorry' was so inadequate. Quiet was better.

"Well, never mind, go back to sleep," Kat ended. "We can talk another time."

Ever since they'd started talking about race, Katrina found herself remembering things she'd buried. And the painful reasons that she'd buried them. She struggled with the same internalized racism that her auntie had felt looking at her, that her mother had wanted to arm her against by teaching her the skills to fit in a white-centric world. She raged in her head and heart against the messages of white-centered education.

Kat wrestled with knowing, looking in the mirror, that she would not trade her lighter skin for darker, that she did not wish that her sons were darker. And every time such a thought entered her consciousness, she felt that she was betraying her Blackness.

When Kat looked back on the falling out, the "Why haven't we ever talked about race?" question, she still hit a wall.

Kat still felt like Grace hadn't *wanted* to know. If she did, she would've asked. And Kat had picked up that cue and not brought things up as to not rock the friendship boat.

And, Kat surmised, Grace felt the same, only in reverse: that Kat did not want to dig into potentially painful areas, and she, Grace, simply respected that boundary and did not probe or press.

Did it matter? Or was it a chicken or egg question that would never be answered?

Grace wasn't a bigot, Kat knew that. But she'd been oblivious to so much going on around her.

How could Kat have explained the slights, the benign questions that assumed a stereotypical "package" when first meeting a Black woman. The slightly lifted eyebrow when Kat had replied "I'm an attorney" to the "Do you work?" question at PTA or some social gathering. The smiling surprise, along with the unspoken "Oh, I was not expecting that."

Like she should work at Walmart? Or be a teacher or nurse? But an attorney? A physician? Didn't fit their 'picture'?"

Kat asked herself *why* she'd never vented to Grace about what it was like for her when other women, white women, were *too* polite, *too* careful to make sure she was asked to be on committees so that there was "representation?" On committees on which she was almost always the only woman of color, and thus asked to approve or veto anything that could be interpreted as insensitive to minority students or families. As if being even part-Black provided her insight and authority?

Because, Kat admitted, she had not vented. She had not shared.

After all, the women were trying *not* to be racist. They were do-gooders. What exactly would she have said to Grace? That the other white women, the other smiling, well-intentioned moms, were so frickin' annoying in their uber-politeness and cordial inclusivity?

Kat wondered if Grace was one of "them" when she interacted with other women of color, at work meetings and conferences.

How could she not be? She was white.

Mike

In mid-to-late February, Mike got an email that was a kick in the gut.

Dear Friend,
　　I'm Ian Thomas's wife. I'm sorry to have to tell you this, but Ian died of COVID in December. I'm just now going through his computer and seeing the friends he was in contact with—and you are one of them. He woke up one morning and couldn't breathe. He was placed on a ventilator. He never came back. Ian gave so much to every life that he touched. Thank you for being his friend.
　　　　　　　　　　　　　　　　　　　　　　　Sincerely,
　　　　　　　　　　　　　　　　　　　　　　　Nell

Ian Thomas? Killed by COVID? After evading death in Iraq, after saving other soldiers, after... And so close, so very, very close to the vaccine?

That, somehow, made it worse. Like soldiers killed in the weeks before they were scheduled to redeploy, when they'd already packed their gear in anticipation, when their families had already planned the surprise reunion party. Those deaths had always been the worst.

Mike remembered, vividly, the reunion ceremonies when his brigade had returned from deployments. The bleachers filled with spouses and children and parents, a massive flag as backdrop, patriotic music pumping, soldiers lined up, at attention, exhausted from hours or days of travel, a few words from a commander and chaplain, And, then, the magic word—"Dismissed"—and the frenzied, desperate release as families found each other in the crowds.

Mike had survived several reunions, each a surprise, like how had he made it through another deployment? He and Ian had shared just one reunion.

But now Ian was dead, killed by this damn virus. Mike thought he would wait to tell Molly. She was scared enough as it was.

Mickey

Grace had not engaged with the sauna as Mickey had hoped. She admired it and joined him a few times. But she did not *anticipate* a sauna, did not look forward to the experience of shutting down her mind and letting her body melt in the cedar barrel of heat.

"I'm not sure that it works for me as it does for you," she told him.

"I don't think you stay in long enough to reach that tipping point. You're looking at the timer, counting down to when you can leave," he countered. "You need to close your eyes, try to clear your brain, focus on breathing."

"It hurts to breathe, Mickey," Grace protested. "I end up panting."

"Only the first few times," Mickey assured her. "It's like exercise and endorphins. They come, but only after discomfort."

That had not been the best explanation as Grace rarely got a hit of endorphins. She did not reach that threshold on her walks. And she was not fond of sweating.

But snow was predicted for this afternoon. A lot of snow over the next 24 hours. And Mickey hoped that the visceral combination of the baking heat, and then shock of the cold, rubbing fresh snow on arms and legs that welcomed the relief? It was hard to explain to people who had not developed a certain "sensibility," how a body could stand naked in falling snow and not feel cold because it had been baked like a loaf of bread, because heat had saturated every inch of skin.

The naked part was also a bit challenging for Grace. She had, Mickey had come to realize, a lot of unresolved body image issues. That she could be so critical and unaccepting of her own body, while helping lots of women, hundreds of them over the years, be more accepting and satisfied with their bodies, was a puzzle.

The few times he had seen Grace loosen from her body issues was when she was in the ocean. Somehow the ocean, perhaps because it was so alive, required focus to not be bowled over by a wave, focus to jump up, to leap into the wave, or dive below the wave distracted her. And the water was up to her chest, so the body was covered. Her laughter in the ocean was different. It came from a deeper place, when she was still a girl, before she knew shame.

That evening, he laid their white robes and rubber slippers out on the bed and then called to Grace. When she walked in and saw the robes, she started to protest.

"Mickey, it's snowing, for heaven's sake. You expect me to go out in the cold and snow in a robe?"

"Yes," he answered. "I want you to try."

"Can we wait until it isn't snowing?" she pleaded.

"I want you to try *because* it's snowing. To see if you can spark a little joy."

Grace glared at him. "Marie Kondo is getting a little old."

"Do this for me. I built this for us, not just me." His eyes were pleading.

"Oh, shit," Grace fumed. "You're doing that thing with your eyes."

"Is it working?" Mickey asked.

"Yeah, it is."

"Then get out of your clothes and into the robe. The sauna is all fired up."

When they turned the corner of the house, Grace could not contain an "Ahhhh."

The twinkle lights reflected against the snow, which was coming down in large soft flakes. It was right out of a Hallmark holiday movie.

Mickey opened the door to the sauna. "May I take your robe, madam?" he asked with a smile.

Grace would later try to describe what it felt like to her friends, who would listen politely, but then say, "I don't think it's my thing." She would try to explain how there was a point in the sauna when all you could do was hope that your eyeballs didn't fry as you dished water over the hot rocks to create a blast of heat. How the blast could, even in such a contained space, come at you, and sweep over your body, hit the cedar wall of the sauna, and then bounce back onto parts of your back that you hadn't felt in years.

How to explain how coming out of the sauna, standing naked in the middle of Kansas suburbia, naked and yet invisible, hidden, raising her arms to the sky and opening her mouth to taste snow? Not feeling the cold because your body was radiating heat from the inside. How all of that maybe sounded uncomfortable, but it was actually wonderful. Glorious. How it made her ordinary, a bit chubby, womanly, older body feel reborn.

Somehow, in the middle of a very shitty time, Mickey had created something that sparked much joy.

HISTORICAL CONTEXT: FEBRUARY 2021

Feb. 1: More Americans are reported to have received at least one dose of a vaccine against COVID-19 than have tested positive for the virus.

Feb. 9: Following an investigation of the origins of COVID-19, the World Health Organization says it is "extremely unlikely" that the virus came from a Chinese laboratory.

Feb. 11: U.S. President Joe Biden rescinds the national emergency order used by Donald Trump to fund the border wall with Mexico.

Feb. 12: The Biden administration announces the purchase of 200 million additional doses of Moderna and Pfizer vaccines, bringing the country's total purchase at this point to 600 million, enough to vaccinate 300 million people.

Feb. 13: Former President Donald Trump acquitted in second Senate impeachment trial on the charge of incitement of insurrection after senators vote 57 to 43 in favor of conviction, less than the two-thirds majority required for impeachment.

Feb. 22: The U.S. surpass 500,000 COVID-19 deaths. (This is higher than US deaths in World War I, World War II, Korea, and the Vietnam War combined.)

Feb. 25: An independently reviewed real-world study shows that two doses of the Pfizer/BioNTech COVID-19 vaccine reduced symptomatic cases by 94% across all age groups.

Feb. 27: The FDA grants emergency use authorization to Johnson & Johnson's COVID-19 vaccine, the first single dose COVID-19 vaccine available in the U.S.

March 2021

Katrina

Katrina was scheduled to get her second vaccination today, March 3rd, the one-year anniversary of the start of the worst year of her life.

And to think she used to bitch about a philandering husband and the inconvenience of a divorce. Thinking this, she felt a pang of remorse, something akin to grief. She had a *dead* philandering ex-husband who had come around to where he'd sincerely tried to be a better father to his sons. If he hadn't run out of time...

Katrina had had some reactions to the first inoculation—sore arm, low grade fever, lethargy—but nothing scary.

The hope, fragile and elusive, that the vaccine would cause her long-hauler symptoms to diminish, had not been realized. Yet, even now, despite the odds, despite having felt defeated so many times over the past year, that sliver of hope persisted.

And there were days now when she did not wake up feeling as if her body had just had a workout, all achy and sore. She would stretch her arms, sit up, make it into the bathroom or kitchen without breathing hard. There were even days when her brain felt as if it were working. Not at full speed, but not so fogged. She could frame sentences, find words, complete thoughts. She could almost see fleeting glimpses of herself waving encouragingly over the high, rocky walls that COVID had left in her brain, in her life.

Zed & Cherry

Cherry had a voicemail from Zed. "Cherry, call me. You are not going to believe this. Oh, never mind. I'll just tell you when I get home. I want to see your face anyway."

By the time Zed got home two hours later, Cherry felt like she'd been checking the driveway every three minutes. She tore out the door and was at the car as he was stepping out.

"What, Zed, just spit it out. Is it something with Q?"

"No," he said, "Not Q. It's more local, closer to home."

"What do you mean?"

"Your husband just got the Employee of the Month Award!" he announced, pumping his arms. "How does that feel, Babe?"

Cherry squealed. She took his face in her hands, one hand on each cheek, and pulled it down to give him a big sloppy kiss. "That's how it feels. You are getting hotter every day. We better be careful, or we could end up with another surprise."

"Well, that wouldn't be the worst thing in the world. Maybe a sister for the boys?" Zed suggested.

The last time they had approached this, Zed said, flatly, "We can't afford the two that we have, so a third would be a disaster." That had shut her down. But he was different now.

Still, she never would have predicted *this* change.

"That's a big decision, Zed. And the world feels a little crazy right now." Cherry replied. "And I've been thinking, well, that I want to go back to school once Colton is in first grade."

Zed pulled back from their hug. "Really? You hadn't said anything."

"I'm waiting to see how this whole pandemic thing pans out. But even if I'm home with the kids doing virtual school again, I could do virtual college, just a couple of classes. Like we're all in school together. We'd need another laptop, but..."

"Damn, Cherry, we can swing a laptop," Zed cut in. "Get it at Best Buy with one of those zero interest credit cards. If that's all that stopping you..."

"Well, there is tuition, but they have grants and loans. And community college is pretty low." Cherry realized that they were having a significant life discussion in the driveway, the car door still ajar.

"C'mon. Let's go inside. The kids could be killing each other and we're standing out in the driveway."

As they walked to the front door, Cherry took his hand. "I think we're happy, Zed. This is what happy feels like," she said with a squeeze.

"Yeah, Cherry. We may need to get used to it."

Grace

Grace was taking an early morning walk, bundled up in her down vest and scarf and gloves. There'd been an ice storm during the night, not bad enough to bring down wires, but leaving the world coated with a thin layer of ice. It looked magical, as the early morning sun reflected off trees and branches, like being in an ice forest. An ice palace. It was a magic that would melt in mere hours.

Grace was thinking this morning that it had been about a year— *What was the date we returned?*—since she and Chelle had walked down the gangplank into a different world. She recalled her incredulity at what had been happening, her naivete about the seriousness of the virus.

Would she have wanted to have understood what was coming? What 2020 would become? Would knowing have made her *more* appreciative of feeling pampered? Would she have held tighter to the fleeting moments of uncomplicated joy?

No, she realized, it would have been awful to comprehend what was looming. How every one of the solicitous, hard-working staff were about to lose their jobs and livelihoods, for not just weeks or months, but maybe years. That countless thousands of families in far off countries— when she'd asked, their cabin steward had shared pictures of his smiling wife, three children and parents, in Thailand—that depended on this consistent income would be abruptly penniless.

Benefits like unemployment did not extend to the seas.

Knowing would only have made her anxious and frightened about something she could neither influence nor control. She'd have been constantly checking news updates, trying to sort out facts from needless alarm. She certainly would not have spent languid hours on a lounge on the Promenade Deck, reading, watching the ocean, until her eyes softly closed.

Grace had had eleven days of naïve trust that, whatever was coming, her country would respond to this crisis as they had to on 9/11—with patriotic solidarity—and that the best medical care in the world would triumph, that citizens would be protected.

She had slept the deep, untroubled sleep, of ignorance.

Nell

Nell had put the letter from the state agency into a file and not looked at it again. But the idea had been planted and kept gestating. So, she made an appointment to sit down with a social worker and learn what hoops would be required to adopt as a single parent.

But there were no more hoops, just a little paperwork. She was, she found out, pretty much approved already. She guessed that being an elementary school teacher for a decade-plus helped, great references, being solvent, and being a Black woman who wanted a Black older child.

The next week, she asked her in-laws to supper, both Ian's parents and his grandparents. After supper over coffee and tiramisu, she explained that she and Ian had been planning to adopt and had been provisionally approved. They'd decided to adopt kids who were older, not babies. They'd been waiting to make the announcement at Christmas.

Then Nell asked them if they thought she was crazy to even think about doing this *alone*, because a part of her was pretty sure she it was some kind of grief-reaction and kind of nuts.

They listened, thoughtfully. Then Ian's mom looked at her husband and he nodded, like "Go ahead." It was like they could read each other's minds, like he knew that, whatever she said, he would agree.

"What makes you think that you'd be doing this alone?" she asked Nell. "If you adopt a child, or children, we're here for you, for them. We're family."

"But you have enough on your plates," Nell answered. "You didn't plan on sharing care of a kid. Or kids." Nell used the plural as she had, for whatever reason, dreamed of two children, siblings. It was, she thought, no crazier than taking on one. And she felt, somewhere in her gut, that having each other would be easier for the children.

"Our plates, as you put it, are already cracked," her father-in-law said. "Kids would be a blessing, not a burden."

Nell was quiet. She'd never had this kind of family. Her parents had divorced when she was four. Her father was dead, her mother had "issues."

Nell has always been a strong black woman out of necessity.

"Whatever you decide is your choice," Ian's grandmother said. "But these children will be loved and cherished. They will have family."

"You do remember that we're only 63, right?" Ian's dad chimed in. "And my folks, sitting here at the table, are 84. So, we plan on being around for a while. You adopt a ten-year old and it's just eight years until they're off to college. We're all in."

Max

"Do you know it's been over a year since Katrina got sick?" Max asked Mickey. "How many people get sick for a whole year?"

"I don't know. How many do you think?"

"I don't know. I was asking you."

"If you mean just with COVID, then I think it's about 20 to 30 percent have symptoms for several months after infection. But I'm not sure about a year. Can you google it?"

"Yeah, I'll do that," Max replied. "Do you think COVID is about over? Because we have vaccines now and everybody wants to get vaccinated and once everybody gets vaccinated then people might get sick, but they won't die. Right?"

"Right about probably not dying but not so sure about 'everybody wants to get vaccinated,'" Mickey answered.

"But why? If they know it will protect them, and other people too, why wouldn't they want to get vaccinated? Are they afraid of needles? I used to be afraid of needles but now..."

"It's not needles, Max," Mickey interrupted. "They don't believe that the vaccines work, or they're suspicious about potential side effects, or worry that there are things that they aren't being told."

"Why do they believe that? Do their doctors tell them? Didn't they get vaccinated when they were kids?"

"This is different. They believe the side effects might be more dangerous than the virus."

"That's what some people believed about kid vaccines. That a vaccine caused kids to get autism. But that started with one doctor in England who made up fake statistics. When they found out, they didn't let him be a doctor anymore. But a lot of people still think it's more dangerous."

"Good comparison, Max," Mickey said. "That's about the same thinking. The internet is to blame because anybody can say or write anything. And the crazier it is, the more it seems to go viral."

"But don't people check to see who said it? Don't they check to see if the person is really a doctor or researcher? The internet shouldn't let anyone say anything. They should make sure that people can be trusted. They should only allow facts."

"Which would be brilliant move except that we have this 'free speech' thing."

"I know about *that*," Max replied, a bit defensively. "But there are exceptions, like you can't yell fire in a theatre. Isn't telling people lies about the virus just as bad as yelling fire? People make bad decisions when they're scared."

"It is kind of like yelling fire, but harder to track down how many people end up dead or sick because they believed what someone said. And then you have to show that they intended to hurt the other people."

"But if they kill or hurt someone, does it matter if they didn't mean to do it?" Max pushed back. "Because they did it."

"Are you thinking of being a lawyer when you grow up?" Mickey asked.

"No, I don't think so. But I'll tell you when I find something."

Covid Grief Group

The grief group was having a rocky time. Everyone had retreated, physically or emotionally, to their own little corner of the universe. Some had skipped a meeting, others showed up physically but were flat, emotionally absent. Their depression was palpable. And contagious.

Grace, of course, was ruminating on what she could do, should have done, to counter the slide into—despair? The bottomless dark well that grief could be. She felt, despite all logical assurances to the contrary, that she was responsible for helping them all to heal and, at the very least, mitigating their pain.

It took Mickey to jolt her out of the hole she was sliding into.

"Gracie," he said one evening, "don't take this wrong but there is a bit of narcissism in what you're feeling. An echo of the 'I alone can fix it' mentality? Do you hear that? Just a teeny-weeny bit?"

And while Grace wanted to rail at Mickey that he was all wrong, that this was nothing like that, that what she felt was inadequacy not narcissistic ego, there was an iota of truth in what he said.

Sometimes feeling responsibility for "fixing" came from a place of believing that one had the power to fix whatever it was. And a false belief in one's power was kind of narcissistic. It was back-ass, but there was a connection.

"Do we have vodka?" Grace asked. Alcohol was handy to move a conversation in a different direction.

"Yeah," Mickey replied.

"And coffee liquor?"

"Yes."

"And Irish cream?"

"Yes."

"And heavy cream?"

"No. Where are you going with this?"

"Ok, so we'll have to make them with ice cream. I know we have some in the freezer."

"Making what?"

"Mudslides, Mickey. Life is short. I want a mudslide."

The next morning, Grace sent an email to each of the group members. She didn't know if it would feel intrusive to some, even push them away, but she had to try *something*.

Everyone showed up for the next session. It was raining, so they were taking over a large meeting room in the funeral home.

Each had done what she'd requested. They brought a piece of clothing, or something meaningful, because it spoke about whomever they'd lost.

A show-and-tell.

Cheryl brought Robert's pipe (*Of course he smoked a pipe,* Grace thought), while Beth had her mom's favorite robe, the one that she'd worn drinking her coffee every morning. Beth wore it for the whole group.

Larry brought Jasmine's Hawaiian coffee table book, full of photos. He'd bought it online to cheer her up when she couldn't leave the house except for chemo. They'd gone to Maui for their honeymoon.

"She looked at it every day when she was in chemo. It stayed on the coffee table in the living room. We'd drink fruity cocktails, with little umbrellas, at 5 p.m., with a CD of waves and ocean sounds playing in the background," Larry said, smiling at the memory.

Kayla brought a red dress that Jolene had bought on sale for a "special occasion." Jolene had joked around with it, singing "Someday my prince will come," and dancing with Kayla. It had hung on the back of her closet door, admired from Jolene's bed, like a painting, but never worn, for ten years. "It was still the prettiest dress she'd ever had. I think that her dreams about wearing it were way better than any real date could have been," Kayla said.

Bill and Debra brought two things: Dean's Halloween costume when he was seven or eight—a tiny set of white medical scrubs and a pretend stethoscope—and a photo of Dean when he graduated medical school, both of their arms around him, with the biggest smile a young man could have. "We have to keep reminding ourselves that he was doing what he wanted to do since he was a kid, and that it brought him immense satisfaction and joy," Bill explained. "That he wouldn't have changed anything in his life right up until he got COVID. He was fulfilling his mission."

Shawnee brought an album, filled with photographs of her childhood, when every holiday was spent with the extended family: grandparents, aunts and uncles, cousins, and then the spouses of cousins and kids of cousins. "I was the only kid without siblings. My mom had three siblings and my dad had four—and they each had at least three kids, so it was quite the family. My dad was killed in a work accident when I was nine, and my mom got breast cancer when I was 22. I moved away for grad school, like a new place would erase the pain."

"And now?" Grace asked.

"Now I'm thinking that I may go back to Georgia, at least for a few years. Before they're all gone."

Shawnee turned the pages, her finger pointing to one person, then another, saying nothing. But everyone knew she was pointing out who'd been killed by COVID.

Luis hadn't said a word, but then again, Luis didn't talk much. He was listening, nodding, a brown paper bag at his feet. Slowly, he opened the top of the bag and reached in.

It was an infant's baptismal gown, long and formal, covered in intricate lace.

"This was Mariana's, and, before that, Mariana's mother's. It was handed down. Mariana, even though she'd almost given up, still prayed that someday she would have a daughter to baptize. When she was dying, and she knew she was dying, I brought it to the hospital and asked the nurses to give it to her to hold. One of the nurses, from Colombia, told me that she said, 'Mi hija y yo estamos juntas para siempre. Dile a mi esposo que lo estaremos esperando.'"

Luis's voice broke as he spoke the words as if they burned on this throat. "My daughter and I will be together forever," he translated. "Tell my husband we will be waiting."

"Is that a comfort for you?" Debra asked.

"For me?" he almost barked. "No. I've never had faith. But my wife? She had enough faith for both of us. She carried me on her faith."

It was a terrifically sad meeting, but it cracked the reticence, the pulling back. They were there for each other. They listened and accepted. They did not mouth stupid platitudes. Grace noticed that Shawnee and Luis joined the others when they went out after group for a drink.

They would all return, at least for now. They had weathered this storm. Some would heal. Some not.

Grace had accepted that she could not fix a damn thing.

Grace was on the outside looking in, like the pictures that had blanketed the news of people outside nursing homes and elder care facilities—hands against glass, but never touching.

MICKEY

Turning and turning in the widening gyre / The falcon cannot hear the falconer; Things fall apart; the centre cannot hold / Mere anarchy is loosed upon the world, The blood-dimmed tide is loosed, and everywhere / The ceremony of innocence is drowned;/ The best lack all conviction, while the worst are full of passionate intensity.

Mickey had always had an affinity for Yeats, but lately, this poem, *The Second Coming*, felt like it was turning and turning in his damn head. Yeats wrote it when his pregnant wife came close to death in the flu pandemic of 1918-1919. And when Yeats felt that the world was sliding into anarchy, that evil was running amok.

Like now, Mickey reflected.

Mickey kept hearing pieces, loose phrases... "Like a shape with lion body. A gaze blank and pitiless as the sun...is moving its slow things and..." and...*whatever*. It would come to him later when he wasn't trying to remember.

It was, Mickey thought, a poem about a world descending into chaos, about another Coming but not of a Redeemer. Was it Satan who was "slouching towards Bethlehem?" But why did he keep seeing Donald Trump's head and face as the Satan on the lion who was "slouching..."

HISTORICAL CONTEXT: MARCH 2021

Mar. 1: A former Trump advisor confirms that Former President Donald Trump and First Lady Melania Trump received COVID-19 vaccines in January prior to their departure from the White House.

Mar 2: Governors of Texas and Mississippi both announce they are lifting mask mandates and COVID-19 health measures despite CDC warnings of complacency.

Mar. 2: Dolly Parton receives the Moderna COVID-19 vaccine that her $1,000,000 donation helped to develop.

Mar. 3: Biden says that every U.S. adult will have access to a COVID-19 vaccine by the end of May. The president also calls for every state to ensure that teachers, childcare providers, and school staff receive at least one dose by April.

Mar. 11: Joe Biden signs into law the American Rescue Plan Act of 2021. It provides additional relief to address the continued impact of the COVID-19 pandemic on the economy, public health, state and local governments, individuals, and businesses.

Mar. 16: A series of shootings occurred at three spas in Atlanta, Georgia. In all, eight people were killed, six were Asian women. Several rallies were held in the days following, a new movement emerging called "Stop Asian Hate."

Mar. 17: Vaccinations may lessen, in some people, some COVID-19 long-lasting symptoms. *(National Institute of Health)*

Mar. 19: Center for Disease Control eases recommendations for social distancing in classrooms, saying three feet of space between students wearing masks is a sufficient safeguard in most classroom situations.

Mar. 19: The U.S. has administered 100 million COVID-19 shots.

Mar. 31: US President Joe Biden overturns Trump's restrictions on transgender people serving in the armed forces.

April 2021

Mickey & Grace

"Hey, Gracie," Mickey said, from behind the newspaper, his mouth somewhat filled with an avocado and chicken panini. "They're looking for volunteers for the vaccine clinics. Looks like they're holding them a few times a week out at the fairgrounds."

"The fairgrounds? Which buildings?"

"I don't know, but I expect whatever would work for drive-through. Not like they want unvaccinated people lining up together."

"Okay. Sign me up. When and for how long?"

"I think a few days a week. I'll call about specifics."

When they opened up vaccinations for most adults, the health department had online signups. And thousands of people signed up. The vaccine supply fluctuated, so people got a call back with a time slot once the department could confirm the number of vaccines available. They did not want hundreds of people to wait in line and then run out.

The sun was shining on their first shift as volunteers.

Cars were lined up along twisting routes that went in circles and across the fairgrounds, like lines at Disney World. The mood was festive, people smiling and laughing, as if they had made it onto a secret line for the best ride ever.

Which it was. Their appointment print-out, with a confirmation code, was a ticket to staying alive. It was a ticket to a future, a door to possibilities. Getting their first shot was better than anything Disney World could ever deliver.

Mickey and Grace were assigned different duties: he directed traffic and kept lines sorted out; she checked appointment confirmations, standing next to the cars. Everyone was masked. They were tired by the end of their shifts, but also felt really good to be helping.

They'd signed on for two shifts a week for as long as the clinics would be going.

"It's like giving blood," Grace told Max. "Such a small thing, but it can make a big difference to the person who needs that type of blood and gets it. And helping people get vaccinated is helping to save their lives."

Zed & Cherry

Zed and Cherry had not been spending as much time online. After doing some research, they were wary about getting vaccinated. The vaccines had been rushed through all the usual testing, and it felt like they were being pushed onto the public. They did not want to be guinea pigs for Big Pharma.

Cherry had never been an anti-vax mom, and Zed had never thought about vaccinations one way or the other. They did what the pediatrician told them to do. There was a schedule of childhood vaccinations, and they followed it. But now they felt a responsibility to not just swallow the party line being pushed at them by mainstream media. So, they read whatever they could find, and some of it was pretty scary.

"Okay, Zed, so they are saying that we do not know what long-term consequences could happen. Like they could be much worse than getting COVID. And there are some sites that think that Jeff Bezos is paying a lot and pushing the vaccines because they have tiny microchips embedded and everyone who is vaccinated will be able to be tracked."

"Nah," Zed said. "That sounds like sci-fi shit. Maybe the Dems are putting out some crazy stuff so then whoever doesn't want the vaccine will look crazy and it will be easier to mandate it."

"Or maybe there *are* microchips. Would that be more far out than, 'Trust us, this is going to be fine even though we developed this vaccine in months when every time in the past it took scientists years and years.'"

But, two weeks later, it became a moot point. Home Depot "encouraged" employees to get vaccinated as soon as possible. The sooner everyone was vaccinated, the sooner they could stop wearing the damn masks.

Zed hated the masks. Half the time he felt like he wasn't hearing people and then they got frustrated. Especially if they had an accent. An accent *and* a mask? He wanted to throw up his hands.

Plus, while they weren't mandating vaccines, they wanted managers to be positive role models for the staff and customers. And Zed had heard that staff who were not vaccinated could end up in jobs with less customer contact, like stocking and late shifts behind the scenes. Nobody said he could be demoted, but managers had a lot of customer contact—fielding problems, building customer trust. Not having vaccinated employees could send customers elsewhere.

Cherry had also found out that some of the programs she was checking into at the community college were going to require proof of vaccination for in-person classes and any practicum.

She'd talked to a woman in admissions who'd been what Cherry called disrespectful.

"Do you have questions about the LPN requirements? And how they can segue into an RN program? Are these the programs you're inquiring about?" the woman in admissions had asked.

"Yes," Cherry had replied. "I've got all I need as far as courses and such, but I want to know about the vaccination policy."

"Well, a lot of that policy is evolving. But the programs you're interested in require up-close and personal contact with clients and patients. They are practicum intensive. And a lot of patients are elderly, which means they're highly vulnerable to serious complications. No facility, hospital or otherwise, wants unvaccinated staff in direct contact with patients. Do you have a medical condition that compromises your ability to tolerate vaccinations?"

Cherry admitted that she had no medical exemption, no chronic illness—and the conversation went downhill from there.

"There are ethical issues here along with the science. Our decisions are based on data, evidence-based and medical, not conjecture. We cannot ethically allow our students to interface with patients without providing every available protection for patients."

"What about my right to not have to put a vaccine in my body that I believe could potentially damage my health?" Cherry had asked. "I understand science, but this is different."

"You can debate all you want that vaccines could have potential damage, or focus on hyped-up anecdotal reports, but we do not build our course content on exceptions, anecdotes, and 'possible-but-rare outcomes.' Students in medical programs need to make decisions based on science."

"But there are times when science has been wrong," Cherry countered. "Like when the pandemic started, the scientists and doctors didn't have all the answers, they were as confused as..."

"Look, I expect you are a nice young woman, and you are getting the brunt of my frustration that maybe you do not deserve. But my dad died in January, just weeks before he could have gotten vaccinated. He was only 65, just starting retirement, and a pretty robust man. We expected another 15 to 20 years with him. So, for me, vaccination is a personal issue."

"I'm sorry for your loss," Cherry had said. "And, for the record, vaccination is personal for me as well."

Covid Grief Group

April is, Grace thought, *the start of the anniversaries.* The death anniversaries. An anniversary that would, for each, be etched into their brains.

It had taken years for Grace to not have an "anniversary" reaction to her husband's death, even when she was not consciously thinking of the day, not marking it down on some mental calendar. And that was after removing herself from everything that they had shared—their home, town, friends. In moving somewhere that neither of them had ever been, where *everything* was different, the triggers of their relationship could not grab her by the neck and squeeze—*Here's where you had a picnic; Here's the Saturday morning farmer's market; This was his favorite restaurant.*

It had worked, sort of, but mostly to push the grief down, to hide it. But each November, as the days inched closer to Thanksgiving, she would feel a pressure in her chest, a tightness between her eyes. And she would be impatient, irritable. In Alaska, people would ask, "Are you okay?" Grace would come back with, "I'm fine, okay, just drop it." Which clearly announced that she was anything but fine.

But they had dropped it.

Grace made notes to ask everyone what their anniversary date was, and what they could do, alone or with people, to acknowledge their loss and sorrow.

She was asking them what she'd never asked, or answered, herself.

The group was back meeting in the garden by the funeral home. There was an ease to their engagement with each other.

Grace waited for a lull in their talking before waving her hand around in a circle encouraging them to change focus.

"Okay," she said. "Other than this lovely day as proof that we're finally having some spring weather, for which we are all grateful, does anyone have anything they want to share?"

Luis shifted in his chair and raised a finger.

Grace gave him a quizzical look. Luis did not usually "take the floor." She nodded at him to start.

"I want to share that I am planning to move back to Mexico," Luis began. "Not where I grew up, near Chihuahua, because that is where my father and uncle were murdered, and the cartels still have power..."

"Seriously?" Kayla interrupted. "You're moving? Like right away?"

"No," Luis replied. "In a few months. But, if I say it out loud to all of you, then it will be real for me, not something that is just in my head."

"Why?" Bill asked. "Or, rather, why *now*?"

"Because he's frickin' tired of always worrying when the damn police are gonna' pull him over," Beth cut in. "He's undocumented. Did you not get that? Who else checks their taillights every time they get in their car after dark, huh?"

Beth turned to Luis. "Sorry, Luis. Did I blow your cover?"

"No, I thought everyone knew. People don't ask. So—respectful?"

"Can you share about why you're moving?" Grace asked. "It's a big step."

"Many reasons," Luis answered. "Not one is enough by itself, but put together?"

"We're listening," Grace said.

"Okay, then," Luis said. "I am tired of being afraid. I have been in this country for over 23 years. I came seeking asylum, but I could not *prove* that my father and uncle had been executed, that I would be killed if I did not join the cartel. Before they could deport me, I slipped away, got on a bus. I didn't even know where it was going. I was 19. Alone. And I ended up here." With "here" Luis gestured, as if including the garden in his description.

"But I'm 43 years old now. I am a little…" Luis paused, searching for the right word in English. "Bitter? Yes, *bitter*. I work very hard, always pay taxes, and Social Security, *never* in any trouble. But who I am means nothing. If ICE picks me up, I lose everything. I am treated as a criminal. I could fight deportation, but, the whole time, months of waiting, not knowing, I would be locked up. And, if deported, I am put on a plane with nothing."

Luis looked earnestly at them, as if he needed them to understand, to approve.

"Mariana," he continued "was my world. She was a citizen, and she made me feel less alone, less anxious. For the first time, I had health insurance. We used her accounts to pay bills online. We were saving to buy a house. We had money in the bank. We had a future."

"But now?" Grace queried.

"If I *choose* to *leave*—I go on my own terms. I can drive to the border in my car, packed with my computers, my work equipment, what I want to save from Mariana. I can wire transfer my savings. We had saved almost $50,000. It will mean a lot more in Merida or Oaxaca than Kaw Valley. The world is very different now than when I came here. I'm looking at jobs. I'm very good with computer repair. I speak English. My references say I have 'excellent work ethic.'"

"So, you'll do computer repair?" Beth asked.

"I may do that. But I may also teach. Teaching kids English is a ticket to a better life for them. And public university in Mexico is very cheap. I think about finishing my degree, then studying to be un abogado—a lawyer."

"But can't you do that here?" Cheryl asked, knowing as the words left her mouth that she already knew the answer.

"No. I cannot teach. I cannot be an attorney. I cannot even use my real name. Here I am Luis Lopez."

"What is your real name?" Debra asked gently.

Luis straightened his back and lifted his chin.

"I am Luis Alejandro Morales. My grandfather was a judge. My father, and his brother, my uncle, were attorneys – which is why they were executed. I am not, and never could be, *illegal.*"

Kayla looked like she was about to cry. She'd thought that maybe Luis was undocumented, but felt bad that she'd never asked, never understood the ways that his loss was different.

"What can we do to help you, Luis?" Kayla asked. "I'd really like to help in some way."

Luis smiled. "How are you with garage sales? I want to sell my furniture and TV and such. Many little things. I could use help with that. And, also, with packing? Mariana was the boss with that."

Then he looked at each of them, nodding at each of them.

"This group?" Luis said. "Just being here, listening? I could hear Mariana telling me to open my heart, to not pull back. And now I think she is telling me that it is okay to leave."

Katrina & Grace

Grace, Molly, and Katrina were having lunch in a popular local brewery with very high ceilings. High ceilings felt safer for air circulation. It was also 2:30 p.m., which Grace had determined was the lowest density. There was only one other couple, seated about twenty feet away.

They'd ordered Bloody Marys, which felt decadent for a weekday afternoon.

Molly shared a few Max anecdotes. Grace said how she'd a few clients in her office again given that they were all vaccinated. Katrina had signed on to be part of a longitudinal study of long-haul COVID symptom persistence and manifestation.

But conversation lagged. They hadn't been to any movies, or concerts, or taken any trips. They didn't have office or school gossip to share. They already knew what each other was binging—or not. They didn't have tidbits lifted from their disparate lives to bring to the table. They wanted to avoid the quicksand of politics or the pandemic.

Even ordering from the menu required so many decisions. Would they like a small salad first? What kind of dressing? How did Molly want her burger cooked? Did she want regular fries or sweet potato fries with that? Was the soup of the day—curried squash – okay for Katrina or would she prefer tomato bisque? The salad that Grace ordered came with a sliced chicken breast on top, so would she prefer that fried or broiled? Did she want her salad mixed in the kitchen or dressing served on the side.

Decisions that had been automatic, almost rote, now required conscious thought. As if any of it mattered.

Once the waitress left, they each took a long exhale. Kat looked at Grace. Grace looked at Molly, a 'Get us started here, kiddo' look.

"What is it about 'Critical Race Theory' that has people pissing their undies?" Molly asked abruptly, gesturing at both Grace and Katrina. "As far as I've read, it's simply that racism is embedded in our legal system, law enforcement, healthcare and education, housing and employment."

"Isn't a lot of the blowback about adjusting school curriculums to include history that does not erase or sanitize the experiences of anyone other than whites?" Grace asked, after first trying to defer to Katrina who was pointedly staring at her drink.

"It's not that simplistic," Molly said.

"Really? So, state legislatures are passing laws dictating what teachers can and cannot teach? And provisions for parents to rat teachers out if they think they've violated the law... Is that not happening in real time?"

"Okay, yeah, it is happening. And I can just see some kid innocently recounting what happened in class that day and later realizing that she's the reason her favorite teacher was suspended," Molly's voice faded. "Forget due process, or truth-in-education. Parents need to cleanse schools of radical teachers who do not stick to the script..."

Katrina listened as her dear friends wallowed in white guilt over whitewashed history and white supremacist ideology.

"As an attorney, allow me to say that the phrase, the name, 'Critical Race Theory' is inherently confusing," Katrina interjected, a rescue move for sure, while sucking the last olive out of her drink. "It's an academic term that was never intended for mass consumption. It is not a hypothesis, but a measurable, verifiable, data-based understanding of systemic racism. And since Black folks were not busy assembling data, keeping records, it's based on *white* data. Having 'critical' in the name just sets people off, because we can all debate whether anything is critical or what that means. And *'race'* is a dog-whistle and not in a good way."

"So, what would you call it?" asked Grace.

"I don't know. Maybe 'Undeniable Ubiquitous Imbalances?' Or 'Embedded Ubiquitous Injustices?' Or 'Blatantly Racist Shit That White People Pretend Didn't Ever Happen and Doesn't Still Exist?'"

"You do like that word, 'ubiquitous,'" Grace noted.

"You noticed, huh? I do, actually. I like to say things like, 'Would you agree that 'blank' is ubiquitous?' And then watch folks take a second to process. Like 'Do I agree or not?'"

They paused as their lunches were served. They declined to order a second drink. Grace doused her salad with blue cheese dressing that probably had more calories than a pile of fries.

After a few bites, Katrina waved her fork at them.

"Have you ever heard of Omar Ibu Said? He was enslaved, in Senegal, in 1806. Brought by slave ship to Charleston. He was a Muslim scholar. He died at 93, still enslaved, but owned by a man who'd bought him because he was intrigued by this slave who was writing, in exquisite Arabic, with charcoal, on his prison cell walls. Said wrote an autobiography in Arabic. There's a collection built around him in the Library of Congress. Maybe 20%, even 30%, of all slaves were Muslim, often educated, faith-focused, literate—but in Arabic, not English."

Katrina had been speaking in her lecture voice.

"No," Grace answered slowly. "I never heard of him." Molly nodded "no" in agreement.

"Well, don't feel too bad," Kat retorted. "Until last week I hadn't either."

Grace

Grace's dream was both fuzzy and clear. She was sitting in a chair in the corner of a hospital room, half-hidden behind those curtains that get pulled around beds. But she could see a patient, with lots of wires and machines and tubes. Lines were moving and changing on the machines, repeating, repeating, repeating. The machines were making background machine noises. Someone was perched on a chair next to the bed, completely covered in PPE, leaning forward. One hand was stroking the forehead of the patient, the other holding their hand. The person leaning in was talking, soft and low, reassuring. They did something with a machine, maybe, but their body blocked her view. Then the person in the PPE stood up, noticed her, nodded at her and walked out of the room. His eyes, over the PPE, looked like Theo.

Grace woke up abruptly, disoriented.

It was not a scary dream, more slow-motion, almost peaceful. But there was a message. Her unconscious was working out *something.* She sat up, swinging her legs over the side of the bed, wrapping a blanket around her shoulders. After a few minutes, she knew she would not be going back to sleep. It was 5:30 a.m. Better to make tea and watch the sunrise.

It took her an hour to slowly process all the different interpretations of what the dream might have meant.

A dream is just a dream, she thought. *But dreams can communicate things our conscious mind might push away.* Like the questions she'd never asked. Questions like, "Is Theo Murphy helping people to die?"

Once a question like that took root, it couldn't be ignored.

But did she want to know the answer? Would the answer open a Pandora's Box of crap that could never get pushed back in?

Grace had a professional code of ethics. She was a mandated reporter. In her experience, that usually applied to a child's safety: reporting if a kid was in danger or in an abusive situation. But the ethical code also required reporting if she was aware of a client with intent to harm. She'd made reports in the past when a spouse in a contentious custody battle had made verbal threats. And a few times when clients had admitted to "losing it" and abusing their spouses or kids—confessions made, not from remorse, but to justify their behavior.

But this was more complicated. More ambiguous.

If she believed Theo was mercy-killing? Even if the patients were terminal?

If she reported, Theo would be suspended from work. There would be an investigation. All the cases he'd worked would be reviewed. His co-workers would be interviewed. There would be a blanket of suspicion over him that he would never shake off, even if no charges were ever brought.

And the other hospital staff, doctors, and nurses? Could they face legal charges or censure if they'd suspected and not reported?

My imagination is getting out of control, she told herself. Theo had never said anything incriminating. He'd just talked about ethics. About his patients. About flaws and holes in the system.

I had a dream. And my gut said that something was off. How is that credible?

Grace found herself remembering everything that Theo had shared on ethics. She could now hear how he'd been working it out for himself, what his ethical responsibilities were when surrounded by ethical chaos.

He'd been, even if he didn't ask directly, looking for guidance. Or a debate. Looking for *something*. And she hadn't seen it, nor heard it, at the time.

Molly

When Molly went to the mailbox on April 11th, there was an envelope addressed to her. The return was an address in Florida, but no name was on the envelope. She recognized the street but did not know if the house number was for Mike or his parents.

Mike had never mailed her a letter. He'd sent a few holiday gifts, but they'd been shipped by UPS, and she'd never even looked at the return address.

Molly walked back to the house, putting the rest of the mail, all bills at this time of the month, on the entry table by the front door. Then she went into the kitchen, poured herself a glass of iced tea, and sat down at the kitchen table. She realized that with email and the constant availability of text and chat, a mailed letter felt both formal and anachronistic. And, somehow, like a phone call too early in the morning or too late at night, likely to bring bad news.

Was he telling her that he'd met someone? That their regular calls had been a useful crutch for surviving COVID but that he wanted to get back into something more normal with someone he could reach out and touch? That would be a pretty human response.

She took a knife and, with one quick motion, slit the envelope open. She unfolded the paper and started to read.

> *Dear Molly,*
>   *I was trying to write this with a pen, but my penmanship is more chicken scratch. So, I'm writing on my laptop, but at a picnic table overlooking the beach on Sanibel. I've taken a day off to get away to think. I remember you describing a vacation you took, alone, to Sanibel, after your mom moved back, your first break in years. Yet, despite living here for a few years, I've never made it across the bridge.*
>   *First, I want to say that I value you, and our friendship, more than...*

Molly's eyes blurred with tears. *Shit*, she thought. *Shit-shit-shit.* It was a "Dear Jane" letter, letting her down, saying how he valued their friendship, but didn't see anything more, and now that COVID was resolving—whatever. Time to get back to normal.

Molly wiped at her eyes with a napkin. *I am such a frickin' baby,* she told herself. *Get real.* Then she picked up the letter.

> *...any other friendship I have ever had, including the guys in my platoon on deployment, although this is completely different, of course. Because that was situational, we were just thrown together and went through stuff we could never really explain to anyone else even if we never talked about it with each other. Anyway...*

What the hell is he getting at, Molly thought. *Just spit it out already.*

> *...what I want to say is that, if you get freaked out by what I'm saying, that it doesn't have to mean anything changes in our friendship. If I am making something up in my head that you do not share, I can take five steps back and just be a friend, like you are a friend to me.*

Here it comes, Molly flashed. *The 'what good friends we are' line.*

So, Molly McDonald, here it is. I think about you every day, every hour. I realized that the time we talk is what I most look forward to. And (this is going to sound sick) I kind of don't want COVID to be over if it means that we stop that. I understand if you want to cut back on our time (adolescent screen addiction?) texting and talking and emails. If you want to have a more normal relationship with a guy than virtual with some dude who can never live where you do. Because you are in a good place in Kaw Valley, with your mom and Mickey right there. You have everything you need to have a good life and raise Max.

Now, I am taking a big risk here, and this is scaring the shit out of me, more than patrolling the perimeter of the FOB.

I love you. Not just as a friend. So much more than that. I want you. I want you in my arms, in my bed, in my life. And I have no right to even say this because I can never move back to Kaw Valley because of what it would do to David. So, for us to have what I want with you, you would be the one to make all the sacrifices, the changes. You would have to move here with Max. Or we could choose someplace new, and both move. But it makes sense to not do that until we know that we can make it work. And I think David needs to be stable until he finishes high school.

I want you to think about something. Do not answer now. Just think about it. Will you come down to Florida for the summer? It's hot here, but so is Kansas. I have a three-bedroom place, so Max can have his own room. It will be an adjustment for the kids, but we can ease them into it, like it's a vacation. And I think we'll know what is right in a month. So, if "right" is that you return to Kansas, okay. If you want to take it slow (because what I'm proposing is crazy-fast) and then decide in a year, okay.

Molly, I want to be with you. I believe that what I feel for you is not just some COVID fantasy. I don't want to spend three years in a long-distance relationship. If there is anything that COVID has taught me is how little control we actually have over our lives. How fragile life is. There are no guarantees about anything. And I've got baggage.

I have to stop writing before I scare you more than I already have. If this is freaking you out, just say so. But if there is any chance you have feelings for me, I don't want to play it safe.

Mike

Molly was glad she was sitting down because otherwise she would've dropped to the floor. She felt like she was hyperventilating and about to pass out. She was crying, choking sobs. Of relief? Joy? Terror?

Mike *loved* her? Mike wanted a *relationship*?

But to have that she'd have to uproot Max and move to Florida? Abandon her mother? The *only* reason Grace had returned was to help Molly. Now she had her casita, and her private practice, and Mickey. She had rebuilt her life around Molly and Max. Molly wouldn't have finished college and started grad school without Grace's support. Her life had been so much better since Grace moved back.

Molly's mind was racing. What would happen to her home? Grace had been the one to say, when Max was still in preschool, that Molly needed a home where she'd never have to worry about Max's meltdowns or being evicted. Grace had made the down payment, and covered the mortgage when funds were tight.

Molly loved her house, the only home Max had known, with its wooden built-ins, the bookshelves on either side of the fireplace, the sunny rooms. It was cozy, welcoming, a perfect fit for her and Max. She felt safe here. How could she up and leave for a man she had spent under two weeks with?

I need to talk to Mom, she thought. But then she reined herself in.

No. STOP. Not yet. Mickey. I need to talk to Mickey.

And without second-guessing herself, she grabbed her phone and called him.

Molly wasn't sure what she said, or if it made any sense at all, but Mickey was at her front door in 20 minutes. She had the door open before he knocked.

"Let's get some tea first," he said, taking her by the elbow and directing her toward the kitchen.

Five minutes later they were seated at the kitchen table, mugs of hot tea with milk and sugar cradled in their hands.

"Now," Mickey said, "tell me what's going on."

And Molly did. How she and Mike had been chatting, emailing, and texting for a few years, but intermittently. How that had expanded after the COVID school closures and shelter in place. How it then became a daily connection. How the Tuesday evening "conference call" she had every week, when Max had supper with Mickey, was not for school.

How she found herself thinking a lot about Mike, and how talking with him—their Zoom calls, no, *dates*, especially—were what kept her sane. How she'd just gotten a letter from him, a mailed letter, with stamps, and immediately thought he was letting her down and that he'd found a real relationship, which would have been perfectly understandable, and how utterly devastated she'd felt at even the possibility of losing his friendship.

"So, what did the letter say exactly?" Mickey asked when she paused to breathe.

"He has feelings for me."

"What kind of feelings?"

"Mike says he loves me. He wants me to come down to Florida for the summer with Max. He wants us to live together."

"Live together as in roommates?"

She started to get flustered. "No, live together as in seeing if we want to be together."

"And does this feel rushed to you? Like what happened to dating?"

She gave him a pointed look. "COVID screwed up dating, Mickey. So, sure, that would seem more rational, but—if this is what I really think I want, why hold back just to jump through some date hoops?"

"Is this what you really think you want?"

Mickey watched as Molly's face softened and she smiled, a wide, beautiful smile that lit up the room. "Yeah, Mickey, I really do think this is what I want."

"So, what's making you so anxious? Is it moving Max?"

"No," Molly replied. "Max hates change, but he loves the ocean, and he's been there twice. Not like he'll be missing his friends. He didn't have any to begin with and he lost touch with the few school friends he had when COVID hit. It will be challenging, but I think Max will do okay. He'd mostly miss you and Mom."

"Then what?"

Molly's face crumbled; tears rushed to her eyes. Mickey thought he'd never seen such a total emotional turnaround.

"Mom. I'm abandoning Mom after she upended her life for me. I'm why she came back here. How can I just pack up and leave?"

With that, Mickey started to chuckle. The chuckle turned into a laugh that became a laughing fit. He reached for some Kleenex.

"What?" Molly asked indignantly. "You think this is funny?"

"Yeah, I do. I think this is friggin' hilarious. You McDonald women are too much."

Molly looked at him, both pissed and confused.

"Your mom came back because you needed her. And she'd run out on you and your brother at another time that you'd needed her. *You gave her a second chance.* But what she wants more than anything is for you to have someone in your life to love who loves you back the way you deserve to be loved. Someone who will respect you and care for you. If COVID hadn't hit, I think she would have hired a yenta."

"Yentas are passé. Now we have Tinder."

"Well, those too. I bet she already has your profile set up and a head shot ready to go."

"But she has a life here, her work, her casita—you."

"And bringing your mother back into my life is something for which I will be eternally grateful."

"I didn't have anything to do with that," Molly argued. "That's on you."

"What I mean is this: Your mother returned to Kaw Valley for you. And she would have stayed for as long as she felt needed. Like forever. But, if you move, then her options open up."

"What about her practice? Her work?"

"You may be giving that more importance than it warrants. Your mom may be ready to cut back. And she wants to travel. COVID's number one lesson is that life is unpredictable."

Molly's mug was empty, the tea gone. She picked it up to sip at it anyway.

"So, you don't think this would be devastating? Mom won't hate me if I move?"

"There is *nothing* you could do for your mom to ever hate you. And following your own path, doing what you feel is best for you, is what she wants for you. Of course, she will want to grill this man, and she may move in down the block until she feels that everyone is settled..."

Molly's eyes widened at the idea of her mother moving down the street.

"Just kidding, Molly. Bad joke."

"How do I tell her?"

"What does Mike think?"

"I haven't told him that I accept his proposal."

Mickey paused. "Wait a minute. Did you say that Mike proposed?"

"No, his proposal to try living together for the summer and see where we end up. *That* proposal."

"So, we're having this conversation and you're leaving the man you believe you love out there hanging? Do you have any understanding of the balls it took to do what he did?" he deadpanned.

Molly squinted. "Umm, yes?"

Mickey abruptly stood up from the table. "I'm leaving and you need to call Mike."

She got up. "What about Mom?"

"This is *your* decision. *Your* life. Your mother will adjust."

"Can you talk to her?" Molly asked, tentatively.

"I will if you really want me to. But I think you can handle this. And so can your mother."

"Should I wait until I've talked this out with Mike and we're sure we want to go ahead?"

"Yeah. Helps to have a plan when talking to your mom. Sort out your head. Figure out how this move impacts school. That kind of stuff."

Molly needed to wait, to think, before calling Mike. Max was with Grace for the afternoon, on a field trip to check out the new baby giraffe at the Topeka Zoo.

Molly sat on her couch, looking out the window at the redbud tree she'd planted when she first moved into her bungalow, at the garden patch where her daffodils had bloomed, the tulips and irises now getting ready to put on their springtime show. A cardinal, so red he looked fake, perched on her birdbath. She'd never felt the deeply satisfying *ownership* of a place as she did here, in this room, this home, this space, this garden.

This kept her grounded.

Could she give it up? Why did she have to be the one who left? Why didn't Mike move to be with *her*?

He would if he could. She knew that. It was impossible, because of David, because Mike could not bring David back to the place where he had been cast out, cut off like a dead limb, from his mother and very large family. Just as she would not sacrifice Max for anyone, he would not sacrifice David. Even for her.

Which is one of the reasons she wanted to be with him. Because he was an ethical man. A caring dad. Kind. Funny. Smart. Fun. Hot.

So very—*hot*. She felt her face flush.

Molly looked out the window, reflecting on her life, and savoring these last moments before so much would change.

Then she picked up her phone.

Mike answered by the second ring.

"Molly?" he asked. Just her name. "Molly?"

"Yes, Mike. Yes, yes, yes. I'll come for the summer. And maybe forever."

And then she heard sounds that echoed those she had made earlier. Choking sobs of relief. And it hit her how terrifying it must have been for him to be waiting, waiting, as his letter moved peripatetically from Florida to Kansas, waiting to know if he was loved as he loved her. The courage it took to say what he had, not knowing, simply hoping.

That's what Mickey had meant by the balls comment.

"I love you, Mike. I want to be with you," she said. "We can do this."

Then they both laughed with the giddy realization of all they had been holding in, holding back. What they had not allowed themselves to admit to feeling filled them—body, heart, mind, and soul.

Nell

Once Nell met with a social worker and confirmed that she wanted to proceed to adopt as a single parent, the process went to "warp speed." A home inspection was done two weeks later.

In early April, Nell started looking, seriously, at the website of children waiting to be adopted. She had, in a dark moment, compared it to picking out a dog at the shelter: the puppies always people's first choice, but the older dogs either lying down quietly, like they'd given up hope, or else scrambling in their kennels, barking "Me, Me, Me."

She tried not to look at the pictures, to be swayed by appearance, but to read the small biographies about the child's interests. She felt she would not be as good a parent to a boy who lived for football because she really did not like sports. She could better nurture a child who was interested in music, books, art. It felt strange to know about things like interests, or whether a kid was shy, or if they needed help with math, or had dyslexia. Parents never got information upfront with babies. Having some data felt reassuring. And there were social workers who were like matchmakers, could sense what kids would be a good fit for what prospective adoptive parents. She'd said she was open to adopting siblings.

Which was how Andre and Aniya came into Nell's life. A social worker called her, saying that a brother and sister, 10 and 8 years old, had just been cleared for adoption. They'd been in foster care since April of 2020 when their mom had died of COVID. Their biological dad had died a few years ago in an accident. They were Black. There was no extended family able to provide care.

And, somehow, that was it. Nell read their little summaries, which mostly said that they wanted to stay together, please, which was all that mattered to them. They were too young to have formed big interests. In their photos, they looked thin, stoic. Their eyes, staring into the camera, were somber. They did not smile.

It was decided that Nell would start having them for weekends until school let out in mid-May. See if they could work as a family. She was approved as a foster parent for the time it would take for the legal adoption to process. Ian's family pitched in and, in one weekend, delivered everything they would need for two bedrooms, assembling bunk beds in Andre's room so the kids could sleep in the same room if they wanted to. When Nell shared their clothing sizes with her in-laws, who told the rest of the family, the closets and drawers filled up in an evening. One of Ian's cousins brought over two boxes of kid books for the bookshelves. In a week, Nell's home looked like kids lived there.

All that was missing was Ian.

HISTORICAL CONTEXT: APRIL 2021

Apr. 1: Data shows that months into the nation's vaccine rollout, those most affected by the pandemic are not being prioritized for vaccination.

Apr. 8: The B.1.1.7 COVID-19 variant, Alpha, first identified in the United Kingdom, is now the dominant strain in the U.S. The variant is considered more contagious than the original strain.

Apr. 8: President Joe Biden says, "Gun violence in this country is an epidemic," as he unveils package of executive actions including restrictions on "ghost guns."

Apr. 8: Dr. Anthony Fauci thanks American health workers for their sacrifice during the pandemic, acknowledging their more than 3,600 deaths.

Apr. 10: Dr. Anthony Fauci says people may need booster shots for COVID-19 down the road.

Apr. 11: 20-year-old Daunte Wright is shot and killed at a traffic stop by a police officer in Brooklyn Center, Minnesota, who mistook their gun for a taser.

Apr. 14: President Biden announces he will be withdrawing all U.S. troops from Afghanistan by September 11, saying, "it's time to end America's longest war."

Apr. 17: The global number of deaths from COVID-19 surpasses 3 million.

Apr. 19: All U.S. adults are now eligible for COVID-19 vaccines. 50% of all U.S. adults have received at least one vaccine dose.

Apr. 20: A Minneapolis jury convicts Officer Derek Chauvin on murder charges.

Apr. 27: The CDC issues updated mask guidelines for vaccinated and unvaccinated individuals. Indoors masking is still recommended for both vaccinated and unvaccinated individuals.

May 2021

Theo

Theo had pulled up a chair next to the patient's bed to have this difficult conversation. It was 6 a.m. He'd worked a 3-to-11 shift and then stayed on.

"We're going to have to intubate you," he said, trying to explain the facts but also convey empathy and reassurance. "Your lungs are failing. Your oxygen levels are dangerously low, and nothing we have tried has made a difference."

Theo looked at the woman on the bed, saw the fear filling her eyes.

Yesterday she'd been hostile, saying that she would be just fine, that she hadn't even wanted to come to the ER except her husband made her.

"Can't you give me that stuff you gave the president?" she asked between short, panting breaths.

"Which stuff do you mean?"

"I don't know, that cocktail, like they gave the president, the one he said made him feel so much better."

"I'm very sorry but we've already tried all the treatment options we have, and there is no magic cocktail. Plus, the president's doctors started treatment on him at a much earlier stage. If Donald Trump himself walked into any ER as sick as you were when you arrived, he'd be in the same circumstances."

She now glared at him, hate mixing with the fear. "You're lying. There is a cocktail and you're not giving it to me because you're a Dem."

Theo closed his eyes and counted to ten, inhale, exhale. *Diffuse the tension*, Grace had said. Don't react, don't escalate.

"I'm going to ask someone else to explain this to you because I've been working for 15 hours and I'm about to say something inappropriate," Theo said, standing up and turning to leave the room.

But he stopped in the doorway and pivoted. "We have done

everything we possibly could to treat your serious illness," his voice was not so much angry as defeated. "There's no magic cocktail for how damaged your lungs are. Donald Trump screwed you over. He screwed his country. And he won't pay for his lies. You'll pay. We're all paying."

In the corridor, Theo leaned up against the tile wall and briefly closed his eyes. He was so, so tired. His head felt like one of those bobbles on a car dashboard. He started to regret losing it with the patient. Or did he? Did he really give a shit if he went off on a patient who was accusing him of deliberately withholding care? He wasn't sure anymore.

The woman was going to die. He'd seen the X-rays. The ventilator was a last-ditch move. Nothing else had worked. But her lungs were too damaged. It was a matter of days, maybe even hours.

In these moments, Theo hated Donald Trump. He hated Tucker Carlson and Sean Hannity. He loathed every smarmy-self-righteous-right-wing conservative who spewed lies and undermined trust in medicine. And he hated himself for getting angry at some woman who'd been sold a pack of lies and was paying for her blind loyalty with her life.

Last night, a resident had tried to show her the X-rays of her lungs so that she'd have informed consent.

"How do I know those are my X-rays? Maybe you use them for everyone when they won't agree with your idea of treatment," the woman had rebutted, wheezing heavily.

How can you respond to that? So, every doctor, nurse, and RT in the U.S.A. was part of the big conspiracy? Why would they do that? What did they get out of it? They were the ones at highest risk. This wasn't some political game.

It was a different atmosphere in the ICU now than last fall, or, really, anytime in 2020. Then, everyone was a victim of an insidious, aggressive virus. Staff couldn't differentiate between patients who'd spent months scrupulously following every CDC protocol and patients who'd flaunted the guidelines, trusted Trump, bought into Fox News or QAnon. Unless they announced their convictions, which many had.

But now? Almost everyone in the ICU was someone who'd refused the free vaccine that would have saved their lives. Patients were in disbelief, like "How could this be happening to *me*? It's not real, just some leftist, communist bullshit!"

It was harder and harder to summon up compassion.

He felt his phone buzz in his pocket. It was a text from Grace McDonald.

Molly

Grace still didn't know about Mike. Molly was evaluating, using social work paradigms, gathering data to present.

She had a list of pros and cons. She had long-term versus short-term costs and benefits. She had a financial work sheet. She researched MSW programs that she could commute to from where Mike lived. She talked to her graduate advisor whether it was feasible to finish classes virtually if she secured a placement or internship out of state.

She looked at the school system and what kind of services they had for kids on the spectrum, their virtual school options and support groups.

Molly wondered if COVID made it easier to move. Like with school. Not having in-person classes with fellow grad students meant no "Wanna have a study session and then get some drinks?" Not that she got invited to study sessions, or that she had many friends to begin with. Being a mom *and* a student made it difficult to make the same kinds of connections other students forged.

She was asking herself how she'd ended up back in Kaw Valley? She'd never made a deliberate decision to settle here. She'd gotten pregnant and this had felt like the safest place to be, less expensive for sure than other options. A university so she could return to school when ready. And, deep down, she'd felt like her mother would return. She had not expected it would take years for Grace to get around to it.

Her tie to Kaw Valley was her mother. Molly relied on her, felt protected and reassured in having her close. Was it fair to transfer that to Mike? She'd never seriously expected *anything* from Mike. Maybe that was what made the relationship so easy. No expectations, just show up for a phone call. Play nice.

And that thought made her panic.

Was she ready for their dynamic to change?

Yeah, it was easy to talk to Mike, to feel that they could share anything. They didn't have to share a bathroom, share chores, to clean up each other's messes, pick up the load when the other shut down, get into arguments because he forgot to defrost the chicken before she got home. It was a fantasy relationship, adolescent even. It was easy to listen and offer empathy and advice about each other's demanding kids when they didn't have to actually *live* with said kids.

It was a circle of doubt that tested her longing. The longing was heart, visceral, not head. She wanted to be with Mike, no matter if the cost-benefit analysis came up short. Changing universities in the middle of a graduate program? Leaving a community where she had support and employment? Driving off into the sunset with her kid to live with a man who she'd never dated, never been intimate with, didn't know as far as his annoying habits?

It was so *not* sensible.

Cons: Haven't had sex with Mike, she'd written.

But the warm flush that she'd felt just linking *Mike* and *sex* together in a sentence made her cross it out. That line item would not, she anticipated, be problematic.

And not relevant to any discussion with her mother.

In the end, the "facts" were just words on a page. Sure, it made more sense to *not* uproot herself and her son, interrupt her grad program, leave all her security, just to be with a man. If she put it that way, it sounded wacko. *So not feminist.* If Molly had a client who was about to do what she was, she'd probably be advising caution, to go slow.

Molly never did complete her evaluation. Her mother pre-empted the process.

"What's going on, Molly?" Grace asked after supper when they were washing up the dishes. "Is something bothering you? You seemed happier the last few months, more relaxed. But these last few weeks it feels that something is weighing you down. Can we talk?"

At that point, Molly's eyes filled with tears, and she started crying, a sniffle at first and then harder.

Grace looked perplexed for a second, and then scared. Like *really* scared.

"What is it? Just spit it out. Are you sick?" Her tone was insistent. "Are you pregnant? *What happened?*"

At the word "pregnant," Molly started to laugh through her tears. Like she could've gotten pregnant during COVID?

"What is so funny?" Grace demanded.

"Pregnant," Molly choked out. "That's funny. I mean, seriously? When the hell did I have time or *privacy* to get pregnant? Another immaculate conception?"

Grace looked at her, exasperated. "Fine," she said. "Then *what?*"

"I'm in love with a man I've never even dated," Molly blurted out. "And I'm going to Florida to be with him for the summer and maybe forever."

With that, Grace was speechless. Mother and daughter just sat and looked at each other, one sniffling and the other trying to process what she thought she'd just heard.

"What?" Grace asked. "Who?" Her tone was incredulous.

"You know him. Mike Flores. David's father. The guy who moved to Florida when his custody case blew up in his face and..."

"I remember Mike," Grace interrupted. "Just not connecting the dots here."

"What do you want to know?" Molly asked.

"What alcohol do you have here, or do I run home to get a bottle before we start?"

It took almost three hours, interrupted by getting Max into his PJs and to bed, ordering two of the crusty, artisanal pizzas from Old Mill, and Grace slipping home to fetch more tonic for a third round of vodka tonics and lime, to cover what Grace wanted to know.

Grace was initially suspicious as she posed questions. She was not big on surprises, and this was one. A big one. She felt protective of Molly and did not see how uprooting her life was in her best interests.

The switch came when she asked, "What is it about him that makes you consider this?" And, just as Mickey had, Grace saw her daughter's face soften, blush, open. It was if Molly herself could not believe what she was feeling, did not have words to explain. It was different than anything Grace had ever seen with Molly, certainly not with the immature boy who had fathered Max and then flaked out.

Her daughter was in love.

How that had happened didn't matter.

In that moment, Grace accepted this new and startling change in their collective reality. She could not absorb *all* the implications, the ripples, but she saw that Molly's life was transforming, that it would be different than either of them had visualized.

Molly had spent so many years consumed with parenting, juggling school and work, that she'd given up any fantasy of "true love."

And Grace remembered Mike, how hard he'd worked to build a relationship with a son who'd rejected him. Mike was a decent man, a good father, a good son. He would be a trustworthy partner. Yes, he was flawed. But that often came after combat.

She realized that she was less concerned about the character of the man, and more the process of how the relationship had evolved. Grace had not been a part of it: observing, critiquing, ensuring that her daughter was not being used or duped.

This happened without my knowledge, out of my control, she thought, *and that scares the crap out of me. So, I have to trust Molly. She's not a girl anymore. She is a responsible mom. She'll make the best decision for herself and Max. She does not need protecting.*

"Oh, Molly," she said, so softly that Molly had to lean in to hear. "This is the most beautiful gift I could ever have imagined for you. You deserve it. Of course, you have to go."

And with that, Grace moved from unsettling, amorphous ambiguity into what she did best: solution-focused problem solving. Lists.

"So, how do you see this happening?" she asked, reaching for a paper and a pen. "In stages, first for just the summer, then more permanent? Or all at once?"

Covid Grief Group

Bulbs in the circle garden, tulips and iris, were blooming. The redbuds were out. Hostas had emerged from hibernation, pushed up through the soil, and were spreading their large striped leaves.

"I'm moving back to Georgia," Shawnee was saying. "I've arranged for a year leave of absence from the university here, starting in a month. I gave a two-month notice to my landlord. I'm going to apply for some positions with colleges in Georgia, but too late this year for anything tenure-track. I'm keeping my options open."

"That's pretty decisive," Grace said. "What was the tipping point for you?"

"I got a card from a cousin. She said that she was thinking of me, that being alone up here must be extra hard. That she didn't know how I'd coped with losing my dad and mom so young because she's 41, married, with a couple of kids, and she still feels like she was hit by a semi when her mom and dad died. She was apologizing for not being more supportive back then. She wrote that she remembered, when we were kids, we were so close that she pretended I was her sister because she just had three pain-in-the-ass brothers."

"That's one packed card," Grace quipped.

But Shawnee was serious. "It's taken a year for me to uncover some stuff. I did feel that my extended family didn't understand how hard that was for me. I'd felt abandoned. But I'd overlooked that I was away for four years in college. They don't show love with letters or cards. They bring you a 'dish.' Comfort food. And then they sit down at the table and eat it with you. They don't ask questions. They just show up."

"And you were too far away for that?" Grace asked.

"Yes, and I'm too far away for that now. I joined this group to deal with all the dying in my family in Georgia. But I'd buried the dying that happened years ago. Then I felt like I had to hold myself together, that no one else could help with that or do that. No siblings. I had to be a *strong* Black woman."

"Not a lot of space with that to grieve," Grace added, turning to face the rest of the group.

"How does this resonate with the rest of you?" she asked, making brief eye contact with each person in the circle. "What messages did you get that told you how you 'should' act or feel? Were they current or injunctions you'd internalized a long time ago?"

And then she shut up.

Everyone in the group spoke, some interrupting each other with "Yeah, that's how it was for me," or "My friends were the opposite." But everyone spoke. The quieter ones were invited to speak, drawn out, and the more talkative stayed silent and just listened.

Luis was more open, more engaged, than he had ever been. More *himself?*

Damn, this is a good group, Grace thought. And to think she'd tried to weasel out.

Theo & Grace

Grace had texted Theo asking if he could come in for a session because she had something she wanted to talk about.

"Sure," he'd texted back. "After night shift next Wednesday? 9 a.m.?"

But then one of his kids had been sick and they'd had to postpone a week.

Now they were going to meet, in ten minutes, but Grace no longer felt the urgency that she had after the dream. In fact, it now felt awkward to have summoned him to a session. She was not sure how she'd approach the issue.

"Hey, Theo. I wanted to ask if you're euthanizing patients?" didn't sound therapeutic. And she wasn't a cop.

When Theo arrived, coming through the back gate to the patio, she was waiting, with a thermos of decaf coffee as he might have worked all night and need to get to sleep soon.

They exchanged niceties, Grace asking how his daughter was feeling, Theo commenting on the flowers in the front yard.

"So, what do you want to talk about?" Theo asked.

She took a deep breath. "I've been thinking a lot about the stressors of your work, and your discussion of bioethics..."

"You mean my rant?" Theo interrupted. "Damn, but I was in a stoked-up space that day."

"What had you so stoked?"

"Wasn't it obvious?" Theo asked, his eyebrows lifting.

This isn't going to be easy, Grace thought. *Get it over with.*

"I have a question that I want to ask you directly, in person, because the answer may have implications for my ethical code," Grace began. "I'd like you to think carefully before you respond about possible consequences."

Grace suddenly realized that this was just another wording for

"Anything you say may be used against you in a court..." That law enforcement disclaimer, when you're told you have the right to an attorney.

But Theo was way ahead of her.

"Do I need an attorney?" he asked. But his voice was soft, not angry.

"Oh shit, Theo, no, I don't think so. Do you need an attorney?

"Maybe, someday. Who the hell knows?" he retorted.

Grace lowered her voice and leaned in. "Are you helping people—die? Are you..."

She couldn't even finish the question.

"You think you know the answer, or you wouldn't be asking," Theo stated. "You tell me."

"I had a dream, Theo, and it was disconcerting. And you've been quite articulate about the lack of ethical guidelines, or protocols, for end-stage COVID. How so much has ended up in the laps of frontline medical workers. And how..."

"I don't know about any dream," he snapped. "But I'm concerned about continuing medical treatment when a patient is *terminal*. There's an assumption that people who are sedated are not in pain. But we don't know how much they rise and fall in terms of consciousness when sedated. They can be sedated enough so they can't talk, but not so much that they're not suffering."

Theo paused to take a long, slow breath.

"People dying of COVID can be 'dying' for a long time. People dying of cancer often are dying for a long time. But with cancer and other terminal illnesses, it's acceptable to transition from treatment into hospice. We stop trying to keep someone alive, especially if they are in pain, and help them to die. We don't make people dying of cancer scream in pain until the bitter end. We make use of comfort meds, like morphine. We don't euthanize, but we meet death halfway."

Grace saw the anguish that was in Theo's eyes. And then she remembered when Mickey had brought Jocelynn to Kaw Valley, and her naivete in questioning Mickey when he said he was giving her morphine.

"What?" Theo asked.

"I remembered something. Just last October. I helped with hospice for a friend. I witnessed a good death."

"Then you know the difference."

Grace nodded, then asked, "Do other staff know what you're doing?"

"What *exactly* do you imagine I'm *doing*? Is it something that they're *not* doing?"

That brought Grace up short.

"Are you concerned about getting caught?"

"*Caught?*" Theo asked. "For what? Patients die every single day. They don't need any help from me. And do you think any hospital wants to advertise that *their* patients suffer when we know they'll never recover? Because—and why is that exactly? Pre-pandemic protocols? Or those 'one-in-ten thousand' ventilator miracle survival stories that gets everyone clinging to false hope for Daddy?"

Theo was breathing heavily now.

"But optics aside, which 'decisions' are more ethical? Which are merciful? Which are, to be blunt, sadistic? Or do you have the key to some magical ethical compromise that I've missed?"

"I am not questioning your ethics, Theo," Grace replied. "You are one of the most ethical men I've ever met. I'm working through *my* professional ethics."

"Do whatever you have to do. We both have to make choices that let us sleep at night."

With that, Theo stood up and walked away.

Grace took two days to process the session with Theo. She reread the Code of Ethics of the National Association of Social Work. She googled the obligations of a mandated reporter in Kansas, which centered on harm to children, the disabled, elder abuse, domestic abuse.

And then there was *Tarasoff*. This 1976 case in California had cracked the sacrosanct client-therapist privilege. If a therapist believed that a client intended to harm someone, they had a duty to notify that person, to warn them—to attempt to stop the anticipated harm.

Tarasoff was a hot potato: not warn and the therapist could be liable; warn and the therapist could be sued for breach of confidentiality.

Grace was pretty sure that a dream and a conversation about ethics wouldn't hold up in court as far as credible threat. Especially when she had no idea who was at risk or when the intended harm might occur. Or even how *it* happened.

Or if *it* was *harm.*

But she also knew her rationalizations could be ripped to shreds if she ever ended up on a witness stand. If there ever was a hearing, a trial, she'd probably have to testify as Theo's therapist. She could wiggle out with client confidentiality to a point, but not if subpoenaed. She could lose her license if found negligent.

She went into the bathroom to wash her face and brush her teeth. Halfway through, assiduously brushing, she glanced up and saw her face in the mirror. She stopped, toothbrush hanging of her mouth. Then she put down the toothbrush, rinsed out her mouth and looked again.

What the hell was she thinking? Did she, deep down, believe that Theo Murphy was *harming* anyone who was not already dying?

When she'd made reports in the past about some kid who was being abused, she'd felt an *urgency*, a need to protect the child. Same with domestic abuse. But she felt no urgency here. This wasn't about protecting *other* people

Theo had gotten mixed in with her phobic fear about "missing something" and her other phobic fear of being seen as culpable.

Was all this angst—this drama in her head—about wanting to cover her own ass?

Yeah, she concluded, wiping at a smudge of blue toothpaste on her chin, that's exactly what it was.

Screw it. Whatever might happen with the damn licensing board, so be it. Losing her license as a therapist would not be the end of the world. And if there was legal blowback, she'd survive that too.

Theo Murphy was an ethical man in an ethical vacuum.

The next day, Grace looked for a card to send to Theo. This was something she needed him to hear, and a mailed letter or card had more gravitas than email.

She chose a graduation card, which didn't really fit the situation, but, maybe, sort of, worked? The cover was the back of a young man walking down a road that disappeared in the distance. The card read, "Wishing you the best in your journey. You will make a difference in whatever you choose."

On the inside, she wrote:

Theo: I needed to work it out for myself. I realized that I'd trust you to make the right decision for me or anyone in my family. I would, literally, trust you with my life. If you need a reference for grad school, let me know. If you want to talk, email anytime. It has been an honor to work with you. I learned a lot. Grace

Max

When Molly told Max that they were going to Florida for the summer and would stay with Mike and David like they had a few years before, he reacted better than Molly had anticipated. She'd expected him to freak out, have a meltdown at the sudden change in routine. But when she told him the news, his eyes lit up.

"Can we go in the ocean *every* day?" he asked. "Can I play with Moses again? I want a dog like Moses, Mom. I really like Moses."

"Yes, we can go in the ocean a whole lot but not every day," Molly said, smiling.

Molly had learned the hard way to not make promises—and saying yes to a casual question was, to her son, a promise. Max forgot nothing. It could come up months later, when he wanted to go to the beach, and she said, "not today" and he would then bring up this very conversation and quote her verbatim and how she'd said they could go to the ocean *every* day.

"Why not *every* day?" he persisted.

Molly sighed. "Because there will be reasons that I do not know right now, like we have to do something else, or bad weather, or—stuff. There will be times when it does not work out to go to the beach."

Max looked despondent for a moment, then perked up.

"But we can go *almost* every day? And bring Moses? Right?"

By the next day, Max was wrestling with the news that Grammy and Mickey wouldn't be coming. That wasn't something he'd factored in when Molly first announced the vacation. It was one thing to go for a week and another to go for a whole summer.

"Why aren't they coming? Huh?" Max asked. "They need a

vacation too. I heard Grammy say last week that she couldn't wait to bust out of here. She was serious. She wasn't joking."

Molly explained that Grace and Mickey might come down later in the summer, but they had work and stuff for a lot of the time. Max did not buy the explanation, but his mother gave him that, *I am coming to the end of my rope* look, along with saying, "I cannot discuss this now, Max, so drop it."

Max decided to wait a day and try again. This was really, really hard because he did not have a "drop it" kind of brain. And his brain would chew and chew and chew until he got the answers that made sense to him.

Grace

Ever since Molly had shared the startling news that she was moving, Grace's head had been exploding. Not in a bad way, but she was realizing how this could change the trajectory of her own life. She'd moved back to Kaw Valley for Molly. If Molly had remained, she was in it for the long-haul. But if Molly was leaving? And Molly had a partner and support?

Where did that leave Grace?

Grace had, decades and decades ago, moved to Kansas with her boyfriend, Gil. He had a job offer with a local paper as a journalist, with hopes to move up to a bigger city. The plan was three-to-five years, and then move on.

But that had not materialized. Gil did not take to the tight deadlines of newspapers, churning out articles. He'd found a better fit with a local press as an editor. By that time, Grace had finished graduate school. They'd married. She balanced teaching a few classes at the university with a private practice. They had a home that they loved and were renovating, room by room, and two little kids. Raising kids was less complicated in Kaw Valley. No traffic jams. Less stress. More affordable.

They'd put down roots.

But none of those reasons mattered anymore. And Grace could think of a dozen places she wanted to experience, not for a quick visit, but to settle in for a few months.

Once Molly and Max left, was she no longer tied down? She imagined a balloon on a string that is let go. Where does it come down?

But Molly might return, Grace considered. She might discover that a Zoom relationship was not enough to build a life on. She'd want her home and school back. If so, Grace wanted her to have a safe place...

In that moment, Grace realized that she did *not* want Molly to return, to fail with Mike. Not just because she hoped for happiness for her daughter, and to return would be a painful disappointment. But for herself.

This "want" was selfish. Just as Molly had not expected love, neither had Grace. But if released from her obligations—although that word always sounded so *obligatory* and did not include the joys of being a part of her daughter's and grandson's lives—Grace could do things she'd once dreamed of. Things that she had buried as impossible after Gil had died.

But now was different from then.

What did she want to do—with Mickey—*now*?

Covid Grief Group

It hit Grace that, *if* she was considering—even if still was a *what if*—traveling when Molly left, she'd better not wait until she was packing to inform the grief group. They were people who'd been hit hard with the unexpected.

She didn't see herself as doing much anymore for the group. They'd navigated their own pain, reached out to each other, provided a safe space. They never offered platitudes, assurances that things would get better. Never anything stupid about God's will. No empty words.

They even had a few inside jokes that Grace wasn't in on. Back in February, Grace remembered a session where Kayla had looked at Larry and asked, "Done any baking lately?" Larry had instantly flushed, and Kayla and Beth had laughed. But not in a mean way. It was more like some funny story that they shared.

Grace thought that, even if she did not travel, the group was at a natural closing point. It had been a year. They'd weathered their first holidays alone and the first anniversaries of the deaths. They were leaving in better shape than when they started. You didn't want a group to drag on until people drifted away.

She would tell them tonight that there would be three more meetings in June, and the group would wrap up by the 4th of July.

It was the right decision, a sound decision, but Grace felt a pang of loss. She had changed as well. The group had taught her, shown her, how to grieve.

HISTORICAL CONTEXT: MAY 2021

May 3: COVID-19 cases have declined significantly in more than half of U.S. states.

May 4: President Joe Biden announces new goal of 160 million people, nearly of 70% of adults, to be vaccinated by July 4.

May 5: President Joe Biden announces the U.S. will support temporarily lifting patent protection on COVID-19 vaccines with the World Health Organization.

May 10: F.D.A. authorizes the Pfizer COVID-19 vaccine for 12-to-15-year-olds.

May 12: Republicans vote to demote their No.3 Liz Cheney from party leadership after she publicly rebuked Donald Trump for lies about the election.

May 13: American Federation of Teachers calls for fully opening school buildings the next school year for instruction five days a week.

May 25: The one-year anniversary of George Floyd's murder prompts observances in cities around the world.

May 25: CDC says half of all U.S. adults are now fully vaccinated, with 61% having had their first shot.

May 31: Tulsa, Oklahoma, marks 100-year anniversary of the historically ignored massacre of hundreds of Black residents by white mobs in Greenwood.

June 2021

Grace & Katrina

Grace and Kat were driving south to the 100th Anniversary of the Tulsa Race Massacre. Kat had asked her a few weeks ago if she'd be willing to go and to drive. Driving to Tulsa from Kaw Valley took about five hours. That was too much for Kat to manage alone.

It was a pretty drive, past fields of spring flowers and sprouting crops. It had been a wet spring, and the land smelled loamy. When they pulled off for coffee and gas, the sign on the door of the Chuck's Stop said masks were requested. But they were the only people, other than the clerk at the register, wearing one. They hit the bathroom, sanitized, grabbed coffee, and left.

Grace made the mistake on the way down of calling it the 100th *Commemoration*, which Kat had quickly corrected.

"There has been no commemorating for ten decades, just silence and secrets," Kat said. "It's finally getting serious attention. Hell, it's finally not being labeled a 'race riot.' It was a massacre. The only time in U.S. history that citizens bombed other Americans. Low-flying small planes flew over Greenwood and dropped kerosene balls onto the roofs of businesses and homes, had target practice on anyone trying to escape. 35 square blocks destroyed, at least 1,200 homes torched."

"How is it that I never heard of this despite all those classes in U.S. History in high school and college?" Grace asked.

"Are you being serious or sarcastic?" Katrina rebutted. "You never heard because it was erased. Not one white person was prosecuted yet about 300 Black residents were killed. The newspaper framed it as a Black uprising. Not angry white supremacists—pissed as hell that Greenwood was thriving—destroying it. The police didn't protect property or people. They even deputized some of the mob. And what does that remind you of?"

"January 6th?" Grace asked. "Although I heard last week that we didn't see what we did see with our own eyes. It wasn't a Trump-loving MAGA mob, it was 'Antifa' dressed up like MAGA folks.' And the real MAGA folks didn't trash the Capitol, attack police, and hunt for Mike Pence. They were tourists exercising their right to free speech. Is that an epic whitewash?"

"Nope. Grand scale gaslighting," Katrina said. "Finally white people getting a taste of what Black people have swallowed for centuries: historical gaslighting. Being told that what you know, even what you even saw with your own eyes, didn't happen."

By 2 p.m. they were exiting into downtown Tulsa. They checked into their hotel, glad to find a little kitchen and a table with chairs, alongside their two queen beds.

Kat exhaled deeply as she lowered herself onto one of the beds.

"Oh Lordy, this does feel good," she moaned, extending her legs and pulling an extra pillow over to support her neck. "All the body parts level and none of them hurting."

"I'm going to make some tea," Grace said from the bathroom where she was unpacking toiletries. "And we passed a Panera at the corner. I think I'll meander over and get some food. Maybe split a salad and sandwich? You have a favorite?"

Katrina didn't respond. When Grace looked over from the doorway, her friend's eyes were already closed.

"Okay, then, I'll decide for you," Grace continued, lowering her voice. "Maybe get soup as long as we have a microwave. And they do have those sinful croissants..."

The anniversary events spanned several days, centering on the opening of the Greenwood Rising Black Wall Street History Center.

That night there was an evening vigil, but Kat tired out halfway through.

On Tuesday, she rallied, and they went to an economic empowerment conference. Katrina had registered them, saying that it was one thing to "wake up" to the racism that fueled the horrific attack back in 1921 and another to understand the economic impact that spanned generations. There were three tracks: institutional investors, entrepreneurs and businesses, and individuals and families.

"There's an intense reaction to *any* discussion of reparations, but nobody mentions that families lost everything they spent their lives building," Kat said. "And insurance never paid a cent. All those paid-up policies were worth nothing because the city labeled it a 'riot' and, gosh, how convenient, there were clauses in the policies that excluded damage from 'riots.'"

Grace planned to keep her head down, listen and learn.

Katrina found herself looking as much at the attendees as the speakers. It was rare for her to be at professional events where the majority of audience and speakers had dark skin. And this much style. Kat wondered if she would ever wear high heels again. They looked dangerous. But there were also women in capri pants and sandals, a blouse under a blazer. A more casual look for this lovely June day.

The men, however, were almost all in suits. Most Black professional men learned early on that a high-end suit could counter the impulse of white folks to assume they worked for the hotel or conference center, asking where to find coffee or bathrooms.

I could get used to this, Kat thought.

Katrina made a note on the back of her program to rejoin the Black Women Lawyers' Association of Chicago. She'd gone to a conference, some years ago, but then? The timing was off for a few years, work was busy, traveling alone and hotels alone got pricey. And it felt—indulgent? Well, bullshit to that. She was joining back up and going to every damn conference they offered.

Katrina tried to focus back on the presentation. A huge screen was changing every few minutes with statistics. Some statistics were depressing but expected.

Others were startling.

Could only 1.4 percent of all the wealth funds in the U.S. be managed by people of color or women? So, 98.6 percent managed by...white men?

That couldn't be true, Kat thought. *Could it?*

As the morning sessions concluded, Kat went up to one of the speakers to get his card and ask a question.

"Elijah Wilson," he said, handing her his card.

"Katrina Baptiste," she responded, reaching into her bag for a card to give him.

"So, what's your question?" he asked, sliding her card into a pocket.

"I want to understand more about the investment options you were talking about, redirecting funds to companies that support Black entrepreneurs and start-ups," Kat said. "The statistics were hard to hear. I expected there were barriers, but when the numbers were laid out it got more real. Like redlining: if Black folks live there, it's high-risk. But if Black families want into a 'low risk' neighborhood? No welcome mats out."

"Yes, that bias persists. In rating start-ups and investment options or opportunities, *anything* Black is rated as less reliable, lower potential, higher risk, despite data that shows otherwise."

"How did I not know this? Why isn't it on the front pages of..."

"The data is buried," Elijah interrupted. "But put it on a big screen? It becomes painfully irrefutable. My favorite message about Greenwood? Black Wall Street? It was 100 percent entrepreneurs. But your question is much broader. Can I join you for lunch to continue the discussion?"

Katrina eyed the man. Obviously intelligent and accomplished or he wouldn't be a speaker at an economic empowerment conference. Decent looking. Good smile.

"Are you checking me out as far as lunch or..."

Katrina laughed. "I think it's been over two years since a man suggested lunch, so my reaction time has slowed considerably. And the last time did not end well."

"I'm not buying, just joining the table," he deadpanned. "But do tell about your prior lunch invite."

"A white lawyer," Kat replied. "At a conference. Strode across the room, no preamble. 'I want to take you to lunch,' he said. 'I think we could really hit it off.'"

"Based on what exactly?"

"Well, it wasn't my keen intellect."

"What did you say?" Elijah was smiling as he asked.

"Thank you for the kind offer but I have another commitment," Kat's voice, remembering, became sweet and fake, along with the plastic smile she'd plastered over her real feelings.

"And then?"

"He started to cajole, like 'Are you sure? Can you reschedule? I really think we could enjoy each other.'"

"Ouch," Elijah said, cringing.

"Exactly. Then I said, very quietly, 'Sir, you are about to cross a line. Please go away.'"

"And did he?"

"Only after saying, in a loud voice, 'Well, you don't have to be so rude. I was just asking you to lunch. No need to get an attitude.' Then he strode off. People from five tables turned to stare."

Elijah looked at Katrina and started to laugh. Seriously laugh.

"You didn't run after him to soothe his wounded ego?" Elijah asked.

"Ego or entitlement?" Katrina asked. "They do tend to blur."

Grace had returned, carrying three box lunches. She pointed to a table. "I'll leave these and get some drinks. Iced tea okay with you? Or Coke?"

"Tea is fine," Kat replied. "Thanks."

"And what would you like?" Grace asked Elijah.

"Tea would be great. Thank you."

They sat down at the table and opened their box lunches.

Katrina reached into her purse and took out a pill holder. It was for seven days, with three sections per day. Together, it contained all of her prescribed medications, along with vitamins and supplements, all designed to bolster a variety of bodily functions and mitigate pain in small enough doses that she could still function.

It was, Kat abruptly realized, the size of a small book. Elijah was staring at it.

"That is one impressive set-up," he commented. "Do you know what every pill is for? Because I don't think I could keep track."

"I'm a long hauler," Kat said by way of explanation. "Not sure if you know what that means, but I had COVID in March of 2020 and..."

"I know what long-hauler means," the man interrupted. "My brother is in the same boat. He had to retire—more he got pushed out. The man had stamina. Now he has to sit down after walking around the yard. And his heart is having issues that were never there before."

"I'm slowly improving," Kat went on. "I had some symptoms lighten up after I got my second vaccination. Just a bit. Which seems weird, but..."

"Not really. We heard about that happening with some folks. My brother was hoping he could be one of them. But two doses and nothing has changed for him."

Elijah looked at Kat's nametag. It had no corporate logo. "Who do you work with?" he asked. "Here for business? Networking?"

"No, more personal. I'm an attorney. I work mostly with white folks. All the judges in my district are white, only a few Black attorneys. Only about five percent of the residents are Black."

Katrina paused, then continued.

"COVID isolation clarified how disconnected I've become. It was different when I was raising my sons, maybe because I didn't have time to think. I was raised Catholic but joined an AME church for my boys. Having church once a week was enough to remind me that I'm Black."

"What happened?"

"I slowly stopped going when my kids left for college. Without family, I didn't feel like I fit in anymore. I do not have a deep and trusting faith. So, I felt phony? And, for some reason, I wasn't invited, included, unless I reached out. Being divorced didn't help, either."

"And being light-skinned didn't help either, I bet," he said.

Katrina laughed. "Well, it's refreshing to hear you say it, out loud and to my face. Yeah, that's been there my whole damn life. But my family was a buffer zone when I was a kid."

"My mama was light," he said. "Always felt like she had to prove herself, that others felt like she had more privilege than if she'd been darker."

"Well, it's true," Kat said. "I can't disagree. I remember my first waitress gig, as a teenager, for a fancy place in New Orleans. Lots of white tourists that wanted authentic Cajun but in a place that made them feel comfortable. I swear it had a 'plantation' décor. There were about 15 of us, the high school summer hires. We all started in the kitchen and cleaning tables. One-by-one, we got moved up to waitress, or helping an experienced waitress, but only one made it to hostess. That was me. It wasn't because of my skill set, and the other girls knew it and I knew it. But did we discuss it? No."

"Did it make a difference with the other girls?"

"Yeah, it did. They worked together, worked hard, and they wore uniforms. I wasn't carrying heavy trays of food all day or dealing with cranky customers. I smiled pretty in my cocktail dress, showed people to their tables, handed them menus, and asked if they wanted someone from the bar to come take a drink order. But, at the end of a long shift, I got the same percentage of tips as they did."

"That must've caused a little rift."

"They didn't bring it up, but they didn't include me if they were going out together after their shift either."

"Did you bring it up with anyone?"

"Like who? The managers had a system that had been around for decades. It was as if every position was color-coded. Was it fair? Or right? Hell, no. But we were expendable. If you needed the work, you just smiled and kept your mouth shut. Darker the skin, more likely you'd spend more time in the kitchen. Darker the skin, more likely some customer would comment about the service. It was all in the tone: 'Hey, missy, can we get some more water around here?' versus 'May we have some more water when you have a moment?'"

"And you got treated polite?"

"Oh, yes. I got smiles and compliments," Kat replied, flashing him another big, toothy, fake smile.

Grace had, meanwhile, returned with the iced tea, opened her lunch box, and started in on a sandwich. But she was listening.

Grace had reluctantly accepted that she could never totally "get it" because she was white. At least *that* much she got.

Like, at this very moment, Katrina was talking with a man she'd just met about restaurant work as a teen and being both Black and lighter skinned. In the decades they'd known each other, she'd never brought it up.

And Grace, for all her liberal, do-gooder, social work values, had never picked up on how much was unspoken.

Grace took a swig of Diet Coke and another bite of her ham and cheese. It was a damn good sandwich, and she wondered what they'd put in the mayo to give it that kick.

When Katrina got up to go find a bathroom, Elijah turned to Grace.

"You haven't said a word," he said. "So, how do you fit into this? And what is your name again?"

"Grace McDonald," she replied. "I'm here with Katrina. I wouldn't have known about it without her telling me."

"Do you work together?" he queried.

"No. We've been friends for years," Grace said, prepared to leave it at that. But then she plunged ahead. "But we never really talked about race until..."

Her voice trailed off. How could she encapsulate all of what had happened with their friendship? Their talking?

"Until?" Elijah asked.

"After George Floyd. When it became apparent that I was 'blind' to a lot more than I'd realized. And we're both skilled at avoiding uncomfortable subjects."

"But now you're talking?"

"Yeah, now we're talking."

"How is that going?" he asked, intrigued.

"I don't know. I think okay. Katrina is a lot more open. It's day-by-day."

"What's the hardest part for you?"

Grace stopped to think about that. There had been so many moments when she'd felt—ignorant? Defensive? But the hardest? So *many* choices.

"Facing my own complicity? Realizing that my motivations—if and when I was doing something, anything, to counter racism—were often driven by some twisted marriage of optics and saviorism? Do-gooder white lady to the rescue?"

Well, you're not alone. Optics drives many people. They want to show how they're 'woke', feel good about themselves, get recognized."

As he said that, Katrina returned to the table and slid back into her chair,

"Who wants to show they're 'woke'?" she asked.

"White people," Elijah said. "You know, the ones that show up at meetings..."

"Got it. The folks who feel so special for showing up, who come with their insights and suggestions? But, if not appreciated as they feel think they should be, they fade?"

"Shit," Grace said. "Just hearing that and I felt this—what does Brené Brown call it—'wash of shame.' I've done that. I can remember fizzling out, rationalizing my retreat by thinking that I didn't 'fit in,' forgetting meetings, making excuses."

"Which makes you—what? White. Ordinary white," Elijah reflected. "You'd never intentionally do anything disrespectful. You want approval and acceptance, maybe to offset that white guilt because you're 'woke' enough to be aware of the many benefits you have that you did nada to earn."

"Yeah, Elijah," Kat added. "My girlfriend can be dense, but she's never mean. And as for fizzling out? For Gracie, that's not just about race, that's about boundaries and not being able to say 'no' when she damn well needs to."

"Hey, I'm starting to feel a little ganged up on here," Grace retorted.

"Didn't Brene also say something like, 'the only way to resolve shame is to talk about it'?" Katrina continued as if Grace had not spoken. "I've faced down more self-shame in the last year than ever before."

"It's that shit that makes me crazy," Elijah added. "It's toxic. Not enough that the world is putting me down, but I gotta' do it to myself?"

Grace opened her mouth, then shut it. Katrina and Elijah were talking to each other. This was not her conversation.

The week was busy, compelling, making connections—and also a blur. But life for the last fifteen plus months had been a blur. Katrina was used to time warps.

What Katrina would remember most, and share with her sons, was the *Greenwood Rising: Black Wall Street History Center*. Perhaps someday she'd have grandchildren to bring as well.

For the opening ceremony, she and Grace got to the corner of Greenwood and Archer early enough to snag some chairs in the shade. The many rows in front of the stage were filled with descendants of the massacre victims and survivors.

There was the usual array of speakers. They welcomed the descendants, some of whom lived in Tulsa. But there were also descendants who had never been to Tulsa, for whom the city name was bitter on their tongue. Their grandparents and great-grandparents had fled from the massacre with the clothes on their backs, abandoning homes, cars, jobs—everything they'd worked hard for and cherished—to start over with nothing. They'd become refugees in their own country.

The speakers thanked all of the sponsors, the members of various committees, the worker bees who made this all happen. There was music, a Ray Charles rendition of "America the Beautiful," after disclaimers that America might not be as beautiful for some as others. There was 100 seconds of silence for the 100 years that the massacre had been invisible, unrecognized, unspeakable. There were stories of pain, and stories of glory.

Before the program wrapped up, Grace slipped out to try to score a table at Wanda J's Next Generation, a tiny family-owned institution in what remained of Greenwood. Locals promised that they served the best fried chicken and peach cobbler in Oklahoma. She lucked out with a two-top just before a line started to form.

Kat would not last if she had to stand in line.

Grace wanted to bring Max to Tulsa. He'd love the majesty of the Philbrook Museum, both the art and gardens. And he'd want to do *everything* in The Gathering Place, which was, Grace thought, the best city park for kids she'd ever seen. She wanted to take him to eat here, to Wanda J's, which carried a story on every plate. Then maybe go across the street for a haircut from Willie Sells at Mr. Tee's Barber Shop. Definitely a big-boy cut.

But mostly to bring him to Greenwood Rising, to learn the history that was not taught in most classrooms. It would be hard for Max to process, and he would be upset. "How could people do that to each other? Why were they so angry?" he'd certainly ask. But truth-in-history was essential. No more secrets. No more lies.

The night before they left, they went to a concert in Guthrie Square. It was a Black jazz band. Black families lounged on blankets and lawn chairs next to white families. Kids danced in front of the stage. It felt like a quintessential, albeit integrated, Norman Rockwell painting.

Grace felt a cognitive dissonance. *Which family had grandparents and great-grandparents who'd hunted down and killed Black people?* Grace thought. *And which families are the descendants of the murdered and hunted?*

So many families, so many stories.

On Sunday morning, they left Tulsa by 9 a.m. and took Highway 75 north. They were both ready to be home.

Grace looked over at Kat, now dozing, her mouth slightly open, the lines between her eyes still tight from the pain that never completely left her. But that would change. Whatever it was that had invaded her body, left her depleted and wounded, was abating. Grace had to believe this, to bury her doubt and fear.

Kat had been her lifeline at the hardest time in her life. They'd been through some—to use Molly's expression—"heavy frickin' shit." There had been times when neither knew if the friendship would survive. But it had survived. And they had survived.

This last year had been harder than either could ever have imagined.

Grace accelerated, feeling an urgency to be home. She wanted to plant hostas. She wanted to be in her casita with Mickey. She wanted to hug her daughter and grandson. She wanted to cherish every hour they had together before Molly and Max would get in the car, wave goodbye, and drive off to start a new chapter.

Grace wanted to feel—deeply, every day, for the rest of her life—gratitude.

She wanted to live.

Abuelo & Abuela

Mike's parents had not been as jolted by surprise as Grace when their son told them his plans.

They'd heard the shift in their son's voice, seen his more frequent smiles, observed how he'd been, well, lighter. And they'd met Molly when she'd visited with Leah. They respected that she was a single parent, that she and Mike shared those roles and responsibilities.

He'd told them, months before, that he was talking with Molly, but that they were "just good friends."

They'd felt the tension and anxiety that their son had carried back from deployments incrementally dissipate.

Mike was looking forward, not just backward.

When he told them that he had serious feelings for Molly, and that he was going to tell her, and at the same time ask her to come to Florida to live with him and David for the summer, Abuela and Abuelo were more than unsettled.

Mike had almost been permanently broken when David's mother had severed her parental rights to her son. He blamed himself, thought it was his fault, that he'd put in motion what eventually happened.

So, they'd felt an anxiety that bordered on panic. What if she didn't reciprocate? What if Molly just wanted to remain friends as Mike had originally told them? That she couldn't uproot her son and herself, that she was in grad school, that he was asking too much?

They believed that their son *was* asking too much of Molly. But they also realized that he was a man who had asked for so little his entire life. He had never wanted to put people out, even them, his own parents. Could he reap all the karma he had earned?

If not, they would be there to help him regroup, to pull through.

So, when Mike had walked in the front door of their condo, his face happier than they'd seen in years, and announced, "Molly loves me. She's going to come," relief and gratitude had washed over them.

When it got down to the details, they were less assured. Molly was not sure what to do about school; there was no set date for this impending move; Molly was researching special-education services for Max; Molly was trying to decide what to do about her house.

But, like Grace, they recognized that this was out of their control. They had to step back and let Mike and Molly work it out.

Grace

Meanwhile, Grace was working through her lingering concerns the way she usually did these last few years: having internal dialogues with herself and then rehashing with Mickey.

Grace was the queen of the "reframe," which had proven to be productive for so many years in her clinical work with clients. She was good at taking what appeared at first look to be really difficult and changing the perspective or the context.

"Mickey, I was thinking how my parents never really dated," she said while sautéing garlic, onions, and peppers. "My mother graduated high school and started working in New York City, and my father enlisted in the Navy after Pearl Harbor. They met before he left for basic training and then were separated for most of three years."

"So, what's the point? And why are you bringing this up now?" he asked, glancing up from his newspaper.

"Because they wrote letters," she replied. "Well, mostly *he* wrote letters. I think her patriotic duty was dancing with guys at the USO three nights a week and keeping poor, lonely soldiers entertained. But the point is that, during war, all the usual stuff we think of as 'normal' goes kaput."

"Kaput meaning what?" Mickey put the newspaper down.

"Meaning that forced distance—when people are deployed, or far from home, or uprooted—leads to the unconventional. My father wrote a hundred missives on that skinny blue air-mail paper and, in the process, decided that he was going to marry the object of his affections."

He furrowed a brow. "Didn't you tell me that your parent's marriage was not made in heaven?"

Grace rolled her eyes. "I'm not saying he made a smart decision, but it was common. People returned from combat and, within weeks, many married. And after World War II and Korea and Vietnam, thousands of soldiers returned with war brides. The fear of dying, the realization that life is fragile and short, propels people into relationships. What was 'normal' prior to war—like get introduced, date, meet the families, date, build a relationship, propose, plan a wedding—was upended."

"Are you saying that your daughter is a war bride?"

"No, although Mike's parents have never gotten to know her, and if it wasn't for that custody case from hell, I'd have no idea who he is," Grace answered, a tad exasperated. "But if we look at the pandemic like it's a war, then what they're doing has a historical precedent. It's kind of sweet and old-fashioned. They've talked for 18 months and never had sex. And they're in love."

"From the look on Molly's face when she talks about Mike, that sex part will work itself out. Just in case you're worrying..."

"Stop being a jerk," Grace interrupted. "I mean that hasty and premature sex, which is what hook-ups are, have nothing to do with intimacy..."

Grace realized that Mickey was laughing, was putting stuff out there just to get her wound up.

"Just set the damn table," she said. "I'll put the pasta in after we have our salads. And pour me some of that Bordeaux."

Grace & John Martin

Grace was in the produce section of the grocery store when she heard a male voice ask, "Excuse me, but aren't you Grace McDonald?"

When she looked up from the tomatoes, the man seemed vaguely familiar, but she never could tell with a mask. She nodded. Then he quickly lowered his mask, smiled, and lifted it up again. She did the same. It was a post-vaccination compromise.

"John Martin," he said. "It's been about 18 months since I came to talk with you about my mother? That would have been just before the pandemic hit."

"Yes, John, of course. Takes me a little longer to connect the dots these days. But your mom was in Wisconsin? Correct? With—Fred? And you were concerned about conspiracy beliefs and that she was being isolated?"

"That's me. I'm surprised you remember all that."

"Just takes me bit to reboot. Once my brain locates the file, it all comes back," Grace said. "So, how's your mother? It's been a tough time for everyone."

"It was that, for sure. But with COVID we had so much to deal with here, with the kids and work and virtual school—and we couldn't have safely visited anyway—that we had to let it go. So, we decided to just send a box every month, with letters from each of us, and baked treats, and pictures from the past. Memories. But no mention of *anything* political. Just small surprises, reminders that she has a family that loves her no matter what."

"Did that help? Or make a difference?"

"I can't say for sure, but it might have saved her life."

"Now you have my full attention," Grace said, putting down the tomato.

"The crazy talk continued, in spurts, all though 2020. COVID was a hoax, there was a conspiracy to keep treatments that worked from people. Whatever Trump spouted. Ivermectin. Bleach. If Trump didn't win it would be a rigged election because it was clear that he..."

"I get the picture," Grace interrupted. "So, what changed?"

"When vaccines became available, it was clear that Fred opposed them. He thought it would put something in his body so he could be traced and then controlled by the feds. A left-wing hoax. But then, in April, he got COVID. My mother took care of him, so she got COVID also. He got very sick and ended up in the ICU. But Mom just got a little sick for a week or so. Fred died after two weeks on a ventilator..."

"Whoa," Grace cut him off. "Fred's dead?"

"Yes," John answered. "Fred is dead." The rhyme made each of them bite their lips to hide a smile of dark humor.

"But your mother didn't get that sick?"

"My mother had secretly vaccinated. She'd driven to another town because she didn't want to be ratted out if anyone saw her. Waited until he was off ice fishing. Never told Fred. Never told us." John was enjoying recounting the story. "Told us later that one of the pictures we sent her was of us three kids all lined up at the family doctor to get vaccinated. It made her remember how grateful she'd been to be able to protect us from those awful diseases."

"So, your mother snuck out and got vaccinated? Now *that* is a story!" Grace exclaimed. "Where is she now?"

"My sister persuaded her to come stay with them for a while. That was about six weeks ago. My sister has NPR on the radio, and they don't 'do' TV news. Nobody mentions Fox or QAnon. Just keeping Mom busy with craft projects and such. And she doesn't ask. I think she'll end up moving..."

"What about her house in Wisconsin?"

"Turns out Fred *did* control the money," John explained. "But he didn't leave a will. He had no kids, so everything goes to Mom. I think he manipulated her by saying if she left him, she'd have nothing because it was all in his name. And it was: bank accounts, stocks, house, cars, boat. All in his name only."

"Happens a lot," Grace added. "Don't push her. It may take a while for your mom to share. It feels shameful to get sucked into a bad relationship. Just love on her."

"That's what we're doing," John said. "But I want to thank you for that advice, to not confront, to just quietly persist in showing her that she has a family. I almost said, 'Screw it,' and gave up. My wife put together the first three boxes by herself."

"Sometimes photos trigger deep memories," Grace said. "Deep feelings."

"Well, that one photo saved her life, and I'll never believe otherwise."

That evening, telling Mickey about the produce aisle encounter, Grace reflected on how good it felt to know how that had worked out. With so many clients, she was intimately connected for a short time and then never knew how the issues resolved or lives played out.

Like 1,000 plays with no third act.

Zed & Cherry

It felt to Cherry and Zed as if life was returning to some semblance of normal. The library was open, with masks required. The city pool was opening as soon as they could train a few more lifeguards. Families were reconnecting. Restaurants were busy although most had patios that filled up first. Some sports for kids were back (baseball being popular, as it was inherently socially distant).

Home Depot had strongly encouraged their employees to get vaccinated, especially management. Zed wanted to be a team player. He was busy working and spending evenings with the boys and Cherry. They ate dinner together most nights, and the kids were eager to be outside. Now that life was opening up, he didn't have hours to research. They agreed that Zed would get vaccinated.

A few days after he got his first shot, when he asked Cherry about her day, she surprised him.

"So, I was getting toothpaste and shampoo at the grocery, and that section is right by the pharmacy? And there was a sign for free vaccinations anytime? And I thought, 'Oh, just get it over with. You'll probably have to do it sooner or later.'"

"You got poked?" he asked, incredulous. "Which kind?"

"Pfizer. Like you. I think it's been the most tested."

If Cherry were honest with herself, she didn't know anything for sure. She'd spent a few days trying to track down the sources for a lot of what she'd read online. She wanted to be able to prove to that lady at the college that there were verifiable, legitimate, evidence-based alternative positions.

But the more she searched, the more confused she became. Like A said their positions or statements were based on B, and B said they got the data from C, and C said to check out D, but then D quoted A. And none of them were from large universities or medical centers or agencies, just private clinics. Some were written by doctors who had gone to great medical schools, but they were out on their own. And three of the most quoted studies seemed to have started from someone in Mexico who had an alternative healing center for people with cancer.

Although she'd decided to not debate vaccines, Cherry still believed in protecting children from abduction and abuse. She checked for updates on some sites every few days and wrote letters to politicians about the unreported pandemic of missing children. There was a march coming up that they wanted to go to. And she and Zed had signed up to be volunteers with a new group, "Child Rescue," or something like that. They were going to go to a training in Missouri next month.

Cherry could not imagine a higher purpose than returning an abducted child to grieving parents. That was something worth some effort, worth a sacrifice.

In so many ways, life was—good? Zed was an assistant manager, steady hours, steady pay, good medical insurance. Cherry had applied to the community college and was scheduled to start in August, a few days after the kids' school opened. Plus, there was some new government program, part of infrastructure or pandemic recovery, that was going to give parents a subsidy to help their kids, which, while they could not believe it would actually happen, would make a huge difference in their lives. They would have a financial buffer. It would help with school. Maybe even nursing school. And childcare. Maybe even cover tutoring because Cody was struggling with math. He'd fallen behind during COVID. It would take a lot of the worry out of paying bills every month.

They were coming out of the tunnel. Cherry could see light, sharp as sun on snow, and they were close, almost there.

Nell & Andre & Aniya

Nell, Andre and Aniya had been living together for a month. The kids had clung to each other during the first few "adjustment" weekends. But after they'd moved in, their guard started to drop. With each meal, each day that passed, they became less vigilant. It was as if they were slowly accepting that this really would be their home, that after a year of awful loss and social workers and foster homes where they never really belonged, that this woman was going to keep them safe.

The third night in their new home, Nell awoke in the middle of the night to find Aniya curled up like a dog at the foot of her bed. She gently picked her up and put her into bed with her, covering her with the comforter. "Anytime you want to cuddle, or feel a little scared, just climb on in," she whispered to Aniya. When Nell woke in the morning, she could feel Aniya snuggled up against her back.

Today they were headed to their first extended family gathering to celebrate Juneteenth.

Nell was a little worried that Andre and Aniya would feel overwhelmed. Ian's collective family could be a bit intimidating, if only in sheer size. She remembered first being introduced, as Ian's fiancé, and being swallowed up, looking over her shoulder at Ian laughing as the 'girl cousins' pulled her into their circle.

She'd sent out an email saying that the kids were kind of shy and might end up sitting together, just watching, and that was okay. Just let them ease into the Thomas clan.

They were gathered in a park, with three picnic tables in a row, and folding chairs in circles in the shade of the elms. The kids were playing kickball, some already meandering over to the swings.

It was a good day, sunny, but not so baking hot that they'd sweat sitting in the shade. The meal would be traditional: barbeque meats, red beans and rice, red cabbage slaw, red velvet cake and strawberry pie.

Andre and Aniya stayed close to Nell at first. But after watching the other kids playing tag, swinging, doing what kids do, they tentatively joined in. When they ate supper, they wanted to sit next to her, but they took in everything from slightly-lowered eyes.

It was almost sunset, as they were packing up, that Nell realized she had not seen Andre for a while. Aniya was sitting at a picnic table with a book. But Andre?

Nell felt an abrupt panic. She looked methodically, in a full circle. As far as she could see, there was no Andre. Many of the cousins had already packed up their cars and left. She felt his name filling her throat as she opened her mouth to yell.

But then she saw him. He was with Pops, Ian's dad, and they were coming around the corner from the restrooms behind the swings. Andre was talking and Pops was leaning over, just a bit, to catch every word. Pops put his head back and laughed, and his hand slipped down to ruffle Andre's hair. Andre started to laugh as well, and Nell thought it was the first time she'd heard him laugh, really laugh. It was a different sound, less constricted, more open. Pops stopped and pulled his arm back and then extended it in a fist-bump. Andre fist-bumped back. They were grinning about something.

Nell finished packing up her cooler. Aniya was getting sleepy and Nana helped her into the back seat and fastened her seatbelt. Andre slid in next to her, still grinning.

Nell thanked Pops and Nana—which she, too, now called them—and started up the car.

"Ready to go home, kiddos?" she asked. They nodded. As she backed out of the parking space, she glanced at the empty front seat next to her, wishing, as she did every damn day, for Ian to be here, with her, to share in this new life.

Max

I decided what I'm going to be when I grow up," Max told Mickey as they settled down for their weekly supper-and-a-movie night. "A bioinformatician. It's like being a detective. They find strains of different viruses. There is a really big database called GISAID, created by scientists for scientists, with, like, millions of genome sequences..."

"What does GISAID stand for?" Mickey interrupted.

"I don't know but I think Global-something."

"Where did you learn about genome sequencing?" Mickey asked. "I'm not sure I even understand it."

"I read about it online. You need to know the genome sequencing to create a vaccination fast, because coronaviruses are way different from other viruses. They can combine inside a person and become a super virus. With superpowers. Any person can be the guinea pig for viruses combining and not even know it. Two viruses have to infect the same cell. It sounds like that would not happen much, but it happens a lot. And the person doesn't know that they're spreading a more dangerous virus. A virus can have a super-power, like an invisibility cloak that protects it from being seen by antibodies who are out to fight it. Nobody knows until a bioinformatician finds out..." Max had been speaking in a rushed voice, as if this was urgent information that had to be shared urgently.

"How did you choose bio-inform-a-tician?" Mickey asked, stumbling over pronunciation. "Why not a doctor?"

"I don't like touching people, and doctors do a lot of that," Max replied. "Pandemics kill people all over the world. Doctors just treat the virus in the people. It will be the bioinformaticians from all over the world that will be the superheroes. Nobody sees them, like nobody can see the virus. But they save way more lives than doctors."

"You're gonna' make a great superhero, Max," Mickey said. "We can talk more about it when we come to visit you in Florida. Okay?"

"I came in from the yard yesterday and Mom was sitting on the couch crying," Max told Mickey, a tight segue to Florida. "I asked her what she was crying for, and she said she was just a little sad about going to Florida for the summer."

"That make sense to you?" Mickey asked.

"She doesn't like packing, and she is packing a bunch. And she told me that we're having a garage sale with Grammy next weekend, and she is going to purge a lot of stuff. I had to look up that word. Purge: 'To rid something or someone of an unwanted quality, condition, or feeling.' But that didn't fit. Or 'to remove from an organization or place people considered undesirable in an abrupt or violent way.' That didn't fit either."

"Well, purge can also mean to clean out stuff, like clean out closets of clothes that don't fit anymore," Mickey added. "Get rid of things that you don't need and let other people have them who might actually use them."

"So why don't they call it a 'purge sale?' We don't even have a garage."

"Well, you do have a yard," Mickey offered. "Would yard sale work?"

Molly

Molly was packing, or at least trying to assemble what needed to be packed. She was looking at what would fit in her car and what was essential.

Her car was decent, a Kia Soul that her mom helped her get when her last clunker finally died. It was perfect for her and Max, and usually felt spacious, especially with the back seats down. But this was daunting.

There were multiple piles: 1) clothing, summer only, no winter gear; 2) plastic bins with Max's electronics and games; 3) Max's "important" books that he kept in his bedside table in case he needed them in the middle of the night; 4) Max's comfort items, like stuffed animals he'd had for years, his favorite pillows and comforters. Molly's computer, chargers, files and such, were in one stuffed tote bag.

In between making lists, Molly had moments of shaking self-doubt. Molly and Mike both had *baggage*. They had two challenging kids. This was not just to see if they would work as a couple, but if the four of them could work as a family.

Molly imagined what she'd tell a client who announced she was going to relocate across the country to move in with a man she'd visited twice in three years. But the client explained that they'd been Zooming and chatting on the phone for the last year, and she "felt" something? Duh?

Molly would tell her to slow down, get off the roller coaster. "This is your life we're talking about," she'd lecture.

But what Molly feared the most was—if it didn't work out—losing her best friend. Were they taking way too big a risk? Was the fear in part because she'd been risk avoidant? And she'd found something wanting in any guy by a second date? Was it by *not* dating, by just *talking*, that Mike had rooted himself in her heart?

She'd been talking to herself: *You can step back; you don't have to move now. Explain that you aren't ready. See if he'll wait. If this is not just some COVID reaction to not having other options...* But at the thought of postponing a year or two, Molly felt a sharp, jagged loss, immediate regret, and she wanted to howl.

She wanted Mike. Whatever issues came up, they could work through. They could talk. And, she'd realized, being able to talk, to trust that the other person would listen, that they would *hear* what you said and be *influenced* by it—not just pretend and blow you off—that was so much more important than sexual compatibility.

Sex could be learned, practiced, as long as they could talk. She kind of looked forward to practicing. *Lots* of practicing, until they had it down. She did not see sex being an issue. Not when she still remembered their one and only kiss.

There were two possibilities: 1) she would, if this did "work out," return to pack up some furniture, have another garage sale, rent a U-Haul, fill it with whatever pieces of her life she wanted to bring to Florida; or 2) she would return from what would be forever labeled a summer vacation, and slip right back into her stable, comfortable life, her mom just steps away, on call whenever she needed. Do grad classes by Zoom, postpone her practicum until in-person was possible, be a mom. All with a support system that would be there for her.

She had a soft place to fall.

Yet, Molly found herself, in each room, saying goodbye.

Mickey had offered to watch Max for as much time as she needed. Molly had a strong feeling that Mickey was doing this more for himself than to help her out. Mickey was the only grandfather that Max had ever known, and they'd grown close ever since Mickey had moved to Kaw Valley.

Molly wanted them—she, Max, Grace, and Mickey—to go to Lone Star Lake, pack a picnic, swim off the dock. Pedal around on noodles sipping drinks.

She wanted a whole afternoon to stroll downtown with her mom, unhurried, no agenda. To stop on a whim in every store that caught their fancy. They would buy earrings because that was the only jewelry that Grace actually wore, and because it was a way to mark the day. *Remember when we bought these at The Striped Cow, that afternoon...*

It had hit her that this might be the last time she and her mother would ever live in the same town. Their contact would be visits, not the everyday, informal, spontaneous "Yoo-hoo" they now shared.

Covid Grief Group

When Grace arrived at the circle garden for their last session, everyone was already there and seated. That was unusual.

"Did you all get here extra early?" Grace asked.

"We wanted to talk about something," Kayla replied.

"Like what?" Grace asked, lowering her bag and easing into the remaining chair.

"You," Kayla answered, looking Grace in the eye.

Grace made a small, tight, laugh.

"That's no fun," she said, waving her hand as if shooing away a fly.

"Maybe not fun," Beth said. "But here goes. And if you truly do not want to talk about this, then we'll stop."

"What are you talking about?" Grace asked, looking around the circle.

Beth glanced at Larry and nodded.

"I was on a jury," Larry said. "About 14 or so years ago? Spring? It was a homicide case."

Grace felt her face flood with the memory of shame, a shame that persisted still. She felt for the sides of her chair to stop from falling over. She looked around the group.

"Have you—all known? This whole time?" Grace asked, her voice cracking. It felt mortifying to think that they'd all read about her past life, and she hadn't known.

"No, we were too busy with our own grief to check you out," Beth replied. "Larry didn't say anything until last week. But no specifics. Said he wouldn't if you didn't say okay. So, is it okay?"

Grace did a quick scan. Everyone was looking at her. No going back now. She nodded at Larry.

"I was on a jury. A murder. Seemed like a domestic," Larry continued. "A husband was found dead on his kitchen floor. He'd been shot, twice. The wife was found in the grass outside the house when the

EMTs arrived. A neighbor phoned it in when he'd seen the front door wide open and then the woman."

Grace listened as if she was hearing this story for the first time. And, in a way, it was a first. Such a concise, dispassionate summary. The only time she'd heard those facts presented was in court when a DA and defense attorney had created dramatically different scenarios.

"They never found the gun. When the wife was taken to the hospital she was cleaned up before the cops thought to test for gunshot residue. The DA painted it as a domestic, that the wife found out he'd had an affair, which was true, and had lost it. The defense pointed out that she was a respected member of the community for decades, no indication of any violence, and that the real murderer was still out there."

Larry's words were describing a scenario out of a Made-for-TV movie. Nothing to do with her life.

"Defense said she'd never owned a gun, no record of ever purchasing a gun, didn't know how to shoot, and the gun was never found because the real killer had it. Prosecutor said she'd had time after the shooting to drive a quarter mile to that small bridge over the river and throw it in or bury it in the woods. Something like that."

Larry paused to collect himself. "But it came down to DNA. The wife's blood was found at the far side of the kitchen, where the shots were fired from. But she testified that she'd never crossed the kitchen, that her husband's blood was on her from when she reached for him, by the entrance, not the back door."

Grace felt as if she'd stopped breathing. Her lungs were working, but with no direction from her brain.

"The DNA trumped the 'logic' of the defense. DNA doesn't lie. We, the jury, voted to convict. I started out not buying it—pieces didn't fit. About half the jury felt the same. But we caved to what seemed back then to be irrefutable evidence.

I wanted to apologize, Grace," Larry continued. "When they found the man who did kill your husband, I kept thinking 'How could I have voted to convict? Why didn't I trust my gut?' At our first meeting, I thought, 'That can't be her. I heard she moved away.' But I took out a box where I put everything related to the trial and looked and it sure was you."

"Why didn't you tell us?" Kayla asked Grace.

"I intended to," Grace answered. "Just not right off because I didn't want to put my loss in the middle of your losses. But then time passed, and it seemed like it would be weird to say. 'Oh, by the way, my husband was murdered, blah-blah-blah....'"

"Didn't you trust us to accept...?" Kayla asked.

"No, no. It was more that I did such a lousy job with my grief, with my kids. I ran away. I believed my kids were better off without me. I'd just hold them back. I rationalized that if I paid for their apartments and tuition, they'd be okay. But it wasn't okay. Nothing that I did was okay."

"But you live by your daughter now? Right?" Debra asked. "You've talked about her and your grandson."

"My daughter got into a relationship with a very immature boy, got pregnant, dropped out of college. I helped her financially, but she was 90% alone raising Max. Only when she had a breakdown did I finally *get* how hard that was. I moved back to Kaw Valley. I live in a casita—really a renovated garage—behind her bungalow."

"What about your son?" Bill asked.

"We were estranged for many years, but now we're talking. I was booked to go visit him but then COVID swept in and..."

"Why were you estranged?" Kayla interrupted.

"He believed that I'd murdered his father. He's a 'science doesn't lie' kind of guy and I could not explain prosecution DNA. It was all so insane. When I was exonerated, I think he felt ashamed. But he lived in Austin, and before we could work it all out, I sold the house and drove off."

"So, you each felt betrayed?" Beth asked.

"That sums it up. And we're both stubborn."

"Sounds like you've been through as much as any of us," Beth said. "Maybe more. You lost everything—your husband, your family, your community, friends. And it was public, front page of the newspapers. You were blamed. It sounds awful."

"It was awful. Very, very awful. People I'd thought were friends turned their backs. I lost all credibility, lost my practice, my work. The actual trial felt surreal. When I was in prison, I wanted to die. But after? It felt like the entire town was a prison. I was the woman who maybe didn't murder her husband after all. So, I got in my car and left. No destination, just escape. Road trip—except I put the house up for sale.

Kept going until I got to Homer, Alaska, where—and I mean this literally—the road ends. Got a job waitressing. Rented a little cabin. Closed off my heart like it was a back room I didn't need any more."

"And you thought what you did made you *less* competent to facilitate a grief group?" Bill asked.

"Well, yeah," Grace rebutted sarcastically. "If you look at lists of what *not* to do when grieving? I did them all."

"Could be that makes you more credible," Bill pointed out. "Also not perfect."

"But you came back. You made it right?" Debra persisted.

"I've tried. Every damn day."

With those words, Grace cracked. The mask she'd been wearing, the carefully constructed professional mask of restrained empathy, slipped off. She was present in this group as she had not been before.

"My daughter is driving to Florida on July 5th to live with a man she mostly knows over Zoom but has fallen in love with," Grace said, evenly. "He loves her as well. And I want her to do this. I want her to have a good relationship, a partner. But I'm just now understanding how many years I've avoided grieving. And I didn't get that until now, after a year with all of you."

"Well," Beth said, "welcome to the club. And, since we're being transparent here, I knew too. I was working at the legislature back then. Had to read a dozen newspapers every day and summarize for the boss. It was a juicy case. When we first met, your name sounded familiar, so I googled it and, well, you know what comes up."

"So why didn't you tell me?" Grace pushed.

"Not my life," Beth retorted. "Would I want to rip open my heart in 15 years to tell my story? No idea. Maybe if you'd screwed up? Maybe then I would have ratted you out."

Later that night, after the group shared where they imagined they'd have ended up without the safety net of the group—which included scenarios of jail, divorce, isolation and more—and sharing also what they valued about each other—Grace could not stop thinking of the millions and millions of people who had no place to share their stories. Not just about a death, but everything or anything they'd lost. The high school kids who never had a prom or graduation. The college kids who missed out on the "college experience" or didn't get jobs. The millions of people who lost their work, their security, their future.

Books could be written about what people had lost—had missed—since this damn pandemic began. Many, many books.

Mike & David

Mike and David were walking on the beach with Moses, who was running in and out of the frothy waves, turning to bark at them to hurry up. His retriever coat was already coated in sand.

Mike had talked to David before he ever wrote Molly the letter. But he'd been ambiguous, asking David how he'd feel if Molly and Max came down for the summer. David had met them twice, the same as Mike, when they'd visited. Pre-COVID, of course.

"That's okay," David had said. "It could be fun."

Now Mike needed to be more explicit.

"Remember how I asked back in April if it was okay with you if Molly and Max came down for the summer?" he started.

"Yeah," David answered. "What about it? They're coming, right?"

"I think so," Mike said. "Early July. But there's more to it."

David stopped walking and turned to face his father.

"Like what?"

"Like I have feelings for her, and the summer is to see how we do together, how we *all* do, living together. If it feels right, if we *all* feel good about it, then she and Max could stay."

"Stay how?"

"Stay as in we all live together, and Max goes to school here."

"So not a visit, but they *move* here? Like permanently?"

"That's what I'm hoping," Mike said. "There will be a lot of adjustments, but..."

"Have you guys even dated?"

"Not in the traditional sense, but we've spent a hundred hours Zooming and talking. I feel more for Molly than I ever have with anyone."

"Do I have to share my bathroom with Max?"

"Probably."

"Will Max get your office? Because I am not sharing my bedroom."

"Yes, Max will have his own room."

"And where will Molly sleep?" David was looking at the ground, but Mike could see the corners of his mouth twitch. The kid was messing with him.

"Wherever she chooses," Mike replied. "And I see you laughing, smart ass. So, are you okay with this?"

"What if I'm not?" David asked, his voice suddenly serious.

"Then we need to sit down and talk out all of your concerns. See what can be answered. Maybe with Abuelo and Abuela. Because it means a lot to me to have you on board," Mike replied. "I'm not going to cancel the summer. But if you feel strongly after a month or so that you do not want Molly and Max living with us, I'll respect that."

"What would they do if I say I don't want them living with us?"

"Maybe go back to Kansas. Maybe rent a place nearby and we take it slow. Depends on how they feel as well. Nobody wants to be where they aren't wanted."

As soon as he said the words, Mike realized they would be heard differently by David. He hadn't been wanted. He'd been cut off. But he would have fought to stay. He was never given a choice.

"That's not what I meant, David. I'm sorry. It's that they would..."

"I know, Dad. I'm good to give it a try, but it's a little scary. It helps to know I have a choice, or at least a vote."

"You are number one in my life, David. I will not force anything on you."

"Is that why Molly is moving here?" David asked. "Because we can't move back?"

"Yes. She understands. I made that clear from the beginning."

They were walking again, Moses now farther down the beach.

"What do Abuelo and Abuela think?" David asked.

"At first that I was crazy, that there was no way she would agree. They were worried that I was going to be hurt. But after she said she'd come for the summer, and they saw I was happy, they shifted," Mike replied. "It might be a good thing to talk this out with them, because you may share a lot of the same feelings."

"I'll do that," David replied. "Molly must care for you a lot if she's uprooting her life to be with you. Does she have a clue what she's getting into?"

"I'm hoping not. If she did, she might run the other direction."

David was now scanning the beach for Moses. He pulled out a silent dog whistle and blew. Far down the beach, a yellow head popped up from the sand, alert, searching the beach for them, then heading back.

"I love that stupid dog," David said.

"Yeah, me too," Mike agreed. "Ready to turn around? I think Abuela is baking cinnamon rolls this morning and they should be coming out of the oven any time."

"You know, Dad, I can help with Max," David added a few minutes later as they walked. "I used to be pretty good with the younger kids. I kind of miss that."

Mike & Abuela & Abuelo & David

"What are you doing to prepare? To make Molly feel welcome?" Abuela asked Mike at 8 a.m. one morning, a few days later, bringing over chocolate croissants as an excuse to stop by.

It was the start of the fourth week of June. Abuela been patiently waiting to see if her son had a plan, but Molly was driving down July 5th.

Abuela was now invested. She did not want her son screwing up a good thing. He'd never lived with a woman, never shared a bathroom with a woman. His mattress was ancient and had a slight aroma of old socks. The pillows were worse. His dresser was from a garage sale. Most of the furniture in his place was garage sale. He'd gotten David new stuff, but not himself. Ever.

"I figure I'd wait until she gets here and then see what she wants to do," Mike replied.

Which was a good approach, Abuela considered. Very respectful. Unless she doesn't feel she had a right to change things up, do a makeover, until she's *positive* she's staying. Because she'll be respectful as well. So, she lives for months in what may be her new home with that mattress, that sofa, the cracked, mismatched dishes? It was a long list.

"Hijo, es la verdad," Abuela continued. "Molly can change

whatever she wants. But don't put her in a position of wishing she could make changes but not yet feeling she has the right to do that."

"Why do you think that?" Mike asked. "She'll tell me."

Oh, sweet Jesus, Abuela thought. *The assumptions men make.*

"Better to woo her," Abuela continued. "Will her eyes light up when she sees *this* as her new home? She is giving up a lot for you." When Abuela said "this," she gestured at the saggy couch, and her nose wiggled as if from a bad smell.

"I know, Mom, but it's only a week away. Too late for those kinds of changes."

"Remember the photos you showed me of the garage sale she put together two weeks ago?" Abuela asked. "Yes, she'll return to pack her home and move some furniture *if* she decides to stay. But you want to leave room for as few doubts as possible."

"So, what are you proposing? In one week?"

"Get your shoes on and grab David. I'll get Abuelo. I saw those pictures of her living room. She likes IKEA."

Abuela was at the door before Mike had time to react. "Get a move on," she said over her shoulder. "We need to be there when they open. There is a lot to cover."

By 1 p.m., Mike was drained. There were so many choices. They'd methodically progressed through the store, following the footprints: couch, chairs, coffee table, dining table, bed, dresser, desk...

Abuela was energized.

"I've been wanting to do this for years," she confessed. "Indulge me. You can pay me back in a few years when you are a rich teacher."

They took a break for lunch in the store restaurant, eating Swedish meatballs and noodles. But just when Mike thought, *Well, that wasn't so awful. Now we can go home,* Abuela said, "Now we go downstairs."

"What's downstairs?" he asked. "It's not as big as upstairs, is it?

David laughed. "You really have no clue, do you, Dad?"

Actually, David had been making a lot of the choices. When Mike had waffled, David had been decisive: "Go with the yellow chair. It's a happy color."

When they got to the lower level, David bluntly asked his father, "Do you give a shit? Like what color dishes?"

Mike rolled his eyes and shook his head.

"Okay, then, because we'll get out of here a lot faster if you let me and Abuela choose," David continued. "You already look frazzled."

In 90 minutes, they had sheets, a comforter, towels, silverware, a set of sea-glass green dishes, serving bowls, pots and pans, baking sheet, muffin tin. David pointed out a large print for the living room that would go well with the couch. Abuela was delighted with a mirror for over the dresser. A bathmat and shower curtain. A rug that looked like waves.

When they got to lamps, David grabbed four of the same ones. "Two for your bedside tables, one for me and one for the living room," he explained. Then he grabbed a standing lamp on their way out of the section. "Too cheap to pass up."

They filled three big carts. Meanwhile, Abuelo had gone ahead with his hefty list from the top floor to get help with the furniture.

"How do we get this all home?" Mike asked, as they stood in line with three overflowing shopping carts.

"Everything in the carts we fit in the car now. The furniture they'll hold until tomorrow. Delivery will take too long. I just reserved a U-Haul for four hours in the morning," Abuelo answered. "David and I will run back."

Mike would later contend that they could not have completed the makeover without the help of Abuelo's bocce friends. Victor and Marcello showed up the next day at noon for Abuela's Salvadoran enchiladas and pupusas, and to help assemble the furniture.

Victor studied the instructions as they unpacked. By the time they'd hauled the boxes to the curb, he was barking out precise directions, step-by-step, so that assembly flowed. Meanwhile, Marcello and Abuelo sat on the floor and manipulated the tiny wrenches with experienced precision.

Mike and David just did whatever they were told to do. Hauled in boxes from the garage. Hauled out the old furniture to the driveway as it was replaced. Held parts in place for Marcello. Cleaned up as they went along.

Mike put up a sign up for the furniture at the curb. "Free—or leave a donation for food bank in the cookie jar." The old dining table was covered with dishes and kitchenware.

"Who's gonna' want this stuff?" Mike asked.

David shrugged. "You did. That's how it got here."

"You can be a smart ass," Mike retorted. "You know that, right?"

As they came back into the house, they could hear Abuela humming, happily, as she cooked their supper with the new pots and pans.

When Mike was profusely thanking the Bocce Boys—as they called themselves—and offering them payment, which they declined, he asked how they'd gotten so skillful.

"I was an engineer," Victor replied. "Designed machines for large scale production. IBM mostly. Lots of parts."

"I was a surgeon," Marcello chimed in. "Shoulders, knees, hips. Needed fine motor skills and hand-eye coordination. Now they use those damn robots half the time."

When Mike woke up the next morning, he was disoriented. The room was unfamiliar. He'd slept deeply on the comfortable new mattress that rested on a low metal frame that did not creak every time he turned in his sleep. There were square tables, with shelves, and lamps on each side of the bed. His "office" fit a corner of the bedroom: a white stand-or-sit desk, tall bookcase, and a small rolling cart for files that fit under the desk. There were two dressers: a narrow one for him was against the desk wall, and a longer, waist high one, for Molly, on the opposite wall. A mirror hung over it.

Mike's bathroom—*their* bathroom—now had a new shower curtain and bathmat. Two cabinet drawers, with drawer organizers, were empty, ready for Molly. A white cube was between the sink and the shower, neatly folded towels filling two of the cubbies and baskets the other two.

Max's room had Mike's old desk and lamp. Three cubes lined a wall, where Abuela said he could put his clothing, and books, and toys—all where he could see them. The bed had a new royal blue comforter. Blackout curtains hung in the window. Mike remembered Molly saying Max needed it dark-dark to sleep.

When Mike walked into the living room, he stopped. Abruptly. The space looked so much bigger. The new couch was teal, comfortable but not overstuffed. More streamlined. The area rug with waves was in front of it on the hardwood floor, with a two-tiered coffee table, magazines on the bottom shelf. There were two bright yellow armchairs across from the couch, a small table and lamp between them.

He thought of the living room of yesterday: an overstuffed, ripped in parts brown tweed couch, a coffee table he'd found by the side of the road, a red-checked tall-backed chair he'd scored at a garage sale, a recliner that didn't recline any more but had been covered with an old blanket and become Moses' chair.

Oh, shit. Moses, Mike thought. But then he saw, in a corner behind a potted plant, a large, plush doggie bed, with Moses snoring contentedly.

David had been on top of it, he realized. David had the "planning" gene. He and Abuela both.

In the kitchen, he slowly opened the cabinets. He felt as if he was checking out a new Airbnb to get acclimated. There were matching plates, bowls, small plates, mugs. Two different sizes of glasses. Wine glasses. Silverware in a divider in a top drawer. Cooking utensils in a brightly colored vase and knives in a block were on the kitchen counter.

Mike could not recall a single thing that was missing. But there was a lot more space. And a lot less clutter.

"I'm throwing out all the old food and spices," Abuela had called out to him while they'd been busy assembling the furniture yesterday. "Just cleaning up the closets. Stuff that has to be pitched. Okay?" She'd recruited David to help her organize the kitchen.

"Great, Ma," he'd called back.

It all felt so—welcoming? He imagined Molly's face when she walked in the front door. Her eyes would light up with surprise. With delight.

Abuela was, as usual, spot on.

HISTORICAL CONTEXT: JUNE 2021

Jun. 3: New U.S. COVID-19 cases have dropped to the lowest level since March 2020.

Jun. 7: UN International Labor Director said the global impact of the pandemic four times worse than 2008 Economic Crisis, pushed 100 million workers into poverty.

Jun. 15: U.S. COVID-19 related deaths surpass 600,000.

Jun. 17: US President Joe Biden signs into law the Juneteenth National Independence Day Act making June 19th a federal holiday commemorating the emancipation of enslaved people in the United States.

Jun. 25: Almost all COVID-19 deaths recorded in the United States are among those who are not vaccinated, according to the Associated Press.

Jun. 25: Judge Cahill sentences Officer Derek Chauvin to 22 and a half years in prison.

Jun. 26: The first cruise ship to board passengers at a U.S. port in 15 months sets to sail from Miami. Celebrity Cruises say at least 95% of those boarding the ship have been vaccinated and the ship will run at reduced capacity.

Jun. 30: Data indicates Medicaid enrollees are getting vaccinated for COVID-19 at lower rates than the general population. Polls also indicate higher levels of vaccine hesitancy among lower-income individuals.

Jun. 30: The Delta variant, first identified in India in late 2020, has become the predominant virus strain, accounting for 51% of all cases. Delta is believed to be more than twice as contagious as previous variants.

Jun. 30: Over 140,000 children in the U.S. have been orphaned due to COVID. This number will grow to over 200,000 by summer 2022. Worldwide, over 10.4 million children will be orphaned by May 2022.

July 2021

Max & Molly & Grace & Katrina

Max was excited. Today was the 4th of July.

This year Kaw Valley was having fireworks again. And his 'pod' was having a family barbeque. Mickey was grilling burgers and hot dogs. His grammy was baking brownies, and his mother was making coleslaw and baked beans with onions and peppers. Katrina was coming.

Their car was packed up for the drive to Florida and they were leaving early the next morning. "Before the sun comes up," his mom told him. "You can stay in your pajamas until we stop for breakfast if you want."

His mom was really in a hurry.

All that was left to put in the car was a bag of bathroom stuff, his backpack of favorite electronics and books, and one carry-on suitcase with extra clothes, pajamas, and swimsuits for the drive down for when they stopped at a hotel.

"Yes, Max," she'd told him. "The hotel will have a pool. I promise."

Max was trying hard not to get *too* wound up, because then just one thing that was not what he expected could throw him. But he felt like he could handle things better than he used to.

One Saturday, in May, Mickey had taken Max to his garage and pulled out two lawn chairs. They sat down and Mickey took down his toolbox. He'd explained what was inside, and what each tool was good for. There was a hammer, five different sizes of screwdrivers, wrenches, pliers, a plastic box of nails, another one of screws and bolts.

Mickey told him how anything that broke needed the right tool to be able to be fixed. So, a man needed a toolbox with different tools. And he needed to know what tool worked best for which repair. And it was no help at all to have all the tools but not know what they were good for or how to use them.

Mickey said it was the same thing for people. That Max had an imaginary toolbox in his head filled with different tools for different problems in his life. One tool was to listen closely to understand the problem. One tool was to hug. Another tool was to make a list of what was good or hard about the problem. There was a tool of asking questions, like to unscrew what was locked up inside someone else. Reading a book could be a tool. Or writing about the problem.

"The objective," Mickey had said, "is to not get overwhelmed by the problem. You have to believe that there's a solution, and that you'll figure it out. If you see the problem as impossible, no tool is going to work."

"Hammers are not good tools for people problems," he'd added. "Hammers make things worse."

It was just an idea, but it made sense to Max. And he liked that Mickey used words like "objective" when he talked to him. Max had found that, when he did remember he had a toolbox with a lot of tools, he was better at fixing his problems instead of having a meltdown about them.

"It will take a while to figure out all of your tools, but you're on the right track," Mickey had told him. "You're the only one who can say what tools work best for which problems for *you*. A hell of a lot of grownups don't even know they have a toolbox or what's in it."

At 8 p.m., they were lying on a king size comforter, with pillows, at a favorite spot by the river. The fireworks would not start for a while, but a band was playing music and a lot of families had come. It wasn't as crowded as Max remembered, but that had been a long time ago.

"It's just two years," his mom told him that morning when she was chopping up the cabbage for the coleslaw. "2019. Now it's 2021."

The numbers were right, but it didn't feel that way. It felt like a lot *more* time, but also like *nothing* had happened to fill the in-between time. It was *hard to remember* time.

It was *nothing* time.

The barbeque had been fun. Mickey let him flip the hamburgers and roll the hot dogs on the grill. Grammy baked his favorite brownies, with walnuts and caramel pieces. His mom set the table with big, divided plastic plates so the beans didn't touch the coleslaw.

What Max did not understand was why they kept toasting.

"To surviving 2020!" his mom started, and they clinked their glasses of lemonade.

"To vaccines!" Mickey chimed in. "To all the people who developed the vaccines!"

"To Dr. Fauci!" Kat added.

"To being together on a beautiful day," his grammy concluded. "To many more just like it."

Then Grammy and Kat and Mickey told stories of 4th of July barbeques they remembered from when they were kids themselves. His mom told some of when she was a kid. Grammy told one about his grandpa, who he'd never met. Katrina told about when her husband was teaching their sons how to flip the burgers but somehow overreached and flipped the whole grill over. She'd washed off the burgers and then tossed them in the oven to broil for a few minutes.

"Tasted fine," Kat finished. "I got most of the grass off."

Even after they finished the brownies and ice cream, nobody wanted to get up.

When the first firework was shot, Mickey pointed to a pair of earmuffs in a bag. "In case the noise gets to be a bit much," he whispered to Max.

But the noise was not too much. Molly was lying between Katrina and Grammy, and they were all holding hands. He was between his grammy and Mickey, and they were each holding one of his hands.

It was BAM! POP! BAM! POP-POP-POP-POP-POP. BOOM. BAM. POP-POP-POP-POP-POP. BOOM. BOOM. Like that. And all different colors.

They'd agreed to not have a 5 a.m. pre-dawn send off. Molly just wanted to get in the car and go. She didn't know if she could take her mom crying. Or maybe it was more her own crying. And then Max getting upset because everyone was crying.

Grace and Molly had said good-bye the night before.

"Be safe," Grace had whispered into her ear. "Don't rush. It's going to be a wonderful journey."

Molly didn't think she'd been talking about the drive.

But Mickey was sitting on her front steps in his pajamas when she opened the front door to carry the overnight bags to the car.

"I won't cry, okay?" he said. "Just making sure you have what you need for the road."

Mickey gently carried Max, in his PJs, from his bed to the car. He was a skinny kid for his age, and definitely too old to be carried. But Max wrapped his arms around Mickey's neck, his legs up around Mickey's waist, and clung. Max was almost awake, but he pretended he was still asleep, his eyes shut tight. When Mickey lay him down in the back seat, he snuggled under the comforter his mom had laid out.

If he opened his eyes, he would have to face saying goodbye, and he didn't want to. It would hurt too much. It already hurt.

"He'll sleep for another two hours," Mickey whispered to Molly. "You have maps? Phone? Car charger? Snacks? Water? Coffee?"

Molly looked at this somewhat disheveled man who'd shown up in her life out of nowhere, who loved both her mother and her son, and who she now loved. How could she leave him? Leave her mom?

"Your mom will come visit after you guys have time to settle in," Mickey said as if reading her mind. "No second-guessing? Okay? It's going to be okay. For everyone. I promise."

Molly slid into the front seat of her Kia, took a last look at her home, turned the key, and backed out of the driveway. Mickey stood in the driveway and watched until her car turned the corner and was out of sight, tears now filling his eyes.

Grace & Mickey

Grace awoke when Mickey slid out of bed and tiptoed out of the bedroom. But she did not immediately get up and follow. Molly had said goodbye last night and had been clear that she did not want a tearful farewell.

"We're just going to Florida for the summer, okay?" she'd insisted. "No big deal."

Grace wanted to respect Molly's request. Too many times, she'd made choices where she'd imposed what she thought was the better choice over what Molly had said, however quietly, that she wanted.

It was hard not to do that now.

Grace lay in bed and imagined her daughter, who had inherited her mother's skills of list-making and car-packing, driving off. She imagined a final hug, fiercely tight, and saying "I love you," her words a dam to the tears that could follow. She imagined Molly, saying goodbye, but also seeing in her eyes an eagerness to go, to be off, to drive into her future.

When Grace woke up two hours later, she was disoriented. What had she been dreaming? Something about driving, but being lost, without maps?

Gee, she thought, turning over in bed and trying to will herself back to sleep*, doesn't take a professional to connect-the-dots on that dream.* But she couldn't get back to sleep. Her brain had been triggered, and, once that happened, she might as well get moving.

Mickey was in the kitchen. She could smell brewed coffee. And something else?

"Is there something in the oven?" she asked.

"Got a caramel pecan coffee cake at Muncher's," Mickey replied. "Just warming it up."

Grace made a face. Chastising but also grateful? It was a mixed message.

"Yeah, I know. We overdid it yesterday," Mickey said. "And we need to cut back and eat more sensibly. But this is a morning when I thought coffee cake might be comforting."

As far as Grace was concerned, caramel pecan coffee cake was an essential coping tool. They could start the sensible stuff tomorrow. The face had been her conscience acting out.

"Let me brush my teeth and get a robe," she told Mickey.

Grace sat with her coffee, lifting her face to the morning sun. In a few hours, it would be a scorcher. This was the best time to enjoy it.

"Did you see Molly and Max off?" she asked, already knowing the answer.

"Yeah, I just wanted to make sure she had everything she needed."

"Did you give her 'emergency cash' for the road?" Grace asked. Mickey was old-fashioned that way.

"No, I did not give it to her," Mickey answered, somewhat

defensively. "I put it in an envelope in the glove compartment. I'll text her later and tell her it's there."

"Was Max sad?"

"The kid didn't fully wake up. I carried him out to the car."

"You carried him?" Grace was almost laughing. "How is your back after that?"

"It's fine. Last time I'll ever carry the kid."

"Oh, Mickey," Grace said softly. "I think this is harder on you than on me."

Later than morning, Grace walked the steps between her casita and Molly's bungalow. She slipped her key into the back door lock and wiggled it to the left to open.

The house was clean. Molly had seen to that. It was hard to tell anything was missing because most of what Molly had packed were clothes for the summer and Max's books, toys, and electronics. Everything else would remain as it was until she decided if they were moving to Florida or staying in Kansas.

Molly had made a point of saying it like that, as if both options were equally possible. But Grace thought that was more for her benefit, to ease Grammy into the new reality. She did not see Molly returning other than to pack up the house and move.

They hadn't decided yet what to do with the bungalow. To sell it meant that Grace would have to move out of her casita. Grace liked her casita. She didn't want the larger—although a bungalow was hardly large—home. Grace thought it made sense to hang onto it for at least a year to make sure Molly was not coming back. Maybe keep it as a rental? Would Mickey want to take it over for a year or two?

No matter for now. They weren't making any decisions for at least two to three months.

Grace walked through the house, taking a few minutes to really see each room. She remembered what it had been like when they bought it when Max was two. Every room needed fresh paint, and the bathroom needed tile, but Molly had vision.

Molly had fallen in love within minutes. "It has such good bones," she'd said to Grace, as if she could see through the very walls. "Look at the wood! All hardwood floors! Built in bookcases! Look at the yard!"

Every sentence had been an exclamation.

And it was a very good home. Molly had painted every room within three weeks. After apartments with a kid prone to meltdowns, a home where she did not have to worry about annoying her neighbors was a relief.

Grace was sitting in the living room, looking out the front window at the bird bath, the island where perennials had replaced the spring bulbs, when she heard Mickey coming in the back door.

"Yoo-hoo" he called out. "Are you here?"

"How are you doing?" he asked, plunking down next to her on the couch. "What are you thinking about?"

"About when I first showed Molly this house," Grace answered. "She was so happy. And I wanted her to be happy so that I could stay in Homer."

"Well, you got another five years, right?"

"Yes, I did. And I haven't regretted moving back. I needed to be here for her."

"But that may be changing?"

"I think so. She's directing the next act of the family play."

"Is this Act Two or Three?"

"Two for her, Three for me."

"And what does your Act Three look like?" Mickey asked, his voice a little more serious.

"I don't know. The curtain hasn't gone up yet."

"Maybe we need a longer intermission?"

Grace looked at Mickey and smiled. He was really working the metaphor.

"What do you mean with 'Maybe we need a longer intermission?'"

"I realized when Molly drove off this morning that we haven't had a break since before COVID. And, as of this morning, we have no responsibilities here. There's a chance that Molly and Max could return in a couple of months, so..."

"Cut to the chase, Mickey," Grace said.

"Where would you like to go, Gracie? I want to go away with you, to have a little adventure. If this an intermission, where do you want to be?"

Grace considered, weighing options. They'd cancelled their trip to

Panama fifteen months ago. But Panama still had very strict quarantine protocols and restricted entry.

"What do *you* want, Mickey?" Grace asked, turning to him, moving her fingers across his face, palm briefly resting against cheek. "What do you want for your 'little adventure?'"

"*Alaska,*" he replied. "I want you to show me Alaska."

Grace sharply inhaled at the word Alaska. She felt an almost imperceptible tremor deep in her gut.

"Alaska?" she asked. "Why Alaska?"

"You lived there for years but I've never been," Mickey answered. "I can't visualize where you were. I've always wanted to go. And it's the last frontier."

"So, we'd just..."

"Pack a bag, go to the airport, fly to Anchorage. Pick up a rental car," Mickey replied. "It's not complicated."

"But what about planning? Like lodging and..."

"Planning is overrated. Lots of Airbnb availability. Not many people taking trips yet."

"You've researched this?" Grace quizzed him.

"Just in case. Once Molly said she would be gone for the summer."

"A-la-ska," Grace repeated, dwelling on each syllable.

"You know you want to go. I can see it in your eyes." Mickey was now grinning.

I'm gonna' go to Alaska, he thought. *We're going to have an adventure.* It had been a long time since he'd felt this loose, life so full of possibilities.

"I'll go check flights," he said, abruptly standing up.

He was almost out the back door when he heard her call out. "Mickey, wait. Come back for a minute."

His heart plummeted. He did not want caution, reason, weighing pros and cons.

"What?" he asked from the doorway to the living room.

"I've been keeping a secret," she said. "And I want you to know before we..."

"What secret?" Mickey asked. His mind was racing to dark places, dark words, like cancer. Harsh, terminal, life-shattering words.

"It has to do with a client, one I've discussed with you."

"Sweet Jesus, Gracie, don't do that again. Client stuff is not worth a heart attack."

"Five minutes, okay? I don't want you blindsided in case this ever comes back to bite me."

"For this I need to sit down," he said, returning to the couch. "So, what's this secret about?"

It took Grace five minutes to sum up Theo, his ethical rant, her dream, her conundrum. Then talking with Theo. She described her "moment of truth" in the mirror.

"I wasn't worried about the patients. I was more worried about covering my ass, to not be culpable," she continued. "I made my decision. I don't need your approval. But I wanted you to know."

"Can you tell me some more about your thought process?" Mickey was probing now, gently, as he would with a suspect—or witness—who he wanted to disclose what they might not even know was relevant.

"The ethical codes are useless. They don't cover what's been happening on the medical front lines. And I freaked out remembering how, after Hurricane Katrina, medical staff were indicted for murder, for holding their terminal patients and giving them morphine—ending their suffering—after five days of horrific conditions in 110-degree heat, no electricity, no water, no treatment, no rescue."

"Anything else?"

"Theo's hospital has a hospice unit. I think it's 4th floor, 4 East. It's for people who are dying but need more care than home hospice can provide, more scrupulous pain management. Or patients who don't have a home hospice option." Grace's voice was calm and thoughtful. "COVID patients don't get a hospice option, because families want to try every last-ditch intervention, 'just in case.' But also, because they're highly contagious. Yet many COVID patients are terminal, not *if* they will die but *how soon*. In hospice, they'd be given comfort drugs so they're not gasping for air."

"But Theo doesn't work on the hospice unit," Mickey's voice was matter of fact.

"Correct. But can ethical medical treatment on 4 East be a crime on 3 West?"

They were each quiet, for a moment, as if waiting for a cue.

"When did all this happen?" Mickey asked. "The dream and such?"

"The dream was back in April, the session with him in May."

"Oh," he said. "And you didn't feel you could tell me?"

"Yeah," Grace replied. "And there's more."

Mickey's face squinched up, as if he'd sucked on a lemon.

"Go ahead," he said.

"Remember how when I started the grief group, you asked if I'd shared that Gil was murdered? And I said I hadn't and gave some excuse why but said I'd tell them soon? And you said something like 'Don't let it be a secret'?"

"I vaguely recall that, yes," Mickey answered.

"Well, I never told them. Then, in our last session, one of the members, a man, said he'd been on the jury. He'd never told anyone else in the group. And then another group member said that she'd known too. She'd remembered the case."

"Small town," Mickey said. "Happens all the time."

Grace glared at him. "Seriously? Sarcasm?"

"Just a feeble attempt to lighten this up. Please continue."

Grace closed her eyes and paused. The tremor in her gut that began when Mickey said the word "Alaska" had not abated. She felt that she might throw up.

"I never told them about Gil because I was ashamed. I've always thought that leaving Kaw Valley was running from grief. Or trauma. But I was running away from shame. I didn't leave my kids because of grief. We could have grieved together. But the shame paralyzed me. I hadn't seen what might have saved my husband's life. I found out from a cop that Gil had had an affair—me, the marriage counselor, was totally in the dark. Which nobody believed, jury included. My friends, my colleagues, my own son. Everybody believed that I was capable of murdering my husband."

"Katrina didn't think that," Mickey said. "Molly never did, not for a moment. And I didn't."

"I barely knew you," Grace said. "We'd met once under strained circumstances. You don't count."

"Okay. Sorry. Go on."

"When I drove off, I was trying to get as far away as humanly possible from the shame. I told no one in Homer about what had happened. I didn't believe that I could ever be a therapist again. How could anyone trust my judgment? How could I ever trust my judgment? I'm the damn therapist who gave my clients Brené Brown's books on shame, on imperfection. And I never connected-the-dots for myself?"

"But now you have?"

"Yes. And so when you said *Alaska?* I've had two lives, and they've never overlapped. My Alaska life was a different woman. I was broken. No one there knew about my past. No one from here ever visited me there. I used my one-bedroom cabin as an excuse. And after returning here? I've never gone back. My life has so many secrets I can't even keep track anymore."

Mickey was silent. Grace felt a stabbing fear that this would be too much.

"What are you thinking?" she asked,

Mickey reached over and took both of her hands in his.

"You're a complicated woman, Gracie McDonald," he replied, lowering his face until their eyes could meet. "Your life has been messy. But so has mine. You're not the only one with secrets."

And with that, his acceptance, Grace felt her body lighten. She could see a bridge, not an abyss.

"What do *you* want to do?" she asked. "What can *I* do?"

"Start packing. You're good at that. I'll go find us some flights." Mickey's voice was matter of fact, but his heart was racing again. *Please do not go all rational and adult on me,* he thought. *Please...*

For a second time he stood up to go, but then turned in the kitchen doorway, waiting for a sign.

Grace still sat, hands now in her lap, looking out the window. Two cardinals were sitting on the edge of the birdbath. They began to splash themselves, lifting their wings, dipping their tiny beaks. Then they started to preen each other's heads, a delicate ballet of affection.

"I need twenty minutes with you at the kitchen table to help with the lists," Grace said, looking up at him. "It's a lot cooler in Alaska than Kansas. It's wetter too. And we'll need hiking boots."

"We can buy boots in Anchorage. I hear they have stores."

"Did I ever tell you about Ulmer's Drug and Hardware store in Homer?" Grace asked, rising from the couch, taking five measured steps to face him. "Hardware, paint, hunting, auto repair. Entire aisles for fishing lures. The pharmacy is tucked in the back beside the greeting cards."

"We'll go to Ulmer's, Gracie. They carry boots, I assume?"

"You can get just about anything in Ulmer's," Grace replied. "Did I ever mention that I worked the checkout there for a year?"

"No, you did not," Mickey replied.

"It was part-time. I was also waitressing at Two Sisters' Bakery."

"You are full of both secrets and surprises. What else do I need to know?"

"That's it for now, but I'm sure more will spill out when we're there."

Grace took one more step to stand in front of him. Their bodies were twelve inches apart. Their eyes locked.

Commitment time.

"So, Gracie McDonald, we're doing this? No backing out?" Mickey wanted definitive, irrefutable agreement.

"Yes, Mickey Donahue, we are so doing this," she said, her eyes taking in his weathered face. "Intermission could end soon. Let's get a move on."

Epilogue
Fall 2021

Covid Grief Group

On September 17th, Bill saw an article about the artist who'd done the massive flag exhibit in Washington, D.C., in fall of 2020. Grace had shared photos and an article with the group. Suzanne Brennan Firstenberg was her name.

Now the flags were returning. *In America: Remember* would be on Washington's National Mall from September 17th until October 3rd.

In fall of 2020, there had been 267,000 flags, a number that then had seemed horrific. Unfathomable. In 2021, the installation would begin with 675,000, with more flags to be planted as the death count rose.

Bill sat for an hour staring out the window in his living room. He was tired of talking, tired of feeling locked down. He looked again at a picture he'd printed out from the article, of last year's flags, and tried to imagine twice that number on the National Mall.

"We can do this," he muttered. "We're vaccinated, we can stay together. Let's make this happen."

"Deb," he called out. "Come here, please. I want to show you something."

Two hours later, Bill emailed the other members of the grief group.

Hey all:

Do you remember that exhibit, the one with all the flags in Washington D.C. that Grace showed us last year? It's back, on the National Mall. It closes October 3rd. We need to go, to write a flag for Dean, Mariana, Jasmine, Jolene, Ruthie, Robert, and Shawnee's family. We didn't get funerals. We didn't get hugs or pies. We deserve to go, to stand in the middle, to scream if we need to. We deserve flags.

I've already looked at options, and round-trip flights are cheap. I booked a 10 bed, 6 BR, 4 BA Airbnb. Debra and I are covering the flights and lodging (no arguments, you'll be doing us a mercy as we can't face going alone). And Dean had life insurance.

Looking at a long weekend, fly out on September 30th, come back October 3rd? Can you make that work?

And most of them could.

Luis had moved to Merida in late July. He'd driven from Kansas to the border at Brownsville and crossed into Matamoros. It was a lot easier to cross the border into Mexico than the reverse. He took his time driving down the coast, swimming in the ocean almost every day. He'd found an apartment in Merida. It was about 45 minutes to the beach. "Please make a flag for Mariana and take pictures of it. 'Amada esposa y madre, preciosa para mi. Sonrieme hasta que pueda ir a ti,'" he wrote to Bill.

Shawnee had moved back to Georgia, but she emailed that she hoped to join them on Saturday.

Bill called Grace and left messages, wanting to ask her separately if she wanted to join them, but she didn't reply. She'd dropped off everyone's radar.

So it came to pass, 12 days later, that the grief group—random people who would never have known each other except they'd lost so very much, with little in common, really, except that loss, but who now felt like family to each other—boarded a non-stop flight, MCI to DCA.

They'd shown up for each other. That was all. They had simply shown up. And they were showing up now.

"Haven't you flown before?" Beth questioned Kayla, after overhearing her ask a flight attendant if her purse had to go in the overhead bin. "How is that possible?"

"Because my mom and I are what other people so politely call 'low-income,'" Kayla retorted, half-pissed but relieved that that she could stop pretending that this was not a weird experience to be having for the first time in her twenties. "I had no dad, and my mom worked two jobs that didn't pay shit. We shopped garage sales and made two runs a month to the food bank. So, no line item in the budget for airfare. Okay?"

"Oh, sweetie, I'm sorry," Beth said. "I wasn't thinking. That was rude of me."

"Oh shit, Beth, it's fine. I get anxious when I don't know exactly what's coming and this trip is a lot of firsts for me. I'm watching everybody to see what they do so I don't screw up."

"Well, seatmate, I will talk you through it so no surprises. Very softly, if you don't want the others to know."

"No need," Kayla said. "Hard to keep secrets with this group."

"Hey, all," Kayla announced, loudly, turning to face the crowded aisle. "I may have forgotten to mention that I've never flown before *and* I have an un-godly fear of heights. Never even made it off a diving board."

The response was enthusiastic clapping, and some whistles, a "you go, girl" from the far rear of the plane. The cheering came mostly from the group, but some strangers celebrated with her too.

"That's a sendoff to remember," Beth said.

By 9 p.m. that evening, they were settled in the Airbnb. They would go to the National Mall in the morning.

The next morning, before dawn, Kayla dressed silently in a bathroom. She slipped out the front door, leaving a note that she was going to the National Mall and would meet up with them later. She had her cell with her so they could call and coordinate.

She followed a route that she'd marked on a map, walking briskly, trying to look like she knew exactly where she was going to compensate for feeling anxious.

When she got to the National Mall, the sky had lightened. There were flags, small and white, moving in the wind. Hundreds of thousands of flags. An unfathomable number of flags, one for each person who'd been alive—breathing and eating, loving, working, before the pandemic—and was now dead.

Kayla sat on a white bench and closed her eyes. She conjured up her mother: her smile, touch, voice, laugh, stubbornness, and independence. *What would Jolene think of this?*

About 7 a.m., Kayla saw a figure walking down one of the paths that crossed the mall. A woman, tall and slender, with long, blondish hair, a blue wide brimmed hat on her head—was it a cowgirl hat? —and a soft blue blazer in the cool morning air. *She looks familiar,* Kayla thought. *But from where? I don't know anyone in D.C.*

The woman was carrying a basket. Was it a basket of flags? In that nano-second, Kayla knew where she'd seen her. In an interview. Some CNN or PBS thing.

She was Suzanne. Suzanne something or other, a long last name. The artist who had made all of this happen. This *one* woman had decided she had to do *something*. And, somehow, there were now about 700,000 flags planted on the National Mall.

Kayla was off the bench and walking before she'd consciously decided to move.

"Are you Suzanne?" Kayla asked, catching up to her.

"Yes," the woman said. "And you are?"

"Kayla. We came yesterday, from Kansas, our grief group. But they're still asleep back at the Airbnb and I wanted to come alone..."

"Who are you here for, Kayla?" Suzanne asked, gently.

"My mom. Jolene."

"You're young to have that big a loss," Suzanne said. "That's a lot of pain to carry."

"Yeah," Kayla said. "It was just the two of us. Always just the two of us."

"Oh, that makes it even harder. Can you tell me about her?"

Kayla had not expected the question. She deflected.

"What are you doing?"

"I like to be here early, to be here alone sometimes," Suzanne replied. "This morning I'm planting flags that were dedicated through our website. People who can't come to dedicate flags themselves submit messages and our volunteers create flags for them." Suzanne paused, then gestured to her basket. "Do you want to help? I'd like the company and you can tell me about Jolene."

"I don't want to intrude," Kayla blustered. "I mean, if you want to be alone."

"That was before I wanted to hear about Jolene," Suzanne answered. "C'mon, let's walk."

Suzanne asked questions about Jolene, and what they'd enjoyed doing together. Kayla found herself talking about photography and camping and how much her mother loved color and art. How the hardest thing for Jolene about living in rented places was not being able to paint all the walls different colors. How they'd cut pictures out of magazines and had a scrapbook for when they would finally buy a home. How Kayla had dreamed of making enough money to put together a down payment.

And then they planted flags. Suzanne handed Kayla a handful, and they alternated pushing the metal stems into the loamy grass and reading, out loud, what someone needed to say.

"Norm was the good guy," Suzanne read. "Good brother. Good friend. Nobody really noticed, but now we see how much he held us together."

"Gary: The best son any parents could want," Kayla chimed in, her voice strong. "We'll look out for Diane and the kids, but life will never be the same."

"Mommy, I miss you every night and every day. I hate coming home from school when you're not there. And I need help with math."

"Harry: Like those damn cranes, I mated for life. My sky is empty without you."

"Mr. Huang: You were the father I never had, the best possible father. I am going back to school to make you proud. I miss you so very, very much."

"Ian: You would so love your kids. They never met you, but I'll tell them all your stories."

"Life is flat without you, Vicki Victorious! The wrong sister died, but don't tell her I said that. Your big-big-big brother, Arnie."

With that one, Kayla paused.

"How do you do this?" she asked Suzanne. "I mean, *seriously,* how do you look at the flags, read all the inscriptions and epitaphs, and not get overwhelmed?

"You're doing the grieving, Kayla. I'm here to witness. And I'm hoping this makes people understand the incredible extent of this needless loss."

Kayla was understanding: while each flag was for *one* person, a dozen relationships, a hundred relationships, had also died with that person.

"When I couldn't stand it anymore, I made some big posters—DID YOU KILL MY MOTHER ?????—with her photo," Kayla blurted out. "I sat outside the convenience store where she used to work, and I held it up every time some guy passed with no mask or a mask hanging below his nose. But I don't think they understood."

"Really," Suzanne said. "And then what happened?"

"The police came and took me to the station but didn't have anything to charge me with. And it would probably be bad PR to charge an orphan for holding up a sign that just asked a question. Not like I was naming names or anything."

"Good point," Suzanne said.

"Did you ever dream that you would do something this *big*?" Kayla asked. "Did you ever see *this* in your future?" When she said *this*, Kayla flung her arms out, as wide as she could, as if one gesture could encompass 22 acres of flags.

"No, I never saw it coming," Suzanne said. "Until it was here."

The group arrived a few hours later. They'd seen the pictures, so, in theory, they knew what to expect. But no picture could capture it. Climbing out of the Ubers, they were stunned into silence.

In the wind, the flags were moving, sounding like marching. Or was it dancing? The noise was visceral, and they could almost feel their bodies vibrating in response.

"Oh, sweet Jesus," Beth whispered, tears flowing down her face. "We are so not alone."

Larry turned to Debra and Bill. "Thank you," he mouthed.

They'd agreed to meet up with Kayla under a giant red sign: "In America: How Could This Happen?" It had the death count from COVID, which changed every day. Today it would pass 700,000.

Next to it were white tents, reception stations, with a few tables in each, and volunteers to answer questions. One table was to sign in. The other table was to get a flag, and to *write* on *your* flag.

Beth and Kayla and Bill and Debra and Cheryl and Larry each took a flag. They sat down at the table and wrote, wrote their message of love, or a memory, even what might have been written on a tombstone.

Bill filled one out for Luis, putting down exactly what Luis had emailed him to write for Mariana.

Shawnee had texted two days prior that she'd been exposed to COVID and couldn't travel. And thirteen flags would be a bit much. But Debra filled one out for Shawnee anyway: "I didn't know it would hurt so much until you were all gone."

When they finished, they stood up and walked out, collectively, to plant their flags. As they gathered outside the tent, Beth stopped. "Hold on," she said. "I'll be right back."

Just then Kayla spotted a familiar hat by the next tent.

"Suzanne," she impulsively called out. "Come here. I have people for you to meet."

Suzanne looked up at the sound of her name, located the voice and smiled. The girl from this morning. "Two minutes?" she gestured with her fingers, her face lifting into a question. Kayla gave her a thumbs up in response.

Two minutes later, just as Beth reappeared clutching another flag, Suzanne walked over.

"I wasn't going to do one for him," Beth was explaining to the group. "I've been so angry. But it doesn't feel right now that I'm here. He was an asshole, but Mom never held grudges."

Kayla waved her arms to get their attention.

"I want you all to meet Suzanne Brennan Firstenberg," Kayla announced, dropping into a curtsey, as if introducing the queen. "She's the social justice artist that conceived this, designed it, and made it happen. *For us.*"

Beth's head swiveled to make eye contact with Kayla.

"When did you meet?" Beth mouthed, lifting her eyebrows in surprise.

"This morning," Kayla mouthed back, with a grin that was both delighted and smug. "We planted flags together."

"So, I've heard that you're all from Kansas," Suzanne said. "May I come with you to plant your flags?"

There was a moment as they looked at each other before nodding.

"That would be good," Bill answered. "Lead the way."

They walked for a bit and then Suzanne led them down a side aisle, to some open space at the end of a walkway.

"How is this?" she asked.

"It's perfect," Beth replied, speaking for the group, still trying to figure out how the artist she'd read about in a CSIS interview was hanging out with them.

"Can you share who you are, who you lost? Read what's written on your flag as you plant it?" Suzanne asked. "And anyone chime in with whatever they want to add."

It took fifteen minutes to plant them all. Each person read their flag, but then said more. They stood together, comforted each other, and witnessed.

"I have to get back," Suzanne said after they planted the final flag. "But it was an honor to meet all of you. There's a lot of love standing right here."

Then Bill, Debra, Larry, Cheryl, Beth, and Kayla separated, wanting time to process, individually, what they'd experienced. To walk through the flags.

They'd meet back at the Airbnb later.

"Pizza and salad coming at 6:00," Debra said. "But don't rush back. It will keep."

An hour or so later, Cheryl was sitting on a bench, along the sidewalk, her hands crossed in her lap, as Larry approached.

"Do you want to be alone?" he asked, hesitating.

"Not really. I'm having that guilt thing again where I feel I don't belong. Because I'm not hurting. Not like you."

"I'm going to walk back to our flags. I forgot to take a picture. Would you like to come?"

"They're taking the flags out in a few days," Larry said as they walked. "I wish they could leave them up. But it's made me think differently about getting a grave for Jasmine. Maybe some of her ashes, with a small marker. A place to go, maybe under a tree."

"That sounds nice, Larry. My parents have graves back in Oakley, and I stop to visit them whenever I drive through."

"Are you thinking of a grave for..."

"No," Cheryl said, not needing to hear the rest of his sentence. "I can't see visiting with Robert. He never really talked *with* me, more *at* me."

They made a few wrong turns before finding the right aisle.

They found their flags, the groups' flags. A small handful in the acres and acres of loss and grief.

"Well, I do like to visit. So how is this?" Larry turned to face his flag. "Jasmine, I'd like you to meet Cheryl. I met her at this grief group

I've been talking about, and she's a friend of mine now. I think you'd like her too. A little shy. More 'proper' than you are, but you'd loosen her up. A little rum punch. Some music. Tell a few of those stories from the islands."

"Anything you want to say to Jasmine?" Larry asked, not really expecting that she would. But she surprised him.

"I'm sorry I never got to meet you, Jasmine," Cheryl said. "You would have been a wonderful friend, and I haven't had those. But I will. It's not too late."

They stood for a few more minutes, then turned to start back, or to walk around the mall, in whatever direction they would happen to turn.

As they turned, Larry reached down and took Cheryl's hand in his. It was a big hand, Cheryl thought, not skimpy. Warm. Not tight, just a soft holding.

It was then that she realized that she'd never walked holding hands with Robert. He didn't like to be slowed down, and she'd always been trying to keep up with his long. hurried strides. "Can't you keep up?" he'd often barked over his shoulder at her.

"You're a good friend," she said to Larry, giving his hand just the slightest squeeze. "And you have a nice walk."

"This is a stroll," Larry replied, "and I'd like it to last. Unless you have somewhere you need to be?"

Grace & Theo

In mid-November, Grace found an email from Theo:

I wanted to let you know that I received your letter. I've realized that you were my only sounding board, but I held a lot back. It was a hard time. Anyway, I've been accepted into a graduate program in Bioethics at Creighton University, in Omaha. Start in January. We're moving up there. Josie has a new position, and I'll work a few shifts a week and try to finish the program in 18 months. We found a little rental house outside of the city with a few acres. Josie wants chickens, and a big garden, and we have a line on a pony for the kids. Life is fragile, and we're not going to postpone what brings joy. Oh, and Josie is pregnant. It's crazy to bring a baby into this crazy, fucked-up world, but we're happy about it.

Theo

Grace sat at the table, looking past her computer and out the window. *Theo made it out in one piece,* she thought. *He's going to be okay. They'll have chickens and grow tomatoes. I can stop worrying.*

Spring 2022

Grief Group

In the following year, the grief group continued to grieve. But it was then a second spring, second Thanksgiving, second Christmas. A second anniversary or birthday. A second death day.

"You need to move on," was a familiar refrain several heard from well-meaning friends and family.

They never, ever, said that to each other.

In early January of 2022, Beth invited Kayla over for supper. They ate barbeque beef that Beth had simmered in the crockpot all day, with coleslaw, beans, and biscuits.

"I haven't had a meal this good in ages," Kayla said, patting her belly. "You've got crockpot magic!"

"I have a question, Kayla," Beth asked after they finished the dishes and sat back down at the table with hot tea. "Are you back in school?"

"I was for fall semester but I'm working second shift, 3-11, at Pizza Perfect," Kayla said, putting down her tea. "It was too much with classes being in-person, then on-line, then 'hybrid,' and papers due but no time to write them. I dropped two classes, finished two others. But I got a B and a C," she explained. "It's frustrating because I was straight As in high school and my first year of community college."

"Are you staying in this semester?" Beth asked.

"I'm going to sit out, save up so that I can go back when I can just work part-time. It will just take a little longer. I'm not giving up or anything."

"Come with me," Beth said, standing up, and walking out of the kitchen.

Kayla followed, up a staircase, down a hall past a bathroom, wondering what Beth wanted to show her.

Beth opened a door.

The room was square: a big bay window looked over the back yard, a long desk in front of it, a double bed against a wall, a side table with a lamp, a large mirror over a dresser. A framed print of aspen trees, sunlight coming through the branches and a stream, hung over the bed.

"Would this work?" Beth asked.

"What do you mean?"

"I mean that I'd like you to live here, with me, for however long, so you don't have to work. Just focus on your classes and finish the damn degree."

Kayla looked stunned. "I can't do that," she said.

"Because I'm too much of a pain in the ass?" Beth asked. "The room not working for you?"

"No," Kayla protested. "It's super nice. It's lovely. But I can't just mooch off you for two years. I'm okay. You don't need to worry about me. I'm not a dog that needs to be rescued."

"This is NOT about rescuing some dog," Beth said. "I'm alone here. My daughter will be in Germany with the Army for two years having the time of her life. And then she will go somewhere else. I love her, and I want her to go live her life, not feel sorry for me. The room is empty. *Empty.* And I'm paying the same utilities if there is one person here or two."

"I couldn't," Kayla insisted. "It wouldn't be right."

"Listen to yourself, girl. 'Right' by whose crazy definition of 'right?' Would your mama say, 'No, Kayla, you stay in that tiny studio apartment you had to move to and waitress until your feet throb and take five extra years to finish college? 'Cause you gotta' go it alone and stand on your own two feet? Because *that's* what's *'right?'*"

Beth paused to take a breath.

"Or would your mom say, 'This is great, Kayla, you so deserve it. And you'd be doing that poor woman a favor because she obviously has no one to cook for and it's a big damn house to take care of all by herself. Must be lonely. It would be a blessing for her to have you to talk to, binge a show together, share a meal, help her in the garden in summer. I know because you were always a blessing for me."

Beth stepped back and put her hands on her hips.

"Which of those do you think your mama would want for you?"

Kayla had started silently crying, tears of relief, of disbelief. It had been so hard, so unbelievably hard. Nineteen months of struggling to be strong, to push herself. Nineteen months of worrying whether she could pay rent or electric if the car broke down. So much worrying. So alone.

"I miss her so much," Kayla said.

"Yeah, I miss my mama too. Maybe we can make them both happy by helping each other out. Will you at least give it try?"

So, Kayla moved in. Her apartment lease wasn't up until June, but Beth said something to the management company about mold issues and they let her leave early and even gave her back her deposit, which had never happened before. Beth didn't share what else she'd said but Kayla thought it might have included where she worked and who she would talk to if they were buttheads about it.

And that mold was not something they wanted documented in landlord-tenant mediation.

Kayla enrolled full time and took an extra art class just because she wanted to. She had time to study, for the first time ever, and time to read. Time to get caught up on the TV she'd missed. She decided to take summer classes before transferring to the university in Kaw Valley in the fall. She was back to getting all As.

Kayla was also getting to be a darn good cook. She'd found that she liked baking bread, rolling flour and yeast, pounding it, leaving it to rise in a bowl with a damp towel over the top. Beth loved coming home from a long day in Topeka, walking into her house, and inhaling whatever it was that Kayla was concocting.

One Sunday afternoon in late April of 2022, Bill and Debra came over for lunch. Kayla and Beth had used it as an excuse for a spring-clean, and Kayla made angel hair pasta with a light pesto sauce and shrimp.

They sat around, Beth and Kayla and Bill and Debra, and talked about the group, talked about how hard it felt, crazy even, for people to keep saying that it was time to "Get back to normal."

Like that was even a thing.

Bill and Debra were considering becoming part-time expats, living overseas for six months of the year. "We love spring and fall here, but it would be nice to go someplace warmer in winter and cooler in summer," Debra explained.

After lunch, Beth and Kayla walked them through the back yard to admire the raised garden beds they were building with scrounged lumber and then out to the driveway. It was hard to say goodbye, even with the assurances that they would do this again in a month. They'd been present for each other at the most horrible time, the worst time. It was a different kind of family, but that's what they had been for each other.

When they got to their car, Debra reached into the back seat and pulled out a small, wrapped box, handing it to Kayla.

"What?" Kayla asked.

"Just open it," Bill said.

Kayla pulled off the lemon-yellow tissue wrapping paper and opened the box. There was a key chain with her name on it, and two keys.

"We flew to New York City a few weeks ago and drove back Dean's car," Bill said. "It'd been sitting in a friend's side yard for almost two years. But it's running fine after a tune-up."

Kayla began to flush, her face feeling hot.

"What do you mean?"

"All the way driving back, we thought of how Dean loved giving more than getting. He was just that kind of boy, then that kind of man. And it would make him happy to see his car being enjoyed by a cute, smart girl. He'd just bought it a few months before COVID, never drove it in the city, but expected he'd need a car when he finished his residency."

"I can't take a car," Kayla said in a rush. "I could pay you, like payments, but it will take a long time…"

"You are taking the car," Debra said. "You need a car, obviously." With that Debra gestured at Kayla's 2005 Focus, which, literally, had duct tape on a fender, and an impressive assortment of dents and dings over what may have been paint at one time but was now more rust.

"It's that one," Bill said, pointing to the curb. "You like it?"

Bill was pointing at a Honda CRV, a hot red Honda CRV, parked in the shade of an elm at the curb. It looked brand new.

"You are very, very kind and very generous but…" Kayla blustered.

"No 'buts' young lady," Bill said in stern voice that Kayla could not recall ever hearing. "Your mom is watching out for our Dean, and we're going to watch out for you. That's what is happening. No. Back. Talk. No debate. *Understand?*"

"He had a stint as a drill sergeant," Debra said, out of nowhere. But Beth and Kayla understood immediately that she was referring to Bill's voice.

It was definitely a drill sergeant voice. No arguments with that voice.

"Yes, *sir*," Kayla said, giving Bill a lopsided salute, heels bumping together, her mouth spreading into an impossibly wide smile. "But you'll be getting fresh baked goods and supper delivered every Sunday you're not overseas. *Understand?*"

Fall 2022

Cherry & Zed

In October of 2022, when asked by a reporter from the *Kansas City Star* what had pulled them into QAnon, Cherry pondered over her response before she replied.

"Purpose," she said. "It felt like our lives had just been meaningless chores, just staying afloat. With QAnon, we were part of something bigger. We understood how the system and people in power were corrupt. That there were people pulling the strings who benefited from keeping us all in the dark. That the media was feeding us lies."

"And do you feel that same way now?"

Cherry paused, looking at the reporter. "We did what we thought was right. But we were betrayed."

"Who betrayed you?"

"The people who told us about the lies, told us what needed to be done, but then disappeared when we were accused...nobody spoke up for us, defended us. We just wanted to help the kids. We believed we were part of a righteous cause."

"Was it worth five years in prison?" he asked.

"If what we believed is true, then yes. We were acting out of principle."

"But if it wasn't true?"

"Then I ruined my life and lost years with my kids for nothing."

"Which is it?" the reporter prodded.

"I still don't know. Maybe I don't want to know," Cherry stated, her tone shutting down the question.

"What about your husband? Would he say it was worth it?"

A trace of smile, of memory, flitted across her face, but morphed into a grimace.

"Zed," she replied. "Zed had a good heart. He didn't plan to get killed."

"Your kids are with your parents, is that correct?"

"Yes, they are."

"Do you get to see them?"

"My parents bring them to visit once a month. At least they do when there are no virus outbreaks. But then they let us Zoom."

"What do your parents believe?"

"They think that Zed and I were crackers. I have to pretend that I agree, say that I now understand that we made a horrible mistake, that everything we believed was fake. That we were brainwashed. Like in a cult. That's what they need to hear to let me see my kids. So that's what I say."

"But is that what you believe?"

"Some days, yeah, maybe it was a cult. But other days I remember how it felt to seek the truth, to question, to choose what to believe."

"Do you regret what happened?"

Cherry felt a stab of anger at the very question.

"Of course, I regret it," she barked. "We were there for a training, to learn how to recognize signs of kids being trafficked. We were camping by a lake, out in in the woods, in Missouri. We'd never even met the guy they came looking for."

"So, you're saying you didn't know that the place 'out in the woods,' as you put it, was a para-military training base?" the reporter persisted.

Cherry remembered the two-mile gravel drive off of a rural road, looking at a print-out of a hand-written map. "Do you have any idea where the hell we are?" she'd asked Zed. But she'd been laughing, not pissed.

"Yes, that's exactly what I'm saying," Cherry answered. "Zed never owned a gun. He didn't even know how to use a gun."

"But someone in the group had a gun. And when the FBI showed up, they pulled it out. An agent was shot. And you were a part of that."

"We were there, but we weren't a part of anything except wanting to protect exploited kids. Zed was trying to put his hands up, not reach for something. It wasn't like they made it out to be."

"So, do you see his death as an accident? Or was it intentional?"

"I'll never know, will I?" Cherry was now staring at the wall across the interview room, a room that the prison had spruced up, not just for interviews but for "special" visitors. Three walls were painted a light blue, the fourth a navy accent wall. Two large prints of country road scenes, fabric mounted on thin wood—no glass—were on the walls. There were two chairs, where she and the reporter were sitting, and a low, padded sofa. Light wood. Matching coffee and end table. Casual but serene. It needed some throw pillows, a few candles, a few decorative touches, but the administration would never allow that.

Cherry missed being in rooms like this, in pleasant, welcoming spaces where the walls were not harsh and punishing. She wanted to tell the people who ran these institutions that women, especially, did better when they had some pretty things. When they felt respected. It wouldn't cost much.

"You said that, with QAnon, you and your husband felt part of something bigger," the reporter said, closing his notebook, reaching for his briefcase. "Was something missing that made it so...compelling?"

Cherry had pulled back in her chair, her eyes, heavy-lidded, looking at the floor. When she lifted them, her gaze was penetrating, but also bewildered.

"Maybe we'd lost touch," she replied. "Maybe that's all it took."

THE END

Acknowledgements

When We Lost Touch has been the most complicated novel I've ever attempted to write. I could not contain it, remember it, in one linear sequence. Each plot line was written in separate documents, as I ricocheted back and forth among them, and then, after two years, assembled them into this book. Even then, some spilled over, demanding an Epilogue.

While each of my other novels have had socially provocative themes, and required research, this book demanded much more. So, I am more grateful than ever for the support I've received.

With gratitude to:

Ashley Honey, personal assistant, for editing, cover design, social media, encouragement, focus, dragging me back from the edge, and insisting on Oxford commas.

Thea Rademacher, JD, of Flint Hills Publishing, for her editing, patience, and pragmatism.

Dan McCarthy, cover artist (*The Days We Are Living In*, www.danmccarthy.org). I saw the print in a shop window in Kansas and felt an immediate pull. I tracked him down in Boston. His art mirrors my words.

Pam Grout, *New York Times* best-selling author, for her pointed, provocative, author interview.

Jim Wheeler, of Wheeler Audio, for his expertise and patience in guiding me through my first author narration of an audiobook.

The diverse professionals who graciously answered my questions, providing insight, context or background: Suzanne Brennan Firstenberg, social justice artist extraordinaire; Nick Hilpman, Registered Respiratory Therapist; Rachel Thomas, for race conversation feedback, guidance, and critiques; Katherine Dee Kinard, Ph.D., epidemiologist; Ann Wallace, Ph.D., on long-hauler issues; Mary Lee Berner Harris, Ursuline Convent Archives and Museum, New Orleans; Rose Foster, M.S.W., grief counselor; Tulsa Race Massacre 100th Commemoration and Economic

Empowerment Conference speakers and organizers; U.S. Representative Lloyd Doggett, for a succinct timeline of Donald Trump's coronavirus responses; Walter "Ricky" Johnson, Craig Johnson, and Debra Johnson of Johnson Funeral Home, a third generation, Black-owned Houston institution, and Taylor Bridges for connecting us; Peggy Hilpman, for insight into grandparenting in a pandemic; Sherman Smith, editor of *Kansas Reflector*, for insight into Kansas pandemic responses; Joel Dominguez, for descriptions of the pandemic response in Panama; Wink Grace, multimedia artist and barista at Brews in Eureka Springs, Arkansas, who inspired the character of Kayla; and Mr. Anonymous, who continues to do what he is called upon to do, work that few of us could ever, ever face, who educated me about DMORT and more.

The creative, essential, and technical: Nathan Pettengill, my editor at Sunflower Publishing; Jen Sharp, web design; Michaela Harding, social media support. Readers who provided valuable feedback: Nathan Pettengill; Jeffrey Ann Goudie; Peggy Hilpman; PK McPherson; Michelle Berg, Donna Davenport; Anne Culp. And I have far too often taken for granted the editing skills of my daughter, Sarah Barthell, who finds errors not only in language but content and timelines. Her research skills are formidable.

I read dozens of books, articles, and columns while writing *When We Lost Touch*. I cannot acknowledge all of them. I can't even find all of them in the piles and files that have taken over my office. But I do wish to acknowledge the following writers, many for multiple books and articles, that I found instructive in assembling the diverse narratives of this novel: Isabel Wilkerson, Robin DiAngelo, Layla F. Saad, Ibram X. Kendi, Tarana Burke and Brené Brown, Jim Wallis, Ta-Nehisi Coates, Nikole Hannah-Jones, on racism; Lawrence Wright, Philip Rucker and Carol Leonnig, Michael Wolff, Bandy Lee, *The Washington Post* Fact Checker Staff, Bob Woodward, the *New Yok Times*, National Public Radio, on Donald Trump, COVID, political division, etc.; Hope Edelman, Alan D. Wolfelt, Elizabeth Kubler-Ross, Brook Noel, Joan Didion, Atul Gawande, on grief; Malcolm Gladwell, Ethan Kross, Brené Brown, on self-talk and understanding how we think, feel, and communicate. This is the point when I wish I'd kept better notes of what I was reading as I read it."

Bob Butler and Robert Lowe for their gracious hospitality and loan of their casita in Santa Fe to write, and Anne Culp for connecting us; Dairy Hollow Writers' Colony in Eureka Springs, Arkansas, and then director Michelle Hannon, for a nurturing space in COVID; Kate Brilakis for inviting me to the cozy studio over her garage and keeping me hydrated and well-fed as I burrowed into writing.

I am blessed to have a village: Peggy Hilpman; Michelle and Mel Berg; Jeffrey Ann Goudie and Tom Averill; Harriet and Steve Lerner; Margaret and Will Severson; Alice Lieberman and Tom McDonald; Marcia Cebulska and Tom Prasch; Anne and Rex Culp; Kelsey Kimberlin; Emily Kofron. My extended family: Kate, Mark, Tess, Zoe, Ross; Marjorie and Amy; Nancy, Danny, and the nieces—Alyson, Megan, and Lindsey—and John; and my Panamanian family, Antonio, Pamela, and Joel Dominguez.

My pod: my daughter Sarah, son Ben and his partner, Dean; and my husband Frank, both trusted reader and critic and COVID-binge-companion. We're still here!

About the Author

Susan Kraus is a therapist, mediator, and writer. Her novels tackle polarizing social issues, always raising more questions than answers as she makes the political personal. While her plot lines are both reality-based and riveting, it is her characters who engage readers' hearts.

Susan is the author of the Grace McDonald Series: *Fall From Grace, All God's Children,* and *Insufficient Evidence.* She is also a prolific travel writer.

www.susankraus.com

Book Group Discussion Questions

LITERARY

1) Kraus calls *When We Lost Touch* a genre-bending novel. What genre or genres do you think this book fits into?

2) There is a genre evolving called "socially conscious fiction." It is literature that prioritizes factual accuracy, addresses bias, and tackles polarizing or misunderstood social and political issues. Do you see *When We Lost Touch* as fitting that category? Did it cause you to reflect differently on any issue?

3) This novel is told in third person with shifting points of view. Does this work for you? Were there too many narrative voices?

4) The characters experience time in different ways, and Kraus utilizes "Historical Context" fact-notes at the end of each chapter to ground the novel in a particular moment in time. What has been your own experience of time during the pandemic? Were the "Historical Context" notes useful? Distracting? Do they help to explain a collective cognitive dissonance?

5) There are multiple endings in *When We Lost Touch*. Some bring closure while others leave the reader hanging. With the latter, did you rewrite the ending in your head? What kinds of endings did you construct?

6) There are multiple protagonists, each with their own story. But who are the antagonists? Are they different for each major character? Is the over-reaching antagonist the virus? Or more those positions of leadership and how they managed the pandemic?

7) Are there some characters who are stereotypes? What characters did you initially see as possibly stereotypes but for whom you developed empathy or attachment?

8) Setting is part of every story. This novel is mostly set in Kaw Valley, a university town in Kansas. Is this a novel about a particular place or a representative place? How do the experiences described mirror or differ from your own 'place' and setting?

9) How did flashbacks contribute to the different narratives? How did they influence your understanding of a character?

10) Were there any symbols used that made an impression? What about the bootie Theo found in the waiting room—that has a story all its own?

COVID & QUARANTINE

1). Grace returns from her cruise to find her country turned upside down by the COVID-19 pandemic. How did you react to the pandemic in the spring of 2020? What were the hardest changes in your life?

2) Mickey does research on "pods" and how to stay safe—home sanitization—early in the novel. Who was in your COVID pod? What measures did you take to protect your family from COVID?

3) Did you binge watch any shows or movies? Which ones and why?

4) How did your sense of time expand or constrict while at home during COVID?

5) Katrina cannot get tested for COVID despite her severe symptoms. Did you or anyone you know struggle to get tested early in the pandemic?

6) Did you or someone you know struggle with long-haul COVID? After reading this book, has your understanding of long-haul COVID changed?

7) Has the possibility of long-haul COVID caused you to feel more anxious?

8) Max is a boy on the autism spectrum, and his perception of COVID is framed differently. How did you react to Max? Was there anything in his responses that provided perspective?

9) Mickey builds a backyard sauna as his quarantine project. Did you take on a creative project during COVID?

10) The pandemic made painfully clear the great disparities in health care and socio-economic stability in our country. But this book is mostly about middle-class responses—and middle-class concerns. Can you recall some issues that were mentioned but not fully explored?

RELATIONSHIPS

1) Grace compares Molly and Mike's online relationship during COVID to her parents' relationship during World War II. Do you see similarities in this comparison, or is it a stretch?

2) Molly and Mike are both single parents who built their relationship online over Zoom and text rather than in-person. What do you think about how this relationship evolves? How does it compare to relationships in hookup culture? Do you think their relationship will last?

3) Amber, one of Grace's clients, is in an abusive relationship. Do you think leaving the state and taking the kids is fair to her husband? Do you

agree or disagree with Amber's decision and Grace's advice?

4) There are many mothers in this novel. What are some of the challenges they face as mothers during COVID? Is there a particular character or struggle that resonates with you?

5) Mickey and Max develop a special relationship during COVID. How is it different for Max as he has never had a father figure? For Mickey as he never had a biological child?

6) Grace and Katrina's friendship is challenged. How have your friendships been challenged by social or political issues?

7) Molly and Grace forged a deep bond. Do you see their understanding of each other as grounded and accurate? Are they missing things as well?

8) Mickey and Grace are a couple who never expected to be "coupled up" again in their lives. Have do you feel about their relationship?

9) Max and Jocelynn forge an unusual connection. What is it about Max that makes that possible?

10) Do you see the Katrina and Crystal relationship as realistic?

POLITICS

1) Grace's client, John, is concerned about his mother's growing distance from her children and grandchildren. He blames her husband and QAnon for this. Has your family been challenged by clashing political beliefs? How have you attempted to resolve these differences? What did you think about Grace's advice?

2) Many of the characters in *When We Lost Touch* discuss or debate different issues. Were there any issues mentioned that made you feel uncomfortable? Did you find yourself agreeing more with certain characters?

3) Zed and Cherry found connection and validation in QAnon. Did you experience empathy for them? Judgment toward them?

4) How did you respond to Betty's "revealed" assertions about Donald Trump "being Satan?" Is Betty someone you see as grounded? What do you think about Grace's advice?

4) How have your political views influenced your responses to COVID? Do politics have a role in medical science? In what ways?

Fiction has no requirement to be 'balanced' politically. Does historical fiction need to be balanced? Does history always reflect the race/culture/bias of whoever has power and writes the history?

HEALTH CARE AND ETHICS

1) Theo and his wife are frontline medical workers during the pandemic. Did this book give you a more intimate view into some of the challenges of frontline medical workers?

2) Theo struggles with the medical ethics of COVID treatment. What do you see as some of the main ethical struggles? How do you think they were or were not addressed in this novel?

3) Take the expression, "the ends justify the means," and apply it to different characters and choices in *When We Lost Touch*. Are people entitled to break rules under certain circumstances? Are ethics sometimes situational? Have you had times or experiences in your own life where the ends justified the means?

4) What end of life care do you want for yourself or your family members? What ethical principles do you believe should be applied to dying?

5) In the legal system, there are often cases that apply standards of contribution. Do you agree or disagree that standards of contribution could be used in the future to triage medical treatment? In other words, if people reject science and CDC guidelines, do they have the same entitlements as people who have done everything they can to avoid infection?

6) Imagine yourself on a jury in a case of a frontline medical worker charged with homicide or manslaughter who was faced with making decisions of which patient had the best chance to live. Do you have religious or ethical principles that would influence your judgement.

GRIEF, LOSS, & DEATH

1) Did you know about DMORT before you read this book? Were there other "surprises" in the novel as far as your understanding of our national response to COVID?

2) There is an entire chapter devoted to Jocelynn and what a "good death" looks like. It illustrates the profound differences between a "good death" and a "COVID death." How do you think that grief has been compounded by being unable to give people they love a "good death?"

3) What are *your* thoughts and feelings as you compare the two?

4) Did you lose someone, family or friend, to COVID? How did the experiences and responses of the COVID grief group members resonate

with your loss? If you have not lost anyone to COVID, what surprised you about their reactions?

5) The issue of accidental infection was raised with Sofia and also with Katrina. Are you aware of deaths or severe illness as a result of accidental infection?

6) Do you believe that people who refused to follow protocols were complicit in their own deaths?

7) Beth and Kayla, especially, blame certain people for infecting and killing their mothers. Is this a reasonable position? Unreasonable?

8) Which member of the grief group did you feel the most connection with or empathy for?

9) Did you feel that each member of the grief group had their own unique experience of grief? What were some commonalities between their experiences?

10) What was your response to their act of "baking rebellion?"

11) Some of the characters in *When We Lost Touch* have experienced trauma. How do you see certain characters as "traumatized?" What have you experienced in your own life, whether you define it as traumatic or not, that has impacted how you feel, think, or react?

RACIAL ISSUES

1) Grace and Katrina have open discussions about race in this book. Have you talked about race with your friends and family? Why or why not? Would you consider doing so after reading their conversations?

2) Kraus quoted statistics from multiple sources during the race discussions. Were those facts new or surprising? How did the discussions mirror some of your own experiences of living in your "skin?"

3) How has your own upbringing (community, religion, race, ethnicity, heritage) informed your sense of security? How about your trust or distrust in law enforcement and the legal system? Have your assumptions changed since the murder of George Floyd?

4) For white readers, how have you benefitted from white privilege? Can you come up with ten examples of privilege from your daily life?

5) White people often assert that they are "color blind" as a positive, meaning an absence of bias. Has reading this changed your perceptions of how being blind to race is more about being blind to the privileges that come with a white skin?

6) Susan Kraus is a white woman, raised in a white town, who attended white schools (much like Grace.) Yet she has written a novel that includes the thoughts and feelings of a biracial woman who struggles with colorism. Do you see Katrina's narratives as realistic? Does it feel like appropriation?

7) What does "Critical Race Theory" mean to you? Does it trigger a negative response? Do you see the American history that you were taught as balanced? Why are fact-based curriculum changes controversial?